THE WEHRMACHT
and
THE WOLVES

The war was lost. Captain Schmitt knew it; his twenty men knew it. They stood in waist-deep snow and bowed their shoulders under the icy wind pouring down from the tangled, black mountains. The wind carried the desolate howling of hungry wolf packs.

In those mountains, men like wolves—the savage Czech partisans—were holding Schmitt's general.

Schmitt and his men had orders to rescue the general. The mission meant death, but they were soldiers—

"March!" Schmitt shouted.

"A MAJOR WAR NOVEL,
EVEN MORE MEMORABLE THAN
THE CROSS OF IRON."
Washington Star

CRACK OF DOOM

BY WILLI HEINRICH

Translated from the German by Oliver Coburn

BANTAM BOOKS · TORONTO · NEW YORK · LONDON

*This low-priced Bantam Book
has been completely reset in a type face
designed for easy reading, and was printed
from new plates. It contains the complete
text of the original hard-cover edition.*
NOT ONE WORD HAS BEEN OMITTED.

CRACK OF DOOM

*A Bantam Book / published by arrangement with
Farrar, Straus & Giroux, Inc.*

PRINTING HISTORY
*Farrar, Straus & Cudahy edition published June 1958
Bantam edition published May 1959
2nd printing .... May 1959
3rd printing .... January 1967*

*Bantam Books are published by Bantam Books, Inc., a subsidiary
of Grosset & Dunlap, Inc. Its trade-mark, consisting of the words
"Bantam Books" and the portrayal of a bantam, is registered in the
United States Patent Office and in other countries. Marca Registrada.
Bantam Books, Inc., 271 Madison Avenue, New York, N. Y. 10016.*

PRINTED IN THE UNITED STATES OF AMERICA

CRACK OF DOOM

CHAPTER

1

There was a bridge over the little stream which ran through the valley. There the valley dwindled to a narrow shaft, between mountains with pointed peaks that shut off the sky on all sides; their slopes were overgrown with pines, bent under a thick layer of snow. The vehicles of a retreating army had pounded the snow on the road to a solid blanket; but on the bridge it lay in black lumps, frozen hard as stone with the return of extreme cold during the past few days. The mountains stood out so brightly against the sky that their silhouettes cut like sharp blades through the clear starry night.

The men under the trees were freezing. They wore the white winter uniforms of the German army and flat fur caps, which they had pulled down over their ears; a thin sheet of ice covered the short squat barrels of the tommy-guns they carried. Now and then a man would step out of the wood and look impatiently at the bridge, about twenty yards from the wood's edge. The others remained motionless, except when one of them, with a cigarette concealed in the hollow of his hand, brought it to his mouth and took a hasty puff. A whole hour passed, and not a word was spoken. Then there was a sudden movement among them.

In the distance they heard the noise of car engines.

In silent accord the men ran out of the wood, across the bridge, and disappeared in a ditch the other side of the road. It was a few seconds before headlights shone out from behind the next bend in the valley; then the beams blazed on the bridge. The two cars were still fifty yards away when a man suddenly appeared in the road, flung both arms in the air, and brought them to a stop. They were open command cars, and the first of them carried a flag on its right wing. A face under a peaked cap emerged from behind the windscreen, and a sharp voice asked: "What is it?"

The man on the road blinked in the glare of the headlights. The lower half of his face was hidden by a black beard, and he had his fur cap drawn down over his brow. Now he went up to the first car. There were four people sitting there, and the man sitting next to the driver spoke again in irritation: "Didn't you hear me? Who the devil are you?" The man with the beard took a step backwards. He observed two faces staring at him from the other car. Turning back to the first car, he said: "You can't cross the bridge, it's gone."

"Gone!" The man next to the driver looked at him suspiciously. Another voice joined in from the back of the car: "Must be partisans again, General."

"General?" asked the man with the beard quickly. There was a note of satisfaction in his voice. "Don't move."

"What's that?"

"I said: don't move." He raised his left arm, and a dozen men jumped out of the ditch. The general looked at their tommy-guns, held ready to fire, and at the bearded man's face. He said quietly: "Are you crazy? Who are you?"

"You can call me Andrej," the man told him. "Your gun!" The general did not move. Suddenly he turned his head. The engine of the second car howled into action. The men just had time to jump aside, then it was past them, racing on to the bridge. Despite their surprise they fired after it at once. Taking advantage of the momentary confusion, the general jabbed his driver, but this time the man called Andrej was quicker. He fired into the back of the car and at its wheels. The car sagged as the air hissed out of the slashed tires. The driver was pulled out, and the butt of a tommy-gun smashed his skull. Before the general could recover from the shock, he too was dragged out of the car. His face was white as chalk and his voice quivered as he said: "You'll hang for this."

"After you," remarked Andrej. He pulled a crushed packet of cigarettes from his breast pocket and held them out to the general, who shook his head.

"As you like." Andrej lit a cigarette himself, then addressed the others. "Prostý." They pulled the dead men out of the car and searched them.

The general watched with tight lips. He had a big, hard face, and his voice was still trembling when he said: "It won't pay—a few hundred of your countrymen will hang for this."

Andrej shrugged his shoulders. "There'll be a dozen of you for each of us."

"You're no Czech," said the general with barely suppressed rage.

"What makes you think that?"

"You speak too good German."

"My mother was an Austrian," answered Andrej. "You people put my brother against the wall in Prague. They caught him when he was trying to throw a bomb into a general's car. We have a weakness for generals in our family."

Meanwhile the man had been searching the car. They undressed the dead and threw them into the ditch. "We may need their uniforms," said Andrej. One of the men brought him the general's map case, and

3

he scanned the papers. "It *has* paid," he told the general.

The men dragged the dead driver across the road, and flung him on to the others. Some were quarreling over the victims' watches and wallets. The general watched scornfully. "Is that why you do it?" he asked Andrej, without looking at him. Andrej crushed the cigarette beneath his boot and went over to the men. He tore a watch out of the hand of one of them and flung it across the road. "We don't need anything from the Germans," he said sharply. He came back quickly. "Your gun!"

The general pulled the pistol from its holster. "What are you going to do with me?" he asked.

"We've got friends who are interested in you." The general hesitated, and his face worked. "Don't try it!" Andrej said, and aimed the barrel of his tommy-gun at the general's stomach.

The general looked at the pistol in his hand and flung it into the snow.

Andrej stared at him. "Pick it up," he said quietly. When the general did not move, he addressed the others: "Help him!" They pounced on the general, pummeling him with their fists till he fell on his knees. His nose was bleeding and he spat two teeth into the snow; his breath came in gasps. "Come on," said Andrej, pointing to the pistol. The general bent over, and before he could straighten up again, the butt of a tommy-gun came down on his back. He fell on his face, but Andrej pulled him up by the collar. "That's something you'll have to learn," he said. "Now, come on with that pistol." The general gave it to him.

"Why couldn't you have done that in the first place?" asked Andrej, and said to the others: "We'll be off, they'll be coming soon." They took the general in the middle. After walking for some time in the direction from which the cars had come, they struck off on to a narrow track leading steeply up-hill from the road. Walking in the deep snow was difficult and they made slow progress. The general was sweating. Blood still came from his nose and mouth; he wiped it off with the sleeve of his coat. Once he stopped and looked round. Andrej went over to him. "Tired, General?"

"You won't get far," was the answer.

"Wait and see." Andrej's hands described a wide circle. "The mountains don't talk."

"The snow does."

Andrej regarded the deep tracks they had made. "Oh, we've thought of that too. Can't you smell it?" The general looked at him blankly, and he laughed. "We've got a good nose for it—there's snow in the air. By tomorrow morning there'll be nothing left of the tracks."

"Don't be too sure."

"Even then it wouldn't help you. Like to know where we're taking you?" He pointed beyond the snow-covered trees and said: "Ku diabolovi." The men grinned.

For weeks the division had been fighting in the Carpathian Mountains. Then they evacuated their last positions and marched past the town of Uzhorod into the extreme eastern tip of Czechoslovakia, to take up new positions in the wooded slopes of the Sovar Range. While the battalions were settling into their sectors, Captain Schmitt, commander of the second battalion, was called to regimental headquarters; there he was informed that his battalion was not to settle in the new positions with the rest, but was to be placed as a divisional reserve under direct command of the general. He was instructed to take the road over the Durkov Pass and proceed to Košice, where he should report directly to the general at divisional headquarters.

He left with his men while it was still night. After extremely hard fighting in the West Carpathians the

5

battalion's fighting strength amounted to just over a hundred and fifty men. No replacements had yet arrived for the officers killed or wounded at Turka, and the four companies were being commanded by three sergeants and a corporal. The battalion reached Košice in the early morning. Proceeding to divisional headquarters, Captain Schmitt heard from a lieutenant that the general had gone to a conference at Dobšiná, further west, and would not be back till evening. Schmitt asked for Major Giesinger, the divisional adjutant. He had met Giesinger in Dresden, where they had worked together collecting a reserve battalion from a crowd of men unfit for military service. The major received him in shirt sleeves, with a cigarette in his mouth. "Sit down," he said jovially, but with that slight inflection of superiority in his voice which always succeeded in irritating Schmitt. But he suppressed his annoyance and looked round the room: "You've got a nice billet."

"Naturally." Giesinger grinned. "Aren't you satisfied with yours?"

"Good Lord, yes," Schmitt answered emphatically. "I suppose I have you to thank."

Giesinger nodded. "That's right. When the general talked about pulling a battalion out, I thought of you at once."

"I'm grateful to you. My men were just about finished, and as for me—well, you know how things have been going. You get on well with the general?"

"I'm quite satisfied."

"You were always adaptable," Schmitt remarked drily.

"I do what I can." Giesinger smiled and looked at Schmitt disparagingly, thinking how the barrel had been scraped for an infantry battalion to be commanded by a sort of cripple. A year ago it would have been unthinkable, he told himself, but times had changed, and so had the war. Schmitt had come to the division three months earlier, after making vain efforts to do so for a long time. He was a hunchback and had bandy legs, so he kept being pushed from one garrison to another. Only Giesinger's sponsorship had persuaded the general to ask for Schmitt as a battalion commander. Giesinger couldn't quite analyze why he had put himself out on Schmitt's behalf. The man's appearance disgusted him, and their work together in Dresden hadn't always gone smoothly. He had only been a lieutenant in those days and Schmitt was his superior officer. Perhaps this was the reason for his contradictory behavior: it gave him satisfaction to rub Schmitt's nose in their new service relationship at every opportunity. When he talked to Schmitt in the presence of a third person, he did it in the pose of a good-looking man who has himself photographed stroking an ugly animal. "You're lucky to find me," he said now. "Originally the general wanted to take me to Dobšiná. But then he changed his mind; I'm indispensable here. A year ago I was just an assistant adjutant running errands for the general, and today he can't do without me. From first lieutenant to major within a year. You wouldn't have thought that in Dresden, eh?"

"I certainly wouldn't," Schmitt looked past him. "But I remember that you've always been ambitious."

Giesinger gave him a cautious look, narrowing his cold, bulbous eyes. Then he reached under the table and, bringing out a bottle, remarked in a hearty voice: "You'll have something to drink, won't you?"

"No thanks, I'd better be going. Will it be enough that I've seen you now or do I still have to report to the general this evening?"

"He wants to speak to you personally," said Giesinger. "I wonder what news he'll bring from Corps. . . . What do you think of the Ardennes business?"

"Let's hope for the best."

"We can do that all right," observed Giesinger condescendingly. "In four weeks the invasion army will be back in the sea and then we'll have the Russians on the run again. I've been looking forward to that for a long time."

He stood up. "Better come about eight, the general is sure to be back by then."

Back at Schmitt's quarters, his adjutant, Lieutenant Menges, was waiting for him impatiently. With a puzzled face Schmitt took the signal Menges thrust at him and read it.

"From division," he said, his face growing even more puzzled. "Odd that Giesinger didn't say anything about this. I left him only half an hour ago. Well, inform the company commanders: strict confinement to billets for the whole battalion. Looks as if we won't be here much longer." He sighed. "By the way, I didn't see the general yet but I will this evening."

Dismissing Menges, Schmitt went over to the window. While he gazed at the hills surrounding the town on all sides he thought about Giesinger. The former lieutenant with the broad shoulders was just the same as ever. He recalled that he had always taken a special interest in married women. How many of them had there been in Dresden? There was the Nazi official's wife who had deceived her husband with him almost every night; the surgeon's wife who felt neglected because her husband sawed off bones and patched up holes till the early hours of the morning instead of bothering about her psyche; the wife of the air force officer with his legs amputated—Giesinger used to have a good laugh at the casino describing how she would run away screaming whenever her husband took his trousers off. There were several others, not counting those Giesinger hadn't talked about. Oh yes, he had developed his weakness for married women into a fine art. But, after all why not? Schmitt smiled bitterly. The ambitious major was endowed with every quality a woman looks for in a man: charm, intelligence, brutality. If you were dragging around a hunchback on the other hand, it was irrelevant whether you covered it with a general's uniform or a captain's.

In deep self-disgust he contemplated his face staring back at him from the window pane: pale eyes, brows that met over the top of the nose, a high forehead heavily lined, gaunt cheeks with skin like crumpled parchment and a thin mouth pinched down at the corners as if in constant pain. An old man's face. Nobody would have thought of putting him twenty years younger; women wouldn't either, not even the one who had stuck it out with him for fourteen months, whether from a whim, sympathy or some perversity in herself he could never find out. She had married him when he was thirty-five—more than six years ago—but even then she had treated him as if he were seventy. Yet she had made him happy for fourteen months. He felt his eyes grow misty and was surprised again at the way he had never got over it, not over the woman and not over the hunched back. Forty-odd years, he thought, what a strange creature a man is.

He abandoned his idle brooding and had his orderly bring him his meal. Afterward he decided to take a stroll through the town.

Košice disappointed him. It was a town like all the others between the Bug and the Dniester that he had seen in the last months: grey houses with small windows reflecting the winter sky.

As he walked he inhaled deep draughts of the cold, clear winter air. His gaze stayed on the gently rising hills, thickly wooded to their highest points. He loved this land with its deep valleys and the bizarre shapes of its seemingly endless chain of sheer mountains—

9

stretching one behind the other as far as the horizon, with the vault of a dark December sky above them. There was a silence full of melancholy hanging over the whole scene, a palpable sadness; and something of that in himself too when he suddenly remembered that in two days it would be Christmas. For the sixth time in this war, and still no . . . but yes, the end *was* in sight. He could not share Giesinger's optimism; he was not much impressed by the offensive in the Ardennes. His mathematically trained brain refused to be taken in by the latest bulletins of German successes. The respective weights remained the same, and trivial shifts made no difference now on the scales: there was no longer any doubt about the result.

Deep in thought, he crossed a road and almost bumped into another man, who muttered an apology, started, and then quickly turned his face away. But Schmitt had already recognized that sharp profile with the high cheekbones and the deep scar running from the right eyebrow almost down to the chin. Schmitt gripped him firmly by the arm.

"Stop," he said sharply. "Where do you think you're going, Sergeant Kolodzi?"

The man was silent. Schmitt released his arm and took a step back. "I asked you a question," he said. His voice became still sharper. "Lost your tongue? Didn't you know I'd expressly forbidden any wandering around?"

"Yes, I heard it from Lieutenant Menges," answered Kolodzi. He spoke slowly, rather slurring his words. Since Lieutenant Jung had fallen at Turka, he had commanded the sixth company. He had held the post down excellently, and Schmitt was sorry to have to talk to him like this. But the place where they were standing was a good five hundred yards from Kolodzi's billet. Schmitt noticed that some civilians had stopped and were looking at them. "Come on," he ordered tersely. They walked a bit further, and Schmitt asked: "Were you coming to see me?"

"No, sir," said Kolodzi.

"Too bad—you've just missed a chance. Where were you going then?"

Kolodzi stopped and looked down the street. "To visit my mother," he said curtly.

"Your mother?" said Schmitt in amazement.

Kolodzi nodded. "I live here."

"Here?"

"Yes."

"In Košice?"

"In Košice."

Schmitt stared at him incredulously. "Why didn't you tell me that before?"

"You didn't ask me, sir."

"Don't be impertinent," said Schmitt. He reflected. "All right," he said, "show me the house where you live. In case I need you I've got to know where to find you."

The sergeant began to walk fast, and Schmitt had some difficulty in keeping up with him. On the way Schmitt pointed to a building which stood out above the houses in front of it. "What's that?"

"The town theatre," Kolodzi answered.

"And that over there?"

Kolodzi's eyes followed Schmitt's outstretched hand. "The Dominican Church," he said moodily.

Schmitt looked in his face. "You meant to desert."

"If I'd meant to do that, I'd have done it long ago."

"Why didn't you?"

"Why didn't I." Kolodzi's face twisted to a grimace. He waited till they came to the next crossroads. There he pointed left with his chin. "Do you see the tree?"

"What about it?"

"They hanged my father from it."

Schmitt stared at him. "Your father?"

"Yes."

"Who's they?"

"The Czechs," said Kolodzi quietly, and walked on. Schmitt ran after him in bewilderment. "Why?"

"Just for the fun of it. He happened to be a Nazi."

"Are you one too?"

"Not me. But later on, when the war got going, I joined up. They won't forgive me for that here. They'd hang me just the same way the first chance they had."

Schmitt had to digest all this. After a pause he asked: "When did this happen to your father?"

"Thirty-eight, before we became Hungarian again."

"And they'd still hang you today?"

"There are more Czechs here than anything else. You don't know the local conditions."

"I certainly don't," Schmitt admitted. Then he said: "Kolodzi sounds Polish."

"Yes, sir. After her first husband's death my grandmother married a Pole with German nationality. Then my father married a German woman."

"Complicated," observed Schmitt.

Kolodzi gave a dry laugh. "There are lots like it here. Poles, Hungarians, Czechs, Slovaks, Austrians, Russians, all in a jumble. Volksdeutsch!" he concluded bitterly, and pointed to a house. "This is where I live. Over there."

Schmitt looked at the building. It had a mean and neglected appearance.

"Seventeenth century house," declared Kolodzi sardonically. When Schmitt made no comment, he asked: "How long, sir . . ."

Schmitt considered. "Let's say till tomorrow morning. Assuming I don't need you earlier, of course. If I do, I'll send someone for you."

"Thank you, sir."

Kolodzi crossed the road, and went into the house. For a moment Schmitt stared thoughtfully after the sergeant. Then he returned to his quarters.

Kolodzi went up a few steps from the hall and opened the door of a room. There was his mother, still sitting by the window. He took off his belt and put it on the table, then pulled a second chair up and sat down so near her that she couldn't help seeing him; their knees were touching. Yet she did not move. After gazing at her for a long while, Kolodzi gently took hold of her hands, which were lying in her lap, and said: "How are you, Mother?"

She raised her head a little; now he could look right into her face, and he thought: how old she's grown. For a second he felt her looking *at* him, but immediately afterward she was looking right through him again like glass. He went on sitting by her till dusk, still clasping her hands. She took no notice of him and kept her eyes on the window, which framed a piece of grey winter sky, gradually being swallowed by the night. Kolodzi watched the darkness eating black holes into his mother's face, and he heard her quiet breathing. As always, seeing her before him in all her helplessness and decay, he began to reproach himself. Things might have turned out differently if only he'd stayed with her. But then he hadn't been able to stand it any more, having her sit there by the window day and night waiting for father, having to watch the grief affect her brain until she failed to recognize her surroundings.

He left the room. It was pitch dark in the hall. He felt his way up a staircase and opened another door. The room he entered smelled stuffy. He groped for a lamp and lit it. Hesitating, as if afraid of a shock, he looked round the room. In the left-hand corner stood a wardrobe; on the other side was a bed with a book shelf next to it; and over that there was a picture which showed a young man with a scar on his face going from the right eyebrow almost to the chin: it was a portrait of himself, Stefan Kolodzi. He got the scar in a fight when he was twenty-five. He and Maria had been sitting in an inn, and two drunken lumberjacks tried to kiss her; when he stopped them, one of them went wild and drew a knife. As he recalled this now, he could feel the scar itching and smarting, even though nearly eight years had passed. He had known Maria all that time.

She was still almost a child then, only seventeen, and they had wanted to marry early. But the business with father happened, and because of it Stefan's boss had immediately sacked him. Soon afterward Košice became Hungarian, but even then the chances of another job were barred to the son of an anarchist, as the Czechs called his father. Orid Krasko, Maria's father, once said: "Anyone in Košice who falls out with the Czechs has fallen out with the whole place." There was a good deal of truth in that, and things hadn't changed during the period of Hungarian rule. As Krasko had also said, "The Czechs will return."

Stefan had never bothered much with politics, and he remembered all the quarrels about that between him and his father. "There'll be no peace in this hell kettle till we're all German," his father maintained. He had joined an officially proscribed movement which sympathized with the Germans and wanted to make Košice into a self-governing German colony; neither Stefan's mother nor Maria's father could talk him out of these crazy ideas. One day he gave up his job, and from then on he was often away for weeks on end. "With friends in Olmütz," he would sometimes explain—till that dreadful day. After that, when his mother got worse and worse, Stefan volunteered for

14

the German army, although Maria opposed it. But he had told her: "When the war's over, we can live in peace. Till then it's better I make myself scarce round here. One's got to take one's stand somewhere, and I prefer the Germans to the Czechs."

He was so deep in his thoughts that he failed to hear the door opening behind him. It was a suppressed cry that first made him turn round. A girl was standing in the doorway looking at him in breathless amazement. Her thin, beautiful face went first red and then pale. Kolodzi took a step towards her. "Good evening, Maria." The girl ran over to him, flinging her arms round his neck. "Stefan," she murmured, "Stefan, Stefan." He kissed her mouth and her eyes. "Stefan," she said again, laughing and crying at the same time. He drew her over to the bed, pressed her down on the pillows, and gazed at her. She was wearing a dark dress that was a little short for her and only came down to her knees; thick woolen stockings covered her slim legs.

She smiled through her tears. "It's stupid of me, but I still can't believe it. Where have you come from, why didn't you write to me, have you got leave?"

"What a lot of questions at once!" He sat down by her side. "I'd have gone to you now. I didn't write to you because till yesterday evening I didn't know myself whether I'd be able to come home. We're stationed here."

She gave a cry of surprise. "You're stationed here?"

"Yes, but not for long, perhaps only till tomorrow."

She started. "Only till tomorrow!"

"Maybe longer, though. Do you still come every evening?"

"Your mother," she said, and then broke off.

"I know. She's in a bad way. She didn't recognize me. Has she never spoken of me?"

"Oh yes. Only a few days ago she asked me if . . ."

15

"Yes?"

She reached for his hands. "She asked me if I'd taken you some fresh flowers."

"Flowers?"

"Yes, she thinks . . . she believes you're dead."

He stared at the floor. "What does she do when she isn't sitting at the window?"

"She stays in bed. She's never got over her last stroke. She can't walk any more."

"So you've got to cope with that too," said Kolodzi. She put her hand over his mouth. "Please don't, Stefan. I'm glad to do it," she said hastily. "I must go now and buy some things to eat, otherwise the shops will be shut. And you could make a fire while I'm gone. It's too cold in here."

"Too cold for what?" he asked. She blushed, kissed him and got up. "Oh, I'm so happy, Stefan. I just can't tell you how happy I am," she said and ran to the door.

The fire was not yet burning properly when she returned. She put her shopping bag on the table, asked: "Are you hungry?" and put two plates on the table. "I've got some sausage," she said, "made of horse meat, but it tastes good. The bread's already stale, though; still, one's glad to get any at all. Would you like any tea?"

"No."

"No tea?"

He shook his head, without taking his eyes off her. She came over to him and sat on his knees. "What *would* you like then?"

"You," he said, and carried her to the bed. "There are worse things than dry bread, horse meat sausage and no tea."

"What sort of things?"

"A year and a half without you. It feels to me like half a lifetime. Does it feel the same to you?"

She nodded, pressing her face against his chest. "Wait," she said.

He watched her pull up her dress and roll down the thick woolen stockings. He looked at her long auburn hair beneath him. "How brown you are," he said.

She laughed. "And yet I've hardly been in the sun, brown doesn't suit me. Wait, my shoes, and don't tear my dress, it's my last."

"I'll buy you lots of dresses later on."

"How many?"

"A dozen or two—as many as you like."

"What should I do with two dozen dresses? I'd have to spend the whole day changing from one to another."

"Only so that I could undress you again. You're beautiful, Maria."

She lay by him with her eyes closed, and trembled under his hands. "Don't hurt me," she murmured.

"Not even like this?" She didn't answer, but she came to him so suddenly that he was overwhelmed. And then his sensations became misty and the darkness lost its contours as he slipped deeper and deeper into the intimate game of hide-and-seek and kept his eyes closed because her mouth ranged so violently over his face. . . .

Later she asked him: "Are you happy?"

"Very."

She laid her head against his chest and looked up at him. "Will you stay here?"

"I can't. They'll denounce me and hand me over to the Russians when they come."

"Then I'll go with you," she said quietly.

He stroked her face. "How do you think you'll do that? As a camp-follower, like the Russian women we've got with us?"

"Not like them. But when the Russians come, I can't stay here either. The people will tell them that there was a German soldier I used to. . . . I notice it everywhere I go. The baker always gives me his stalest bread, and in some shops they won't let me have anything at all. Father's frightened. He's already forbidden me to look after your mother."

"Has he!" Kolodzi gave a start, but she pressed him back on the pillows. "Father's getting old," she said hastily. "Since the front's been so close, he's all for the Czechs again. He thinks we'll become Czech again when the Russians are here."

"Are *you* for them too?"

"I'm for *you*. But you must tell me what to do. I can't go on, it's all so. . . ." She began crying quietly, and he didn't try to stop her, simply caressed her face and her bare shoulders. When she had grown a little calmer, he said: "Father had good friends in Olmütz. We've got relations living there too, a brother of his. You go to Olmütz with mother, and after that we'll see." He turned his head abruptly, thinking he had heard somebody call his name.

Maria had started too. "What's that?" she asked in a scared voice, climbing out of bed.

"Get dressed," he told her. "I'd like to know what the devil. . . ." He got into his clothes. As he was putting on his jacket, he heard the sound of heavy feet coming upstairs. There was a knock at the door, and someone said: "Sergeant Kolodzi."

Motioning Maria behind the door, he flung it open, and saw a man from his company, panting hard. "You're to report to the captain at once, sergeant," the man said breathlessly. "We're pulling out."

Kolodzi felt his hands beginning to tremble. He took a step forward. "Pulling out, you say?"

"Yes, that is, we're to be sent off on trucks. Special mission. . . ." The man swallowed noisily and concluded: "That's all I know."

"When?"

"In an hour."

18

"All right, I'm coming." Kolodzi shut the door in his face and turned to Maria; she was only half dressed. "I was afraid the town was being evacuated," he said.

"Stay," she said. He looked at her in amazement. She put her arms round his neck. "Stay here, Stefan," she faltered. "You mustn't go away now. If you put something else on, we can go to Olmütz together. They won't look for us in Olmütz, and the Russians . . ." She stopped, out of breath; she was trembling and clung to him.

He tore himself away. "What are you talking about? It's swarming with army patrols. Do you want them to hang me as they did my father? You go on to Olmütz and later on. . . ."

"And my father," she interrupted him. "He'll never let me go. He'll be mad."

"Are you scared of him?"

"No, not scared, but . . ."

"But what?"

She leant against him wearily. "He is my father," she said softly.

"I know." He patted her shoulder. "But you've got to decide now who you belong to. Perhaps you could persuade him to move to Olmütz with you."

"No, he'll never leave Košice. He's got something on here. I don't know what it is, but it often frightens me. There are such a lot of strangers who come to him."

"What strangers?"

"I don't know, they always come at night. I hear them talking when I'm in bed. I'm frightened, Stefan."

He looked down at her, frowning. "What do they talk about?"

"I don't know that either, I don't understand what they say, I just hear them talk."

"Czech?"

"I think so."

"Some day he'll put a rope round his own neck,"

19

muttered Kolodzi. Then he shrugged his shoulders impatiently. "What do I care, let him do what he likes. Listen, Maria," he drew her to him. "You've still got time to think everything over," he said roughly. "You can go back to your father again. It may even be better for you if. . . ."

She quickly closed his mouth with a kiss. "I'll never leave you."

He took her face gently in his hands like a big shell. "If we lose the war, I'll have to hide somewhere. Wait in Olmütz, if possible, till you hear from me."

She lifted her face to him, and he saw that she was once more weeping.

"If I get through this," he said huskily, "you'll never have to cry again." She clung to him, and he had to wrench himself away from her. "Look after Mother," he said, then rushed off. She called something after him, but he did not stop.

There was nobody about. He walked quickly and slightly bent, past dark windows and unlit lampposts. Snow lay in the gutters, dirty heaps blown along by the wind. The streets were lifeless shafts between silent façades, in which only the cold was alive, a cold which pierced through his uniform, through his skin and right to his heart, congealing it with fears. He forced himself not to turn his head, not to think that *she* was standing in the doorway and gazing after him, as she had always gazed whenever he left her in these many years of war—with the mute pain of all women in her face, all the tears that had been shed, tears of uncertainty and endless waiting. Always he had felt her gaze upon him, she had been with him on all the roads of war, following him through the hot breath of the steppe, over the curving lines of the horizon, all the way to the remotest places. He had met this gaze in each valley of loneliness, had felt it in all his thoughts; and she had been looking at him out of every face.

His steps slowed more and more. In his thoughts he saw the lights behind the narrow windows, saw the men as they used to sit and laugh in front of their houses on the long summer evenings, nodding to the girls as they went by with their short skirts and red boots up to their firm, brown calves, bodices tightly laced over their young breasts. With every beat of his heart the past came more to life in him.

Turning, he stopped and looked back on the way he had come. He felt as if he need only take a few steps and he would find it all again. He bit his lip. But then, as if some irresistible force had taken control of him, he could feel his body turning; and without once stopping he strode back to the battalion.

Shortly before eight o'clock that evening, Schmitt and Menges set out for Schmitt's postponed appointment with the general. The captain was silent and Menges did not venture to intrude on his thoughts. "God, it makes me sick," Schmitt exclaimed suddenly. "The whole thing makes me sick. How much longer are we going to play our part in this damn swindle?" Being used to such outbursts, Menges did not feel an answer was called for, but Schmitt gripped his arm and said: "Do you hear me?"

"What do you expect me to say?" Menges answered, feeling he had enough on his mind already. Any day now his wife would be having their child, and he was anxiously waiting for her next letter.

"I've got other worries," he muttered grumpily.

Schmitt smiled in the darkness. "Oh naturally. Everyone's thinking about his own affairs, and everyone behaves as if all that were no business of his."

"If you'll excuse my saying so," said Menges coldly, "I think you're making life unnecessarily hard for yourself."

"You think so? Personally I feel as if I'd always made it too easy for myself. Always the line of least resistance, always closing my eyes to the problems and . . .

but I'm not going on with it much longer, I can tell you. You can't alter the law of gravity by constantly shifting your weight, and no more can you switch off your reason by pretending you haven't got any. I've tried to do that long enough. If this Kolodzi isn't a complete fool," he said erratically, "he'll stay where he is now."

"You sent him away?"

"I gave him leave till tomorrow morning. He lives here."

Menges stopped in amazement. "That surprises you?" said Schmitt. "Surprised me too, at first. But it's all the same where we live. You may be able to hide from the informers, but you can't hide from yourself." He hurried on, so that Menges was obliged to run after him. It was cold in the streets, and the lieutenant dug his hands in the pockets. Suddenly he exclaimed: "Look at the crowd!" The two men had reached the division headquarters, and his remark referred to the unusually large number of guards who were standing outside the front door or patroling in small groups. "It wasn't like that this morning," said Schmitt in astonishment.

A sergeant asked for their papers. "Those are my orders," he said in polite but firm tones when Schmitt protested. Inside the big house they had to pass a second check-post. "Completely crazy," declared Schmitt angrily, pushing his wallet back in his jacket. They crossed a long hall to a door which again had two men standing in front of it.

"Schmitt!" The captain turned round and saw Giesinger, who had come running after them. "There you are," he said, panting. "I've just been phoning your HQ." He shook hands with Schmitt, nodded curtly to Menges, and pushed the door open. Inside, seven officers were seated at a table. Giesinger made hasty introductions before sitting down himself. Then he leaned toward Schmitt and said in a hollow voice: "They've caught the general—partisans."

Schmitt looked up incredulously. Glancing around the officers' faces, he noticed for the first time how worried they looked. "How did it happen?" he asked eventually.

Giesinger pointed to an officer who had his right arm in a sling. "Captain Meisel was there. He was in the second car, and the general in the first with Colonel Schnetzler and Captain Sitt."

"They're. . . ."

"Dead. But the general's a prisoner."

"Then we're left without our general staff," Schmitt said to Meisel, who grimaced and felt his bandaged arm with his left hand. "Yes. A week ago the bombs and today the partisans. If it goes on like this. . . ."

"And they let you go?" asked Schmitt.

Meisel gave a harsh laugh. "Like hell they did. If it hadn't been for my driver we too would be lying in the ditch now."

Giesinger winced slightly, and said to Schmitt: "Captain Meisel's nerves are rather strained. He was lucky to get away with his car, but he went back afterward. The partisans were gone, the general with them, and the others . . . well, it's as you've just heard." He sat up stiffly. "Apart from the fact that the partisans have collected all our positional plans, the general's fate is also completely uncertain. I've been on the phone to Corps, and they want to send us General Stiller, who's a complete stranger. Until he comes, it's my job to carry on." He reached for a map on the table, and pointed with his finger: "That's where it happened, between Denes and Szomolnok, about thirty miles from here. We presume the partisans' hide-out must be somewhere near, and in any case somewhere between those two places—which means we've got to decide whether it's north or south of the road. My guess is that it's

25

north, because the Hungarian frontier's to the south, and it's obviously Czechs we're up against. The compass please." Giesinger drew a semi-circle around the point where the ambush had taken place. "This is where one must start," he declared confidently. "They're sure to be somewhere in this region. Don't you agree?" When nobody answered, he flung the compass down on the table. "I called you to a conference, not a lecture. What do *you* think?" he asked, addressing Schmitt.

Schmitt rubbed his nose and said hesitantly: "I don't feel sure the partisans are as stupid as that. If I were they, I'd have chosen a place for the ambush as far away as possible. . . ."

"As far away as possible!" interrupted Giesinger. "Don't talk nonsense. You seem to forget there's several feet of snow in the woods. Under the circumstances, they wouldn't take a long walk."

"If they had skis perhaps."

"Skis!" Giesinger turned quickly to Meisel: "Did you see any skis?"

The captain shook his head. "I don't think they did have skis. Unless they laid them by somewhere."

"Hardly likely." Giesinger looked at Schmitt. "You over-rate these scum. It's all right for a dozen of them to attack defenseless people, they can think that one up—but their imagination won't stretch any further. We'll give them a lesson they won't forget in a hurry."

"I wouldn't do anything drastic without getting Corps' consent," said Major Fuchs, commander of the reconnaissance unit. Giesinger waved this aside. "If we can inform Corps that we've freed the general, everything will be quite all right, my dear Fuchs. We haven't got time to wait for any bureaucratic decisions. Colonel Kolmel said nothing about our not taking any action."

"Nor about our taking any," commented Fuchs, and several of the other officers nodded approvingly.

Giesinger sprang to his feet. "I wonder what the general would make of your attitude," he snapped.

Fuchs looked lazily up at him: "What's the matter with you? You don't imagine this thing leaves me cold, do you? It's just that on principle I'm against ill-considered actions. Besides, as you very well know, it's only an hour since my men got back, frozen and exhausted. I wouldn't dream of sending them out in the cold again now."

Giesinger decided it would be wiser to give way for the moment. "Nobody said anything about that," he answered, "I was thinking of Herr Schmitt. The reconnaissance unit were the rearguard," he explained to Schmitt, "and they only returned an hour ago. But your men have been rested, have they not?"

Schmitt had seen it coming. He sat up straight, and said coldly: "Would you like to hear my opinion?"

"Yes?"

"Then I must express strong disagreement. My men are also dead tired, and I protest against their being sent into action so soon again."

"They'd still have been in action now if I hadn't brought them to Košice."

"I know. But then they wouldn't have been on the road all night."

"They'd have been working the whole night in their trenches."

"Not as bad as twenty-five miles' march in snow. You seem to forget . . ."

"And *you* seem to forget," said Giesinger loudly, "that I didn't call you here for a debate."

"Please, gentlemen," put in Fuchs; but Giesinger would not be deflected. "So you don't want to?" he said, looking down at Schmitt.

"No."

"Interesting. Captain Schmitt doesn't want to. Captain Schmitt is asked to rescue his general from the partisans, and he doesn't want to. I must say you've established your independence pretty quickly. But we can perhaps make it simpler: I now give you an official order to leave with your battalion immediately and make all possible efforts to recover the general. Has anyone here any objections?" His cold eyes ranged over the officers' faces. They were silent. Sensing their irresoluteness, Giesinger threw caution to the winds: "I'll take responsibility."

"If it goes wrong," said Fuchs, "well, you know what can happen to you."

Giesinger bit his lip. For a moment he felt uncertain, and his heart began thumping. But this was the chance of his life: suppose he succeeded in freeing the general! The idea intoxicated him. "That's my worry," he said, "Has anyone else any objections?"

"We're talking too much," declared Meisel, laying his injured arm on the table. "If I were able to, I'd get going at once. Giesinger's right, we must teach the rabble a lesson. If you'd seen how . . ." He stopped for a moment and stared in front of him, then raised his head. "They can't have got far yet, we mustn't lose any time."

"Indeed we mustn't." Giesinger sat down again, and said to Fuchs: "You'll admit yourself that it would be futile to ask Corps first. We'd have lost hours before the gentlemen made up their minds, and by then it would be too late. No, we'll handle it ourselves this time. What we need is success, and that depends wholly on you," he told Schmitt, who was listening with a stony face. "Look." They bent over the map. "It happened here," said Giesinger, "in this spot. You and your battalion will comb the country within the circle between Denes and Szomolnok, going over the houses in every village. I'll have you taken to Szomolnok in trucks, and I suggest you start the search from there. Divide the companies into small groups and send them off. It's important the men climb the mountains too and don't bypass them. How many walkie-talkies have you?"

"Three per company."

"Excellent," said Giesinger. "Then you can make up eleven groups, keeping one walkie-talkie at your headquarters. You will thus have continuous contact with your men, and can direct the groups as and where they are most needed. Is your headquarters radio in good order?"

"Certainly."

Giesinger turned to an officer seated opposite him. "Look after the radio logs, Herr Pfeiffer, I need a continuous connection with Herr Schmitt." He turned to Schmitt again. "If for any reason you have to leave your headquarters, then take signals men with you. Communications between us mustn't be broken off for a moment. Is everything clear?"

Schmitt cleared his throat. "Perhaps I might remind you that in this difficult country I need three or four days to carry out the task properly. And suppose I find nothing?"

"I'm not sending you to find nothing," Giesinger answered angrily. "I'm sending you to get the general back, and you don't need four days for that if you're worth your place as battalion commander." He got up abruptly. "How many trucks have we here?" he asked a young lieutenant.

"I'll have to go and see," was the answer. "All the vehicles are out."

"Where the devil have they gone?"

"You gave the orders yourself, sir. The trucks are taking building material to the positions."

"Then see if there are any here now. I need. . . ." He turned to Schmitt. "What's the strength of your battalion?"

"About a hundred and fifty men. The officers. . . ."

"Yes, I know," Giesinger broke in irritably. "We're waiting for replacements daily. Let's say forty men to a truck, then. See if we've got four trucks here," he told the lieutenant. "Have you any suggestions to make?" he asked the others. There was a silence. "Perhaps you have some yourself, Herr Schmitt?" said Giesinger.

"Not for the moment."

"Herr Fuchs?"

The Major kept his hands clasped over his stomach, and squinted at Giesinger: he was taking his time. "I should have handled it differently," he said at length.

"That's very interesting. How, pray?"

"Do what you like. I'd rather be out of the whole thing."

"The simplest way of shirking responsibility. Don't you think General Stiller may like to learn how his officers would behave if something like this happened to him?"

"No, I don't think so for a moment," said Fuchs. "Stiller's a realist and hasn't any use for sentimental nonsense. Once in Berlin he had an officer punished, and do you know why?" Giesinger gave him an uneasy glance. "The officer in question," Fuchs explained with deliberation, "tried to save a woman's life, a Jewess. She'd jumped into the river Spree, because they'd got her husband. The officer saw her and jumped after her even though he couldn't swim. If there hadn't happened to be other people about, they'd both have been drowned. When Stiller heard the story, he sent for the officer and had him put under house arrest for a month. Not, by any means, because it was a Jewess he'd jumped after, but because he did it when he couldn't swim. And that, you see, is what Stiller is like."

"You know him?" asked Giesinger in dismay.

"Of course I know Stiller. I met him before the war."

"And you only tell me that now?"

"You didn't ask me before."

"We were agreed he was a complete stranger," Giesinger said furiously.

"We *were*?" Fuchs raised his eyebrows. "You took it for granted; there was no suggestion of agreement. We've never yet agreed about anything, not important questions anyhow."

You swine, thought Giesinger. Suddenly he felt he was making an enormous mistake, and his determination to send off Schmitt and his battalion began to waver. The other officers stared past him with impassive faces, and even Meisel, who had been for the plan till then, now avoided his eyes. Giesinger struggled within himself. Don't do it, a voice warned him. All was quiet in the room, and he could hear his own breathing.

The lieutenant returned to report: "There are two vehicles here, sir. But they're already loaded with building material."

"Loaded?"

"Pit-props and barbed wire."

"The fates are against you," remarked Fuchs smoothly.

Giesinger stared at him. In this second he made up his mind. His voice turned into steel: "Do you think so? Unload the trucks," he told the lieutenant. "There'll be more back by the time you've done that." He addressed Schmitt: "Load up in front of your quarters, and be ready to move. The radio logs," he said to the signals officer, and turning again to Schmitt: "Take mortars with you, enough ammunition and rations for two days. Don't explain to your men the purpose of the operation till you reach Szomolnok; and don't attract attention to yourselves." He paused and glanced over at Fuchs. Something in Fuchs' face seemed to warn him again; but he had already ventured too far, and said with a firmness he did not feel: "That's all, gentlemen."

The officers rose, and Giesinger went over to Schmitt. "You know your mission."

Schmitt exchanged a glance with Fuchs. "The mission is completely hopeless."

"We'll talk about that when you get back," said Giesinger. "In the presence of the general."

"A spiritualist séance, eh?" mocked Fuchs.

Giesinger picked his things up off the table. He would have liked to produce some crushing retort, but at the moment he could hardly speak for fury. When he saw that Schmitt was still there, he shouted at him: "Well, what are you waiting for?"

The battalion was informed that it should be ready to move in half an hour, and Schmitt directed a man to the house where Kolodzi was staying, with orders "to run as fast as you can and bring the sergeant back at once."

Schmitt went off to pack his own things. He was still at it when the man who had been to Kolodzi returned, reporting smartly: "Orders carried out, sir."

Schmitt glanced over his shoulder. "Did you see his mother, too?"

"His mother, sir?"

Schmitt turned round impatiently: "Sergeant Kolodzi's mother."

The man grinned. "I don't know if she . . . no, I don't think so."

"What don't you think?"

The man looked embarrassed. "There was a dress lying on the floor," he said hesitantly.

"What's that?"

"I only saw her legs behind the door," the man said hastily. "She hadn't anything on."

"Who hadn't?"

"The wom— I mean his mother."

"She hadn't anything on?"

"No, sir."

Schmitt bit his lips and dismissed the man. A little later Menges appeared. "All in order," he said.

Schmitt sat down at the table. "Log forms?"

"On the way."

"Ammunition?"

"More than we need."

"Let's hope so," said Schmitt. He pointed to a chair. "I wonder if I'll win my bet."

"Your bet?"

"A bet I took with myself. I laid odds on Kolodzi coming back. But now I'm not so sure."

"Why not?"

Schmitt lit a cigarette. "Put yourself in his place. Let's suppose you live here and have been given leave till tomorrow morning, you're in bed with a woman, and then someone rushes in and says: you're to come straight back to battalion. What would you do?"

"Come straight back," said Menges.

Schmitt nodded, as if he had expected this answer. "You're a good officer, Menges, but you haven't much imagination, have you! Know what I'd do?" He bent over the table. "I'd say, to hell with it—and so would you if you were only half a normal man. What do you bet he doesn't come?"

Menges looked irritated and said nothing.

"It is now"—Schmitt looked at his watch—"five to ten. If he's not here by quarter past ten, you've lost your bet."

"I've not taken any bet."

"My God, what a prig you are."

"I'm an officer," Menges said coldly.

Schmitt smiled: "A gallant German officer, eh, *sans peur et sans reproche*—every little shop girl's dream."

Suddenly he lost his composure. "But Menges, man, don't you realize how little this make-believe suits you? God Almighty! It doesn't seem to worry you that several millions of human beings have been slaughtered these last years, and that more and more are dying every day. Our whole world is going down the drain, and you simply look on and say: 'I'm a German officer!' Don't you realize how absurd it sounds, man?"

"There are some things. . . ." Menges began stiffly, but again Schmitt did not let him go on. "Who are you telling that to? There *are* some things, Menges, yes, and thank God there always will be. Things for whose preservation one should let oneself be torn to pieces if need be. But only for those things, not for the people who merely pretend to be fighting for them. And if you haven't yet learned to recognize the difference, then I'm damned sorry for you." He stared through the window, breathing heavily.

Menges relapsed on to his chair. "Exactly what do you want?" he asked helplessly.

Schmitt swung around. "I want you to stop fooling yourself now and dying of it later. The muck on our boots still stinks even if we shut our eyes, and we've waded around in more muck than we let ourselves dream of. Every day we . . ." He broke off and looked quickly toward the door. It opened, and Kolodzi appeared in the doorway. Schmitt stared at him. "Leave us alone together," he told Menges, without taking his eyes off Kolodzi. His voice sounded strangely quiet. He went to the table, sat down at it, and pointed with his chin to the second chair. "Why didn't you knock?" he asked.

Kolodzi sat down. "I did knock, sir."

"You heard what was said?"

"Every word," said Kolodzi indifferently. Schmitt leaned back in his chair. "How's your mother?"

"All right, sir."

34

"And the woman with the naked legs behind the door?"

"I didn't realize it was an informer you sent me," said Kolodzi, unruffled. "My fiancée was with me, sir, if you want to know."

"Where is she now?"

"At her father's."

"I see." Schmitt put a map down on the table in front of him, and his voice became business-like. "Partisans have kidnapped the general; we're to hunt for him. This is the district where it happened, can you see?"

"By the bridge," said Kolodzi.

Schmitt looked up quickly. "You knew about it already?"

"Not about the general. I know the district, I was there several times before the war."

Schmitt nodded. "All right. Well, listen to this." He told Kolodzi briefly what had happened. "And so," he concluded, "we're moving off as soon as the trucks are here. Where would you look for the partisans if you were given the job?"

Kolodzi reflected and eventually shrugged his shoulders. "Hard to say. There are thousands of places for hide-outs round there."

"Exactly my own opinion," said Schmitt. "Unless we're damned lucky . . ." He pushed the map away and lowered his voice. "While the major search is going on, I want to start a little minor operation. Have you some reliable men?"

"How many?"

"Two or three will be enough."

"I can think of two, sir."

"Who are they?"

"Sergeant Vöhringer and Corporal Herbig."

"Vöhringer." Schmitt thought for a moment and then remembered. "Your deputy?"

"Yes, sir."

"Now listen carefully: you'll ride with us to a place we've still to decide on, if possible right in the center of the suspect area. There we'll drop you off and you'll wait till we've searched the houses. We'll pretend to the civilians that we're looking for three German deserters. That's you and your two men—get me?"

"No, sir."

"You will in a moment. So—we search the houses; naturally we don't find anything, and on we go in the trucks. You and your men wait a good hour, then go into the first houses you come to. What do you suppose their occupants will think of you?"

"That we're deserters."

Schmitt smiled. "You are a gifted child. And that's just what I want to happen. If there are partisans in the place, they certainly won't keep you waiting long. They'll try to make contact with you, and if they don't, you must take the initiative yourselves. In either case you let me know at once, though of course without arousing the partisans' suspicions—I rely on your common sense. Once we've got hold of one of those boys, we'll soon have him telling us what we want to know."

"I wouldn't be too sure, sir."

"You can leave that to me. There are one or two tricks to make even the dumb talk."

"You don't know Czechs."

"I know people. It's worth trying anyhow. If it doesn't work, then we'll just have been unlucky. And now about the place." He bent over the map again. "We haven't a big choice. Including Denes and Szomolnok there are about four villages. The first two won't be any good for you because we're supposed to be searching there. So where shall we send you?"

"To Oviz, sir," said Kolodzi, without looking at the map.

Schmitt gave him a sharp glance. "How d'you work that out?"

"It's a place I used to know."

"I see." Schmitt studied the map. "Oviz lies outside the circle . . . a good six miles from Szomolnok. A bit far, I feel; must be over four hours' walk in this snow. Can we get there at all with the trucks?"

"The road's good, it goes past Svedler."

"Even so." Schmitt gnawed at his lower lip. "It lies outside the circle," he said again.

Kolodzi yawned. "The partisans certainly won't be bothering about your circle."

"You may have something there. Still, we've got to limit the space we search in. What sort of a place is this Oviz?"

"Pretty small, a few dozen houses. In the middle of the forest, with mountains on all sides—the perfect partisan village."

"All right then, that's the way it will be." Schmitt leaned back and stared at the table. "Excuse my excessive curiosity, but you said there's a girl you're engaged to, didn't you?"

"Yes," said Kolodzi.

"Then I'm surprised you didn't stay with her. What will happen to her when the Russians come?"

"She's going to Olmütz the day after tomorrow."

"And your mother? Or was that only an excuse?"

"I don't need excuses. She'll be with my mother."

"And if the Russians get to Olmütz?"

Kolodzi did not answer. At last, Schmitt rose. "Let's get ready then. You'll ride in my truck. Wait a moment." He went to a corner where his belongings were lying. "An heirloom," he said, picking up a large pair of binoculars; Kolodzi had often seen him wearing them. "A sort of mascot; my grandfather used to take them along with him whenever he went out hunting. So I don't want to lose them." He held them undecidedly in his hand, then gave them to Kolodzi. "You might need them in Oviz," he said casually. "You can give them back to me afterward. But don't lose them, they mean a lot to me, and this is the first time I've let anyone else have them."

Kolodzi looked into his eyes and saw a strange expression there. "You'll get them back, sir," he said quietly.

"Good." Schmitt put a hand on Kolodzi's shoulder. "You're certainly going to be very useful to me just now. Which is why I'm glad you came back. Is there anything else you want to know?"

"I can't think of anything, sir."

"All right then."

Returning to his billet, Kolodzi found Vöhringer lying on his bed ready for the move. He sat up when Kolodzi came in, and asked: "Was she pleased to see you?"

"My mother?"

"Her too."

"Yes, quite pleased." Kolodzi sat down by Vöhringer on the bed. "What d'you think they're going to do with us?"

"Something awful, I suppose. Do you happen to know?"

"Yes, Schmitt told me. Guess."

"Don't feel like it," grunted Vöhringer.

"We're clearing off—deserting."

"At last."

"What do you mean by at last?"

"At last you've seen sense. If I'd had my way. . . ."

"Oh, shut up," Kolodzi interrupted. "If you'd had your way, you'd have had us hanged long ago."

"We can always make Wertheim." Vöhringer felt in

his pocket and brought out a folded map. "Found it here," he said ponderously, "map of Czecho. We can mark out a route."

"The devil we can. In this snow you have to keep to the road, and on the road you'd run into plenty of patrols. Besides, what should I do in Wertheim? You've got your family there, but what about me?"

Vöhringer was silent.

"How far is it to Wertheim?" Kolodzi asked after a pause.

"Nearly six hundred miles."

"Nearly six hundred." Kolodzi laughed. "You must have a screw loose. Maybe you've chartered a plane?"

"Then don't talk such crap to me," said Vöhringer sullenly. "You started all this."

"Not in the way you meant. We're deserting on Schmitt's instructions."

Vöhringer stopped in the middle of lighting a cigarette. "What!"

"Just what I said." Kolodzi lay back and explained the whole thing, while Vöhringer listened with mounting astonishment. "It's pretty crazy, I suppose," Kolodzi said, "but I like the plan. It'll be a good break for us."

"Good break!" Vöhringer leapt to his feet. "Good break you say!" He flung his arms in the air. "The partisans won't play, of course, but the thing is terrific, absolutely terrific. *The* opportunity—well, isn't it?" Without waiting for an answer, he dashed to the table, spread out the map and studied it closely: "From here," he said feverishly, "we go by Linz, Passau, Straubing, Regensburg, Nürnberg, Fürth, and so to Wertheim. We can do it in a month."

"*You* can," said Kolodzi. He had his hands clasped behind his neck, and was blinking up at the light.

Vöhringer's thin rat-like face glowed with excitement.

"Don't be pig-headed," he said urgently, sitting down by Kolodzi. "You don't want your number to come up just before the curtain comes down, do you?"

"No, I don't, and that's exactly why I'm staying here." Kolodzi leaned on his elbow, and said firmly: "I've told you over and over again that I wouldn't do it. Besides" —he pointed to Schmitt's binoculars on the table in their dark leather case—"I promised to bring that thing back again."

"Where did you get them?" Vöhringer asked irritably.

"From Schmitt; he says they're an heirloom. And one more thing: Herbig's coming with us."

"Herbig!" Vöhringer jumped up again. "You're kidding."

"Why not?"

"But that's crazy, man." Vöhringer cried beseechingly. "Herbig of all people. Can't the two of us manage the thing alone?"

"Two people aren't enough. One of us might have to go and report to Schmitt; then it would be useful to have someone else there."

"But not Herbig."

"He's reliable."

"He's an informer," cried Vöhringer. "A damned informer."

"Why are you so damned set against Herbig?" asked Kolodzi. "Just because he was a Hitler Youth leader, that doesn't make him an informer."

"I can't stand the man," Vöhringer declared furiously. He sat down at the table and stared disconsolately at the floor. "I can't make any plans with him around. Do you know I haven't seen my son yet? Can you imagine what that feels like?"

"How old is he?"

"Eight months. So you insist on Herbig?"

"Yes."

"That's your last word?"

"Yes."

"Well, I suppose I'll have to come all the same," said Vöhringer with a sigh. His anger spurted up again. "But I warn you, if he starts talking any of his damned muck, I'll let him have it."

"He could put you in his pocket," said Kolodzi.

"I don't know what you see in that bastard," Vöhringer said sulkily.

Knowing he was jealous, Kolodzi smiled. "If anyone's going to find the general, it'll be the three of us together. Wait and see if I'm not right."

"The general can stay lost for all I care. He was a stupid bastard anyhow."

"He never got in my way," Kolodzi remarked.

Vöhringer stood up. "I'll go and tell Herbig."

A few minutes later he returned grinning. "The man didn't believe it. Told me he didn't want to be a deserter, not even a fake one. I told him he was always keen on medals and this was his big chance. But listen," his face grew serious and he sat down. "I've just thought of something—what are you going to do about your Maria?"

"How do you mean?"

"I only meant, what is she going to do when Ivan comes. And your mother, too."

Kolodzi regarded him with an expressionless face. "They're going to Olmütz."

"And then?"

"I've no idea."

"D'you imagine Ivan won't get to Olmütz?" Vöhringer asked scornfully.

"Of course he will."

"And then?"

Dropping his fists on the table in a helpless gesture, Kolodzi said: "Don't ask so many questions. It worries me enough as it is."

"I expect it does," Vöhringer said. "Of course, you might have sent them to Wertheim."

Kolodzi jerked his head round. "To Wertheim?"

"Yes."

"Who to?"

"To me," Vöhringer said simply. Kolodzi gaped at him, and he went on in urgent tones: "Well, why not? After all they could stay quite a while at my home, perhaps till the war's over. I'll write my wife. Well, it's an idea, isn't it?" He had talked himself into a fine glow of enthusiasm for his plan. Kolodzi, who had gone on staring at him, now bent over the table. "You damned fool!" he said, and his voice shook.

It was the last thing Vöhringer had expected. He flushed and was about to speak, but Kolodzi forestalled him. "You had all the time in the world, we've known each other long enough. And you have to come out with it now, just when it's too late. If you'd only opened your mouth a couple of hours earlier, before I went to see them! How am I going to let them know? Perhaps you can tell me that?"

"Damn!" cried Vöhringer, and began furiously scratching his neck. "Got a cigarette?" Kolodzi threw a packet on the table. "Oh damned!" he said, taking a cigarette out and lighting it; he flung the match on the floor, and stamped on it with his heavy boots. "But after all you might have asked me," he said. "How d'you expect me to think of everything? How was I to know what your plans were?" The more he tried to justify himself, the less confident he felt. He cursed again. "For God's sake say something," he cried angrily. "You've got a head on your shoulders too, haven't you? Just think a bit! Why don't you simply write to Olmütz?"

"Of course I'll write now," Kolodzi answered slowly, "and it's very good of you to offer. Only how can I be sure the letter will get there in time? It would all have been so different if you'd just opened your mouth before; there would have been none of this damned uncertainty." The thought renewed his exasperation. "Two hours earlier, and I wouldn't have anything to worry about now." He stopped abruptly as the door burst open and Herbig entered, his white camouflage coat already over his uniform. He was a tall man with a lean hard face and fair hair that fell untidily over his brow.

"We're to board the trucks immediately," said Herbig, putting a heavy rucksack down on the floor. "Company commanders report to the captain."

Kolodzi glanced resignedly over at Vöhringer. Then he hung Schmitt's binoculars around his neck and went out.

The company had already fallen in. "We won't waste any time now," Schmitt said to them, "you'll be told the plans later." He took Kolodzi to one side and pressed a document into his hand. "I took the precaution of having a movement order to Oviz made out for the three of you, just in case you run into any German troops. Only make use of it as a last resort, though—it would put the locals wise as to what's happening." He stopped and looked down the road, from where car engines could now be heard. "Here come the trucks," he concluded. "You'll sit with me."

Four big six-wheelers stopped on the other side of the road. Schmitt went over to the first, climbed on the step and spoke to the driver in the cab. "Which route are you taking?"

"Through Jaszo, sir."

"I want you first to take us twelve miles further on, to Oviz."

The driver pulled a face. "We haven't been told anything about that, sir. Our orders are to take you to Szomolnok and then come straight back to Košice."

43

"Half an hour more won't make any difference."

"We've still got to get building material to the lines tonight, sir," the man objected.

"And you'll still have time for that if you drive fast. Anyhow, those are your new orders. Ready?" Schmitt asked Menges, who had just come up.

"All aboard, sir."

The trucks moved northward over snow-covered roads and through half a dozen dark villages. To their left snowy slopes lifted toward a black sky; single trees flashed past, and telegraph poles, with wide fields and woods in the background. The driver turned on the windshield-wiper. "It's started to snow," said Menges, with a note of insensate satisfaction in his voice. Snow-flakes could be seen dancing in the headlights; they fell thicker and thicker. Then buildings appeared again on both sides—it was nearly midnight. "Szomolnok," announced the driver. Schmitt looked through the misted-over windows. The road was getting narrower, and led up the mountain side in a series of sharp bends. "Hope we don't get stuck," he said apprehensively.

"Not with this bus, sir," the driver reassured him, pointing ahead with his chin; "we've almost made it."

Kolodzi had dozed off, and woke to a shout from Schmitt. The truck had come to a stop, and the captain was just climbing out.

Looking back down the road to see the other trucks come up, Schmitt told the driver to switch off his lights, then signed to Kolodzi to get out. "You're there," he said. "See that light down there?"

Kolodzi got his bearings with a single look. There was a thick pine-wood rising on one side, while on the other there was a steep drop from the road to a deep valley completely surrounded by woods and mountains. Through a gap in the trees he at once saw the light Schmitt was referring to. It twinkled along the bottom of the valley, vanished in the snow storm for a few seconds, and then seemed to bob up again in a different place.

"That must be Oviz," said Schmitt. "We'll drive on along this road; you stay somewhere near till we've searched the place. When we've finished, we'll fire white Very lights—that'll be your signal. But remember to wait a good hour after that before you go down."

Schmitt dug his hands in his pockets and remarked with a shiver: "Wild enough country to leave you to your fate in."

"It isn't new to me, sir," Kolodzi answered. He went to the back of the truck and called his two men down.

"I'll see you get special leave all right if you find the general," Schmitt told them.

Kolodzi said nothing, and Vöhringer spat rudely on the ground; only Herbig braced his shoulders a bit. Schmitt hesitated for a moment, then shook hands with each of them in turn, and climbed back into the truck. He put his hand out of the window, and motioned to Kolodzi to come over to him. "Don't forget these," he said quietly, looking into his face and tapping the binoculars hanging on Kolodzi's chest. The trucks moved off.

When the rear light of the last truck had disappeared behind the trees, Kolodzi bent down for his rucksack.

"What now?" asked Vöhringer.

Kolodzi pointed into the darkness. "Let's get off the road." They tramped off into the wood and down the steep slope. Once Kolodzi stopped and raised his head, listening. Far ahead of them, certainly on the other side of the valley, an animal was howling plaintively. "A dog," said Vöhringer, unable to hide the quaver in his voice.

Kolodzi shook his head. "Sounds more like a wolf. I remember them from the last time I was here."

45

Vöhringer shuddered. "Are there wolves here?"

"Wolves *and* bears, but when you've got a tommy-gun you don't need to get the wind up."

They moved on. Although it was a laborious business walking in the deep snow, they made good progress owing to the steep incline, the chief obstacle being the close-set pines. After about ten minutes they suddenly came out of the wood, and found themselves looking down on the houses of a small village. They could no longer see the light they had noticed from above, but the sky had a vague brightness.

Kolodzi stared hard into the valley. A few lights went on suddenly in the village, then more and more. "All according to schedule," he observed with satisfaction, wiping the snow off of his face with his sleeve. "We'll wait here." He looked around the country. They were still on the edge of the wood, the snow was falling softly and regularly. Further to the right the wood fell back a bit, while on the left it went as far as the first houses. The terrain between was bare, undulating slightly and on a steep gradient.

They sat on their rucksacks and looked down again into the village where there was now a light showing in almost every window.

"They've finished," Kolodzi said after what seemed a long time. A Very light whizzed over the roofs, and seemed to drift uncertainly through a glittering cloud of snow, before gliding to earth. "A quarter past one," said Kolodzi, glancing at his watch. "We'll get going in an hour's time."

They fell silent again. The snow settled in thick wads on their caps and shoulders. Somewhere in the distance a wolf's long-drawn-out howl was repeated at irregular intervals, and each time the men would look up and hold their breath. "If only it weren't so damned cold," Vöhringer said, his teeth chattering. "This whole thing's crazy." He gave a sidelong glance at Herbig, who sat on his rucksack, neither moving nor speaking. "The war's lost anyhow," Vöhringer said fiercely.

Herbig turned his face around and stared at him.

"Anything the matter?" Vöhringer asked in an aggressive voice.

"Shut up," Kolodzi broke in. "First of all, that doesn't make any difference to us now, and secondly we're not at that point yet. Don't forget the Ardennes offensive."

"Yeah," jeered Vöhringer, "and Santa Claus."

"Don't forget the V-2's either," said Herbig, speaking for the first time.

Vöhringer sat round so that he could look Herbig full in the face. "Haven't you noticed everybody's stopped talking about it? Haven't you noticed that yet?"

"They're developing the V-3," said Herbig.

Vöhringer affected a laugh. "That's nothing new, my boy, we've had it all the time. Know what V-3 stands for, don't you?"

Herbig looked at him coldly, but said nothing.

"Voodoo third-class. The propaganda they've been feeding us with the whole war—that's your V-3, so shut up about it, can't you?" He turned angrily to Kolodzi. "What do *you* think?"

"Leave me alone, I've got other things to worry about."

"Oh. . . ." Vöhringer scratched his head and immediately felt guilty again. He felt inhibited by Herbig's presence and lowered his voice. "There must be a chance, don't you think?"

"No, I don't think," Kolodzi answered.

"If I were you . . ." Vöhringer began, but stopped at once because he noticed Herbig regarding him with interest. Kolodzi looked up: "Yes?"

His unfriendly tone overcame Vöhringer's caution.

47

"Well, you've still got time," he said firmly. "Perhaps you'll pick up a truck on the way, then you can be back here by this evening."

"Has this got anything to do with our mission?" Herbig asked, and when neither of them answered, his hard face assumed a watchful expression. Pensively stroking the barrel of his tommy-gun with his fingertips, he fixed his eyes on Kolodzi. "What's this all about?" he said.

"Nothing to do with you," Kolodzi answered, and then, turning to Vöhringer: "You're crazy."

His tone more than his words aggravated Vöhringer's guilty conscience and made him stick to his idea. "I admit it was dumb of me not to have thought of it before," he said quickly. "But after all, you could still have talked to Schmitt about it before we drove off. Schmitt could have sent a messenger or told the supply column to send someone. Why on earth didn't you say anything to him?"

Kolodzi was silent, thinking: of course what he says is quite true—a word to Schmitt would have done the trick; only it simply hadn't occurred to him, he always missed the obvious. He couldn't even blame Vöhringer; because he would still have had time then to send word to Maria.

Vöhringer watched him, pleased to have found a way of displacing some of his own sense of guilt. With the magnanimity born of relief he said: "No point in our both blaming each other. But now it's up to you. Ivan will be in Olmütz soon enough anyhow, you can bet."

Kolodzi was still silent, his eyes narrowed to small slits. "I'd never make it by this evening," he said.

"With the pace *you* walk! Besides, when you're on the main road, you're sure to get a lift."

Kolodzi's resistance was crumbling as the first shock

48

gave way to calm reflection, and he heard himself say: "But I just can't . . ."

"And why can't you?" Vöhringer broke in. "You don't seriously think, do you, that if the partisans show up at all, they're likely to come today?" When Kolodzi made no reply he addressed Herbig: "Got a cigarette?"

"No."

Bastard, thought Vöhringer, and turned back to Kolodzi; "Have *you?*"

"No smoking now," Kolodzi answered absently, his brain feverishly working.

Vöhringer was right, this was the only thing he *could* do. Only he must hurry, he mustn't dither about it a moment longer. He got up, picked up his rucksack, and hoisted it on to his back.

"Not more than half an hour gone," observed Herbig coldly.

Kolodzi swung round. "Let's get this quite clear," he said deliberately. "As long as we're here, there's only one person who has any say, and that person's me. It's time you got used to the different uniform—you're not in the Party now—understand?"

Herbig got up without a word and hoisted his rucksack. He said nothing as they stamped through the snow toward the houses. On the way Vöhringer suddenly stopped. "What's that?"

"What's what?" asked Kolodzi, looking round.

"Up there in the wood. A house?"

Now the others noticed it too. The building Vöhringer had seen was about three hundred feet above the village on the other side of the valley, and despite the darkness could easily be distinguished by its pointed gable, which peeped out above the trees.

"Perhaps the sanatorium," said Kolodzi thoughtfully.

"A sanatorium?"

"For heart cases, I think—I remember hearing of it.

49

Sure to be empty now. You can't see it from down there."

"It might do for us," said Vöhringer, eager for action. He stared at it in fascination; the picture excited him in a way he couldn't analyze. "Some place," he continued. "Like a castle, a snow-capped castle."

"You and your imagination," said Kolodzi. "What d'you think you'd find up there? The rooms would be so cold we'd freeze to death."

They went on. The point where they reached the village was near the edge of the wood. There was a large house, standing rather on its own; Kolodzi passed it and crossed the road before looking round. The other houses were well spaced out and on both sides of the road. Besides the houses on the road there were about a dozen more, hidden between small clumps of pines; these others had been built on both sides of the valley's steep banks, but they were sunk so deep in snow that they could hardly be seen. It looked as if the village had about eighty houses altogether.

Kolodzi made up his mind. He went to a house about thirty yards away from the big house, standing in a garden surrounded by a chest-high fence. Behind it, only a few yards further on, the wood began. He had always liked the idea of living next to a wood. The garden gate was open, and the snow in the drive had been trampled down by many boots. "Our comrades," said Vöhringer with a meaningful grin.

Kolodzi stopped outside the front door. "Be careful what you jabber about," he whispered. "The locals may understand us, and we're deserters, remember." Then he knocked on the door and waited.

Inside there was complete silence. Kolodzi took a step back and glanced over the front of the house. "Give them a bang with your tommy-gun." Vöhringer hammered against the door so hard that the noise reverberated through the house. A light went on behind one window, and a little later the door opened. "Damn," said a sleepy voice.

"Grüss Gott," Vöhringer grunted, switching on his flashlight and shining it on the man in the doorway, who was only half dressed. He was a tall, lean man with a dark face and a long straggly beard. The light seemed to dazzle him, and he muttered a few incomprehensible words.

"We want to sleep here," Kolodzi said to him, putting his right hand on his cheek. "Sleep," he repeated in Czech.

"Nix sleep," came the sullen answer; and then in Czech: "No room."

"What's he say?" asked Vöhringer.

"I can't understand him either."

"But you. . . ."

"Quiet," said Kolodzi sharply. He pushed the man aside and went into the house; the others followed him. There weren't many rooms, and they tried each in turn, ignoring the man's violent protests. "What a stink!" said Vöhringer in disgust. He looked into a room half filled by two large beds. An old woman was sitting in one of them; she hastily pulled her sheet up to her neck and looked at the men in terror. "Wrong number," Kolodzi remarked, closing the door behind him. The next room looked fairly tidy. He shone his torch on the walls. "How will this do?"

Vöhringer sniffed. "It stinks too," he said.

"You ought to be used to that," grunted Kolodzi. "This is where we'll stay."

There was a large tiled stove; when Kolodzi put his hand on it, he almost burned his fingers. Around it was a wide bench stretching as far as the window, under which there was a heavy table. Among the room's other furniture was an old, brightly painted chest and a spinning wheel. On the walls, in rough frames with much of their gilt flaking off, hung the images of saints, whose round faces smiled out through the dusty glass.

Kolodzi lit an oil lamp. Without worrying about the civilian, who stood in the doorway watching their every movement, he dumped his rucksack and extracted two reserve magazines of ammunition and pushed them under his belt. His look fell on Herbig, who was standing about uncertainly. "What are you waiting for?" he asked impatiently. "You two are staying here."

"And you?" asked Herbig warily.

Kolodzi ignored him. He went over to the civilian, and asked: "Can you understand us?"

"No," the man answered.

Kolodzi laughed and looked at Vöhringer. "Did you get that?"

"I'll say I did. He's even stupider than he looks."

The man stared at them in fury. Suddenly he turned and left the room.

"That got rid of him," said Vöhringer. "He understands every word."

"Looks like it." Kolodzi lowered his voice. "So you must be careful when you talk to each other."

"Perhaps he's one of them."

"We'd never have that much luck. But he'll certainly know if there are partisans in the place, and that's what matters." He slung his tommy-gun over his shoulder. "I don't want either of you to leave the house. When I come back, we'll see how things go."

"Where are you going?" said Herbig.

"Just for a walk," Kolodzi answered coolly. His eyes met Herbig's, who was still leaning against the stove, a cigarette hanging at the corner of his mouth. He hadn't taken off his coat, and his pack also stood by him ready to hand. I should have brought someone else, thought Kolodzi again: Herbig's obstinate and unpredictable, it's a risk leaving these two alone together. A warning voice registered faintly inside him.

He straightened up, and the other two watched him walking to the door, tall and supple. "If I'm not back by tomorrow morning," he said over his shoulder, "go to Schmitt at Szomolnok." Then he was gone.

Andrej Zarnov, leader of the group which had captured the general, had not been a partisan from the start. Living on a tiny farm in Oviz with his father Jozef and his sister, Margita, he had long ago lost touch with his brother Pavol, a lawyer in Prague and a strong Czech nationalist. In 1941 Pavol was shot for trying to throw a bomb in a German general's car. Andrej was comparatively little affected by this, unlike old Jozef, who took his elder son's death very hard. He would like to have given the rest of his life to the farm and his two surviving children, but the solace they could provide him was very short-lived; Margita indeed had long been a source of anxiety to him.

Before the war Margita had worked in the sanatorium at Oviz, where rich men from Prague and Brno came to take cures for their over-fatted hearts and to recover from their latest *affaires.* There Margita had met a fine young gentleman from Rožnava, who stayed in the sanatorium a few weeks every year and who had promised to marry her; but one day he suddenly disappeared, and was never heard from again. Since then Margita Zarnov had become little better than a tart—so people said—who slept with a different "patient" every night. So old Jozef was almost glad when the Germans marched in and cleared the sanatorium of its occupants; but even then things with Margita had gone no better. She was still a beauty, and there were plenty of young men in Oviz and Svedler who had an eye on her; only she would have nothing to do with them, and spent all her time plotting and planning with Andrej and Nikolash, the Russian whom Andrej had brought into the house.

Nikolash had demanded Jozef's room, saying contemptuously: "The old boy can sleep in the stable"; soon he treated the whole house as if it were his own. Jozef was getting too old to work on the farm, which he saw going to rack and ruin, but he had to be satisfied if Margita still cooked his meals for him, and if she and Andrej still gave him a bit of their company at Christmas time. He could still take pleasure in the preparations for Christmas, cutting down a pine from the wood—he had chosen a particularly big one this year—dragging it up to the house, and decorating it as in old times when his wife had still been alive. Of course Nikolash mocked at these capitalistic rites, but here at least Andrej defended his father against the arrogant and overbearing Russian.

Nikolash had come to Oviz two and a half years ago, determined to persuade Andrej that he should avenge Pavol's death by leading a partisan group as Pavol had done. "You owe it to your brother," he insisted. "We worked together for six months, and I tell you he was a hero, a great Czech."

"We're not Czechs," Andrej objected. "Mother was Austrian, and father's remained a Magyar."

"We're all brothers," Nikolash answered. "The men and women who have been subjugated by the Germans are all brothers and sisters. Do you want them to stay here forever? Think of the others. What did the Germans do to Austria, or to Hungary? Didn't you hear how their soldiers raped the women in Vienna, and in Budapest?"

Andrej shook his head. His work on the farm was hard, and he had never bothered much with what happened in the wider world. Nikolash told him more about the Germans—how they had massacred the Poles and burned up the churches in France, and showed him pictures of Russian women who had been killed by the Germans. Andrej was shocked; he had never seen such terrible pictures before. "This isn't a national war any longer," Nikolash said. "It's a crusade against evil; and anyone who hates and fears evil must do something against it, as your brother Pavol did. You're a Czech citizen, and so is your father. The land you live in gives you your bread. One day your children will live in this land, and their children will have Czech parents only. Do you want them to talk ill of you?"

"What do you want me to do?" Andrej answered; and that was how it started. Margita too made friends with Nikolash; in fact, she fell in love with him. This distressed Andrej, who was very much attached to his sister and knew she was only a diversion for Nikolash. Andrej's dislike of him grew with the easy way Nikolash spread himself in the house, and picked up in his coarse hands anything that caught his eye: their best crockery from the cupboard, old Jozef's suits, the pictures of Andrej's dead mother, and then finally Andrej's own sister.

Moreover, the longer they lived together in that house, and the nearer the front came, the less restrained grew Nikolash's talk. He ranted at the Czechs in the same breath as the Germans, calling them a miserable pack that couldn't be trusted, who didn't deserve to be liberated by the victorious Russian army. Andrej suppressed his anger. In the course of months he had become more and more convinced by Nikolash's views, and now there was no Czech in the country who desired the downfall of the Germans more fervently than Andrej. In contrast to the others, who out of patriotism became partisans, Andrej developed from a partisan into a patriot. But recently he had begun to show a shrewd independent judgment which the Russian was coming to find very tiresome. He tried to water down Andrej's newly aroused national consciousness with Marxist doctrines; but Andrej showed that in two and a half years he had absorbed practically nothing of Nikolash's views on the dictatorship of the working class. "Dictatorship sounds bad," he declared on one occasion. "We Czechs are against every dictatorship, whether it comes from the Germans or the workers. What d'you think we're fighting for?"

"You'll never be anything but a stupid yokel," Nikolash said furiously. "None of you can see beyond the dung heap in front of your own house. You people simply can't be made to listen to reason, you have to be taught a lesson first."

"What exactly do you mean by 'you people'?" Andrej asked, but Nikolash gave no reply. And ever since that day Andrej's suspicion had grown.

It was the day they had captured the general, when they sat together for a while celebrating with loot champagne at Zepac's house, that Nikolash said the long-awaited words: "The day after tomorrow our friends will be coming!"

His words were a bombshell. The two men sprang up, and Nikolash enjoyed their surprise, his leathery face wrinkled up into a broad grin. "I heard it an hour ago," he said cheerfully. "Why are you getting so excited? Didn't I tell you a month back that it wouldn't be long now?"

"Of course you did," muttered Andrej. He fell back on his chair, looking rather stunned. "What will happen to *us* then?" he asked after a pause.

Nikolash was rolling himself a cigarette. "You can do what you like," he answered in an indifferent voice. "In case you feel like coming with me, I'm going to

Dobsina. We're starting again there. I'd be glad if a few of you came along."

"And the prisoners?" asked Andrej.

"You'll hand them over when the first of our people come."

"I thought *you* would be doing that."

"I've changed my mind. We don't know how far our divisions will advance. In case they reach Dobsina, I'll have to be there before them; otherwise the whole organization will go up in smoke. I can't even count on Pushkin now, he's got too much on his mind." Pushkin was the head of the entire organization.

"Then we might have taken the general to the others straight away," said Andrej.

"No, he's worth far too much to me," said Nikolash. "You don't catch a general every day. If he's given company, he might start getting ideas." He lowered his voice so that only Andrej could hear. "We'll take him up tomorrow."

"To the mountain?"

"Yes. And you'd better call your people together tomorrow. I've got to know who's coming with me to Dobsina. I can count on you, I suppose?"

Andrej frowned. Going to Dobsina was something he couldn't decide about on the spur of the moment. "I'll think it over," he said evasively.

Nikolash picked up a bottle, and drained it. "Best thing about the Germans, their champagne," he said, wiping his mouth. "When we get to Berlin, we won't drink anything but champagne. Let's go."

Nikolash stamped off into the darkness, and Andrej noted with satisfaction that snow was falling. He turned to Zepac, a tiny, gnome-like figure of a man with the belligerent air of a small fighting cock.

"You were very quiet," Andrej said.

"You know why," Zepac answered. He had had a grudge against Nikolash ever since Nikolash had called him a miserable Slovak yokel. "I'll be glad when we're rid of him," he added. "Think I'm going with him to Dobsina? I wouldn't dream of it, what should I do there? I've got a wife and children here. Let the others carry on."

"We're not free yet."

"Free!" Zepac laughed. "What is free? Certainly not what *you* imagine. You're a Czech, but we Slovaks want something different."

"Perhaps you want the Germans," mocked Andrej.

"Oh shut up. You know we don't want Germans *or* Czechs. Why d'you think I've been fighting against the Germans?"

"Well, why *have* you, seeing that your Tiso is all for them?"

"He's not our Tiso. Tiso's working for the Germans and the Hungarians, not for us. So shut up about Tiso," he shouted, and disappeared into the house.

Andrej walked on smiling, remembering all the times he had bickered with Zepac on this subject. Zepac didn't know what he wanted, in fact he only joined the partisans, according to Kubany, so as to impress his wife, who wore the trousers at home. Still, he was a good man with a tommy-gun, and Andrej was satisfied with him.

But that reminded Andrej that they wouldn't need tommy-guns any more: no tommy-guns and no organization. The thought was so painful he felt like crying, and he trudged through the snow toward Elizabeth's house hardly noticing where he was going. He had never realized it would mean so much to him, but of course it wasn't surprising. As time went by he had become a leading figure in the local partisan activities.

It was a well-planned organization, and much bigger than Andrej had at first supposed; all its men were chosen with great care. Andrej had picked *his* section from Oviz and two neighboring villages; they were supposed to take prisoners so that Pushkin, in Dobšina, could supply his contacts in Prague with exact information about each new division the Germans moved up to the front through Košice.

Until a month ago, the prisoners had been shot after questioning. Then Nikolash gave instructions that those with the rank of captain and up should instead be taken to a safe hideout. The place chosen was a hut in a remote wooded valley northwest of Szomolnok, which was guarded by four reliable men from Košice; it could also be used as a reserve base should things become too hot in Oviz. Nikolash, however, had been anxious to take extra precautions, so he and Andrej built a strong log cabin near the highest mountain peak in the vicinity; it was extremely defensible, and they brought up enough arms and ammunition to give them a breathing-space in any emergency. They did not tell the others about it, because, said Nikolash, "They'd be the first to betray us if their necks were in danger— I know this rabble." Nikolash didn't know that in less than a week Margita had wormed the secret out of her brother.

Going straight to Margita's room, Nikolash lit the lamp, went over to the bed and called her name. The pillows moved, as a slim face appeared with dark tousled hair and black eyes which blinked at him sleepily. "Nikolash!" she sat up with a start. "Is Andrej back?"

"Yes. With his woman, I think. Come on over." He went into the next room, where he took off his shoes. Margita came in. She had only a nightgown on and sat down on his knees. "Did you get the general?"

"Yes."

"Andrej's a good man," she said proudly.

Nikolash smiled. "It wasn't very difficult. The Germans are stupid as geese. Aren't I a good man?"

"Show it."

He pulled her nightgown up over her knees. "Like this?"

"Yes."

"Or like this?"

"Like that too."

He laughed heartily and put her back on her feet. "I'm hungry," he said.

"You pig!" exclaimed Margita in disappointment. "You think of nothing but eating and drinking." She leaned over his shoulder. "Do you still love me?"

"And how!"

"Show it."

"Let me eat first."

"No, show me straight away." She bit his ear.

"You little bitch. Let me alone, or. . . ."

"Or what?" He did not answer, and she took a step back. "Nikolash!"

"Yes."

"Look this way." He turned around and saw that her nightgown was on the floor. "Am I beautiful?" she asked.

"Your legs are."

"Nothing else?"

"Your breasts are."

"You've got another woman," she said angrily.

He wiped his greasy fingers on his trousers and laughed. "Any objections?"

She ran toward him. "If you've got another woman, I'll kill you."

"You will?" He put his huge hands round her throat. "One squeeze, and you're dead."

"Let me go."

"You see!"

He sat down and she climbed back onto his lap and said: "It occurred to me this afternoon, you've never told me why you aren't married."

"Women marry, men love. Like this."

She groaned beneath his hands. "Nikolash. . . ."

He carried her over into her room and threw her on to the bed.

Afterward Nikolash returned to his room, took a half-filled bottle out of the wardrobe, put it to his mouth, and drained it. Then he stared pensively at the ceiling. He had a lot to think about. Moving the organization wasn't going to be easy, he told himself, and he had to decide which of the men to take with him. Krasko's men were out. They were to blow up the German HQ tonight. That was the last job they were to get from Nikolash, though they didn't know it yet. Even old Orid Krasko didn't know. He couldn't take more than a few men from Košice, because the Germans had a field Gestapo at Dobšina and a lot of new faces there would attract attention. Besides, Orid Krasko might well have a foot in both camps, he used to sympathize with the Germans—even had his daughter running round with a German soldier.

As for Andrej and his men—Nikolash bit his lip in annoyance. He rose and went to the window. A fierce wind had blown up and shook the bare trees. You couldn't have wished for better weather, he thought; again Andrej had been dead right. He had never known anyone better fitted for leading a section of partisans. . . . If only they weren't at loggerheads all the time. From the first day he had talked to Andrej on confidential terms and in his own strange way felt something like friendship for him. But these feelings were not reciprocated, nor could he win over Andrej to his ideological views. Nikolash found himself rather in the position of a rejected lover, and with his easily offended vanity could never forgive this humiliation. He had begun to hate Andrej.

Nikolash wondered if he might persuade Margita to come to Dobšina without Andrej. After all, he was convinced she loved him. The war might still go on for a long time and he meant to keep her with him as long as he could . . .

Nikolash looked out the window and suddenly saw the lights of the trucks.

They moved slowly into the village, and a moment later the streets were swarming with German soldiers. They're coming for Andrej, Nikolash thought, and just for a moment this gave him satisfaction; then he realized the danger he himself was in. He rushed into Margita's room and over to her bed, felt for her head in the dark and pulled her up by her hair.

She whimpered, then started hitting out at him. "Stop that!" he told her; "the Germans are here." At once she became wide awake. He jumped out of Margita's room into the garden, and still in his bare feet raced to the front, where there was a garden shed; above it was old Jozef Zarnov's room. Nikolash levered himself on to a beam, walked precariously along it and knocked at the window, through which he could see Jozef sitting by the stove. The old man got up and came hesitantly toward the window. When he saw Nikolash's face, he shrank back. Without letting him speak, Nikolash pushed him roughly aside, and with an eloquent gesture toward his throat said: "Don't you breathe a word about me, or else. . . ." He fancied he could hear voices downstairs. Crossing his arms, he remained standing by the window, and told Jozef to sit down.

He looked at the pine standing in a bucket near the window. "Why don't you take it to bed with you?" he mocked. "Tomorrow I'll stick it in the stove." He listened again for the noises from below and heard Margita pouring out abuse.

The little she-devil, he thought fondly. He decided to get her away to Dobšina at all costs, by force if necessary. From below came the sound of one of the

Germans laughing loudly, then, a moment later, a door slammed and all was silent.

Nikolash met with Margita halfway down the stairs. She gave a rather forced laugh. "Nothing to do with us. They were looking for three German soldiers."

"Three German soldiers?" Nikolash was baffled.

They went to the front room and looked out the window. All they could see were the trucks' rear lights, which got fainter and fainter in the snow-storm and finally disappeared altogether.

"That might easily have gone wrong," said Margita.

"It was very clever of you to keep them downstairs," Nikolash pulled her toward him.

The front door slammed and a second later Andrej came bursting into the room. When he saw the two of them standing there, his face relaxed. "Did they come here too?"

"Yes," said Nikolash. "Where were you? At Elizabeth's? Did they come there?"

"Three soldiers. They didn't want anything of us, they were looking for their own men."

"Deserters perhaps," said Nikolash slowly.

"And the Very light?"

"What?"

"They shot a Very light when they were finished. Didn't you see it?"

Nikolash shook his head. "What color?"

"White."

"Odd," muttered Nikolash, uneasy again.

Andrej nodded. "A sign for someone or other. We must watch out."

4

Kolodzi had thought very carefully about his route to Košice. Altogether he reckoned it must be a good fifty miles, a distance he couldn't possibly cover by the evening on foot and in this snow. But he trusted to his luck, for about six miles past Svedler the road met the railway line to Jelnice and there he might find a freight or a truck going to Košice.

The road to Svedler was easy enough, downhill all the way; and at half-past one he by-passed Svedler on a footpath.

Back on the road he quickened his pace again. The snow gave him little trouble. During the four years in Russia his leg muscles had gained the toughness and resilience of steel springs. The division had marched two thousand five hundred miles from Upper Silesia into the heart of Russia, and almost as great a distance on their retreat now. There was a layer of calloused skin on his feet almost as thick as the soles of his boots, and on the march his body worked like a machine.

However, gradually the snow storm grew worse until he could hardly see ahead of him. He kept having to wipe the great, wet flakes out of his eyes; they lay on his shoulders and chest like a white armor. He started to sweat and stopped to catch his breath.

It was so quiet he could hear the snow falling on

the trees. On one side of the road a bare hill rose so steeply you could not see the top; it was like a white sheet hanging down to earth and fastened somewhere in the sky. A slight wind came up over the mountains, sweeping the snow along in front of it and making the telegraph wires whir like airplanes.

Never before in his life had he felt so alone. The cold seemed to be seeping right into his marrow and he suddenly threw away his cigarette, finding it tasteless. He sighed. His thoughts strayed to Herbig and Vöhringer, who would now be lying on the warm bench by the stove and sleeping. As he thought of them he caught himself wanting simply to turn back and give up the whole crazy plan. The snow storm persisted and the wind whirled big flakes along, and Kolodzi registered subconsciously that he would have the wind behind him if he stayed on the road to Košice. Perhaps it was a sign. He was not superstitious, but at this moment of utter forlornness he made up his mind to go with the wind; and as always, once he had decided something, he wasted no more time and marched on.

About an hour later he came to the railway line. The railway now ran northward parallel with the road, and Kolodzi strode on even faster, afraid that a train might go past before he reached the station. But his luck held; nothing stirred on the line. At last he saw a light dancing through the snow. It twinkled on the right of way, and when he got nearer he saw that it was the lantern of a man going down the line.

He called out, but the man took no notice and walked on with big strides; Kolodzi sent an oath after him. His legs began to hurt, and the snow clung to his boots in big lumps and made the going harder. At last the first houses came into view. It was Nagy—he remembered now. The station, a long wooden hut, was at the other end of the village, and he could see at a

glance that it was not in use. The windows were
boarded up, iron grating had been put in front of the
door, and the wind howled over the dark, deserted
platforms. It was half past three by now. From a sort
of desperate obstinacy, Kolodzi went back to the road
and marched on. The road ahead led unendingly into
the middle of the snow storm. He began to feel very
drowsy. Somewhere there were houses with warm beds
in them, and people lying in those beds now, not worrying about the snow falling outside and the wind howling in the telegraph wires. It would be wonderful to be
in bed. His shoulders drooped as he went on down the
road, while the snow fell into his tired face and on
his bent back, which hurt under the weight of the
heavy gun. He walked on as in a dream and it began
to seem to him that he had been walking on this road
all his life, through the same night and the same snow
and always the same wind on his back and the howling
of the telegraph wires in his ears.

Finally he saw a light twinkling near the line. This
time it wasn't a lantern; the light came from the window
of a signal tower between the tracks. He crossed the
rails and found himself in front of a door. He opened
it, went up a steep staircase in the darkness and bumped
into another door; when he opened it a current of warm
air hit him, making him blink before his eyes became
used to the light. One side of the room contained a
battery of switch and signal levers. There was a red-
hot stove with a man sitting by it, the man was staring
at him and now lifted a pistol and pointed at Kolodzi.
"What d'you want?" he asked loudly. He wore the uniform of a railroad man, with a service cross in his button
hole.

Kolodzi pulled the door shut behind him. "Put that
thing away, I don't like it," he said.

The signalman hesitated, then lowered the barrel of
the pistol. "Who are you?"

"Lot of questions you ask, I'm a *Landser*—can't you tell?"

"You've got a funny way of talking," said the signalman. Kolodzi pulled his paybook out of his pocket and threw it over to him. The man looked at it, compared the photograph with Kolodzi, then handed it back. "One has to be careful," he said apologetically, and pointed to a chair. "Come and warm up."

His manner had changed instar.tly. "We don't often get anyone straying this way," he remarked chattily. "And when we do, it's almost always a partisan. The trouble we have with them here! A week ago they blew up a whole signal tower. Three men killed. Cup of coffee?"

Kolodzi nodded. He was beginning to feel extremely comfortable.

"Where have you come from?" the signalman asked, as he poured out the coffee.

"Oviz."

"Not on foot surely?"

"Yes, on foot. Thought I'd pick up a lift somewhere, but there wasn't a thing on the road the whole damned way. And I want to get to Košice too."

"There's nothing along here before dawn, I'm afraid. There aren't any trains that stop here. None of them stops before Jelnice."

"When's the next?"

"Can't say. One side of the line's snowed up, and there should be a snow plow coming, but God knows when."

"It goes beyond Jelnice?"

"Right to Košice."

"Does it, by God!" said Kolodzi, massaging his numbed fingers and holding them near the stove. "Can't you stop it?"

The signalman laughed. "What d'you think?—there's no stop here. Are you in a hurry?"

"I'll say I am. I live in Košice, and they suddenly gave me home leave on compassionate grounds. Only I've got to be back in Oviz by this evening. We're supposed to be looking for partisans there."

"If it were only up to me," said the man. "One might try to stop the plow. But I'm sure my partner won't agree. We don't get along too well. He's out on the line now."

"I believe I met him," Kolodzi said. "With a lamp. I tried to talk to him but he wouldn't stop."

"I'm not surprised," nodded the signalman. "You don't know how careful we have to be. All the locals here are in with the partisans. And they put only two of us up here, it's crazy. We hardly ever get any sleep."

Kolodzi glanced at his unshaven face and noticed for the first time how pale and bleary-eyed he looked. At that instant the door flew open to show a tall man, who stooped to come in, with a gaunt face and piercing eyes, his coat heavy with snow. He slammed the door behind him and stared at Kolodzi who suppressed an immediate feeling of antipathy and exclaimed, forcing a smile: "Ah, so there you are. A moment ago you wouldn't even talk to me."

The man went on staring at him. "That was you, was it? What do you want here?" He took off his great-coat and went on, not waiting for an answer: "You can't spend the night here. We've no room and besides it's against regulations."

"I don't want to. I only wanted to ask about trains."

"The station's at Jelnice," the man said in a surly voice. He sat down on the chair which Kolodzi had been occupying. His partner began to explain. "He's got compassionate leave till tonight, his people live in Košice. But he has to be back in Oviz by this evening."

The man stared at Kolodzi.

"Compassionate leave, eh? Got a leave pass?"

"Want to see it?" Kolodzi asked, as calmly as possible.

"He's shown me his paybook," the first signalman hastily put in, "and it's quite in order. Perhaps the plow can take him?"

"It doesn't stop here," the tall man rapped out. "How can you say that it might take him?"

"I only said perhaps," the other defended himself.

It was obvious that the tall man was in command and Kolodzi decided to lose no more time. He rose and picked up his gun. There seemed no further point in hiding his feelings so he turned to the tall man and shouted: "Lucky there aren't many like you. I'd prefer a Gestapo man."

"Well, we can always fetch one. Let's see your leave pass."

"What d'you mean?"

"I want to see your leave pass," repeated the tall man, reaching for the pistol which the other had put down on the table.

Kolodzi calmly lifted his gun, pushed back the safety catch with his thumb, and aimed the barrel at the man. "Here it is," he said. "No need to get excited. This isn't a question of leave passes, it's a question of principle. Where should we be if every railwayman could ask to see your leave passes, get me? And I'd put that pistol down if I were you," he told the tall man whose face had turned dead white. He dropped the pistol.

"That's better," said Kolodzi, backing to the door. "You'll never make a good Gestapo man," he added and then stumbled down the dark staircase.

At the bottom of the stairs his foot hit something. He bent down and felt a lantern and without stopping to think picked it up and took it with him.

Outside the wind had now increased, but it was still behind him and the snow was not falling so thickly now; the lantern, however, felt very heavy on his arm.

He set off in the direction of Jelnice, keeping on the right side of the rails. Looking around he saw dozens of trees lying all over the wood. Their bases were mostly jagged like broken glass, and only a few had been uprooted bodily. He knew about this; when it was very cold trees would break up at the impact of quite an ordinary storm; they froze so hard right to the core that they snapped apart like icicles. As he was looking at the overturned trees, he suddenly had a bold idea. He continued walking along the right of way until he found what he was looking for.

Two yards from the rails the storm had pulled out the stem of a young beech and hurled it across into the wood, where it was still hanging with its top caught in another tree. It seemed almost impossible to move so heavy a tree: with its branches it was about ten yards long, and its average diameter about a foot. But Kolodzi saw that the tree was not hopelessly stuck. Only the stem of the other tree was caught in its crotch, and he could easily reach up to it. The broken-off end had dug itself into the snow near the stump. Kolodzi found a strong branch sticking out of the snow, which he put crossways under the end of the tree. Kneeling down, he took the upper part of the branch on to his shoulder, went on his hands and knees, and heaved himself upward; the tree moved slowly at first, the crotch slipped off the stem of the other tree and thudded into the snow. Now came the hardest part, turning the tree and dragging it over the line. He stepped into the crotch and wound his arms under a branch pressing against it with all his strength. He succeeded in pushing the whole tree a foot and a half in the direction of the line and then pressed it around so far that it lay parallel with the embankment. The work was exhausting but he allowed himself no break, though his fingers were stiff and numb as he dragged the tree around to cross the rails. Finally it was lying just as he wanted it: diagonally over the tracks, with its broken-off end a foot from the stump. He wiped out the traces of his work with a bundle of brushwood. He could safely leave the rest to the storm, which was whirling clouds of fine snow over the embankment and into the wood. In a few minutes the last traces would be covered.

Kolodzi lit the lantern, then fetched his gun and started walking in the direction from which the train would be coming.

He had walked about three hundred yards when he heard a noise which made him stop. Now he heard it again. It was the shrill whistle of an engine. His heart began hammering, the storm blew snow into his face, but he took no notice and stared tensely into the night. Now he heard the whistle again, much nearer. He held the lantern above his head with both hands, waving it to and fro, as he had once watched railwaymen doing. Now he saw a spark moving forward between the rails; it swelled like an avalanche, a few seconds later it broke apart, and two glaring beams of light swept over the line. The gale howled in his ears, louder and louder, till he realized it was no longer the gale but the noise of the engine roaring down on him. They had not reduced their speed.

He crouched. The beams of light were blinding him, and the wind threatened to tear the lantern out of his hands. In front of him a whirl of snow and light grew to a huge, shining white cloud, which rolled toward him with fantastic speed. Now there was a hot blast on his face. He stumbled, trying to jump to one side; his legs no longer obeyed him. The lantern dropped. A terrible force had gripped him, hurled him aside into an icy black vortex. He felt the snow in his mouth and struggled for air, thrashing round with his arms. His lungs swelled like balloons, the blood rushed to his head so that it seemed to burst. Air, he thought, I must

74

have air. He fought like an animal against the snow that had its icy fingers round his throat, that would not relax its grip, that was doing its best to strangle him. Twice, three times he succeeded in slightly raising his heavy body, but his strength was gone. On the verge of unconsciousness he felt himself being gripped by the legs and pulled upward. He writhed in the snow, still fighting for air, and heard voices above him.

He pushed himself up on his arms. Icy fresh air flooded into his lungs, and opened his eyes to see two men's soot-covered faces above him. Instinctively he felt behind him, where the gun should be hanging; but someone gripped his arm and said: "Take it easy." The voice sounded friendly, it brought Kolodzi completely to himself; he swore loudly. Four powerful hands lifted him to his feet, and steadied him. "Nothing broken?" one of the men asked, a fat man with a huge chest and a good-natured face. Looking past him, Kolodzi saw the engine about fifty yards away, just recognizable in the snow storm. They stopped, he thought, they really stopped.

The two men were regarding him curiously, but he was still too shocked to be capable of saying anything. His legs were still trembling, snow melted inside his coat collar, and the icy water ran down his back. Because he couldn't think of anything better to do, he began to swear. It helped quite a lot.

The two men in front of him grinned. "It's shaken up his brains," said the fat one.

"People shouldn't act like snowballs," the other giggled, his pointed adam's apple jerking up and down. Kolodzi suddenly went into a fury. "Do you always behave like this when someone tries to stop you?" he cried.

The adam's apple came to rest. "Nobody tells *us* to stop," the men answered in surprise.

Kolodzi put his hand to his coat, and was relieved to find he hadn't lost Schmitt's binoculars. He tried to smile. "Not even a tree?""

"What tree?" asked the fat man quickly, his face suddenly losing its good-natured expression. "Is there something wrong with the line?"

"There's a tree across the rails," said Kolodzi. "I tried to drag it off, but couldn't manage it."

"Do you belong to the railway staff?"

"No, I'm trying to get to Jelnice and was walking along the line because it's the quickest way."

"And then you saw the tree?"

"Couldn't help seeing it. When I realized I couldn't get it away on my own, I began walking back toward Nagy, but then you people came."

"And you don't belong to the railway staff?" the fat man asked again, with a sudden note of suspicion in his voice.

Kolodzi looked around for the lantern, but it was not between the rails. Perhaps the engine had dragged it along. In an indifferent tone he asked: "Why *should* I belong to them?"

"What did you give a signal with?"

"With my flashlight. It's around here somewhere." He went over to the snow drift and pretended to be looking for the flashlight.

The fat man called him back impatiently. "Leave it, we haven't time. First we must get the tree away. Where is it?"

"Couple of hundred yards from here," Kolodzi answered. They went along to the engine, and he saw that it had been running backward, pushing a freight car. "In with you," said the fat man, "and if you've been spinning us a yarn, we'll make things hot for you, as sure as my name's Gustav."

"An excellent name," Kolodzi grinned. He climbed

76

the steep iron steps to the cab. The heat coming from
the firebox did him good. He watched the fat man
working the controls. The engine started up laboriously.

"Well, and where *have* you come from?" the engineer asked over his shoulder.

Kolodzi told them the same story as he had told the
signalmen. They listened to him without taking their
eyes off the line. "If that's true about the tree," said
the engineer, "we'll take you with us right to Košice."

The fireman gave a shout. "D'you see it?"

"I'll say I see it." The engineer reduced speed. "Well,
that's true enough," he said.

The engine came to a stop, but instead of making any
move to climb out, the two men stared suspiciously
into the wood. "What are you waiting for?" Kolodzi
asked.

The engineer looked at him. "Ever heard of partisans?"

"Seeing that's why we're in Oviz! We're supposed to
search for partisans there."

"God, you don't need to *search* for partisans!" The
engineer spat through the window. "The bastards are
everywhere. You go out, you've got a gun."

"There certainly aren't any here. The tree was pulled
up by the gale, I've had a look at it."

"Are you scared?"

Kolodzi smiled, clambered down the four iron steps
and regarded the freight car. On the front was a V-
shaped blade, about three yards wide, over which
there were two powerful headlights. He glanced casually at the wheels of the blade, but there was nothing
to be seen of the lantern, perhaps it had been shattered. With studied carelessness he trotted ahead to
the place where the tree lay over the rails. There he
stopped and looked back. The engineer's head emerged

cautiously on one side of the cabin. "How does it look?" he called. When Kolodzi waved to him he jumped out of the engine and came hesitantly nearer.

"Look at the thing," said Kolodzi.

The engineer regarded the tree. "And you couldn't get that away? Why I could pick it up between thumb and forefinger."

"I'd like to see you."

"You shall in a minute." He bent down and put his long gorilla-like arms round the trunk and with a jerk which made Kolodzi think he heard the bones crack, the man tore the heavy tree off the ground, dragged it over the line to the edge of the wood. Then he let it fall, and came back to Kolodzi. "That's how you do it."

"Simple," muttered Kolodzi, much impressed.

They returned to the train.

The fat man went to the door of the freight car, and there turned around. "You can't come in the cab. If you're seen by the stationmaster at Jelnice, I'll be in bad trouble. Don't make a sound till I call you."

"When do we get to Košice?"

"That depends. There may be another tree blocking the line. Otherwise we'll make it by seven o'clock."

"As late as that?" asked Kolodzi in a disappointed voice.

The engineer was insulted. "Late you call it. You can be glad we're taking you with us at all." He pressed open the heavy car door with one finger. "Get a move on," he said crossly. Kolodzi climbed in. "And don't make a sound," the engineer repeated. Then the door rolled shut and Kolodzi sat down in the dark.

The wooden floor was cold. He sat on his cap and stretched out his legs. The car began to move, the engine let off steam, and then the speed increased. There was a small slit in the door, through which one could see white clouds whisking upward.

The wheels' metallic clang, the snow plow's monotonous droning, the engine's occasional whistling, began to fade from his consciousness. A great weariness went out from his legs and climbed over the whole body. Even so, he could not fall asleep. At a certain point in his brain there seemed to be a fine needle boring; it was painful, and the irritation this caused made him wide awake again. He opened his eyes, it was so dark in the car that he blinked to convince himself they were really open. When that was no use, he turned his face again toward the chink in the door, and gazed for a while at the grey-white cloud dancing past outside.

Suddenly he had a distinct sense of being watched, and much as he tried to reject it as imagination, he could not shake the feeling off. He sat up straight and groped for his gun. He felt for the safety-catch with his fingers, and flicked it. At the same moment a voice said: "Don't shoot."

Kolodzi gave a start. The voice had come from the right of the car, and now he could make out a man's figure in the darkness. The figure moved closer and stopped in front of him. "Here I am," it said.

"Well?" said Kolodzi.

"You're from the military police, aren't you?"

"Me? Are you crazy? What are you doing here?"

"Aren't you from the military police?"

"Hell, no," answered Kolodzi impatiently.

"Well, thank God," said the man in a relieved voice. "My name's Alfred."

"Pleased to meet you," said Kolodzi in a noncommittal voice.

They crouched on the floor, each trying to make out the other's face. As far as Kolodzi could see, the man was in the uniform of the German army but he seemed to have no gun. Kolodzi felt uncertain how to treat him, and after a pause asked:

"Where are you making for?"

"As far as I can get, if possible to Erfurt."

Kolodzi grinned. "But you're on the wrong train."

The man made an abrupt movement. "What d'you mean?"

"This thing's going east to Košice. Didn't you know?"

"My God!"

Kolodzi was surprised by the dismay in his voice. "What's your trouble?"

"I told you, I'm sitting in the wrong train."

"We're all sitting in the wrong train." Kolodzi was losing his desire for conversation. The man was a puzzle to him and he had grown vaguely suspicious. So near his objective he mustn't make a mistake. "I've got leave," he said as matter-of-factly as he could. "My relations live in Košice."

The man peered at Kolodzi's face through the darkness. Suddenly he blurted out: "They're after me. I ran into them at Rožnava right in the street. They hunted me like a pack of hounds. Got a cigarette?"

Silently Kolodzi handed him the package.

"Thanks, I don't usually scrounge." Alfred took a cigarette and lit it; for the first time Kolodzi could see his face. It was a thin, intelligent face, but very nervous; his eyes blinked continually as if he were staring steadily at a bright light. Now he threw the match away and took a deep puff at his cigarette. "It was at the station I managed to give them the slip. This car was standing on the platform for Dobšina. They searched for me everywhere, except in here. But now. . . ."

"Now what?"

"I've got an address in Dobšina. I don't understand how it is we're bound for Košice. The train was on the platform for Dobšina."

"That sort of thing can happen," said Kolodzi. "They must just have switched, and you didn't notice. But I still don't understand who . . ."

"The MP's," said Alfred hoarsely.

Keep out of this, said a voice inside Kolodzi: you've got to get to Košice now, and you're not concerned with anything else. Instinctively he moved away a bit. "I can't help you," he said in a surly voice. "You cooked up your own mess and it's you now who has to stew in it."

"Right."

Kolodzi turned his face. He suddenly felt sorry for the man but he fought the feeling. It's not right, he told himself, you can't simply run away and leave others to carry the can. Where'd we be if everyone tried to run away? His momentary uneasiness subsided. It's a dirty business, he thought, and anyone who lets himself in for it must know what he's doing. "Everyone must know what he's doing and which side he's on," he said aloud.

Alfred did not reply.

"Don't you think it's more decent to get a Russian bullet in your brain than to kill yourself?"

"More decent, is it!" jeered Alfred. "What decency have we still got? That we gas the Jews instead of cutting their throats, or hang our soldiers instead of clubbing them to death—is that the sort of decency you mean?"

The subject made Kolodzi nervous. "Listen," he said, taking Alfred by his coat and shaking him, "now just listen to me. Did I start this war? And while I have to stick my own neck into combat, I'm not going to let someone like you come along with stupid stories about the Jews. What are the Jews to me, or the trash that have been put up against the wall? They're no loss. If they'd had *their* way, the Russians would have been in Košice long ago."

"Oh, so that's how you see it, is it?" Alfred's voice grew shrill. "Was it the Russians, then, who started the war? Why are they at the gates of Košice, why has it come to this point with us all? Not because the Russians declared war on us, was it? Are you people really so dense, or are you just putting it on?"

"We're putting it on," Kolodzi answered furiously. "I've been roaming round Russia these three and a half years to have you come and tell me it was all for nothing? If I'd a man like you in my company, I'd make him dig mass graves from morning till night, so that he'd realize why we can't run away—and that's because the ones in the mass graves didn't run away either, although they were neither stupider nor cleverer than the rest of us." Breathing heavily, he grabbed Alfred's coat and shouted: "If you want to run, then go ahead, but leave me in peace. I'll be glad to have seen the last of you." He fell back, trying to calm himself, but then he flared up again. "Did I start the war, blast you?"

"You're one of the people who are keeping it going."

"Me? You're crazy. Whether I go on with it or not is as unimportant for the war as. . . ." Failing to find an adequate comparison, he broke into curses.

"Why do you go on with it then, if it is so unimportant?" mocked Alfred. "You said it was that yourself."

"Unimportant for the war," cried Kolodzi. "For the war, you damned fool. But not for me. It's important for me that I stick where I belong and that's by my . . . by the others for whom it's also important. Can't you understand that?"

There was no answer from Alfred. Kolodzi stared into the darkness. A strange, dull sadness spread through him. Damned, he thought, damned. It had never got him as badly before and he couldn't understand himself.

"I wouldn't like to be in your shoes," he declared.

"One has to take some risks," answered Alfred.

"Perhaps we'll still win the war, then what do you do?"

"Win the war! Don't fool yourself."

Kolodzi felt his sadness increasing. He listened to the monotonous noise of the snow plow, beneath him the floor was trembling.

He tried to reason himself into a peaceful mood. This man has his outlook, he thought, and he, Kolodzi, had his own. One was responsible all the time to one's own conscience only and so long as one had nothing to reproach oneself with, one could listen to a different opinion without committing high treason. He discouraged further conversation.

After a long while Alfred spoke up again in a different tone.

"I have to get out of this crate before we're in Košice. There are sure to be MP's at the station."

"I'm getting out before that."

"Can one?"

"I think so. There are lots of tracks there and the trains slow down to a walk when they're approaching the station. You just have to jump the right way." Kolodzi peered at his watch. They had been traveling for two hours. He rose and went to the door. The darkness made it impossible to get any sort of bearings but it couldn't be long now.

Alfred moved nearer. "Are we there?"

"We shall be soon." Kolodzi picked up his tommy-gun. "That must go out first, I need both hands free. You haven't a gun?"

"Chucked it away."

"That was dumb. A good tommy-gun is worth more than a bad leave pass."

Kolodzi pushed the door a bit more open. Snow-covered bushes flashed past, telegraph poles and wood. "I think this is it," he said. "Get ready!" He pushed the

83

door wide open and stood poised to jump. The engine reduced its speed with a sudden jerk.

Kolodzi leaned out. Signal lights flashed by, then a few houses with lighted windows: in the grey light they looked cold and hostile. There was now only a slight snow fall. The noise of the snow plow had stopped, the engine whistled shrilly, then the wheels rumbled over the switches. A chain of red lanterns appeared round a bend, and further on the glare of powerful searchlights.

Kolodzi swung round, knocking into Alfred, who stumbled back in alarm. "Now!" he hissed, and crouched to jump. But at that instant he noticed some men standing on the line and staring up in his direction. The engine braked sharply, to move past the lanterns at a walking pace. On the other side there were enormous holes torn out of the track. Near it lay the debris of a freight train, there were rails sticking up into the air, and in between many people running to and fro. The engine passed the searchlights, where about fifty men were struggling with a shapeless lump that had a tube sticking out of it. "What's that?" asked Alfred.

Kolodzi relaxed from his tense position. "What was it, you mean. A railway gun. Must have been an air raid. Bad luck for us."

"Why?"

"Because we missed the right moment. There's the station already."

Alfred tried to get past, but Kolodzi gripped him, saying sharply: "Stay here. Sit in your corner, and don't budge. We mustn't make a mistake now."

The locomotive stopped. Looking through the chink, Kolodzi saw the engineer climb down. In a moment he came running up and pushed the door open. "Out with you." He looked tensely around. "Make off across there," he said, pointing into the darkness. In case you're caught, you haven't been traveling with me. See the fence there—get away over that. Don't let them pick you up, all hell is loose here—they blew up the local HQ today."

"Our people?"

"Don't be a fool—the partisans, of course. Now get going!"

With his head bent, Kolodzi ran over the line to a board fence, where he stopped and looked back. He saw the engineer vanishing into a dark shed, followed by the fireman. Further to the right was the main station building, looking black and dirty in the clammy grey of the morning; only its roof was white. He waited, leaning against the fence and looking over toward the shed. He had just decided to lose no more time when he heard a movement behind him. Crouching down against the fence, he looked through one of the cracks. At the back of the fence was a road, and he could see two sentries, steel-helmeted and with tommyguns slung over the shoulder; now they had passed on. Kolodzi waited a few seconds longer, then dashed over the line, round the engine and up to the car. He pushed open the door, and found himself looking into Alfred's face, which relaxed at once.

"Get out! We haven't much time."

They raced toward the fence. Kolodzi stood with his back to it and clasped his hands in front of him. "See if you can see the sentries, two of them, with steel helmets."

"Over there?"

"Where else?"

Alfred climbed on to Kolodzi's hands and pulled himself to the top of the fence. "Nothing," he whispered.

"Then over quickly."

The fence's boards were spiked, and Alfred got his coat stuck. Panting, he wrenched it free, and jumped down to the road, followed closely by Kolodzi—who got his bearings at a single glance. To the left, as he now remembered, the road went steeply downhill, curved sharply and disappeared in a tunnel, to come out the other side of the railway; the two sentries must have gone in this direction. To the right the road went straight along by the fence, while on the other side of it there was a row of trees. Behind them a white plain stretched as far as the mountains, which stood out against the grey sky more and more distinctly.

He stiffened up; from the right the sentries appeared again. They were striding along the fence, the tommy-guns ready in their hands, their faces dark under the tin helmets. Alfred had seen them too; he gripped Kolodzi's arm and hissed: "Let's run for it." They raced down toward the tunnel, and a voice yelled after them, but they kept running. They could not be the same sentries he had seen before, Kolodzi thought feverishly. At his side he heard Alfred panting. It was another fifty yards to where the road branched off into the tunnel. The main road continued on in the same direction, but to his left was the high embankment and on the other side the snowy plane which offered no cover: the tunnel was their only chance. The yelling behind them suddenly stopped. The crack of a tommy-gun shot sounded above their heads, then another, then more and more; they ran for their lives. They charged round the corner, and like a huge black maw the tunnel opened ahead of them, a hundred and sixty yards long. Without a moment's pause, Kolodzi dashed in; it was pitch dark. They kept close to the right wall, and ran as hard as they could go.

Behind them, the dry crack of another tommy-gun sounded, booming through the tunnel like a cannon; a ricocheting bullet whistled just above their heads, then all was quiet. Kolodzi stopped running so abruptly that Alfred bumped into him in the darkness. "What is it?" he asked, and receiving no answer, looked ahead, where the opening of the tunnel appeared like a smudge of grey. Out there one could hear several voices shouting back and forth. Alfred leaned against the wall. "They've got us," he said in a resigned voice.

"Not yet." Kolodzi took the tommy-gun off his back: he needed time to think. It was a novel situation for him, because this time it was not Russians but Germans who were after him. It was a paralyzing thought, and for a moment he felt like a man wrongly suspected of a crime. It was as if he only needed to reach the tunnel exit in order to clear up the misunderstanding with a few words. But then he remembered that he had a deserter with him and had himself left Oviz without leave. He might have been able to explain that, he thought: after all, he had Schmitt's movement order in his pocket, and he could surely try something with that; easy enough to think up a special mission he had been sent on. And he could say he simply had to get to the station so as to look out for a train; only then he oughtn't to have let himself be caught climbing over the fence with Alfred—because obviously the sentries saw them. You're a damned fool, he told himself furiously, why did you ever let yourself in for this at all? You knew it might go wrong.

It was pitch dark in the middle of the tunnel. At its exit, where the patch of grey had grown brighter, the noise had stopped. Kolodzi felt for Alfred's arm and whispered: "Back."

Although they tried to walk quietly, the nails of their boots crunched on the stone ground as if they were walking over splintered glass. They went down on their knees and crept forward on all fours. The ground was cold. Kolodzi felt as if he were crawling through a black pipe; only the patch of grey at the exit showed the direction. His brain was working feverishly, thinking of the two sentries who had fired at them.

Were they waiting outside the tunnel till it grew lighter? Were they getting reinforcements, would there already be machine guns waiting for them at each end of the tunnel?

Kolodzi jumped to his feet, took his tommy-gun in his hand and began to run. Behind him he heard Alfred's scared voice, but he took no notice of that, nor did he remember any longer that it was German soldiers who were out for his blood. He thought of nothing at all now, simply ran fast and steadily, no longer worrying about the noise his boots were making. Schmitt's binoculars knocked against his chest, but he didn't register that either. His tall, sinewy body had become anesthetized by a single thought, and when a tommy-gun cracked off somewhere, he did not even bend his back. Bits of stone were torn up in front of him, but he only shook his head slightly and ran on steadily with a murderous determination. When he reached the tunnel exit, he saw five men race up the road as though the devil were after them, and further up what seemed a solid wall of soldiers was rolling toward them. He heard sirens shrilling, a tommy-gun barked, the shots came whistling through the cold air. At last he stopped and looked round.

Alfred came running out of the tunnel, looked along the street and then turned left. Kolodzi bounded toward him, yelling: "To the embankment!" They clambered up the slope, sinking up to their knees in snow, slipped back, gasped, clutched on to lumps of icy snow; then they were on top. Before them stood the fence, dark and threatening, nearly seven feet high. Kolodzi heard shouting on the road, shots whizzed near them, near his shoulder one bullet struck a hole into the fence; the hole was so big he could have stuck his finger through it. He threw his tommy-gun over the fence and pulled himself up. Taking in at a glance that there was no one on the other side, he jumped down. The snow broke his fall, he was on his feet again at once and retrieved his gun. Looking up, he saw that Alfred had not come over the fence.

He dashed back and pressed his face against a crack, just in time to see Alfred sliding down the embankment slope. Soldiers came running across the road, and it was already so light that he could see the badges on their coats: Military Police. More and more thronged behind them, the whole road was full of them. The first three reached the slope, and he saw Alfred kicking at them; one of them reached out with his gun and there was an ugly sound. Now they grabbed Alfred, and began battering him with their fists, kicking him in the stomach with their nailed boots, and left off only when he had stopped moving and lay in the snow, a lump of bleeding flesh. Then they came running up the embankment. Kolodzi saw their distorted faces, ugly grimaces under bobbing steel helmets: German soldiers. Half mad with terror he pushed the barrel of his gun through the crack and emptied the whole magazine. Then he was running away from the fence across the snow-covered tracks. He was crying but he did not notice it. All he could think was: that's how it is, and again: so that's how it is. Some men came toward him, he raised his tommy-gun with the empty magazine and they ran away in alarm. Instinctively he swerved off into another direction. He scrambled under a string of freight cars, crossed tracks and switches in great bounds, and came up against a wall. He vaulted over it not noticing that his hands were torn and bleeding from the glass fragments on top. He came out into a deserted street. Without reducing his speed, he ran as far as the next crossroad and fifty yards beyond; only then did he drop to a walk. Three civilians were standing under a door and stared at him. He did not see them. Blindly he marched to Maria's house. The front door was open, he went down a dark hall, and saw Maria. When Kolodzi came in, she looked up incredulously. "Yes," he said, "it's really me."

She jumped up and flung her arms round him. "What's happened, Stefan?"

"Nothing."

"That's not true. Just look at yourself."

"I'm all right." His knees were tottering, he dropped into a chair and asked: "Where's your father?"

"I don't know. What's happened? Do tell me, please." She pressed against him, panting. "What's happened, Stefan?"

Kolodzi did not answer. A red cloud hung over his brain, he could taste salt water at the corners of his mouth, and there was a lump in his throat so big he couldn't swallow it. But Maria was with him. Through the thin dress he could feel her trembling. He caressed her shoulders, her neck; and the warmth of her body enveloped him. Her mouth was against his ear, he heard her say something, but shook his head and pressed her to him still tighter. Somewhere there was the hum of boiling water, a clock ticked, a dull light crept through the kitchen window—it was already day.

With Colonel Schnetzler and Captain Sitt the division had lost its two senior staff officers after the general; following the conference at headquarters, Captain Meisel also went off to an army hospital for treatment of his injured arm. For several hours the extensive and complicated machinery of division headquarters was wholly in the hands of Major Giesinger, the divisional adjutant. He was not completely at ease in his new role; he had failed to make the brilliant entrance he had previously imagined, and the quarrel with Fuchs had left him vaguely unsettled.

The HQ was housed in the huge villa of a Czech industrialist, now living with his family on the top floor, where the servants used to sleep. By Czech standards the house was luxuriously furnished. Giesinger's room possessed a wide projecting bay with a big desk, a smoking table and four comfortable chairs. Opposite, built into the paneled wall, there was an open fireplace with elaborate wood carving and graceful pillars on both sides, which had immediately aroused his enthusiasm the first time he entered the room: it was an exact replica of a fifteenth-century chimney piece he had once seen in Florence.

He was a passionate connoisseur, and his flat in

Aachen had swallowed up over half the respectable fortune which his father had accumulated in thirty years of flourishing legal practice. On the other hand, it contained a good fifty treasures, collected from all over the world, any one of which was worth a small fortune: Giesinger stinted neither money nor effort to transform his residence into a private museum.

Now he was seriously considering whether there was any chance of dismantling part of the fireplace and packing it home in a big chest. He mentioned the idea to Captain Hardorff, whom he had invited over for a drink, when the latter arrived.

Knowing Giesinger's hobbyhorse, Hardorff, a lanky man with grey hair, smiled. "The pillars perhaps. Only I'm afraid they wouldn't survive the journey, traveling conditions being what they are."

"No, I suppose they wouldn't," said Giesinger. He took Hardorff by the arm and led him to the table where drinks were set up.

The room was at the back of the house, and had a view on to a large park, which formed part of the grounds. Giesinger went quickly over to the window and looked out. "It's snowing," he said in dismay.

"So it is. Bad for Schmitt."

Giesinger bit his lip. Then he drew the heavy curtains, saying: "Had to expect it." He got one of the bottles, filled the glasses and sat down. "You didn't open your mouth once the whole conference," he remarked.

Hardorff took a sip from his glass. "I know. But what can a dyed-in-the-wool bureaucrat like me say? I can figure out for you exactly the number of superfluous forms that are filled in the division on an average day, but if you ask me how to catch partisans, I'm out of my depth."

Giesinger was disappointed. He needed someone

who could help him regain his self-confidence. "What would you have done in my place?" he asked.

"Probably the same as you. As to Herr Fuchs—but I needn't say anything against him, you can do that much better than I can. Only I feel you let him impress you too much."

"If that's what you feel, you're quite wrong. Herr Fuchs doesn't impress me one little bit. I'm not thinking of him, but the others. They're all against me."

"Appearances are deceptive, you shouldn't get wrought up like this. Hepp's with you, for instance."

"Did he tell you so?"

Hardorff nodded. "We discussed it afterward. I know that goes for Pfeiffer and Hartung too. You needn't care what the rest think."

Giesinger felt slightly relieved. He set great store by Hardorff's opinion. Since he discovered Hardorff's keen interest in his own hobby, he had several times invited him to share a bottle of wine, and they had agreed to continue their acquaintance after the war. Hardorff was a confirmed bachelor with a great taste for literature and art, and an amazing grasp of their history. Giesinger felt something almost like friendship for him; their conversations were seldom intended for other ears.

"You can't rely on their chatter," Giesinger said now. "They talk like that to you because they know you and I are friendly. Hepp, for instance, is typical. I know exactly what he thinks of me and how he usually talks about me. Let him—it doesn't matter in this kind of situation. What *does* matter is the fact that we have a bit more brain than the others. Look at our higher staff officers till now, they were brainy enough and yet. . . ."

The telephone rang. Giesinger went to the desk, and announced on returning to his chair: "That was Colonel Höpper. He says his battalions are hearing powerful engines, probably tanks, on the Russian side, and he wants to send out a patrol. He reports a lot of activity over there."

"In this weather?"

"That's what I said. The people up there may have been hearing anything. Our own artillery perhaps."

"Did he ask for the general?"

Giesinger nodded angrily. "What was I to tell him? Corps doesn't want it talked about."

"Colonel Wieland will be pretty staggered when he hears."

"He will indeed. He's known the general since 1916, they were in the first war together." He noticed that Hardorff had finished his glass. "Sorry, I'm a bad host—why don't you help yourself?"

"I think that's plenty," said Hardorff, stealing a glance at his watch. "It's three a.m. already."

"Oh, stay a little longer. When the new general comes, there'll be a load of work for me, and who knows when we'll have another chance for a chat. Besides I'm afraid. . . ." The phone rang again. Giesinger got up with an oath. "I'll never get any sleep this night."

Colonel Wieland from 318 Regiment was asking impatiently for the general's aide. Giesinger expressed his regrets. "Impossible at the moment, sir. Can I . . ."

"You can tell Schnetzler there's something brewing over here. It's not just imagination, I've been forward myself. If the anti-tank guns don't come, I can't be responsible for what happens."

"We're doing our utmost, sir. Don't you think that in this weather . . ."

"Weather!" yelled Wieland. "When did the Russians ever bother about weather? I need at least two guns for the road. How about that?"

Giesinger considered. He knew the anti-tank section

had lost almost all their guns during the fighting in the Carpathians. But now he remembered that there was a platoon somewhere with a twenty-five pounder, and he promised the colonel this. "In two hours that gun will be with you, and two light guns as well." He hung up, and turned to Hardorff. "I'd like to hear how things look with Scheper. Wieland claims to have observed equally strong movements on the other side."

"That sounds bad," said Hardorff, and listened anxiously while Giesinger was phoning the regiment. "All quiet with Scheper," he told Hardorff over his shoulder. "But Lieutenant Scheuben from the artillery tells me his observers have also heard engines. I'd better inform Kolmel, just to be on the safe side . . ." He asked for corps.

Kolmel answered at once, and directly he heard Giesinger's voice, said: "What's up in Scheper's sector?"

"He hasn't reported anything special. Seems to be more in Wieland's and Höpper's."

"Along the road then," said Kolmel. "Hold on a moment."

Giesinger heard him talking to someone, then he was back. "We're moving Flamingo forward to Košice. Look after their billets. In the east of the town, if possible." He gave a few more instructions, which Giesinger hastily scribbled on a pad. Flamingo was the code name for an assault regiment: this one was corps reserve, at present near Jaszo, its commander being Lieutenant Colonel Kreisel, who held the Knight's Cross.

After ringing off, Giesinger picked up the receiver again, and asked for Lieutenant Hartung. When he eventually came back from the telephone, he exclaimed in affected exasperation: "Damn it, am I a horse? If things go on like this, I shan't get a wink of sleep."

"You're divisional commander and general's aide rolled into one," suggested Hardorff with a smile.

Giesinger threw himself into the easy chair. The telephoning had been a strain, but also rather exhilarating. He was settling down in his new part, and though he wouldn't have admitted this to anyone, he began to enjoy it enormously. He shook his head. "Not my line, my dear Hardorff. I like my peace and quiet, and I'll be glad when the new general's here."

"Didn't Kolmel say anything about it?"

"Not a word, but they're sending Flamingo forward."

"That's good," said Hardorff, relieved. "Nothing can go wrong then."

Giesinger nodded. "Hartung's phoning the district HQ about billets," he said cheerfully. "I'm sure we don't need Kreisel, but still it's quite comforting to have him."

"Especially as Schmitt's not here."

"What's it got to do with Schmitt?"

"I only meant that if you have Kreisel, you certainly don't need Schmitt."

"Don't tempt providence," said Giesinger in sudden anxiety. He went back to the telephone and spoke to Lieutenant Pfeiffer. "The radio connection's working," he told Hardorff, "I can get Schmitt any time." Despite his confident words, he seemed on edge now, and lit a cigarette.

There was a knock at the door, and Lieutenant Schreiber came in. Giesinger regarded him coldly. "What is it?"

"The trucks that took Captain Schmitt are back, sir."

"Not till now! Why so late?"

"The roads are partly snowed up. Also Captain Schmitt went further on than Szomolnok. The drivers report that the battalion was looking for three German deserters in Oviz."

Giesinger turned to Hardorff in surprise. "What do you say to that?"

"Perhaps three men ran off on the way and went . . . but no, they can't have."

"Impossible. If he's been looking for deserters in Oviz, they must have already deserted in Košice." Giesinger's eyes narrowed, and his face set in determination. "Well, we'll soon see." He moved quickly to the telephone.

As he was picking up the receiver, the window panes blew into the room. There was a tremendous roar, more glass could be heard shattering somewhere, then all was quiet. Hardorff slid off his chair onto the floor, Schreiber ducked out of the room, and Giesinger stood motionless, gazing toward the window. Then he jumped to the door and switched off the light. He dashed back to the window, crunching glass beneath his feet. He pulled the curtains apart, and started out into the park through the empty window frames, but could only see the trees and the snow falling in big flakes from a black sky. Somewhere a tommy-gun barked, and there were sounds of commotion in the building: doors being torn open, confused voices shouting. Then Hardorff was at the window too, leaning out. "Can you hear anything?" Hardorff asked tensely, listening to the sky.

"Planes, you mean?"

"Yes."

"There won't be any planes in this weather. It must have been the District HQ. Wait a moment." He groped for the telephone and asked for the district headquarters. "Out of order," he told Hardorff. "We must find out what's happened."

They ran into the passage, where a few excited officers were standing about. They noticed Giesinger, and Captain Hepp came over to him. "The District HQ," he said nervously.

97

"Partisans?" asked Giesinger.

"Seems like it. What shall we do?"

"Go and see."

The district headquarters was in the next street parallel to theirs, and also had a large garden at the back. The grounds of the two houses were separated by a wall, in which the general had had a hole made for direct communication. The officers went through this hole, and after two hundred yards they could make out the other building. At first glance they didn't notice anything unusual, but when they reached its opposite side, they stopped in horrified amazement. The whole front of the house had gone. Where the entrance had been, there was an enormous gaping hole. All the way across the street lay a heap of rubble, remains of furniture and shattered beams. Amidst all this a crowd of soldiers were trying to rescue the occupants of the house. Giesinger saw three of them pulling the upper half of a man's body out of the rubble, while others dragged a bloody bundle across the street, and put it with four others lying there; the sight sent the blood to his head. He swung around, shouting for Captain Hepp, but not finding him, climbed over the rubble to the other side of the street, where wild confusion reigned. Giesinger pushed his way through regardless, and then saw Hepp. The captain stood facing two civilians with blood-smeared faces who were leaning against the wall of a house.

"What's up here?" Giesinger demanded.

Hepp turned. "We've got three of them, the sentries saw them when they were trying to run away."

"Where's the third?"

"Lying there."

Giesinger saw a man on the ground with twisted limbs. "Is he dead?"

"Not yet. He's got a bullet in his back."

"Where are the sentries?"

"Here, sir," said a voice.

Giesinger looked into the anxious face of a soldier, who had come up to him with three others. "You were asleep."

The man turned pale. "No, sir. We were . . ."

"Asleep," cried Giesinger. He turned to Hartung at his side. "Have these four arrested and sent to field headquarters at Dobšina—they can do what they like with them. And now to the scum here." He went over to the two civilians. One was young—Giesinger put him at about twenty-five—and looked stubbornly at the ground. The other had a dark face, prominent ears and a red beard; his glance traveled fearfully over the numerous soldiers who had come up and were standing behind Giesinger in a semi-circle.

"We'd better take them to HQ, hadn't we?" said Hepp. "What shall we do with the wounded one?"

Giesinger went over to the man on the ground. He lay on his side and groaned. Looking at the man, Giesinger felt a cold rage rise in him. He glanced round; there were two trees in back of the destroyed building. He pointed to them. "Hang him."

Four soldiers ran off to the next house, and soon came back with a rope; dragging the man under one of the trees, they put the rope round his neck. "Get going," ordered Giesinger.

The wounded man gurgled. With a stony face Giesinger watched him being pulled up; he kicked with his legs and spat out bloody foam. His movements became slower and slower, like the pistons of an engine running down; then he hung still. For the first time Giesinger looked at the pale faces of the crowd of soldiers standing round and watching; several officers on the staff ran behind the house. He smiled scornfully, and then gave orders that the other two prisoners should be taken along to divisional headquarters. Back there he beat the snow off his coat and told Hepp: "Squeeze all you can out of them, I'll be with you in a moment."

Going into his room, he phoned the adjutant at corps. The conversation took some time, the adjutant wanted full details, and Colonel Kolmel also joined in, asking for the enemy position. Giesinger reported Höpper's intention of sending a patrol forward. "Excellent," said Kolmel, his voice sounding unusually affable, so that for a moment Giesinger fought with himself, wondering whether he shouldn't after all report Schmitt's partisan operation. Perhaps Kolmel didn't know anything at all about the general having ordered Schmitt's battalion up to Košice just before he was caught. Before he could decide, Kolmel returned to the explosion at the district HQ and mentioned that the head of corp's Gestapo unit was on business anyhow in Košice and so was bound to be looking in. "The new general should also be turning up soon," he said. "In about two hours, I'd say."

"As soon as that!" Giesinger let slip.

There was silence for a moment at the other end, and then Kolmel remarked: "You sound rather sorry."

"Oh, of course not," Giesinger declared in haste. He certainly had not expected it so soon. On the other hand he felt relieved, for the latest reports from the front had increased his uneasiness. When Kolmel hung up, he returned to Hepp's room.

Hepp was sitting behind his desk, turning over his spectacles in his hands. The prisoners stood in the middle of the room with a guard on either side, and there were six officers there as well. Giesinger sent them all out except for Hepp, Hardorff and an interpreter; he told Hardorff to go and fetch Kahlmann, the judge advocate.

"They're as stubborn as Tibetan mules," said Hepp. He lifted a cloth which was on the desk. "Take a look at this."

Giesinger saw a roll of copper wire, a small cylinder

with two wires and a narrow tin. "Know what that is?" asked Hepp. Giesinger picked up the tin and examined it. "A detonator."

"Very much so. A detonator for a charge of dynamite, and the rest belongs to it too. We don't need more than that."

"Where did you find the stuff?"

Hepp pointed to the younger prisoner. "In his coat pocket. When he was caught, he tried to throw it away."

"Bad luck for him he didn't do that sooner." Giesinger looked toward the door; Hardorff had just returned with a short, balding man, who came quickly over to Giesinger and shook hands. "You've got work for me," he said. His eyes fell on the prisoners, and he looked them up and down, with a broad smirk.

Giesinger turned to the interpreter. "Tell the two of them we want to find out who's behind them. If they give us the addresses, we'll let them go."

"They won't believe that," Kahlmann interrupted. "You have to go about things more cleverly with this type." He passed a hand over his bald pate and, blinking nervously, said to the interpreter: "Put what the major said differently. Tell them it doesn't matter for us whether we hang them or not, we're only interested in the people behind them; and if they give us the names, it may save their necks."

The interpreter, a young staff officer, translated accordingly. Giesinger watched the prisoners. Their faces were swollen, and the younger seemed to have a broken nose; he kept wiping the blood away with the dirty sleeve of his coat. When the interpreter had finished, they looked silently at the ground. "The inspector won't be any more successful," said Hepp, shrugging his shoulders; "we may as well hang them. . . ." The ringing of the telephone made him break off; he picked up the receiver, and his face became tense. "Right away . . . Höpper on the line," he told Giesinger. "The patrol's back, and they lost four men. He says it's impossible to go ahead, the Russians are massed there."

"Let me talk to him," Giesinger took the receiver.

"What's Wieland's report?" Höpper asked.

"Same as yours, more or less. All quiet in Scheper's."

"Right—well, now we know where we are." Höpper rang off unceremoniously, and Giesinger called corps.

Kolmel was disappointed. "Perhaps Wieland will be more successful. It's imperative we get a prisoner, tell him."

Wieland swore when Giesinger passed on the message. "It's crazy in this weather. I'd rather you sent Schmitt to me. The sector's too big for two battalions."

"The general . . ." began Giesinger, but Wieland had already hung up. "What a muddle they're all in," Giesinger remarked. He returned abruptly to the prisoners. "We're making too much fuss of them," he exclaimed in a sudden fury.

Kahlmann laughed. "That's what I've said all along. We're much too humane. It's not enough to hang a dozen of them if we let ten thousand others go free because we haven't anything on them, or tell ourselves we haven't. It's my experience that every other Czech is in league with the partisans either directly or indirectly." He turned to the interpreter. "Explain to these fellows that in five minutes we're going to string them up. They can think it over till then. . . ."

Lieutenant Hartung stuck his head in the door. "The inspector, sir."

"Send him in," Giesinger said tersely. A powerfully-built man with a placid-looking face entered the room.

"Fine circus you've got here," the inspector remarked, after shaking hands all round. He did not even glance at the prisoners, but came straight to the point. "I've already been to the district HQ—neat work, I must say." There was a note of admiration in his voice.

Kahlmann frowned. "You don't really consider this a work of art?"

The inspector smiled. "I said it was neat work." He turned to Giesinger. "Perhaps you'd like to tell me what you know." He listened to Giesinger's report, and nodded. "I can't stay long over this business, I'm on to something else. Yesterday we received an anonymous letter." He paused and for the first time looked at the prisoners; his face was no longer placid, but sharp-featured, with a hard line over the bridge of the nose. "An anonymous letter," he repeated slowly. "In it were two addresses of alleged deserters who were supposed to be hiding in Košice. The addresses were fictitious, of course. What interests me, however, is why the letter was written."

"Hope you find the sender," said Giesinger.

The inspector grinned. "We already have, and meanwhile they've brought off this stunt with your general. Perhaps there's a connection." His small eyes examined the prisoners again. "You've not got anything out of them yet?"

"Only Czechs could be as stubborn as these two," answered Kahlmann.

"Hang one of the two," said the inspector, "and let the other watch. That method always works."

Giesinger shook his head skeptically. "We've tried it already. I told you there were three, didn't I?"

"Depends on the way you do it, Herr Giesinger. Hang one of them, and let the other struggle and kick for half a minute until he's softened up. Just try."

"If you think it's any good," said Giesinger, rising with reluctance. "I don't really believe in it. Which one do you want to hang?"

"The young chap. He's got more powers of resistance, and probably he doesn't know as much as the old man. You'll come with me, won't you?"

"I have my own stuff to see to." The thought of witnessing another execution suddenly revolted Giesinger. Hepp and Hardorff also suddenly looked very tired. Hepp yawned, extracted his bulky figure from behind the desk, and asked Hardorff: "What are you going to do now?"

Hardorff turned to Giesinger. "Do you need me still?"

"No," said Giesinger sulkily.

"Then I'm off to bed."

"Me, too," said Hepp. Both officers left hastily, with Kahlmann looking after them in consternation. The duty officer appeared in the doorway, with six men behind him in steel helmets carrying tommy-guns. Giesinger saw the prisoners' faces change color under the crust of blood and dirt.

"Where shall I find you?" asked the inspector.

Giesinger went into the passage with him and showed the inspector his room. He suddenly felt himself entangled in an ugly business that was no concern of his. Behind him Kahlmann's voice asked eagerly: "Are you really not coming with us?"

"No."

"Pity."

Giesinger watched them go. The prisoners went first, followed by the firing squad with flashing jackboots, and the inspector, who was talking to the interpreter. Last came Kahlmann, carrying his cigar carefully in an extended hand. Giesinger felt sick and exhausted, and his head was aching. Back in his room, he sank into a chair and stared wearily ahead of him. Suddenly he remembered the three deserters Schmitt had been looking for in Oviz. His eyes went to the phone, but his weariness was too great; he decided to follow the thing up later. One thing at a time, he thought with a huge yawn; perhaps he could mention it to the inspector—considering he'd also been after deserters. He yawned again, then realized how cold the room was, and glanced at the curtain, blowing to and fro in front of an empty window frame. That on top of everything else, he thought—he must get some glass into there as soon as possible, perhaps it could just be put in from the window in another room. He was about to send for his orderly when the inspector and Kahlmann entered the room. Their faces were flushed; Kahlmann was still holding his cigar. "More than we expected," he said jubilantly, and gave Giesinger a piece of paper. "Twelve addresses, eleven in this region and one in Oviz. Where's Oviz?"

Giesinger looked up with a start. "Oviz—but that's. . . ." He went to the phone. "Send me Lieutenant Schreiber," he said in excitement, then told the others more doubtfully: "You may think I'm crazy, but it's really an amazing coincidence. In connection with the missing general I sent a battalion to Szomolnok, and Lieutenant Schreiber told me just now that the battalion went on a bit further, to Oviz, looking for three German deserters there. It was the first I'd heard of it."

"Interesting," said the inspector.

Giesinger sat down again. "I can't quite make it out. Captain Schmitt . . . Ah, here comes Schreiber."

Giesinger asked him impatiently: "What was that about Captain Schmitt in Oviz?"

Schreiber braced back his shoulders. "Captain Schmitt went first to Oviz with his battalion, looking for three German deserters there, and as he didn't find them, he returned to Szomolnok."

"Get me one of the drivers," Giesinger ordered.

"Can't, I'm afraid, sir. They're off to the front again."

"Nuisance." Giesinger turned to the inspector, who had been listening with interest. "It's the drivers of the heavy trucks. They drove Schmitt and his battalion to Szomolnok, and now they're taking building material to the trenches."

"Then there's nothing we can do. I can't stay any

longer, I'm afraid, my men are waiting in the car out-side. What exactly was the idea in sending the bat-talion to Szomolnok?"

"I told you: in connection with the missing general —a large-scale search operation. They're combing the whole area between Szomolnok and Denes. Here's the map."

The inspector bent over it. "Where did it happen?"

"Just here." Giesinger showed him the place.

"And where's Oviz?"

Kahlmann discovered it first. "Here it is. Quite a way from Szomolnok," he said in surprise.

They looked at each other. After a moment the in-spector straightened up. "The prisoner came out with the name of someone called Nikolash, who's supposed to live in Oviz. It was this Nikolash who gave him orders to blow up the HQ."

"A man from Oviz?" exclaimed Giesinger, his brain racing. He was hunting for connections, but his con-fusion merely grew.

The inspector rose. "Unless I'm very much mistaken, we're at last on the track of the band which has given us so much trouble."

"And the prisoner?"

"He's called Krasko, Ovid Krasko, and lives here. I'm taking him with me to Oviz."

"You want to . . . ?"

"What do you think? Where do I find your Captain Schmitt?"

"In Szomolnok!" Giesinger turned to Lieutenant Schreiber. "Tell Pfeiffer to signal Schmitt by radio. . . ."

"Leave that to me," the inspector interrupted. "I'll talk to him myself. But you'll have to deal with the other addresses—or perhaps you'd better leave it to the MP's." He hurried out of the room.

Giesinger handed Schreiber the addresses. "Do the

necessary," he said, sinking wearily into a chair. "What do you say to all that?" he asked Kahlmann.

Kahlmann screwed up his plump face into a broad grin. "Man after my own heart, that. Doesn't say much, but he certainly knows how to get things moving. You missed something. The way that prisoner poured out information when he felt the rope round his neck! We could hardly keep up with him. Yes, the only method. . . ."

"I'd rather not hear about your 'methods,'" Giesinger interrupted irritably. "I'm an adjutant, not a hangman."

Kahlmann got up and began mincing up and down the room on his short legs. Giesinger watched in disgust the way he held the cigar between his podgy fingers. "Chilly in here," he remarked.

"The explosion blew the window in," said Giesinger.

"You poor man!" Kahlmann went quickly over to the window and drawing the curtain aside, said enthusiastically, "Well, there he is!"

Giesinger joined him at the window. About ten yards away, barely visible in the snowstorm, a man's lifeless body was hung from a tree.

"Couldn't you find a better place?" Giesinger asked.

"Does it disturb you? If it hadn't been so far from my quarters we'd have strung him up there as a sort of trademark."

"Oh, shut up," said Giesinger savagely.

Kahlmann laughed. "Lord, you are sensitive. When you had the wounded one hanged you didn't seem to have any qualms."

"That was something different. I saw red at that moment, but now. . . ."

"Are you sorry?" Kahlmann asked curiously.

"Of course I'm not sorry!" They fell silent and looked at the snow-covered body dangling from the tree.

"Ah yes," said Kahlmann, "that reminds me—I must find a little tree. I mean, one isn't sentimental, but still it's part of Christmas. Have you anything planned?"

"I don't know," said Giesinger.

Kahlmann pulled his coat tighter round his stomach. "If you haven't anything special, come to me. Of course the Christmas Eve party is out this year."

"Yes, without the general. . . ."

The phone rang; it was Hartung reporting the arrival of the assault regiment's billeting officers. "I don't know what to do," he said. "It's really the district HQ's business."

"Well—they know about it, don't they?"

"Yes, but everything's topsy-turvy there."

"Then look after it yourself," said Giesinger impatiently. "If there's no room, make some." He hung up. "Nothing but trouble," he told Kahlmann.

"Don't worry, the new general will be here soon. Then you'll have an easier time."

But I don't want that, thought Giesinger, saying out loud: "It does wear one out."

"Yes, it's a big responsibility," nodded Kahlmann. "Well, good night."

After he had gone, Giesinger remained at the table, thinking. In the last few minutes he had remembered a lot of things he still had to do; yet it was already day, and he hadn't had a minute's sleep. He called his orderly and told him to get the window repaired. Then he asked Pfeiffer for reports from Schmitt. The last radio signal was two hours old, there had been nothing through since then. Giesinger told Pfeiffer to signal Schmitt that he should contact division every half hour. After that he studied the regiments' morning reports, and while doing so remembered Wieland's patrol. He phoned Wieland's adjutant, and heard that the patrol had not yet returned. "It'll be daylight in ten minutes," said the adjutant. "I'm afraid we'll have to write them off."

"Let me know when you hear anything definite," said Giesinger, and afterwards began anxiously re-examining the reports. Höpper had strong mortar fire on his positions, so had Wieland; only Scheper reported a quiet morning. He pushed the papers away with a sigh, got up, and went out into the passage. Here there was a hive of activity—orderlies running from door to door, officers with briefcases, a quartermaster lieutenant shouting at a sergeant. Giesinger went into what had been Colonel Schnetzler's office. Some typewriters were rattling away, three officers phoned simultaneously from different phones, others had their heads buried in papers and looked up briefly when Giesinger came in. He wound through the mass of tables to find the lieutenant who was acting for Schnetzler. The lieutenant stood up quickly on seeing him, and said: "I can't get the ammunition supplies here, sir. The road's blocked the other side of Rožnava."

"Snow?"

"Yes. The district HQ is putting the civilian population on to clearing it."

"Tell them to get a move on. How does. . . ." He stopped and looked round. A lieutenant was holding a telephone receiver: "Captain Hepp wants you."

Hepp's voice sounded very excited. "A new calamity. The railway command has just reported two deserters picked up by their guards."

"Our men?" asked Giesinger with interest.

"Apparently not. One escaped, they shot the other down."

"Can he still be questioned?"

"Yes, I think so."

"Inform Kahlmann. Any other news?"

"Colonel Höpper reports increasing artillery fire.

He thinks there must be at least twenty batteries ranging on his positions."

Giesinger frowned. "Has it been reported to corps?"

"Yes, it has. Also, Wieland's asking for the general again."

"He'll have to be patient a little longer. Stiller should be here any minute now."

Giesinger rang off. His nervousness had increased. After a few words with Schnetzler's deputy, he went back into the passage, where he detained a man who was just rushing past. "Tell the duty officer to take the dead man off the tree."

"Dead man off the tree, sir. Right, sir."

Giesinger reached the exit, where the sentries were standing. They saluted. He shouted at one of them who had a coat button open, tore the button off and threw it behind him in the snow. "Report to me after guard duty with your button sewn on."

A second lieutenant came running up the steps. Giesinger recognized him as the assistant adjutant of the artillery regiment. "What's the rush?"

"Lieutenant Scheuben sent me, sir—about the ammunition."

"I'm sorry—the roads are snowed up," said Giesinger. "Try the railhead at Dobšina. Perhaps they can put two trucks on some train or other."

"We don't know where our vehicles have been held up."

"Behind Rožnava apparently. Your supply column's there, isn't it?"

"That's an idea, sir."

"Go and see Lieutenant Pfeiffer and ask him to connect you with them."

Giesinger stood outside; the fresh air was doing him good, and he could feel his headache subsiding. It was already light on the street, and there was very little snow falling at present, but the sky was dense and more could be expected.

Suddenly he heard a peculiar sound. He looked quickly toward the sentries at the gate: they were gazing up at the sky. The sound continued. It sounded as if a distant freight train were rumbling over the rails; but this was no train, nor was it planes. He dashed up the steps, and saw doors burst open in the passage. Hepp's bulky figure emerged from one room; on the other side Pfeiffer appeared, saying breathlessly: "The barrage!"

Scarcely looking at him, Giesinger ran up to his room. As he reached it, he remembered something, and dashed back to Pfeiffer, who was talking excitedly to Hepp. "Where?" he asked.

"In Wieland and Höpper's sectors."

"Not Scheper's?"

"No, sir."

"How about Wieland's patrol?"

"Wieland has lost contact with his sixth company," Hepp interjected. "He doesn't know anything about them."

"Thanks." On reaching his room, Giesinger immediately phoned corps. As he waited for the connection, he watched his orderly putting new glass in the window.

"Where did you get *that* from?"

"Upstairs, sir. The civilians don't need any."

Giesinger nodded. In the room the artillery fire was hardly audible. Corps had now brought Kolmel to the phone. His voice sounded sleepy at first, but became wide awake when Giesinger gave him the reports. "Isn't General Stiller with you yet?"

"No, sir."

Giesinger heard Kolmel talking to someone; then he spoke back into the mouthpiece again. "He should

111

have been there long ago. Look, have you a map, handy?"

"Yes, sir."

"Then send Flamingo to Durkov. In the meantime the general's bound to reach you."

Giesinger took the map and went over to Hepp, who had four other officers with him. "The assault regiment's to go to Durkov. What do you think of that?"

"Durkov!" Hepp looked at his map. "Here it is. Right between Wieland and Höpper." He took off his spectacles and rubbed his eyes. "In this snow the Russians would never try except on the road."

"I'm not so sure," Giesinger objected, then turned to Pfeiffer and asked if there was a line to Colonel Kreisel.

"Yes, sir, we've had one for five minutes now."

"Put me on to him."

Giesinger spoke to the commander of the assault regiment, and then turned to Lieutenant Hartung. "You'll go to Kreisel as liaison officer. The assault regiment is to dig in outside Durkov. . . . There's nothing more to be done at the moment," he told the others. "I'd just like to get the latest bulletins. . . ." He phoned through first to the regimental commanders, then to the artillery commander and the anti-tank section—his face growing longer and longer. "Wieland has no more contact with the front," he told Pfeiffer.

Corps rang again. "No change," Giesinger answered Kolmel's anxious question, "Flamingo is on its way."

"And your reconnaissance unit?"

Giesinger was taken by surprise, but managed to keep his presence of mind. "I've sent it off," he lied.

"Then you've still got a battalion in reserve. You'll have to manage with that."

Giesinger hunted for words. He would have liked to explain that he had sent the battalion off to search

112

for the missing general, but Kolmel left him no time. "The general still hasn't arrived?"

"Not yet, sir."

"Send a car to meet him. Perhaps he's broken down in the snow."

At the door Giesinger bumped into a man and shouted at him: "What d'you want?"

The man began to stutter. He had his steel helmet on, and now Giesinger recognized him. It was the sentry whose button he had torn off. He cut the stammer short furiously: "Get the hell out of here."

He went to Schnetzler's office, and asked the lieutenant who had taken over Schnetzler's duties: "Is the road through Rožnava still blocked?"

"There are five hundred civilians working on it, sir."

"Then they'd better get five thousand working on it, if they're not finished yet. General Stiller must have got stuck in the middle of a column somewhere. Send a car to meet him." He returned to Hepp. "The reconnaissance unit. . . ."

"Ready to leave," said Hepp.

Giesinger looked at him in fury: why hadn't he thought of giving the order himself? "It had better go to Höpper," he said, and stormed back to his room, where he phoned the regiments. What he heard made him more worried still. Wieland still had no contact with the front, and said: "We've hardly ever seen fireworks like this." Höpper too had alarming news.

I must bring Schmitt back, thought Giesinger. He picked up the telephone, but dropped it again as if it were red hot. Instead he went to the signals officer and asked for bulletins from Schmitt.

"Nothing new, sir."

Corps rang through again. This time it was the commanding general in person. His sharp, querulous voice jarred on Giesinger's ears. "General Stiller not with you yet?"

113

"I'm afraid not, sir . . . I can't understand it either. I've sent off a car now to meet him. He should arrive any minute."

"He should have an hour ago," barked the general. "When he's there, call me up at once. Things otherwise?"

"Unchanged," answered Giesinger.

"You have an assault regiment, eight assault guns, a reconnaissance unit and a battalion in reserve. With all that you can plug any gaps."

"Of course, sir," said Giesinger tiredly. He remembered that he had not yet had breakfast, and echoed: "We can plug any gaps."

"Good. And when General Stiller comes. . . ."

"Right, sir." Giesinger put the receiver down.

Now he felt really scared: So the missing general had informed corps about the reserve battalion. He had been a damned fool, he thought, not to have told Kolmel about it just now when he had a good chance. Either he had to call him again at once, or else bring Schmitt back at once to Košice. For a few moments he fought with himself, but still couldn't decide. His head seemed to have suddenly turned into a sieve; all his thoughts ran away before he could properly grasp them. Never before in his life had a decision cost him so much torment. If he recalled Schmitt, he could pack in all his ambitions, and more than that—his prestige on the staff would go right down the drain. He thought of Hepp's face, and of Fuchs, who was only waiting for him to be humbled. He thought of the orderlies' gossip, of the other officers' mocking faces. He clenched his teeth as he imagined it, and for the first time felt how alone and isolated he was.

When he rushed over to Pfeiffer's shortly afterwards, he still didn't know what to do. Pfeiffer shrugged his shoulders apologetically. "From Schmitt . . . no, nothing new. The connection's all right."

"Where is he at the moment?" asked Giesinger.

Pfeiffer went to a radio receiving set, with three men sitting in front of it. "Ask where Captain Schmitt is."

"We'll hear from him again in ten minutes," answered one of the men.

"What's that mean?" asked Giesinger irritably.

Pfeiffer looked at him in surprise. "Radio contact every half hour. We've been . . ."

"My orders were," Giesinger interrupted, "that you should have continuous contact with Schmitt."

"We'll pass that on the next time he reports, sir," said Pfeiffer, offended.

Giesinger went to Hepp, whom he found standing by the open window. Hepp swung round. "Listen to that, it's getting worse."

Behind the haze of black clouds which covered the mountains, there was a rumbling like heavy thunder. Giesinger hunched his shoulders and shivered. "Can't understand where the general is."

"He could have called you up from the road," remarked Hepp. His face twitched nervously. "Hadn't we better send Fuchs off at once?"

"Of course! He must go to Höpper."

"I don't see that he's needed for Höpper. Now, if we still had Schmitt, then I'd say Schmitt to Wieland, and Fuchs to Höpper."

Giesinger took the thrust without flinching. He had suddenly made up his mind. "Schmitt stays where he is," he said coldly. "You know my opinion. If we can't manage it with Fuchs and the assault regiment, Schmitt's hundred and fifty men wouldn't help us either."

"You can't be sure. When you consider that without Schmitt, Wieland has only two battalions, neither of which is stronger than Schmitt's, the hundred and fifty men are just as important for Wieland as the three hundred he has up there now. From a tactical standpoint. . . ."

"Oh forget about your tactics," exclaimed Giesinger. "What we need now is some luck. Without luck Schmitt's hundred and fifty men would be cut to pieces in five minutes. At Lvov Wieland had four hundred casualties in half an hour, and the fact that there weren't even more had nothing to do with tactics; it was simply that those were all the men he had. Well, things aren't much better today. Call up Fuchs, he should get going."

He watched Hepp while the captain phoned the reconnaissance unit. "I'm sorry, Herr Fuchs," Hepp said. "The major wants you to go forward to Durkov to reinforce the assault regiment."

"I said to Slancik," Giesinger cut in sharply.

Hepp shrugged his shoulders. "Not to Durkov then, report to Lieutenant Colonel Höpper . . . yes, in Slancik, his command post is there . . . what was that? . . . Oh, I see—hold on a moment." He looked round. "Herr Fuchs asks if you've found the general yet?"

"Tell him to mind his own damned business."

Hepp grinned. "Did you get that?" he asked into the receiver. "Yes, you're to mind your own damned business . . . no, of course, not me . . . thank you, I'll tell him." He returned from the phone, still grinning. "Herr Fuchs wishes you every success."

Giesinger turned on his heel and left the room. In the next half hour he was not given a moment's peace. Kolmel rang through at progressively shorter intervals. Colonel Conrad from the artillery regiment was in a steam about the missing ammunition. "We'll run out in five minutes when things start here," he yelled. "Then they can fight this goddamned war without us."

"That's all right with me!" His face scarlet, Giesinger banged the receiver down, only to be recalled for a conversation with Colonel Wieland.

"Look here, Giesinger, what the devil's going on up there? I want to talk to the general."

"He's at corps, sir," said Giesinger with effort.

"Then put me on to corps."

"That wouldn't be any good. He's already on his way back here."

"It's about time he returned. And Colonel Schnetzler?"

"With the general."

"Then tell them my gun's been knocked out—direct hit in a broadside."

"Colonel Kreisel is on his way with eight assault guns."

"To me?" asked Wieland in a relieved voice.

"To Durkov, which is very near you."

"Then you could just as well have sent him straight to my command at Rozhanovce."

Giesinger suppressed his anger. "We've also got to think of Herr Höpper. From Durkov the regiment can reach Slancik just as quickly as Rozhanovce."

"But the main road runs through Rozhanovce. Friend Höpper shouldn't make such a fuss, the chief fire is in my sector."

"Colonel Höpper says just the same about his. We must . . ."

"You'll soon see what you must," Wieland interrupted. "When the general comes, I want to speak to him at once."

"So do we all," Giesinger murmured wearily. He replaced the receiver and looked toward the door, where Pfeiffer had come in, waving a piece of paper. "Captain Schmitt's command post in Szomolnok reports no contact with him for twenty minutes."

Giesinger was too tired to get excited about this. His head felt like a lump of lead. He took the paper limply from Pfeiffer's hand, and gazed down at it for a moment or two, then said in a resigned voice: "Just

117

wait a bit, he'll come through again very soon now."

"Our receiving sets are working continuously," declared Pfeiffer.

When he had gone, Giesinger sat down at the table. There was a constant roar from the front, and though it was muffled by the closed window, he felt it had become more violent. Wieland came on the phone again, his voice sounded indistinct and distorted, floating like a thin bubble on a seething whirlpool. Giesinger plugged the other ear with his hand and shouted: "I can't hear you properly, sir." Suddenly there was a silence on the line. He bent desperately over the phone. "The connection's gone, sir," the switchboard announced.

"Then find out what's wrong and get it repaired," he cried, and dashed into the signals office, which was in a turmoil, with a dozen voices yelling across each other. He hunted for Pfeiffer and found him with the men at the switchboard. "What's happened to Wieland?"

Pfeiffer gave a helpless shrug. "We've got three repair crews off to see, I don't know. . . ."

A man came running up to him: "Radio signal from Colonel Höpper, sir."

Giesinger tore the paper out of his hand.

"Something bad?" asked Pfeiffer in anxious tones.

Giesinger looked up distractedly. "Read it yourself."

Pfeiffer studied the signal, and his face went pale. Then he gave it back. "What'll you do, sir?" he said.

"I don't know yet. But I was always afraid the Russians would break out first in Höpper's sector. Where's Kreisel?"

"He should be in Durkov soon, sir."

"Signal him to make for Slancik as fast as he can."

He rushed over to Hepp, who was telephoning. Giesinger waited impatiently till he had finished, then flung the signal down on the table. "Here you are.

Höpper needs immediate reinforcement. I've redirected the assault regiment there."

"To Höpper?"

"Where else? His sector's getting a terrific pasting."

"Wieland's is having it just as badly. Besides, you've already sent the reconnaissance unit to Höpper."

Giesinger gaped—he had forgotten that. He struggled to regain his composure. "I know exactly what I'm doing. Wieland had two light guns on the road and the twenty-five pounder."

"That's been knocked out," said Hepp laconically. "Didn't you know?"

"Of course I knew." Giesinger cursed his thoughtlessness, and it took him an immense effort to add: "He still has the two light guns."

"They may equally well be knocked out. We've no contact with Wieland at present. I imagine he's taking up new positions."

"New positions!" Giesinger started. "You're not serious, are you? But that would mean. . . ."

"That the Russians are through in his sector," nodded Hepp. He got up and opened the window. "Do you hear! No more artillery. I'd give the hell of a lot to have Schmitt here now. Wouldn't you?"

Giesinger moved his lips, then reached for Hepp's phone, and asked for Colonel Conrad.

The artillery commander answered at once, but he was almost speechless with rage when he heard Giesinger's instructions. "I'm to fire, am I? I can't fire with empty cartridges. I'll be glad enough if I can get my batteries out safely—everyone's retreating up forward."

"Who says so?"

"My observers, in case you don't happen to have heard yet."

"Then pull your guns back behind the high point of the pass, and take up new positions. The assault regiment has moved up to counter-attack."

"Without ammunition. . . ."

"You'll get your ammunition if I have to bring it up in person."

Feverishly Giesinger got on to Schnetzler's deputy. "All vehicles, I said," he yelled, when the lieutenant began protesting. Then he phoned corps. "Your pioneer battalion," said Kolmel. Giesinger dropped into a chair, he had forgotten the pioneer battalion too. "I gave it to the assault regiment," he said in a hoarse voice.

"General Stiller?"

"Still not here."

"Thanks." Kolmel rang off abruptly.

Giesinger turned to Hepp. "The pioneer battalion."

"To Höpper?"

"To Wieland," cried Giesinger. In the passage he ran into Pfeiffer. "Signal Kreisel," he ordered. "He's not to go to Slancik, but to counter-attack at Rozhanovce on both sides of the road. Fuchs too," he yelled after him as Pfeiffer dashed back to the signals room. In his own room Giesinger phoned Schnetzler's aide once more. "We need four or five trucks to send up the pioneer battalion."

"The artillery ammunition. . . ." began the lieutenant.

"I said four trucks," Giesinger cut in, and banged down the receiver. He tried to light a cigarette, but his hands were trembling and he used six matches. If only the general would come, he thought for the first time. He was not even allowed to smoke his cigarette, for Pfeiffer burst in to say: "Signal from Höpper, sir. The Russians are through in Wieland's sector. He wants to know if he can pull out."

Giesinger tore the paper out of his hand. "Höpper stays where he is," he said savagely.

Pfeiffer looked at him in horror. "But if Wieland's gone, that leaves Höpper isolated."

"Then he'll just have to dig himself in," cried Giesinger. He remembered Schmitt, and fought against it, but he had been worn down. "Signal Schmitt, he's to reassemble in Szomolnok at once," he said hastily.

"The radio center in Szomolnok has no contact with Captain Schmitt, sir," Pfeiffer reminded him.

Giesinger almost burst into tears. "If the bastards haven't got any in five minutes, I'll have them court-martialed," he cried.

He left Pfeiffer standing and dashed into Schnetz-ler's room. "Four trucks to Szomolnok." The lieutenant leaped into the air, his face scarlet. "But you ordered. . . ."

"I ordered you to send four trucks to Szomolnok," shouted Giesinger, with the last strength he had left. He went back to his room, threw himself into a chair, and buried his head in his hands. When the telephone rang shrilly, he did not move. He had had enough.

After the staged search for the deserters, Schmitt and his battalion had returned to Szomolnok for the night and sent the empty trucks back to Košice.

The next morning Schmitt called together the company commanders and ordered them to divide each company into three platoons, each leaving one platoon behind in Szomolnok with Lt. Menges.

"You, Kaiser, will go north with your other two platoons and turn back when you've gone six miles. You, Roos, will march due west with one platoon and from there climb the Golden Table, meeting me there with the second platoon which will go straight up the mountain." After giving the other two sergeants their instructions, he turned to Sergeant Werner:

"Keep one radio here. I've decided to go with Corporal Baumgartner and we'll take the other radio with us." He turned to Lieutenant Menges. "You'll be in continuous radio contact with me. Let me know if you come up against anything serious but don't act on your own initiative unless it's an emergency."

Menges nodded sulkily. The last remark was quite superfluous.

The men were standing about in small groups; the snow was up to their calves. It was still dark and hardly anything could be seen of the mountains. The single-story houses on both sides of the street crouched under the masses of snow on their roofs and the snow flakes dropped from the vast chimney of the night like flakes of soot which grew lighter and lighter as they neared the ground.

Schmitt's sharp voice rang out. "If you can't get your men to fall in I'll do it myself in the future." He told Roos to collect his men and sent the other three sergeants off. Roos returned with about twenty-five men.

"Is that all?" asked Schmitt. "All right, you take half this lot with you, I'm going with the other half. We'll meet on the Golden Table."

Roos quickly divided the men into two platoons and marched one way. Schmitt ran his eye over the men left behind. "Corporal Baumgartner—you go at the rear and make sure nobody gets lost."

The corporal nodded. He had a lean face with a rather crooked nose which hung peevishly over a thin-lipped mouth. Schmitt noticed his orderly who came running out of the command post.

"What on earth do *you* want?" he asked.

The man brought his short bow legs together—one could have stuck a head between them. He had the fond, submissive eyes of a spaniel and looked at Schmitt pleadingly.

"You're staying here," said Schmitt. He saw the spaniel's eyes grow sorrowful. "Do you have to stick your nose into everything?" he cried. "You're staying here, I said. You can tidy up my things."

The man turned round and crept off to the command post like a beaten dog. Schmitt bit his lip. It was always the same, and he cursed his own weakness as he called: "Corporal Teltschik."

"Yes, sir." The bow legs tried again to join forces.

"Come here," ordered Schmitt. The man stumbled over, his wrinkled face beaming. "If you do anything to annoy me on the way," Schmitt said bitterly, "you'll be sorry forever."

"Yes, sir, forever, sir."

Schmitt turned away and the men grinned.

He led them out of the town on the road going north. There they left the road and struck out northwest to the foothills of the mountains, which were only about two hundred yards from the last houses and stood out against the dark sky like a white wall. Day was slowly dawning. The men went into the snow up to their knees, but Schmitt did not seem to notice, nor did he reduce speed when they started struggling up a steep slope. It was not till they reached the edge of the road that he stopped for the first time and looked back.

Right below lay the houses of Szomolnok. In the dull grey light of the morning they looked like a herd of game which had taken shelter from the cold, crouching in a snow drift. There was nothing to be seen of the other platoons. Schmitt checked the direction, then stamped off into the wood. There was not much undergrowth, and since the snow was also less deep than it had been on the unprotected slope, they made good progress. Most of the trees were beeches; their smooth trunks and tall, curving crowns made them seem like ancient columns. Schmitt let his men extend in a long line, but told them all not to lose sight of the man ahead.

The wood ahead was beginning to clear: a group of young pines skirting it had been practically flattened by the weight of the snow. The platoon went through them, and reached a gorge which was almost sheer, with a mountain stream some seventy feet below, foaming along amid ice and snow.

Schmitt looked around searchingly. A bit to the right was a place which looked suitable. The descent was equally steep, but there were some shrubs growing to which one could cling. He climbed down first, and the men above watched him feeling for a foothold with his boots as he clambered yard by yard into the gorge. Once he almost lost his balance when a great ridge of snow came loose and slid down, but he was able to grip the bushes in time. The gorge was about ten yards wide, with a narrow channel in the middle where the water had eaten through the snow and uncovered the icy boulders. He felt his way carefully across, creeping on all fours from one boulder to the next. It was an odd sight, and the men above could not help grinning. Now he was over the dangerous middle part and climbed swiftly on to the other bank.

Schmitt called out to the rest of the platoon to follow in single file. He had just lit a cigarette when the man carrying the radio lost his balance. He tried to break his fall by gripping a bush as Schmitt had done, but the branch he had hold of snapped, and he fell headfirst all the way down into the stream. The heavy radio set came off his back during the fall, banged violently on a rock, bounced away and disappeared into the snow.

For a second no one moved. Then Schmitt slid down the slope, and waded recklessly through the water till he had reached the man. He pulled him up by the seat of his trousers. Some of the others had followed, and together dragged him back to the bank, where they laid him on the ground. His face was distorted with pain. They took off his camouflage coat and jacket; with each movement he clenched his teeth and groaned. Then they saw that his right arm was broken above the elbow. Schmitt asked him whether he could walk. When the man nodded, Schmitt had someone find a thin branch, with which he set about splinting the broken arm. "Send two men back to Szomolnok with him," he told Baumgartner.

It was hard work getting the heavy man up the steep bank of the gorge; only after the men had cut steps into the snow with their trench picks did things begin to go better. We should have done that at once, thought Schmitt. The incident had taken the verve out of him; he had already come to the conclusion that it was impossible to fulfill the objective of the operation. For a moment he seriously considered turning back and giving up the whole business, but in the end he decided to send off an appropriate signal to Giesinger that evening. He went over to the place where the radio set had fallen into the stream. It was lying deep in the water, and when he pulled it out, he saw that the front of it was smashed in. He let it drop back and turned to the man with the walkie-talkie. "Can you get the battalion with your set?"

"It's too far, sir. In this sort of country we can't do more than a mile."

"Can you at least get Sergeant Major Roos?"

"I don't think so, sir. Shall I try?"

"Yes." Schmitt climbed back to the other side of the stream, sat down and took off his boots. Teltschik came over to him. "Clean socks, sir."

Schmitt gazed incredulously at the pair of dry socks he was being offered. "Where on earth did you get them from?"

"I brought them along, sir."

Schmitt tried not to show how touched he was. "Sometimes you're an angel, Max."

"Yes, sir!"

"You needn't take everything I say so literally."

"No, sir—not so literally, sir."

Schmitt put on the socks, and told the rest of the platoon to get ready again. The man with the walkie-talkie had failed to make a connection. "I thought so," he said with a shrug. "There's too much wood in between, and these things are no use beyond the sight range."

"Fat lot of good they are then," said Schmitt angrily, as he led the platoon off again through the pines and into the forest. He was feeling the strain now, and his muscles no longer responded properly. Later, when the climb was over, things improved a little. Schmitt noticed a good many game trails on the ground, but his thoughts were elsewhere. According to his calculations they should soon be reaching the valley, and he was growing impatient. Then he noticed that the ground was gently inclining and ten minutes later they had arrived at the base of the valley. It was about fifty yards wide and wound northwest with many twists. There was wood on both sides. The trees looked like silver-plated organ pipes and in their branches the snow lay a foot high.

The valley now wound gently round a protruding mountain ridge. He led his men to the edge of the wood, where he gave them a short break and asked the signalman again about contact with Sergeant Major Roos.

"Not yet, sir."

"Then try your damnedest," said Schmitt impatiently. "If you'd told me at once that the things were so little use, I shouldn't have taken them along at all."

They marched off again. The valley became a good deal broader. It went steadily down-hill, so they kept up a fair pace, and after an hour and a half they joined another valley. From here they had to march westward, where the valley climbed steeply, narrowing at the end.

Schmitt told Corporal Baumgartner to see no one fell behind, then stamped off up the valley with long strides. It had started snowing again, and visibility became worse and worse. Schmitt kept close to the left edge of the wood, which followed the valley's bends. Further on, where the valley narrowed sharply, Schmitt saw that the wood went right across the valley. The snow storm made it impossible to see what was beyond that. The men seemed to be marching into a black cloud, which was spreading deeper and deeper into the valley, slowly swallowing it up. The valley had shrunk to a gorge, and Schmitt was afraid this would be a particularly difficult stretch. Luckily it proved otherwise. After only a few hundred yards they came to a narrow clearing, of which only a small piece was in view, because there was a bend to the right. After this bend the valley broadened out to a longish oval, surrounded on all sides by wood. At the far end stood a hut.

Schmitt stopped in his tracks and blinked incredulously, but the picture remained. In front of the hut a man stood motionless staring toward them. He wore a German winter uniform, and a flat fur cap pulled down over his ears, which looked more like the caps the Russians wore.

Schmitt felt a queer pricking under his skin; he knew his men were waiting for an order from him. For a few seconds his power of decision was checked by images which had almost the compulsiveness of a hallucination—he saw the men dashing up to the hut, heard the deafening rattle of tommy-gun fire, the shrieks of the wounded before they writhed in the snow with mangled limbs; he saw himself writhing there among them, the taste of bitter almonds in his mouth and the corrosive smell of gunpowder in his nose.

With an abrupt movement he took the tommy-gun off his shoulder; at the same time the man by the hut also came to life. He ran around it to the right, where the door must be, and returned at once with three others. They had civilian clothes on and were holding sub-machine guns. As though in a kaleidoscope Schmitt saw the four men peering toward him and then disappearing into the wood with huge bounds. Then at last the brain clicked. He dashed off across the clearing, and panting, reached the hut, where he looked round for his men. They were approaching rather hesitantly. When Corporal Baumgartner started to run into the wood in pursuit of the partisans Schmitt recalled him sharply. They can't escape now, he thought, and at the moment their tracks were more important than their heads. Besides, he was glad things had turned out like this; heaven knew what would have happened if they'd shown a bit more courage. They were partisans—no doubt about that.

He told Baumgartner to post two men outside, then took the rest of his men and went into the hut. The room they entered had a small window looking out on the wood, with a snowed-up pine-branch hanging in front of it. Everything pointed to a very abrupt departure by the room's occupants. There were overturned glasses on the table and scattered playing cards. On the left wall, half torn from their hooks, hung three German winter uniforms, like the one the man in front of the hut had been wearing. Four wooden bunks built on top of each other stood in one corner and in the middle of the room glowed a small iron stove.

On looking round, Schmitt discovered a second door. He went up to it and kicked it open. His eyes widened in horrified surprise. Although the room had no window, there was enough daylight coming through the door for him to see the figures of ten or more men. Their unshaven faces stared at him. For a moment he stood in amazement, then he pulled up his tommy-gun and ten pairs of arms immediately reached for the low ceiling as if they had been puppets. In the half darkness Schmitt noticed the men's uniforms: they were German officers.

The realization took his breath away. He seized the nearest officer by the arm. "Who the devil are you?"

"We're prisoners," the officer said dejectedly.

Schmitt stared at him. He felt laughter welling up in his throat and his shoulders began to shake. The tension of the last minutes exploded. "You're prisoners, are you?"

His men behind him roared with laughter.

Schmitt turned and went back out into the open where he stood trying to recover his breath. The officers came rushing after him and, surrounding him, almost tore him to pieces. A fat artillery colonel kept banging him on the shoulder so hard that in the end Schmitt lost his temper and yelled abuse. But the colonel only laughed and slapped him on the back. "After this you can shout at me as much as you like."

"Where's the general?" asked Schmitt, looking keenly at their bearded faces.

"*General?*" inquired the colonel blankly. "We haven't got a general. I can offer you six captains, three majors and my humble self; but with the best will in the world we can't supply a general."

The disappointment was like a blow in the face, and it took Schmitt a full minute to recover. Then he ordered Baumgartner to have the platoon fall in.

"Here, wait a moment," the colonel interjected. "Aren't you going to give us any explanation?"

"Haven't time, I'm afraid. My orders are to find our missing general, and find him now, I will, as sure as my name's Schmitt."

"One way of introducing yourself. But seriously, Herr Schmitt, what do you think's going to happen to us?"

"If you follow our tracks back the way we came, you'll be in Szomolnok in four hours. My command post is there."

"Fine, fine." The colonel nodded sarcastically. "And what do you think of that?" He looked up at the sky, from which snow was falling in large flakes. "If we need four hours, we won't find much of your tracks, eh? I'll make you a suggestion. You look for your general with one half, and give us the other."

"Half of what?"

The colonel looked astonished, and his voice hardened. "Are you really so dense? Half your men, of course."

Schmitt became reckless. "The upper half or the lower?" The colonel's face turned the color of a beet, and in order to forestall his outburst, Schmitt continued quickly: "You seem to have misunderstood me. I have orders to look for the general; for that I need my men. I can give you one, but that's all."

The colonel seemed about to explode, but now a major joined in the discussion. "Perhaps I might make another suggestion," he said to the colonel. "Let Herr Schmitt keep his men, but instead give us four or five tommy-guns."

The colonel nodded, and the swollen veins on his neck went down. "Good idea. We'll take a guide with us, of course. Have the guns collected," he told Schmitt.

The peremptory tone made Schmitt see red. He said coldly: "We have no spare guns."

"Who's saying anything about spare guns? You give us half your guns, then we'll have five and you'll have five. Fifty-fifty, eh?"

"You think so? Only with the small difference that you'll be bound for Szomolnok and we have to go after partisans. Am I supposed to arm my men with sticks?"

"With pine cones for all I care," the colonel answered furiously. "You don't seriously suggest that we go through partisan country like this?"

"*We* did."

"But not unarmed. Stop this nonsense, Captain. I'm not letting myself get captured again just to please you."

"If we hadn't found you, you wouldn't have had the

chance to let yourself get captured again. Why don't *you* throw pine cones if necessary?"

There was a stir among the officers. "Preposterous!" snorted the major, and went up threateningly to Schmitt. The colonel waved him back. "Leave it, thank you, Herr Jung. We'll do this another way." He turned to one of Schmitt's men. "Give me your gun."

"No you don't!" shouted Schmitt, pale with anger. "Corporal Baumgartner, choose a man to go with them to Szomolnok. All the rest come over here."

The men rushed past the officers and took up position behind Schmitt. The colonel's face went livid once more. He took the major by the arm. "Collect the guns, Herr Jung."

"I wouldn't try if I were you," said Schmitt.

The officers behind Major Jung moved grimly nearer. "You'll be shot for this," gasped the colonel.

"Take care you aren't shot yourself before you get back to Szomolnok," retorted Schmitt, aiming the barrel of his tommy-gun at Major Jung, who had meanwhile come still closer. "Don't do anything foolish, Major. I've given my men an order."

"You soon won't be giving any more," said the major with white lips. He was almost close enough to put out his hand and take the gun. Schmitt curled his finger round the trigger. He scarcely recognized his own voice as he cried hoarsely: "If you haven't disappeared in one minute, I'll give the order to fire."

The major goggled at him. For an instant it looked as if he were going to hurl himself at Schmitt; but again the colonel's sharp voice brought him to his senses. "Let it go, Herr Jung. Don't you see that we've got a madman to deal with? We'll make sure afterward that he's put out of harm's way. Come over here."

The major turned without a word. They spoke to the man who was to guide them, and soon they fol-

lowed him across the clearing and disappeared behind
the bend in the valley.

Scowling, Schmitt gave the signal for marching off.

It was snowing hard, but the partisans couldn't be
more than twenty minutes ahead and even if the snow
went on falling like this their tracks would be visible
for some time. Schmitt felt a growing impatience, the
thrill of the hunt had caught him and he would now
have made the same efforts if they had been searching for a mere private.

They went on until Schmitt stopped the men in
order to study the terrain. About twenty yards ahead
of them the wood climbed to a plateau, on which there
was a heavy growth of young pines. The tracks led in
that direction and Schmitt suddenly felt certain that
the partisans were waiting up there.

He called the platoon over to him and divided them
into two groups. With one of them Corporal Baumgartner disappeared among the trees on the left, while
Schmitt circled to the right with the other until he
decided there was plenty of protective forest between
them and the partisans. Then they started climbing,
through trees growing so close together that at first
glance there seemed no way through. In time they
worked their way through the growth and came upon
the partisans' tracks.

The footprints were plainly visible, and Schmitt was
annoyed at having lost valuable time. He called the
signalman over and told him to try for contact again,
and at the same time detailed a man to find Baumgartner. Schmitt stared uneasily between the trees. At
last the signalman looked up. "I've got them," he said
eagerly.

In three strides Schmitt was with him. "Who have
you got?"

"Sergeant Major Roos, sir," the signalman answered.

"Excellent." Schmitt felt tempted to pat him on the

back. "Ask him where he is, and if he's in touch with their platoons." He watched with excitement as the man busied himself with the set. "No contact with other platoons," the man told Schmitt. "They'll soon be at the top."

"Right." Schmitt pulled the map out of his pocket, and worked out the new position and course for Roos' platoon. Baumgartner and his men joined them and gathered around Schmitt, watching tensely as he gave instructions to the signalman. "They can't be more than a mile and a quarter as the crow flies," Schmitt said to Baumgartner. "If they step on it, they'll be here in half an hour. Leave a man here with a Very pistol. In exactly half an hour he's to start firing a red Very light every five minutes. The rest of you: ready to move." The men threw away their cigarettes. "Keep your distances," he ordered, and they set off again.

They followed the partisans' tracks through thick forest and dense scrub, making slow progress through the continuing snow storm. Watching the tracks, Schmitt observed that they had not lost any ground on the partisans. He was not surprised; probably the partisans had worn themselves out at the start, as he could guess from his own condition. He was a tough marcher, and had been on many hikes and climbs before the war, yet he could feel his reserves of energy draining away. The wet boots hung on his feet like ton weights, and his tommy-gun bothered him. He turned to the man behind him and said sardonically: "Good exercise, huh?"

"Yes, sir," said the man, and fell flat on his face. Submachine guns barked off in the wood and Schmitt and the others threw themselves to the ground. Shots whined through the air, plopping against the trees and hissing into the snow. Schmitt pressed his face to his arms, his heart contracted in the grip of a cold hand, and for a second he seemed to be choking. Rais-

135

ing his arm, he described a circle; the platoon understood the circle, for he could hear movements behind him. Out of the corner of his eye he saw dark objects fly through the air, and a few moments later sharp explosions sounded through the wood. Baumgartner and two other soldiers raced through the trees toward a dense growth of scrub, their heads down, their guns firing continuously.

Now Schmitt was firing too. The butt of the gun drummed against his shoulder. The magazine with its slightly curved front lay cool and supple in his hand, giving him a feeling of security. He could think clearly again: the partisans' fire had ceased, there was only a tommy-gun barking.

He got up, gave his men another signal, and cautiously went over with them to the scrub where the partisans had been hidden; they reached it unmolested. As he moved into the undergrowth, he almost fell over a man's crumpled body when Baumgartner panted up. "Got away," he gasped. Then his eye fell on the corpse, and he whistled softly. "Except one apparently. We saw the others, but they were already too far away."

"That's all right," said Schmitt. Numbly he watched the men attending to the casualties. The face of one was disfigured beyond recognition, a second had his legs drawn up to his stomach and was groaning.

"What do we do with the dead?" asked Baumgartner. "Dig a hole for them here?"

"A grave, you mean," Schmitt shouted at him. "Take your men to intercept Sergeant Major Roos. Tell Roos he's to send four of his men back to Szomolnok with the wounded; then you return here with him as quickly as you can. You stay here," he ordered Teltschik, and set out alone to follow the partisans' trail. He simply had to do something; the sight of the dead filled him with revulsion and he could not escape a feeling of personal responsibility. Give up now, he thought, it's no use going on.

He glanced ahead, and saw something surprising. The tracks curved off at a sharp angle, the partisans had suddenly gone off in another direction as if they had bounced off an invisible wall. The trail now led due north, whereas before it had been going westward all the time.

He pulled the map hastily from his pocket and studied it. Yes, I'm right, he told himself: if they continue in the new direction, they're bound to come to Oviz, and that's where Kolodzi and his men are. For a moment the conclusion stunned him, then he came bounding back to Teltschik, who stood by the dead men and now looked toward Schmitt anxiously.

"When Sergeant Major Roos comes," he told Teltschik in breathless tones, "he's to follow my trail, as fast as he can."

"Yes, sir. As fast as he can, sir. Can't I . . ."

"You can stay here and bury the dead," said Schmitt and raced back into the wood. It was beginning to grow dark. He ran like a wild cat, with head thrown forward, gasping, sweating, like one possessed—he was propelled by a cold hatred which took away all weariness and drove him onward.

He ran for half an hour, then another, and then he came to the road—which must be the place where Kolodzi and the other two had gone off on foot the night before. The ground fell sharply away into the valley, and the lights down there were the lights of Oviz. Suddenly he heard shots. They came from the valley, they came in quick succession. He looked round tensely. Although it was dark, the partisans' tracks were still recognizable in the dim light that lay over the snow like a haze. They led straight over the road and across the wood; Roos couldn't miss them. Schmitt thought feverishly. Roos wouldn't arrive for another half hour, and by then it might be too late. The gunfire grew fiercer. When he reached the edge of the wood, he saw the fiery trails of tracer ammunition whizzing over the road, where they bounced off somewhere and shot up toward the sky. The sight surpassed his worst imagination.

As far as he could see, the battle was going on in the street at the right end of the village. He raced down, past dark houses, till he noticed a black mass standing in the middle of the street. As he cautiously approached, he saw that it was a vehicle. On the right side of it a man's lifeless arm was hanging out. Further on, also in the street, there was evidently another man lying. His body was covered by the snow. He must have been lying there for several hours. It was fifty yards to the two houses between which the tracer bullets were whistling back and forth. Schmitt would have liked to go up to the truck, but decided it was too dangerous. Instead he concentrated on the gunfire. In the course of the months he had learned to distinguish the rattle of a German tommy-gun from that of a Russian sub-machine gun, and he knew what he must do.

Turning he raced back into the wood: he needed Roos and his men to help him now or rather to help Kolodzi.

Standing at the window, Vöhringer watched the snow come down and wondered what he could do for diversion. Suddenly he remembered the sanatorium. It was too early for lunch and if he hurried he could be back in an hour. Perhaps he could get out of the house without Herbig noticing—then he could worry his head about where he had gone too. They had squabbled all morning.

The idea pleased him. Picking up his gun he crept to the door. Herbig must be in the kitchen, his muffled voice seemed to be coming from there. With a few strides Vöhringer was in the open, running across the garden to the far side of the house, where the wood began. He stopped for a moment to look back, but there was no sign of Herbig. Then he happened to glance at the big house on the other side of the street, where he saw a swarthy man he had noticed before from the window. The door opened, and another man came out, stopping near the swarthy man; the two of them looked across the street at him.

What on earth are they gaping for, thought Vöhringer nervously. For a moment he felt like putting his tongue out at them. "Be your age," he muttered under his breath, and turned into the wood. What did he care about these damned Slovaks? Let them goggle till their eyes dropped out; if they tried any tricks he'd always have his gun. He caught himself stroking the cold metal. By God, he was not one of those who enjoyed swaggering around with a tommy-gun, but with the Russians after one it was an extremely comforting thing to have.

The climb was hard, and he sweated. This was a good idea, he decided; a climb took one's mind off things. The hill became so steep he had to stop now and then for a breather; after a while he began to think he had missed the way, for surely he should have reached the sanatorium long ago. He wondered whether to turn right or left, and on a hunch decided on the left. The terrain was difficult, impeded by bushes, stunted pines and large boulders; besides which, the snow was falling harder and harder. None of this deterred Vöhringer, whose despondent mood was passing now that he had something to do. In the silence, which lay over the wood like a shroud, his thoughts lost their bitterness. Sometimes he could look down into the valley through some gaps in the forest, and then he saw the houses of Oviz lying far below, with streaks of blue smoke rising from the chimneys into the snowy air, and the mountains on the other side disappearing behind the flaky veil of snow which the wind blew into the valley.

After ten minutes he was convinced he had taken the wrong direction, so he went back to the place where he had come up the hill. Here he made a remarkable discovery: two men had followed him on his climb, the imprints of their unstudded boots were easily distinguishable from his own. They must have followed his tracks so far, but then turned right where he had gone left, for their footprints led across the hillside that way. Probably they were the same two who had stared at him down below. It all seemed rather odd to him. They certainly hadn't climbed the hill just for pleasure, but why had they suddenly struck out in a different direction? He hoped this showed they weren't plotting anything against *him*, but decided to be on his guard all the same.

Taking the tommy-gun in his hands, he followed their tracks. After about two hundred yards he suddenly saw the sanatorium between the trees, and stopped in wonder. It stood in a clearing enclosed by the forest on all sides. It had a great many windows, each with a small balcony outside, and there was a glass-roofed terrace at the back of it. The stone walls were smothered with ivy, which had climbed everywhere between the windows and up to the pointed roof. On every corner there were bay windows with Gothic arches, and thick wads of snow had settled on all the ledges protruding under the windows. The picture surpassed Vöhringer's finest expectations. He had forgotten about the two men, and as he slowly walked up to the building, he was so entranced by the sight that he did not hear the glass breaking at one of the windows. The bullet went in a couple of inches above his groin, piercing his peritoneum and stopping at his small intestine.

Not that Vöhringer felt it as precisely as that. The pain was so violent that he did not even hear the report of the gun. He collapsed as if a scythe had gone through his knees, and began to scream. Then a tommy-gun barked off behind him, but he did not hear that either. He screamed with his mouth wide open. He rolled about in the snow like a worm, as if he could thus rid himself of the pain that had crept upon him, clawing deeper and deeper into his body. He thrashed out with arms and legs. When he couldn't scream any more, because the pain had squeezed him dry, he let his face fall down and licked up the snow like a dog. By the time Herbig pulled him up, his whole mouth was full of it: he had almost choked with snow.

That morning Andrej had gone to Kubany and asked him to come to the house with his men at midday in order to discuss their going to Durka with Nikolash. On his way back Andrej saw something that stopped him in his tracks. Ahead of him, where the street led out of the village into the wood, stood two men in German winter uniform. They wore narrow peaked caps, and carried tommy-guns. Before he had properly collected his thoughts, Andrej heard his name called, and saw Nikolash and Zepac standing outside Zepac's house; he ran over to them. "Come in," said Nikolash. Andrej entered and looked out of the window. "What d'you make of it?" asked Nikolash.

"Where did they come from?"

"They're living at Sztraka's house. They came last night, half an hour after the Germans had gone off with their trucks. Three men," he added significantly. "One of them left again almost at once, and hasn't shown up since. If this Sztraka weren't such a stupid oaf, he'd have let us know at once—he only came to me ten minutes ago."

"It had to be Sztraka of all people."

"Just what I said. Even if they were deserters, it wouldn't suit me to have them living with Sztraka just across the street where they can see everything we're doing."

Nikolash was thoughtfully licking his lower lip and now remarked: "I don't trust them, they prance around too much for deserters. Listen!"—he took hold of Zepac by the collar of his coat—"The general must be moved. You and Dula will take him on to the Golden Table. We've got a cabin up there."

"I never knew that," exclaimed Zepac in surprise.

142

Nikolash took some paper out of his pocket. "Well, you know now. Here's a sketch, and this is where the cabin is—you can't miss it. You stay up there with the general till he's fetched down. I was going to take him there this evening, but now we can't afford to leave it any longer."

Zepac looked gloomily at the sketch. He had lived in Oviz forty-five years, but the idea of climbing the Golden Table had never entered his head—and now he was to do it in deep snow! "Why don't we take him to join the others?" he asked.

"He's too important for that. I'll tell Dula. You must start in half an hour." Nikolash went out into the street with Andrej, and asked: "When will your men be here?"

"At three o'clock."

"As soon as the first Russian soldiers arrive, you can lead them first to the ten prisoners in the lower hut; then go and fetch the general. They know about it already, Pushkin sent a man through to tell them."

"What'll *you* do?"

Nikolash turned up the fur collar of his coat. "I'm off to Dobšina tonight. I've got a sledge coming. And in case you change your mind—there'll be room for two more."

"What does Margita say?"

"Leave that to me," said Nikolash.

Andrej dug his hands into his coat pockets. They walked down the middle of the street, like two men talking about their sheep. The wind drove snow into their faces, Andrej's dark beard was stiff with it. He said: "She'll miss you."

"Perhaps I'll come back one day."

"She'll be married by then."

"If she hasn't any children, that won't worry me. Have you already got a husband for her?"

143

"There are plenty of people around here who'd like to marry her."

"Shepherds!" said Nikolash, with a sudden raucous laugh. "Margita and a shepherd. You wouldn't find a Moscow woman marrying a country bumpkin."

"Our shepherds were good enough for you as long as you needed them," Andrej retorted.

Nikolash did not answer. Before they turned off the street, he stopped and looked across at Sztraka's house on the other side. The Germans had been clever, if things became hot for them, they could quickly reach the wood; whereas Andrej's house was surrounded by a steeply rising meadow, at present blanketed with snow, and was about the same distance from the next house as it was from Sztraka's. This meadow gap could be watched from Sztraka's house, but on the other hand, Nikolash realized, that the window of his room gave a good view of Sztraka's house; he wondered why he hadn't thought of it before. Turning back to Andrej, he replied at last:

"We finished off the White Russians, and now we're finishing off the Germans. None of your shepherds lifted a finger to stop them when they marched in. If we had your divisions, things would have been very different. But it took even you nearly four years to deal with the Germans, despite your hundred and seventy millions."

"We weren't prepared for the attack. The Red Army. . . ."

"Ran away as far as the Volga," said Andrej, "and would have run even further if winter hadn't come. That's something our children learn at school." He swung around and was about to enter the home when Nikolash called him back in a low, excited voice. Turning, Andrej saw him pointing across the street to the edge of the wood, saying: "Over there."

Andrej looked, and saw a man standing dead still,

staring at them. He immediately recognized the man as one of the two Germans. Just then the German moved swiftly to disappear into the wood.

Without a word, Andrej and Nikolash rushed back into the house, Nikolash going to his room, while Andrej tore upstairs. Pulling open the door of his room, he ran to the window, where there was a dark chest-of-drawers, crammed full of sheets and linen; underneath were sub-machine guns. He quickly unbuttoned his greatcoat, putting one of the guns in the belt of his tunic, then buttoned up the coat again, thrust two magazines into the big pockets, and raced downstairs.

Nikolash was waiting for him impatiently. They heard Margita's voice calling something from the kitchen, but they took no notice and ran across the street to the place where the German had gone off into the wood. There they brought out their guns, put in the magazines, and followed the German's trail, which led straight up the side of the hill. When it suddenly took a leftward bend, Nikolash exchanged a brief glance with Andrej. They turned in the other direction, and made for the sanatorium as fast as they could go. On reaching it, they hammered against the door with their fists.

Dula opened up for them. "A good thing you've come. I've got nothing left to drink."

"You'll get blood to drink," Nikolash told him.

Dula locked the door and took them down a long corridor with high windows, through which glimpses could be seen of the snow-covered wood. At the end of the corridor there were stairs leading to a large room. This had an open fireplace and French windows with a balcony outside; some of the window panes were broken and taped over with paper. The room had a door, smaller than the others, leading into a windowless chamber that had contained X-ray equipment. Here they had locked up the general.

"He's asleep," said Dula, motioning to the door.

"Best thing for him," grunted Nikolash, going to join Andrej at the window. "If they find the house," he said, "they're going to be taught a lesson. It's the third man who worries me most. He may have gone for reinforcements."

"You don't believe they're deserters?" asked Andrej.

"I never did."

Dula was listening in dismay. "Has something blown up?"

"Yes, a balloon," answered Nikolash. "Go and get ready—Zepac should be here any minute, and you two have got to take the general on to the Golden Table."

"Up there?"

"Yes. Zepac knows all about it, he'll tell you. We'll come part of the way with you."

Dula cleared his throat. He was a short fat man with a plump face, partly hidden by a huge, straggly beard which went down almost to his chest; all you could really see of his face were the deep-set eyes and the red tippler's nose. "Can't you tell me what this is all about?" he said.

Andrej turned to Dula. "Since last night there have been two Germans in Oviz. One of them is coming up through the wood."

"There he is now," said Nikolash.

Andrej swung around. His movement coincided with the sudden crash of glass. Nikolash had pushed the barrel of his gun through the window and fired. Down below, in front of the house, a man toppled into the snow and began screaming.

"Badly aimed," said Andrej. "Put another one into him."

"Let him croak there." Nikolash showed his teeth in a cruel smile.

Dula pressed past them to the window and looked out. He failed to notice Nikolash leaping to one side, and Andrej flinging himself on the floor. The panes cracked inwards, Dula put both hands to his face and fell flat on his back, a jet of blood spurting from his mouth like a fountain. Outside, from the edge of the wood, a tommy-gun hammered away in what seemed a never-ending salvo. Tearing the strips of paper from the shattered panes, the shots hit the wall. Andrej crept toward the balcony and looked across at Nikolash, who was crouching by the wall on the other side. Their eyes converged on Dula's disfigured face. The blood ran down the beard and dripped on to the floor.

The tommy-gun stopped, and in the abrupt silence a faint sigh could be heard, sounding like the last bit of air being squeezed out of a flat tire. Dula's feet quivered slightly, then turned outwards and stiffened. "Idiot," said Nikolash, not specifying whom he meant. He cautiously straightened up, but as his head approached the balcony door, several shots rattled into the room. "There's only one of them," he said, "I'll make him pay for this. Stay here till Zepac comes."

He crept to the door, raced downstairs and along the corridor, hurled open the last window, and jumped out. Moving stealthily around the house to the place where the German had been lying, he saw a wide trail of blood which led to the edge of the wood; there it stopped, and deep footprints continued instead. Nikolash smiled in grim satisfaction: with a wounded man on his back, the German couldn't escape.

He ran down the hill in great bounds, but at one point he slipped, and slid on his seat some twenty yards further in thick scrub. He was about to get to his feet when the tommy-gun barked off ahead of him, the shot rattling like pebbles against the frozen tree-trunks around him. Nikolash pressed deep into the snow, and did not even move when the noise suddenly stopped: perhaps the German was waiting for him to come out, but he was not that stupid—he chuckled into the snow. After a few minutes he started creeping cautiously through the snow, away from the trail, and having covered forty yards like this, he got up, ran another hundred yards in the same direction, then made straight for the valley.

Very soon he had reached the edge of the wood and came out on to the street. He glanced at the nearest house, and remembered Zepac. He pulled open the door, saw Zepac standing in the hall, was up to him in a couple of strides and seized him by the coat. "What were my orders, eh?"

Zepac trembled, and raised his arms entreatingly. "Please let me go, Nikolash. I was just off, then the shooting started, and. . . ."

Nikolash hurled him against the wall. Zepac ran out of the house. Nikolash caught him up in the street, and gave him a furious punch in the face. "Off to Dula," he said tersely. "You manage with the general on your own. If he's caught, I'll hang your wife and children by their feet. Get me?"

Zepac nodded. Nikolash's blow had made his upper lip bleed. He wiped the blood from his mouth and rushed off toward the wood.

Now Nikolash looked around. He saw Margita and Sztraka standing at the window of Andrej's house, making signs to him; he took the signs to mean that the Germans were back. He raced across the meadow and climbed through the open window, where Margita was waiting. "What's happened to Andrej?" she said.

"Oh, don't fuss," he answered. "Andrej's at the sanatorium. Are the Germans in your house?" he asked Sztraka.

"Yes, both of them. The tall one was carrying the short one. I think he's dead. Did you shoot him?"

"He'd have been pretty silly to do it himself. Is your wife still there?"

"She's hiding in the stable."

"Bring her over here," Nikolash ordered.

A few minutes later Sztraka returned with his wife, who was weeping.

"What's the matter with her?" asked Nikolash.

"She's scared about her house."

"Nobody's going to take the hovel away from her. Did you see the Germans?"

"No, I didn't see them, but my wife heard one of them screaming."

"Then he's still alive. You and your wife go to another house till it's over."

"I can help you people," said Sztraka.

This offer did not displease Nikolash. He had enough sub-machine guns in the house, and although Sztraka wasn't a partisan, it might be better to keep him around. "All right, but your wife must go."

While Sztraka was taking his wife away, Nikolash explained what had happened. "We must finish with them before the third comes back. He may be bringing more with him."

"Then we'd be fools to stay here," said Margita.

"That remains to be seen. Andrej's men will arrive by around three, and if things get bad, we've still the thirty men in Meczenzéf. I could send someone to them—Sztraka for instance."

He was wondering about this when Sztraka returned, apologizing for his wife. "Women are terrible in this sort of thing."

"Not all of them," Nikolash remarked, looking at Margita. She was wearing a shirt with red ribbons on the elbows, a low-cut bodice fitted tightly around her narrow waist, a short skirt hanging down to her knees in many folds, and high red boots reached up to her calves. She's one of the women you can't get enough of, thought Nikolash, and turned to Sztraka. "Do you know your way about in Svedler?"

"I've got a brother living there."

"So much the better. Go to see Hodscha. His house is the third on the right. Tell him that Matuska's to bring his men along. He'll know what to do."

"I've got my coat over in the house," Sztraka objected timidly.

"Give him one of mine," Nikolash told Margita.

When Sztraka had gone, Margita returned and her face was angry. "If I were a man I'd have given him the whip instead of a coat."

"I prefer you without a whip," said Nikolash, putting his arms around her from behind. With closed eyes she let him feel over her body.

Nikolash pressed his face to hers. "How would you like to travel with me to Dobšina, and later to Prague. Would you like that?"

"What'll you do there?"

"I need a change of air. If all goes well, our divisions will be here tomorrow."

She looked at him in amazement. "And you're only telling me now?"

"I've only just heard. Tonight the organization will be transferred to Dobšina. Pushkin's sending a sledge for us. You'll come on it, won't you?"

"Perhaps."

"Only perhaps?"

"At least perhaps. But I'll have to think it over first."

Her reaction disappointed him. He was about to draw her to him, when a tommy-gun barked. He went on his knees, and pulled her down by his side. Then he realized that the shot hadn't been aimed at *them*. There was a clatter at the side window, Andrej leaped into the room like a panther, landing on all fours alongside them. Now the shots whipped through the front window, as the three of them lay pressed against the floor. The rain of shots shattered the pictures on the wall and made big holes in the door that led to Margita's room. Then the firing stopped, as suddenly as it had started.

"I've had enough of this," said Nikolash.

"Why the devil didn't you warn me?" panted Andrej.

"You should have sent us a postcard to say you were coming." Nikolash crept to the window on the street side, and fired the magazine empty. "Just to show them we're still alive."

Sliding along to the door, Margita sat up and leaned against the wall. Still pale with shock, she asked Andrej: "Were they shooting at you?"

"Who else d'you think? There's a car coming here."

Nikolash stopped in the act of putting in a new magazine. "What sort of a car?"

"I followed your tracks. From the place where you came out of the wood one can see into the road on the other side, and there was a car just passing there."

"A truck?"

"No, a small one—like the one of the general."

"Then they'll be here any minute." Nikolash ran to the other window, which gave a view on to part of the road, till it was hidden by the next house. "Has the general left?"

"Yes, I sent Zepac off with him at once. . . ." Andrej broke off, gripped Nikolash by the shoulder and pulled the window open. The German car, with five people in it, was now appearing from behind the next house. Nikolash saw a face behind its windscreen which made him gasp; his face twisted to a grimace as he fired a rain of shots; Andrej was also firing.

It was forty yards to the car, and three men jumped out of it. Above his gun Andrej noticed the windshield blowing in. He aimed at the three men, saw one of them stumble. He had the man right in the sights, and because it was Orid Krasko, he emptied the whole magazine into his body. Krasko fell to the ground, the other two men raced on; before Andrej could change the magazine, they had disappeared. Now he heard a tommy-gun rattling away from the other side of the street; the shots whipped through the room behind him. He swung round, and his heart missed a beat: Margita lay motionless by the other window. Then he saw her move her head and look at Nikolash. She gave a sign with her hand, then all three got up and beat the dust off their clothes.

Nikolash took Margita's arm. "What was the matter with you?"

"I was just shocked," she answered. "The glass came into my face."

"I'll flay them alive for that," vowed Nikolash without smiling. He looked out of the window at the car. There were two men lying motionless on the front seats. He could see the uniform of one, whose arm hung rigidly out of the window. The other had his blood-stained face against the windscreen, and Orid Krasko lay in the street. The other two must have escaped into Sztraka's house. He looked at Andrej, who was standing by him and staring out at Orid Krasko's body. "He's always been a traitor," said Andrej.

Nikolash laughed softly. "Not always; only when he was trying to save his own skin. Now he won't have to worry about his skin any longer."

"Something's gone wrong in Košice."

"We'll hear about it when Poniatowski comes," Nikolash answered, watching the Germans' shots smacking against the door. The fire became briefer and briefer, then stopped altogether.

"They're holding a palaver," remarked Andrej.

Margita put her hand on Nikolash's shoulder. "Shouldn't we clear off?"

"No."

"Then we must wait till Andrej's men come."

"That'll be a party all right," said Nikolash, reaching down inside her shirt. Andrej watched with unconcealed disgust.

General Stiller arrived when Giesinger was about to give orders for the transfer of divisional headquarters to Jaszo. With the general were two new staff officers, and also the corps commander's aide, Colonel Kolmel. After the last telephone conversation with Giesinger, he had jumped into his car and gone after the general; he found him on the road between Szomolnok and Meczenzéf. The road was slippery and winding, and in the middle of the forest the car had skidded at a hairpin bend, rolled down a bank and rammed a tree.

Kolmel invited the general and other officers to travel in his car, and they arrived in Košice six hours late, just as the first supply units were preparing to leave the town on their own initiative. Stiller had two paymasters arrested, demoted five sergeants to the ranks, and arrived at divisional headquarters fuming with rage. He dashed up the steps, followed by the other officers, and yelled for Giesinger.

Giesinger was sitting in Hepp's room, anxiously studying the last flagged positions in the map. When he heard Stiller's voice he rushed to the door.

"So you're Giesinger, are you?" said the general, stepping up to him with scarlet face. "Who gave orders for the supply column to evacuate the town?"

Giesinger looked into his furious eyes. "A precautionary measure," he said breathlessly, "purely that."

"Purely that!" Stiller's voice almost squeaked. He turned to Kolmel and the other officers. "Did you hear that? A precautionary measure?"

"Did you give the order?" asked Kolmel.

Giesinger fought for breath. "Not to evacuate, sir. We simply gave orders to stand by for a move."

Stiller beckoned over Captain Hardorff, who had just come out of his room, and told him to make sure nobody in the division left the town. "Only with my express permission," he added. Then, turning back to Giesinger, he asked how things looked at the front.

It was the question Giesinger had been waiting for tensely the last hour. His haggard face grew taut. "The Russians are through, sir."

"What's that?"

"We did what we could," said Giesinger desperately.

Stiller stepped past him into Hepp's office. "Let's hear the position," he told Hepp, who was standing stiffly at attention by the table. Hepp's account was worse than he had imagined. Colonel Wieland had withdrawn his command post to Durkov and the Russians were in Rozhanovce; Wieland's last radio signal reported the decimation of his battalions. Colonel Höpper, also in great difficulties, had dug in at Slancik. Only Colonel Scheper was still holding his old positions, having sent one of his forward battalions south to protect his open flank. "Here's his latest signal, sir," said Hepp, pushing it across the table to Stiller.

The general thrust it aside carelessly. "Where's the assault regiment?"

"It should be in Rozhanovce by now, sir. Colonel Kreisel was to counter-attack on both sides of the road. He's got the pioneer battalion with him."

"How about the reconnaissance unit?"

"It had orders to go to Slancik, but Colonel Höpper signals that it hasn't arrived yet. Major Giesinger was

156

going to redirect it to Rozhanovce, but we don't know if Major Fuchs ever got that signal."

Stiller turned to Kolmel. "What do you say to that?"

"It's incredible," answered Kolmel, looking at the map. He turned his long, horsy face to Giesinger. "You should have sent the pioneer battalion to Höpper, too. The assault regiment would have been enough on its own for the counter-attack at Rozhanovce."

"When I gave that order, things weren't too bad in Höpper's sector," Giesinger objected.

"Höpper was left high and dry the moment Wieland evacuated his positions."

"So was Colonel Scheper."

"The assault regiment could have taken that over too. If Höpper has dug in at Slancik, the Russians can march through unhindered between Slancik and Durkov."

"The reconnaissance unit. . . ."

"That was far too weak on its own. Besides you don't even know where it is at the moment. And where on earth's your reserve battalion? Is that with the assault regiment too?"

Giesinger moistened his dry lips with his tongue. The eyes of all the officers were on him. He looked helplessly at Hepp, but Hepp had taken off his glasses and was contemplating them with interest: I can't expect any help from him, thought Giesinger. Behind the general he fleetingly noticed the pale face of Lieutenant Pfeiffer, who at once lowered his eyes. It was so quiet in the room that the wood could be heard crackling in the fire. Giesinger hunted for words. Everything he had rehearsed for this moment now seemed trite and unconvincing. The conversation he had been hoping to have with the new general had turned into something like a court-martial hearing; there was no alternative but to answer Kolmel's question. "The reserve battalion should be getting here any minute."

"Getting here from where?"

Again Giesinger moistened his lips. Without looking, he could feel a glance of protest from Pfeiffer. He pulled himself together. "The battalion has been in Szomolnok. We were . . . it was to search for the general."

"For me?" asked Stiller in amazement.

Giesinger looked at his powerful jaw and from there into his eyes, which were glacial. His thick hair lay very straight over a narrow scalp that might have been hewn out of rock. The question offered a temptation, and for a moment Giesinger thought he saw a chance; but then he remembered Hepp and Pfeiffer, who were gazing at him intently. Trying to save what he could, he answered: "Well, I *was* thinking of that, sir, because we were worrying about you."

"Thinking of what?"

"Of trying to find you, sir. The battalion was already on its way, you see."

"To search for General Marx?" inquired Kolmel.

"Yes, sir."

"Who gave the order for that? You perhaps?"

"Yes, sir."

"Without informing me?"

"I take full responsibility."

"For the Russians having broken through?"

"If I may say so, sir, Captain Schmitt with his hundred men. . . ."

"Hundred and fifty."

"With his hundred and fifty men he couldn't have held up the Russians."

"How do you know?"

"Experience. . . ."

"What experience? Yours? In Synewidsko fifty men under one of your captains saved the whole division, simply by staying in the trenches. And then you start talking about experience." He turned abruptly to the general. "This is the first I've heard about it, sir. With that battalion the gap could still have been blocked in time."

"Of course." Stiller came close to Giesinger. "When did you send the battalion off?"

"Yesterday evening, sir. But there are already trucks on their way to fetch them back again."

"Yesterday evening! Without informing corps! Simply sent a battalion off! Have you the faintest idea what you've done?"

Giesinger felt his knees giving. "I was only acting in the general's interests."

Stiller gasped. "As the general's deputy," he burst out, "the division's interests were all you had to concern yourself with, instead of sending your men across the countryside on a wild goose chase."

"Time will show whether it was that."

"What d'you mean?"

"We don't know yet how the search has gone."

"You aren't seriously telling us the general has been found?"

"We shall see when the battalion comes back."

Stiller looked across at Kolmel, who made an impatient gesture. "Even if you were successful, it would be in no proportion to the mess you've made."

"Perhaps it isn't as bad as all that," said Giesinger, who was beginning to feel firm ground again. Growing reckless, he added: "Besides, the position here can't be held much longer anyhow, with the Russians in the south . . ."

"I don't care a damn what the Russians are doing in the south," Kolmel interrupted furiously. "That's the business of the higher command. I am responsible for the corps. Put me on to the corps commander."

Giesinger realized he had overstepped the mark. With ashen lips he went to the telephone. When corps answered, he handed the receiver to Kolmel. The conversation was short, and to his relief Kolmel did not mention the reserve battalion.

Replacing the receiver, Kolmel turned to Stiller: "The general wants me to go up forward and take a look at things. Will you come with me, sir?"

"Of course. To Durkov?"

"Rozhanovce would be better. I must find out where the assault regiment is." He instructed Hepp to collect every possible man from the supply column, take them to Durkov as quickly as he could, and there report to Colonel Wieland. "If the reserve battalion is back by then, take that with you as well." Kolmel turned to Giesinger. "And you'll come with *us*, it will give you a chance to see just what you've done. If we can't push the Russians back over the pass, it will be a black day for you."

Giesinger went to his room to get ready. Before he even had his greatcoat on Kolmel stuck his head in. "Do I have to send you a formal invitation?"

Digging his hands into his pockets, Giesinger sat in the car beside the driver and abandoned himself to a chain of gloomy thoughts. He had hoped the road would get worse and it would be impossible to drive any further. He began conjuring up the grimmest pictures, and saw himself marching off to captivity under escort of Russian soldiers. Instinctively he felt for his wrist watch, which had been left him by his father and was very valuable.

The valley narrowed, and the road began to lead uphill with many sharp bends. A noise shook Giesinger out of his reverie. The general heard it too, and told the driver to stop. He and Kolmel stuck their heads out of the car. Artillery fire was distinctly audible somewhere behind the hills they must negotiate. The harsh bark of the guns, increasing at times to a protracted roar, sounded ghostly enough under the grey winter sky, rumbling like distant thunder behind the dark backdrop of mountains covered by low-lying clouds.

"Must be at the pass," said Stiller.

"Sounds like it," Kolmel agreed.

Ahead of them an ambulance emerged from the snow storm, then another. "Just the people I want to speak to," said Stiller, jumping out on to the road.

The ambulances stopped, and the door of the first was pushed open. A corporal climbed out and reported: apparently they had been attacked by rifle fire a mile behind Durkov.

"Which means the Russians have by-passed Durkov," said Stiller, looking worried. "What else do you know?"

The corporal mentioned that the assault regiment was still in Durkov, at which Stiller shook his head. "What's Kreisel doing in Durkov at all?" he asked Kolmel. "He was supposed to go to Rozhanovce."

"I can imagine what happened, sir," said Kolmel. "Kreisel attacked on both sides of the road, as ordered. When he found his flank being rolled up, he withdrew to Durkov. Wieland really doesn't seem to have a single man left up forward."

"So the road's open to the Russians."

"The assault guns are still on the road, sir," put in the corporal.

"Where?"

"At the crossroads where the road forks off to Durkov, sir."

"How many?"

"Four, sir."

"There should be eight," said Kolmel. "Is the place where you were attacked before or after the crossroads?"

"After from here, sir. The fire came from a clearing on the right."

Kolmel looked at his map, then asked the corporal a

161

few more questions. "A nice cheerful position," he remarked to Stiller. "No pioneer battalion, no reconnaissance unit, no contact with Höpper." He returned to Giesinger with a frown. "I suppose we can write off the reconnaissance unit. Did you at least tell Major Fuchs how things looked in Höpper's sector?"

"When I sent him off, everything was still intact there."

"Then you should have sent a dispatch rider after Fuchs. He must have walked straight into a. . . ." He suddenly broke off. "There's something wrong, though." Kolmel frowned. "You can drive on," he said to the corporal in charge of the ambulance.

The corporal hesitated. "We've seen a sergeant, sir, he had twenty or thirty men with him. I think they were running away."

"Where did you see them?"

"On the road, sir. You're bound to meet them."

Kolmel exchanged a glance with the general, then they both went back to the car. "Drive on," Stiller told the driver tersely, barely leaving Giesinger time to get in. Neither the general nor Kolmel seemed to notice he was there.

For half an hour no one spoke a word. The road was still going through thick woodland, but the gradient was gradually flattening out. Stiller ordered a stop at one point, where the ground fell away sharply on the left, giving a view on to an expanse of snowy landscape. The artillery fire sounded so close here that the reports could be distinguished from the explosion of the shells. The echo too was very distinct now, rolling over the mountains in a muffled thunder; in the snow storm all noises sounded as if they were heard through a wad of cotton batting.

"Let's have a look at this," Stiller said to Kolmel and climbed from the car. They crossed the road and stood gazing down into the valley. Across the narrow, wooded valley huge mountains piled up into the leaden sky. It was a sight of desolate grandeur and the two men stood spellbound until Kolmel nudged the general and pointed to a long line of men who came trudging along the road. About forty yards away they halted and stared at the general.

"Major Giesinger," Stiller called.

Giesinger jumped out of the car. "Yes, sir."

"Bring those men over here."

Giesinger ran over to them and spoke to their leader, a tall man in winter uniform, who now came toward the general, his men trotting miserably behind him. "Sergeant Scheubele of the 2nd Company, 318 Regiment," he reported to Stiller.

"Wieland's regiment," commented Kolmel.

"Where are you going?" asked Stiller.

"We're falling back to regroup, sir."

"At Košice?"

The sergeant did not answer. Stiller tore the sergeant's stripes off and flung them on the ground. "At Košice, of course!" he repeated scathingly.

The sergeant still said nothing. His unshaven, dirt-encrusted face had turned white. Stiller took the tommy-gun from his hand. "Who gave you permission to leave your position?"

"There isn't a position any more, sir. Everything's gone to pieces up forward. We remained in our positions till the Russians were right on us."

"Your regimental commander is still in Durkov."

"I don't know anything about that, sir. The command post was at Rozhanovce. We tried to get there and ran into Russians everywhere."

"You withdrew from your regiment's sector without permission."

"The regiment hasn't a sector any more, sir."

"So long as your commanding officer is in Durkov, and so long as you still have a tommy-gun to shoot with, you've got a sector to hold."

"It would have been irresponsible to . . ."

"Shut your mouth," yelled Stiller. He turned to Giesinger. "Shoot that man for cowardice in face of the enemy."

Giesinger staggered back. His fleshy face turned ashen. He looked at the sergeant, who was staring at the general in disbelief. Before Giesinger could recover from the shock, Stiller's biting voice lashed his ears again: "Didn't you hear?"

Giesinger looked desperately at Kolmel, but the colonel was looking out over the valley. Behind the mountains artillery boomed, and the snow fell in huge flakes from a black sky. Giesinger stalked past the sergeant. For a moment he was tempted to take his pistol out of its sheath and aim it at the general. The scarlet stripes of Stiller's trousers gleamed against the snow. "What the hell are you doing?" he called, when Giesinger hesitated.

"The firing squad, sir," Giesinger answered, his voice shaking with rage.

"*You* are the firing squad." Stiller pointed across the road. "Over there."

"I can't do that."

"Are you refusing to obey an order?"

Looking into his ice-cold eyes, Giesinger again felt the wish to kill him; but his fear was far stronger. "According to martial law. . . ." he began laboriously.

Stiller cut him short. "You can complain later if you wish, but at present you will do what I ordered."

"It'll be your responsibility," rasped Giesinger, and went up to the former sergeant. He pulled his pistol from the holster. The other men dared not move; they stood in the snow like helpless animals, fear and dismay on their faces, staring at the general. Kolmel was looking away; his long face wore a rather sorrowful expression.

With a wooden movement Giesinger took the soldier by the arm. "Come on." He led the unresisting man across the road. They were about three steps from the steep slope, and further below the wood began. Run, thought Giesinger, why don't you run, you idiot? All of a sudden the general was standing next to him, asking icily: "Like to join him?"

Giesinger looked into Stiller's face and from there at the sergeant's head. The man's long hair stood out above his coat collar, and he had a pimple behind his right ear. When Giesinger placed the butt of the pistol next to it, his stomach protested, and sent foul-tasting bile up into his mouth. He was nearly sick, and his arm trembled so violently he had to grip the pistol with both hands. He saw the sergeant's profile before him as in a close-up. The man had shut his eyes tight, his unshaven chin hung slackly down, and saliva trickled out of the right corner of his mouth. Why doesn't he struggle, thought Giesinger, and pulled the trigger.

The short sharp report hit him like a piece of wood between the eyes. He staggered, and looked at the sergeant, who fell down as quickly as if he had dropped from a tree, his feet drumming a crazy dance in the snow. The sight was too much for Giesinger's stomach, and he vomited. Nearby he heard the general's shrill voice shouting an order, then two men came running across the road, aimed their guns at the soldier, and fired.

Giesinger reeled over to the car, put his handkerchief to his mouth, and stood with his face averted until he heard the general's voice behind him: "You bungled even that, eh? I'll send you to the front with a gunner's company, so you'll learn how to handle a pistol."

Giesinger did not move. He heard the general talking to Kolmel and someone giving the order to collect the paybooks. Then the general yelled at him: "Well, get in," and he stumbled into the car.

Stiller leaned out of the window, and looked at the men, who were standing in a disorderly bunch on the other side of the road. He beckoned to one of them. "Your name?"

"Corporal Hebauer, sir."

"Take the men to Durkov and report to Colonel Wieland."

"Yes, sir."

"Bury the dead man."

"Yes, sir."

Stiller dropped back against the cushions and gave a sign to the driver. The car moved off. "*Pour encourager les autres*," he remarked to Kolmel.

"Do you think it will do any good?"

"Those thirty men are going to talk, and within three days the whole division will know not only that it has a new general, but what I'm expecting from it."

They drove for awhile in silence, then Kolmel said: "We should soon be at the fork."

"The crossroads, you mean?"

"It isn't really a crossroads, sir. The main road goes straight on, but there's another one forking off to Durkov. Here, have a look."

Stiller studied the map. Suddenly he started up from his seat; somewhere to the right the crashing of shells could be heard. "Russian artillery," said Kolmel. The road now dipped steeply down into the valley, and climbed up the other side. The driver reduced speed, steering past several shell craters. Five minutes later they came to the fork: the road to the Durkov Pass led almost straight ahead to the top of the hill, while the other road cut a narrow glade into thick pine forest, curving off after a few yards to disappear from view. Stiller noticed some broken trees on the other side of it, and on looking closer discovered the assault guns as well, barely distinguishable in their camouflage. "Stop just by the edge of the wood," Stiller told the driver. As he was getting out of the car, two shells landed not far away. He ducked and ran over to the guns with Kolmel. The dark uniforms of several men emerged from between the trees. They looked at the two high officers, and one of them, with a captain's markings, saluted.

"What's happening here?" asked Stiller.

"We're covering the road, sir."

"So I see. Where are the Russians?"

The captain made a gesture with his hand. "They're banging about all over the place, and I'm stuck here with four guns and no infantry."

"Haven't you any contact with Colonel Kreisel?"

"Only by radio, sir. I've already told him. . . ."

"But you've got eight guns, haven't you?" Stiller interrupted.

"We lost three at Rozhanovce, sir."

"You were at Rozhanovce!" Kolmel exclaimed in surprise.

"Yes, sir. Our advance went pretty well up until then, but after that things blew up on all sides. Colonel Kreisel sent me here with four guns."

"Three from eight leaves five."

"The colonel took one with him to Durkov, sir."

Stiller talked to Kolmel for a moment, then turned to the captain again. "Did you see the ambulances?"

"They came through here, sir. They were fired at."

"Yes, we know. You must give us one of your guns so that we can get through. What orders were you. . . ." Stiller broke off, suddenly hearing a series of sharp reports behind him. Heavy-calibre shells roared over the trees so close that he automatically drew in his head.

"Our artillery, sir," the captain exclaimed. "It's there just behind us in case Russian tanks come."

"Have you seen any?" asked Stiller.

"Rozhanovce is swarming with them, sir."

"Then I'm surprised they're not here yet," remarked Kolmel, who had been listening intently.

The captain pointed to the road. "We've still got a twenty-five-pounder there."

"Any infantry with it?"

"I've no idea, sir."

"All right," said Kolmel. "Listen. There's a reserve unit coming up from Košice, you're to keep it with you. Hold on here and await further orders. Signal Colonel Kreisel that we're on our way. We're going up there now—unless you have any other questions, sir?" he turned to Stiller.

"No, I don't think so," said Stiller, and they returned to the car. He waited till the assault gun they were taking had lumbered past, then told the driver to follow behind it, and remarked cheerfully to Kolmel: "We'll squeeze them—between Kreisel with his regiment from Durkov and Hepp's lot coming from here."

"We must reinforce the reserve unit," Kolmel suggested.

"I'll see. With what I have in mind it'll hardly be necessary. After all we've got the three assault guns down there."

"What about this one ahead of us?"

"We need it for Kreisel. He can't do much with the single gun he has in Durkov. Besides, there's still this mess with Höpper in our rear."

"Yes," said Kolmel. "I'm almost more worried about him than Wieland."

Stiller peered over Giesinger's head at the assault gun. "So long as Höpper stays in Slancik, nothing much can happen. I don't think the Russians are all that interested in Slancik, there aren't any roads leading west from there. If they want to get to Košice, they can only do it through Durkov or Rozhanovce. We're holding Durkov firmly, and we'll get Rozhanovce back. Once the Russians are on the run, we'll push them back over the Durkov Pass as well. And even if we don't, there's always the chance of stabilizing the front along the line Slancik-Durkov-Rozhanovce. When people are ensconced in warm houses, they don't let themselves be driven out so easily—one of the things I learnt in Russia."

Kolmel watched the assault gun traveling up a steep incline. The deep furrows it plowed in the snow made it increasingly hard for the command car to follow: the right wheels kept getting stuck in one of the gun's tracks, while the left wheels skidded in the snow. "If it goes on like this," said Stiller, "we'll bog down here. I don't remember any more whether it was right or left of the road—the clearing where the ambulances were fired on."

"Right, according to that corporal—so we must keep our eyes skinned to the left."

"This is going to be interesting. A mile and a quarter before Durkov: we should soon be at the place."

"Until we see something of the clearing. . . ."

"Always assuming the Russians haven't gone beyond since then."

"I hate operating in the woods," said Kolmel, "you can never feel safe in it."

Giesinger hardly listened to them. Since the terrible incident he had been only half conscious of what was going on around him. He felt in an unspeakable way defiled, his thoughts veered continually between fear and hatred—and the sickening sense of shame, which grew stronger and stronger the further they went from the scene of his disgrace. When he thought of how he had vomited in front of the thirty men, he felt like putting his face in his hands and crying like a child. He

did not dare think of the coming hours. Irrespective of
how the counter-offensive might improve the situation,
he knew it was all up with his position at divisional
headquarters—unless General Marx should be rescued.
His recent humiliations were only a foretaste of what
he could expect if Schmitt came back empty-handed—
he'd be better off then as commander of a gunners
company. For a moment he found this idea less terrible than having to work under Stiller. But when he
had a closer look at it, imagined himself running toward the Russian positions at the head of his men and
being wiped out by a spray of machine-gun fire, he
shuddered. I'd rather go over to the Russians, he decided.

His head almost went through the windscreen, as the
car suddenly braked hard. He saw that the assault gun
had also stopped.

"The clearing," announced the driver.

The assault gun started again and moved on. Kolmel bent toward the driver. "Wait till they're past the
clearing, then make a dash for it."

The driver let in the clutch. The wheels skidded in
the snow for a second, then they gripped and the car
shot toward the clearing. They were past almost before they realized it. Ahead of them the gun was jolting
laboriously up a slope. Stiller sat up straight again. "In
ten minutes we'll be there."

"If we don't have any trouble from the Russians,"
muttered Kolmel, and neither spoke again till they
reached Durkov.

Here the road led into another, the main road between Slancik and Rozhanovce—as Kolmel knew without looking at the map. The assault gun clumsily
turned right, disappearing behind the first house. The
village was in a narrow valley and had about seventy
houses. Men were standing around in the street in
small groups; they stared at the passing officers. The

gun now pulled up on the right of the road, and the car stopped behind it. The men got out and were met by Lieutenant Colonel Kreisel who took them into a room where Colonel Wieland was standing with several other officers. "Your new general," said Kolmel, turning to the astonished colonel. "Sad news for you. General Marx has been captured by partisans." He informed the speechless officers how it had happened.

When Kolmel had finished his account, Wieland stared at the floor for some time. Finally he looked up. "It never rains but it pours. My regiment is in pieces, only about a hundred men left. Oh yes, and there's something here for you, Kolmel."

"For me?"

"Yes, from corps. We got the radio signal through division a quarter of an hour ago." He gave Kolmel the message.

"From the corps commander," said Kolmel. "I'm to go straight back to Dobšina."

"That's all we need," Stiller growled.

Kolmel asked for a report on the present position.

"It went all right as far as Rozhanovce," Kreisel told him. "Then the Russians came at us from all directions."

"From the west too?" asked Stiller.

"Yes, sir—from the west too. Either they were detached groups we'd passed without noticing it, or they simply surrounded us. In the operation I lost three of my assault guns, I sent four off to break through to the west. . . ."

"Yes, we know that. What we don't know is why you decided to come to Durkov. You could have gone back to the road fork with your guns."

"Then the Russians would now be holding Durkov as well, and if we want to recover Rozhanovce, we must have Durkov. There'd really be no point in trying to block the pass at Rozhanovce if the Russians could get to Košice from here without any trouble. Besides, we're sitting on their flank here. I'd rather attack from the south than up a steep mountain from the west."

"Where are your battalions?" asked Kolmel.

"Two in the wood, on both sides of the Durkov-Rozhanovce road; the third here. The pioneer battalion is covering the south."

"Good."

"Leave two companies here," Stiller told Kreisel. "With the rest you will attack Rozhanovce."

"Two companies!" protested Kreisel. "My regiment is too weak as it is. After all, sir, you've got the pioneer battalion here."

"Kindly leave that to me," Stiller answered coldly, disconcerted by the insolent tone of the young lieutenant colonel wearing the Knight's Cross. "I need the pioneer battalion for Höpper," he added, raising his voice. "As for the two companies you're leaving here, they're to protect Durkov from the east. We don't know where else there might be Russians too. It wouldn't surprise me if they suddenly turned up outside our front door. As long as the gap up forward is open, they can march through the woods unimpeded."

"I doubt that," put in Wieland. "What would they want in Durkov when they've got Rozhanovce? To attack that we need every man."

Stiller stared at him. Wieland was a tall, broad-shouldered man with long arms, and a bull-neck indicating stubbornness. When he spoke, his ruddy face with the thin reddish eyelashes worked violently, giving it a nervous look. Stiller was about to retort sharply and put the man in his place, when Kolmel interjected: "Perhaps for the corps commander's benefit, I might ask a few questions. How was the break-through possible at all?"

"Same as usual," answered Wieland bluntly. "Two

battalions weren't strong enough to hold the positions."

"Then I don't understand why General Marx took a battalion away from you."

"I understand as little as you. Perhaps Herr Gie-singer knows."

The eyes of all the officers turned abruptly on Gie-singer, who had been listening indifferently in the background. When Kolmel looked hard at him, he raised his head and commented: "Colonel Wieland had the smallest sector, exactly a third of what the other regiments had."

"But they weren't right on the road," Wieland burst out. "I told you straight away. . . ."

"Let's leave that for a moment," Kolmel broke in. "Apart from the direct hit on your twenty-five pounder, you still had the two lighter guns on the road. Couldn't they hold up the tanks?"

"There was only one left by then, the other got two tanks before being mown down. Also, Russian infantry were swarming about everywhere. If I hadn't ordered the second gun back to Rozhanovce, it'd be gone too. My men. . . ."

"Your men ran away," Kolmel finished the sentence. "They didn't even wait till the tanks had come. We met thirty of them on the way up, and goodness knows how many of them are still roaming round the wood."

"From my regiment?"

"Yes, from your regiment, led by a sergeant, cheer-fully making for Košice. You needn't explain to me why the Russians broke through in your sector. In your place I'd have been up to the forward positions my-self, instead of crawling off to Durkov with my com-mand post."

Wieland looked as if he were going to have an apo-plectic fit. "I didn't move my command post till the Russians were right there."

"If you'd seen to it that your men stayed in their trenches, the Russians might never have *been* there. Your battalion commanders. . . ."

"I've only one left."

"The others are already on their way to Košice, I suppose. It wouldn't surprise me."

"What!" Wieland staggered backward. "You say that to me of all people. Who held the whole damn show together at Turka and at Lvov, where you got my regiment cut to pieces in your counter-attack?"

"Control yourself," said Stiller sharply.

"I protest against Colonel Kolmel's insinuations, sir. If I'm expected as regimental commander to hold a sector, I should be given a regiment to do it with. For six months I've just had a battalion under me, and I can't occupy a regiment's sector with one battalion. If corps can't see that, they should choose another whipping-boy. . . ."

"For the last time I order you to control yourself," cried Stiller. "Where the hell do you think you are?" They stared at each other for several seconds with rage in their eyes, then Stiller turned to Kolmel. "Things are going to be different here, I assure you. In the future I shall treat as a deserter any regimental commander who moves his command post without my permission. As for your sergeant," he told Wieland, "you can collect his paybook from my car and the paybooks of the thirty others he had with him. I had him shot for cowardice. It'll be just the same in the future for anyone I catch trying to run away."

Wieland looked at him, shocked, but Stiller was already addressing Kreisel. "That goes for your men too. With your regiment and the pioneer battalion how could you let yourself be pushed out of Rozhanovce again?"

"First of all," said Kreisel rebelliously, "where my regiment is concerned I must associate myself with

Colonel Wieland's attitude. Secondly, as for the pioneer battalion, I didn't see it until I got to Durkov."

"What! Didn't it attack with you?"

"With me, sir? You must be joking. There was no pioneer battalion there when we attacked. If I'd had it, we'd be holding Rozhanovce now. My regiment on its own was far too weak."

Kolmel turned on Giesinger, whose face was ashen. "You reported to corps that you'd sent off the assault regiment and the pioneer battalion together."

"I told you, sir. . . ." began Giesinger.

"Is that right or not?" Stiller cut in.

"In a certain sense."

"Yes or no?"

"Yes, sir."

"Together?"

"Yes, sir, that is . . ."

"What?"

"We don't need to ask any more," Kolmel interjected. He had taken a notebook out of his pocket and was skimming through the pages. "He didn't send off the pioneer battalion till he'd been reminded by me that he had such a thing."

"Hm—false report," said Stiller.

The officers stared at Giesinger in silence. Wieland gave a bitter laugh. "We regimental commanders get raked over the coals when the whole bungle has started in division. It was like that with the anti-tank gun, and. . . ."

"You have your anti-tank gun," Kolmel told him. "I want to see the commander of the pioneer battalion."

"He's at his command post," said Kreisel.

"Then put me on to him." He waited impatiently for Kreisel to hand him the telephone. While he was phoning, all the officers' eyes were on him. "Just as I thought," he told Stiller after hanging up. "The pioneer battalion didn't leave till the assault regiment had

175

been on its way for some time. When they reached the fork, instead of making for Rozhanovce they came on to Durkov. I suppose it was much the same with the reconnaissance unit."

"I don't know anything about that," said Wieland.

"Nor do I," said Kreisel.

"Then we can write them off. I imagine Major Fuchs tried to take a short cut to Slancik and so ran straight into the Russians."

Again the eyes of the officers fastened on Giesinger. He looked into Stiller's cold eyes, and said: "Major Fuchs was quite well aware I wasn't sending him to any picnic at Slancik. So it's not the case that he ran into the Russians all unsuspecting, if he did run into them, and even that's not certain yet. He and the reconnaissance unit may equally well have lost their way in the wood."

For a moment it looked as if Kolmel wanted to say something, but then he turned abruptly and shook hands with the other officers, pointedly ignoring Giesinger. The general walked with him out into the street. Kolmel's driver started the engine. It was snowing hard, the mountains on the other side were now scarcely visible.

"The pass is up there," remarked Kolmel.

"I'll get it back."

"I hope you will, sir. The pass is as important for corps as for you. The Košice front hangs or falls by it."

"What are you thinking of?" Maria asked. Her clothes were strewn untidily over the floor. The stove in the room was cherry red, and outside the window snow was falling.

Kolodzi started out of his thoughts. He had been thinking about Maria, thinking she had changed. He was remembering how she always used to get dressed at once, almost in a hurry, and had avoided his eyes. Today it was different. She was sitting at his side, leaning slightly forward, and he could see the curving line of her slender back.

"You'll be surprised to hear," he answered, "that I wasn't thinking of anything."

"I know you too well to believe that. Perhaps you're having regrets again."

"Perhaps, but that makes no difference. Only it's about time we made up our minds what we're going to do."

"That's simple enough—stay here."

"I might just as well give myself up to the Russians. And there are too many people in Olmütz who knew me. But I've thought of something. We might go to Pawlowitsch, at Baska. Nobody knows me there. What do you think of that?"

Maria was silent. Pawlowitsch was an old friend of

Kolodzi's. They had been working for the same transport firm, and when Kolodzi was fired Pawlowitsch had been so angry he too went off to another firm. Privately he was pro-German, but he was one of the people you could expect to change their minds overnight. That, however, was something you couldn't tell Kolodzi, so Maria tried a different tack: "It might well be too much for him if all three of us descended on him at once."

"Well, we'll just have to make ourselves very small. Anyhow at the moment I don't see any alternative. As soon as the war's over, we'll go to Wertheim or somewhere else, out of Czechoslovakia anyhow. You'll soon feel at home in Germany."

He rose, went over to the window, and looked out through the curtain on to the street. He heard Maria's voice behind him. "My God, but you've grown thin. Don't you soldiers get anything to eat?"

It upset him to have her watching him as he stood naked by the window, and he quickly went back to her. "Only paymasters and maggots got fat in Russia. Don't you like me any more?"

"Of course I do. It just struck me, that's all."

"You could do with some more fat yourself. How do you do it—growing more beautiful all the time?"

She slapped him lightly on the mouth. "Stefan!"

"Well, it's true, isn't it?"

Her face flushed and she struggled against his hands. He felt her long legs against his knees, and her hips pressing against him, so that there was nothing left that parted them.

"Stay this way."

"I'd like to stay this way forever," she said.

"Good. If that's the case, I doubt whether there could be anything more important."

"Than this, you mean?"

178

"Yes, stay like it, stay just this way. Can you feel what I mean?"

She nodded. "And you must stay like it too, Stefan. You must always stay like it, till the war's over. I want to be without fear at last. I want to stop having to remember about the war. Do you understand?"

"Yes, I do—I do."

"What do I care about the war? You men think of nothing but the war. What do you get out of the war? Nothing, if it's lost—and nothing if it's won."

"If we'd won it, we shouldn't have to be leaving Olmütz."

"You meant to leave Olmütz anyhow. Or was that mere talk?"

"I don't go in for mere talk along those lines."

"All the more reason why you shouldn't care a damn how the war ends."

"One can't think only of oneself."

"You don't have to—think of me, think of us. Other people think of themselves first. I've got blood in my veins: at twenty-five a woman wants her man to belong to *her*, not to the war."

"For this?"

She did not answer, but he could feel her impatience. And he was impatient too. He put his mouth to hers, and his legs lay along her legs. He closed his eyes, and felt he had been right to stay with her, because there had to come a point where all uncertainty ended. And she was so close to him now that he was aware of nothing but the smooth curve of her hips like a high dam against which all his emotions were piling: good emotions and bad, tender and brutal, lofty and base; his whole being surged up against a dam which grew weaker and weaker until it gave, and all his blood drained from him, and his body floated like an empty shell on the raging waters which lifted him and flung

179

him down and lifted him again—until he realized that the whole flood of movement was now only in his brain.

From somewhere a long way away Maria's hands came and clutched his arms. He looked into her agitated face, looked at her twisted mouth and into her feverish eyes. Then she said something, and Kolodzi stared at her.

Of course, he thought, why on earth did I stop? He hadn't realized what was happening, because it had never happened to him before; and while he was still feeling surprised about it, a noise which his ears had registered faintly for some time suddenly burst into his consciousness. Before Maria could stop him, he rushed to the window. There were people standing in the road, men and women, also a few soldiers, and they were all staring in the same direction. The barrage had started.

Heavily, Kolodzi turned around. Maria stood in front of him with an expression on her face he had never seen before. He looked past her at his uniform and then at Schmitt's binoculars.

I must take them back, he thought. Without a word he got dressed. Maria did not move. Not until he hung the binoculars around his neck did she ask: "Where are you going?"

He did not answer. The coffee things were still on the table. The stove glowed with heat, the rumbling outside the window grew louder and louder.

"I'll never forgive you this," said Maria.

"What?"

"This. No woman would put up with it. It's worse than having to *wait* a year or two."

"That's what you say now. Don't you understand that it happened of its own accord?"

"If you loved me, it wouldn't have happened."

"It can happen to any man. It hasn't anything to do with love. I tell you—you don't understand. When you've heard that noise for four years it's just as bad as if someone were firing a gun in this very room. I could feel it long before I actually heard it."

"You heard it at once. You wouldn't have heard it if. . . ."

"If what?"

"You know what I mean. You once told me that at a moment like that you wouldn't stop even if the house were crashing about your ears."

"This is an automatic thing. I can't help it. I heard the firing before."

"Other men wouldn't have heard it."

"You talk as if you'd slept with plenty of them."

She rushed up to him, her eyes blazing. "You know very well that I haven't slept with other men, but I might now."

"Nice of you to tell me!" he shouted.

She wept with rage.

"Yes, I've told you now, and I'll be glad when you're really gone. Go ahead—what are you waiting for? Go to your Vöhringer and your Herbig."

Kolodzi gripped her by the shoulders. "What on earth has got into you? There are millions of women who. . . ."

"I don't care. If they're stupid enough to let their men be shot down, they don't deserve any better. I kept quiet because you told me it was important for both of us the Germans should win the war. But do you find them winning it?"

"You'll see that yet," Kolodzi said desperately. He let go of her and fetched his gun from the kitchen. When he returned to the room, Maria was lying on the bed, sobbing. He said: "It was all wrong the way I tried to tackle it. I promised to go back and I must keep my promise. But I'll be with you again in a few days."

She turned her tear-stained face toward him. "If you're alive then."

"That's what you said yesterday, and I'm still alive today. Be sensible now, you can hear for yourself that there's all hell let loose out there. I can't leave the others stranded at Oviz in this mess. You'll have to go straight off to Pawlowitsch today. And he's sure to find some way of getting Mother to Baska."

"I don't want to go to Baska."

"Why not?"

"I'm not one of your soldiers you can order about. Yesterday you told me we were going to Olmütz, today you come back and tell me it's not Olmütz but Wertheim we have to go to, and now it's not Wertheim either, but Baska. I'm staying here."

"Oh, hell!" Kolodzi exclaimed. "Are you going to be reasonable now and listen to me, or not?"

She was staring down at the floor. "Maria," he said, clasping her hand between his own hands. "I've got just five minutes more, and if we can't agree by then, I'm staying with my company until the war's over. And you can be sure that in that case we shan't see each other again. Now are you going to listen to me?"

"I've always listened to you."

"Well. . . . I said Olmütz yesterday because at that time I didn't know anything about Wertheim, and when Vöhringer suggested it, I ran away from my company to tell you to go to Wertheim, not Olmütz. And now I've dropped Wertheim because you won't be able to get through now. You won't get through, can't you understand that? Just listen to the barrage, I know about that. If it's as bad as this, we can't stop the Russians. They may be here in a few hours. Even now if you went to the station you wouldn't get a train. You must go to Baska—that's not ordering you about, it's speaking in your interest and mine."

"If you really have our interests so much at heart, then why don't you stay here?"

"I've explained that. There are two men waiting for me at Oviz, and I've got to return these binoculars to the captain."

"Is that all?"

"It's enough—quite enough for me. Perhaps you'll understand some time. Would you rather I had to go about with a guilty conscience for the rest of my life?"

"You've no reason to have that."

"Not if I return to Oviz now. I don't want to run into anyone in Germany later on whom I can't look in the eyes."

"Then we'll just have to stay here. Czechoslovakia is a big place."

"It won't be when the Russians come."

"You've let the Germans stuff your head with a lot of nonsense. What do you care about politics?"

"This has nothing to do with politics," Kolodzi said impatiently. "Look at Vöhringer. You could offer him a castle over here, and he'd still stay in Wertheim. And it's just the same with the others: they all know where they belong."

"They're Nazis," Maria objected in hostile tones.

"That isn't true. I could name quite a number of men in my company who I know are against the Party. The Nazis are not Germany."

"Nor are the Czechs Slovakia."

She had him in a corner. He glanced at her sideways, at her face and at her breasts; he felt he had never looked at the breasts properly before. Somehow they seemed fuller now, fuller and more beautiful, with a sweet heaviness which reminded him of ripe grapes. And as he looked at them, he knew he could never be without Maria again. One day he would have to leave Herbig and Vöhringer, but Maria. . . . He forced himself to speak calmly: "I'll explain to you some other time."

"There's nothing for you to explain," she said coldly. "I know what you're going to explain to me all over again, and I don't want to listen to it."

Kolodzi suddenly felt he had a complete stranger sitting by him. He tried to put his arms around her but she pushed him away. "Stop that," she told him harshly. "It's always when you want to. For once it so happens I don't."

"All right," said Kolodzi. He looked at the door. It was only five steps away yet he hesitated because he was frightened by the finality of those steps. He sat there helplessly, not knowing what to do next. To act on impulse was something entirely foreign to his nature. He took time over his decisions, waiting for them to ripen, till they dropped into his consciousness almost independently of him; after which nothing could stop him from carrying them out. And his decision to stay with Maria had not yet ripened, he could feel that now. The line he wanted to draw should be firm and definite, not blurred so that one could quibble about it afterward. Probabilities weren't good enough for him. Only four years ago it had looked as if the Germans were winning the war, today it seemed probable they were losing it, and who could say how things would look tomorrow. But if he went to the door now, that would be final, and he was not going to risk it.

He sat stiffly upright and said: "Why won't you understand that hearing the barrage gave me a shock? I'd have heard it even if my ears had been plugged. Every morning for two years I've woken up with my heart thumping, waiting for the sound. You sit here acting as if it were the only other thing which had happened and nothing else. You don't seem to mind at all that the Russians may be here in a few hours and everything blasted to bits exactly as our forward positions are being blasted to bits now."

She started crying again and rose to pick up her

clothes. Kolodzi jumped up and pressed her to him. "Maria," he began, but couldn't think of anything more to say to her. She pushed him back, trying to break away. Her face was contorted and wet with tears.

"Maria!" he repeated in a louder voice. "Do be sensible, Maria."

"But I've always been sensible," she answered. "That's just why you've got to stay now. You simply can't leave now when it's Christmas tomorrow. If it's so necessary, I'll go to Germany with you—I'd go to Russia with you if you wanted that. It's all the same to me where we're going. Only you mustn't leave me alone. I can't bear to be alone any more. If you're dead, I shall have nothing left, nothing," she said despairingly. "I shall have nothing left."

Her outburst staggered him. He put both his hands on her shoulders. "I'll come to Baska."

"Don't go away," she said. "I'm frightened, you can't leave me alone."

"Nothing will happen to you in Baska."

"But I'll be afraid in Baska too, it's awful."

"What is?"

"Just listen," she answered, staring at him with wide eyes. Kolodzi looked toward the window. The thunder from the front was becoming fiercer. "It always sounds worse in the distance," he told her, knowing it was not true. "At Baska nothing can happen to you, the Russians have nothing against you Czechs."

"They don't bother about that. They didn't bother either whether it was Germans or Czechs when they dropped their bombs on the station the night before last. What would I do in Baska without you? I'd die of fear."

He felt himself beginning to waver again, and hastily bent down to pick up her clothes. "Get dressed now. Pack anything else you need in your small case.

185

Don't forget to call on Mother. She'll just have to manage without you for the two or three days till Pawlowitsch comes to fetch her. Inform the neighbors so that they'll look in from time to time."

"So you're going after all," she said softly.

"I must." He handed her her clothes. "Later you'll understand everything."

"No," she said.

"I'm quite sure."

She let her clothes drop again. Kolodzi went to the door, and there turned around to say: "Good-by, Maria. In a few days you'll be glad I didn't listen to you."

She made no reply. Her face had become small and ravaged, everything about her looked helpless, miserable.

He could bear it no longer and ran out of the house.

10

When he found that Vöhringer had disappeared, Herbig's first reaction was fury: it was crazy to roam around the place on his own like this. Probably he was pretending to be insulted again—perhaps he was waiting for Herbig to run after him. If so, he was in for a disappointment, Herbig thought.

He looked out the window, annoyed at the mounting uneasiness he had begun to feel. Because he felt an urge to do something, he decided at least to go and see which way Vöhringer had gone.

He slipped into his camouflage coat, took his gun and some magazines and left the house. He picked up Vöhringer's trail leading to the edge of the wood, and then found it was joined by two others coming from the big house on the opposite side of the street. Herbig felt his heart thumping. Without stopping to think, he sprinted through the wood to the place where Vöhringer's trail, which he recognized by the hob-nailed boots, deviated to the left before returning and leading in the opposite direction with the other two trails. He raced after them.

When the shot went off, he was so close to the clearing that he saw Vöhringer fall. There was a building at the other end of the clearing which he remembered was a sanatorium; he noticed some faces at one of its windows, and fired at them without aiming. The faces disappeared immediately. In a flash Herbig was with Vöhringer, who was writhing in the snow and screaming. Picking up his tommy-gun, which was lying near him, Herbig dragged him to the end of the wood, and there fired several more shots at the window. Then he hoisted Vöhringer on to his back and panted off through the wood, feeling his load grow heavier and heavier with every step he took. After staggering about fifty yards down the steep slope, he could go no further. He put Vöhringer down on the ground and pulled him along by the legs, past some thick scrub, to a huge mass of rock which looked like a snowed-up hut. Here Herbig flopped in the snow, gasping for breath.

He heard a noise above him, and without waiting till he could see anything, rattled off a new magazine into the scrub. As nothing moved, he again took hold of Vöhringer's legs and dragged him the last two hundred yards to the edge of the wood. There he again took him on to his back, carried him around the house to the entrance, kicked the door open and tumbled into their room. After rolling Vöhringer's inanimate body off his back and on to the floor, he sat panting for a moment, struggling to get his wind back. When he had recovered a bit, he rose and pushed the heavy table up against the door. Now he could attend to Vöhringer.

At one glance Herbig saw there was little to be done for him: his face was the color of straw. Having unbuttoned the corporal's coat and trousers, Herbig looked for the wound. It was an unusually large hole for a bullet, with a bit of intestine sticking out of it.

Herbig bit his lip. It couldn't have caught the poor bastard worse. He took his field dressing out of his pocket and pressed it on to the wound, trying to push the bit of intestine back into the hole. It did not work. He felt as if he had a jelly-fish under his hands. Eventually he gave it up and raised Vöhringer's body a bit so that he could get the bandage around. But since he could not take his one hand off the dressing, he did not succeed. The effort had exhausted him. For a while he squatted there looking at the distended stomach with a mixture of hatred and disgust. Then he tried a different method, lying between Vöhringer's legs and pressing his chin down on the dressing. Now he had two hands to draw the bandage through behind the back, and was able to make a knot. After making sure the bandage was firm, he stood up, reeling. He went to the window and lit a cigarette with trembling fingers.

The house on the opposite side seemed deserted. The two men's tracks were still visible. Herbig crossed to the door and pushed the table away. He hesitated a second before pulling it open; but there was no one in the passage. He went quickly to the front door, turned the key, and ran into the kitchen. The woman was no longer there. A roast chicken lay on the table, the fire in the stove had almost burned out. On returning, Herbig found that Vöhringer had recovered consciousness and was working at the bandage.

"Keep your paws still," said Herbig.

Vöhringer turned his face towards Herbig. "The swine have got me."

"It's your own fault," said Herbig.

"Where did it hit me?"

"Bad enough place," said Herbig. He stuck a cigarette between Vöhringer's lips and watched him inhaling the smoke.

"Give me something to drink," said Vöhringer between two puffs.

"All right." Herbig went to the table, where Vöhringer's flask lay. Taking the cigarette out of Vöhringer's mouth, he let him drink, putting the flask down by him afterward and asking: "Can you feel anything?"

"Can I! I need a doctor. You have to get one."

"If I leave you on your own, the partisans will kill you."

"Just let 'em come. That's what I've been waiting for all along. I need a doctor, otherwise I'll croak here."

"Nobody croaks as quickly as that. You must hold out till this evening. As soon as Kolodzi comes, we'll take you back."

"You want to see me croak," said Vöhringer. "You want that, don't you! Go on, say it, you filthy swine, you're glad they've got me."

"Shut your trap."

"Not while I can still talk. While I can still talk, I'll tell you what I think of you, you cowardly swine, you mean. . . ." He broke off and tried to crawl on his stomach toward Herbig, who stared at him angrily, and said in a hoarse voice: "You're crazy. Why do you think I dragged you all the way back here?"

"That's true." Vöhringer stopped his movements in surprise. "By God, I hadn't thought of that. . . . Thanks."

Herbig watched him feeling for the flask, unscrewing the cork and drinking, spilling half of it over his face. His face was now the color of sulphur, and Herbig wished he had died at once. "Nonsense," he answered gruffly.

After mumbling a few words which Herbig couldn't catch, Vöhringer said: "If you had the pain I've got. . . ."

"You wouldn't have it if you'd stayed here."

"Those bastards, shooting a man in the guts. Oh, those bastards," groaned Vöhringer, beating his fists against the floor.

Herbig had never before been affected by watching someone die, but this time it churned his insides. Another thing was that his own position was getting more and more dangerous. If he only knew whether the two men up there had stayed in the sanatorium or whether they'd come down and were now waiting for him to walk out of the house! The more time I lose, he thought, the smaller my chances will be. There was nothing to be done for Vöhringer, and as far as Kolodzi . . . He looked at Vöhringer, who was making peculiar movements with his head; and as he looked at him, Herbig forgot that he had thought of leaving him to the partisans. He walked over to him, and said, "I'll get you into a bed."

"In the guts of all places," whimpered Vöhringer, his eyes closed.

"Not as bad as in the head. Stop your damned whining, you're not a woman, are you?" said Herbig, wondering where to put him. He went to have a look at the bedroom. If I put Vöhringer in here, Herbig thought, the partisans may shoot him in bed. They might force their way into the house from any side. He regarded the beds uncertainly, and in the end collected a few cushions, dragging them back into the other room. There he stopped in the doorway, looking silently at Vöhringer.

Vöhringer had unbuttoned his trousers, pushed the dressing to one side, and was staring incredulously at his bulging intestines. He looked up at Herbig, his mouth agape, and from there back to the wound. Herbig had never in his life seen such terror in a face; it was dreadful. Dropping the cushions, he dashed over, wildly shouting: "Hands off."

Vöhringer put his head on the ground and began to cry, silently, not moving his mouth. His face now seemed like a squeezed lemon, wrinkled and weary and unutterably sad. Herbig felt it was more than he could bear.

He carried the cushions over by the stove, and laid them on the ground. Returning to Vöhringer, he said: "For Christ's sake stop, I just can't stand watching you.

191

Put your arms around my neck." When he lifted him, he could feel the tear-stained face against his own, which upset him so much he almost dropped the heavy body. "This is terrible," he gasped, dragging Vöhringer to the cushions. Then he bent over him. "Now stop fussing—do you hear?"

Vöhringer did not answer, and as he looked at him, the thought struck Herbig for the first time that it was hideous to have to die this way. He sat down near him on the bench by the stove, and looked out the window. Suddenly he noticed a civilian, who was running over to the house opposite with a sub-machine gun. It surprised him so much that he waited three seconds before leaping to the window. The place where the man had disappeared lay on the right side of the house, of which Herbig couldn't see anything.

The fellow must have a damned guilty conscience, he thought, annoyed that he had not watched more carefully. He picked his tommy-gun off the table, pushed a chair up to the window seat, with its back facing the window, and straddled his legs over it. In the next few minutes he did not take his eyes off the house. Once he thought he could see movements behind one of the windows. He was itching to fire a few shots, but it would only have been waste of ammunition.

Where had the man gone? So far as Herbig remembered, the house hadn't a door on the right. It was annoying he could only see the front of it, which was about ten yards wide with its two windows and the door in between them. On the other hand the house was favorably placed for him, because it was separated from the other houses by an open space. Nor could anyone come up unseen from behind, where the ground climbed steeply to the wood.

"Are they coming?" asked Vöhringer. His voice sounded amazingly clear. He's tough as a cat, thought

Herbig, and answered: "They're in the house across the street. One of them's just run inside it."

"Why didn't you shoot him?"

"I didn't see him till too late."

"I bet they're going to try and smoke us out."

"Easier said than done."

Vöhringer groaned. "Oh, damned—if only I could do something. I can't move my legs any more, it's as if they'd been chopped off. This will be a shock for Kolodzi."

"He should have stayed here."

"Then it might have caught *him*. He's just as much of a fool as you and I are. We're bloody fools, the whole lot of us. We croak here so that the boys in Berlin can keep their fat asses warm."

"No warmer than the boys in Moscow and London. But we'll get them yet."

"Just like they've got me. Wait till *you* have something like this in your belly. Man, how it hurts!" He began to moan again and writhed about on the cushions.

"You have to try to lie still," said Herbig.

"I'll be doing that long enough—till the worms have eaten me. And all because of this damned army, this God damned army, this God damned. . . ." The pain made him scream.

Herbig looked out of the window, gritting his teeth. Another man was going over to the house. This time Herbig reacted quicker. Without even stopping to make a hole in the window he fired at random. The man jumped up as if he had been standing on a springboard, and shot toward the house like the cast of a harpoon. There he vanished on one side just as the other man had done.

Herbig swore. He had aimed badly, disconcerted by the cross-bars of the window. In a sudden fit of temper he fired the rest of the magazine at the house's right

193

window. Then he took a few more magazines from his pack and took up position by the window again. Suddenly the window panes shattered, and in came a rain of machine-gun bullets like a swarm of hornets. Herbig waited till they stopped, then edged nearer to the window so that he could have a better view of the street without risk of a sudden bullet catching his face. Cold air came through the shattered window. Then he heard Vöhringer's voice from the corner near the stove. "I've no time now," Herbig said impatiently. "What d'you want?"

"Can you see them?" asked Vöhringer.

"Of course not. If I could, they'd be dead now."

"Perhaps I can help you. Get me on the table and push it up to the window."

"So they could make mincemeat out of you," Herbig growled. He was much impressed by Vöhringer's suggestion, though it would have been foolish to take it seriously. "You better nurse your belly."

"Oh, that's gone anyhow, I needn't worry about that any more. But I'd like to knock off one of those swine before I go." His teeth chattered as he spoke, but his head had become quite clear. He could feel the warmth of the stove, the soft cushions which gave rest to his tortured body, with a grateful sense of security.

Suddenly the bark of sub-machine guns broke into his consciousness. He heard Herbig's voice yell out something; as if through a soft red fog he saw Herbig dashing to the door, then back to the window, from where he started firing like a madman. Then two men came stumbling into the room, staggered to the wall with faces white as chalk, and stopped there to look at Herbig, who was still firing out of the window.

Vöhringer closed his eyes in bewilderment, unsure whether what was happening was reality or some terrifying nightmare conjured up by his fever. He only

194

looked at the two men again when he heard Herbig's voice asking them where they had left their guns.

"We've only got pistols," one of them answered, a redhead with a weak sagging chin that was covered with pimples. The other one was very fat; in his greatcoat he looked like a barrel. The expression on his bloated face was one of mortal fright.

"Well, I like that," said Herbig. "You pull up here in your limousine as if you were attending a wedding. What's the idea?"

"It was the inspector's fault," said the Redhead dejectedly.

"What inspector?"

"We're from the Gestapo."

Herbig gave a whistle. "Well, fancy that now. What's secret about *you*?"

"The uniform," said the Fat One with a rueful grin.

Vöhringer raised his head a bit and stared at him. Then he dropped his head again and groaned.

The two Gestapo men looked at him in amazement. "What's wrong with him?" asked the Fat One.

Herbig went over. "Anything the matter?"

"Throw the beggars out," groaned Vöhringer.

The Redhead looked at Herbig in confusion. "What's he got against us?"

"He's got something against everyone," Herbig enlightened them. He bent down for Vöhringer's tommygun, which was lying near the door. "Can either of you handle this?"

The two men eyed each other in embarrassment. "Not that one," said the Fat One. "I can manage a submachine gun all right, but . . ."

"This is the same. If you can work one, you can work the other." He showed them how to put the magazine in and set the gun at continuous fire. "A child could handle one," he said. "I wish we had a dozen more here. What interests me most now is why you've come to Oviz."

"Wish we'd never seen the place," grunted the Fat One, and told Herbig how they had driven straight to Szomolnok, where they found only Lieutenant Menges. In Oviz they stopped at the first house, and inquired about the NKVD man.

"You mean to say there's an NKVD man here and you simply drove up in your car?" Herbig asked.

The Fat One made a grimace. "What could we do about it? It's just like the inspector. In Dobšina he. . . ."

"Doesn't interest me," Herbig cut in rudely. From this place near the window he could see the shot-up car, with the dead partisan lying on his stomach a few yards away, already covered by snow. "Looks as if the NKVD chap must have known him," he remarked.

The Fat One cautiously took up position near Herbig and glanced out at the corpse. "Of course—it was he that led us here. We caught him with some others in Košice blowing up the district headquarters. He obviously knew he'd get this sort of reception, otherwise he wouldn't have denied knowing which house the man lived in. If you hadn't called to us, we'd have run exactly the wrong way."

"You should have dropped behind the car, instead of hopping around in the street like frightened chickens. By the way, do you know why we are here?"

"The inspector heard about it from your adjutant. But back at division they think you're real deserters."

"Good God," said Herbig, stunned. "Why hasn't anyone told them?"

"I've no idea. I wasn't present when the inspector talked to your adjutant, we had to stay in the car to watch the prisoner. He only told us afterward that you weren't deserters at all. Weren't there three of you?"

"There still *are* three of us, I hope," Herbig said. "But one of us had better go."

"Where to," asked the Fat One, looking startled.

"To Szomolnok. We need a truck for the casualty."

"Out of the question. You can't set foot outside the door. He can die here as well as in a hospital. Out of the question," the Fat One repeated.

"It'd be plain suicide," the other hastily agreed.

"Then I'll go myself."

"You're staying here." They all looked at Vöhringer. "You're staying here," Vöhringer repeated. With his bloodless lips, yellow skin and shriveled face, he already looked like a dead man.

Herbig went over to him. "Aren't these two enough for you?"

"They can go hang themselves. If a partisan sticks out his tongue at them, they'll faint on the spot. The hole in my belly is enough for me, I don't want my throat cut as well."

"But just now you said I should get a doctor."

"I've changed my mind. We'll wait till Kolodzi comes."

"Hope we don't wait till we're blue in the face."

"Not with that conscientious bastard," said Vöhringer, pressing his hands to his stomach and screwing up his face. "He's just as dense as you."

Herbig turned to the Gestapo men, who had followed this brief conversation with blank expressions. "All right, you can stay here. But you know that the spot we're in will get tighter and tighter. The partisans are sure to be getting reinforcements." Herbig went into the bedroom with them and pointed through the window to the edge of the wood. "They may try to get in this way. The kitchen's next door, but it only has a small window, they won't come through that." After giving them some more instructions, he returned to the front room.

"Do you want a cigarette?" Herbig asked. Vöhringer moved his head feebly. "It'll soon be over," he said.

"No, it's just starting."

"Not for me. My pains have stopped, and when you stop feeling pain with a thing like this, it's the beginning of the end. I'm still thirsty, though."

Herbig brought him some water. "A bucket of brandy would be better for you now. Don't you really want a cigarette?"

"Yes."

Herbig pushed it between Vöhringer's lips, and noticed his own hands were shaking. He went back to the window. "If only I knew what those boys were up to," he said. "And I wonder where the civilians are. The woman isn't in the kitchen any more. Did you notice how she stinks?"

"Like the Russians," said Vöhringer, grinning with his yellow face. It was painful for Herbig to see but he suppressed this feeling and said, "Yes, just like the Russians."

"What we've been through," said Vöhringer, the cigarette dangling from the corner of his mouth.

"Plenty," Herbig agreed.

He looked out of the window again. The dead partisan on the street was gradually being covered by the snow. He had his face turned the other way so that Herbig could only see his reddish hair, parts of which still glinted in the snow like the embers from a heap of cinders. There was nothing more to be seen of the two in the car. A thick blanket of snow had covered up the shattered windshield. Somewhere a dog barked, and Herbig noticed how quiet it was in the room.

"Are they coming?" Vöhringer asked sleepily.

Herbig looked at him. "What's the matter with you?"

"Don't know, I'm so sleepy."

"Then sleep on."

Vöhringer moved his arm a bit. "Damn."

"Does it hurt?"

"No, only I can't get my arm up. D'you mind scratching me, my face is itching."

Herbig rubbed his cheeks. "Here?"

"Yes, that's fine. If only I knew what was wrong with my arms."

"They'll be all right again soon."

"I don't understand it," Vöhringer muttered indistinctly. It was an effort for him to keep his eyes open. "Now it's becoming funny," he went on. "After all, I'm pretty tough."

"Nobody said you weren't."

"They'd better not. But it's so funny. If I close my eyes, I feel I'm falling."

"You've got fever."

"Seems like it." After a while he said softly: "Listen."

"Yes."

"Just in case. She doesn't need to know about getting it in the guts."

"Who?"

"My wife. Just in case, you know. Write to her that it was a head wound."

"All right. If you think so."

Vöhringer smiled at him. "Sometimes one can talk to you. That idiot Kolodzi should make sure he runs before it's too late."

"You can tell him so yourself."

Vöhringer stopped smiling and looked up at Herbig in silence.

"All right," said Herbig grimly. "I'm sure we can manage without him."

"You'll never see sense," Vöhringer answered.

Five minutes later he was dead.

Herbig stayed sitting by the dead man's side for some time, then he took Vöhringer's blanket, laid it over his face, took the pack with the ammunition over to the window, and looked out on to the street. His mind was a blank. He had no idea how much time had gone by when he heard gun fire behind the house. He rushed over to the bedroom, where a glance showed him that the two Gestapo men had nothing to do with the fire. He looked across to the edge of the wood, and saw Kolodzi, standing between the trees with his legs apart, firing his tommy-gun at someone who was out of Herbig's view.

Now Kolodzi dashed across with his head down and vaulted over the garden fence; the sub-machine guns were still hammering away from the left. Herbig chewed his lip excitedly. Kolodzi was making directly for the window. When Herbig yelled out his name, he gave a start, then came bounding along, and hurled his legs over the window-sill. His first glance fell upon the two Gestapo men who stared back at him in amazement. "Who are they?" he asked.

"Gestapo," answered Herbig. He had a strange feeling in his bones, a sort of delayed-action shock from all he had been through.

Kolodzi's face froze, then he realized that the two men, although curious about his sudden appearance, seemed to have no personal interest in him. He looked out of the window. "There are at least ten of those boys," he said. "I found their tracks in the woods. Is it you they're after?"

Herbig sprang to life, remembering that there was now no one at the front window. He rushed back to the other room, and there breathed again; nothing had changed. He heard steps behind him.

Herbig looked at Kolodzi's face and from there to Vöhringer. Kolodzi hadn't seen Vöhringer till then, but now he went over to the corpse and lifted the blanket from his face.

"He said you should run," said Herbig.

Kolodzi slowly turned his face toward Herbig. "When did he say it?"

"Not long before he went. You should have come sooner."

"Did he say that too?"

"No, that's what I say."

Kolodzi dropped the blanket again and sat down on the bench by the stove. "I've run from Szomolnok in two hours."

"You should have stayed here."

"I did more than anyone else would have done in my place."

"Anyone else wouldn't have left us stranded on our own here."

Kolodzi was silent. His hard features looked suddenly corroded, the scar seemed deeper than usual. "How did it happen?" he asked after a pause. Herbig told him.

"One of us must go to Szomolnok," said Kolodzi, gazing at the car in the street. He noticed the dead civilian. "Who's that?"

"Some partisan from Košice. They caught him. . . ."

"I see. . . ." Kolodzi leaned against the wall and looked hard at Herbig. "You haven't yet told me why Vöhringer went to the sanatorium?"

"How would I know?"

"You're more level-headed than he was. Why didn't you stop him?"

"Didn't see him go. I was in the kitchen."

"Cleared off for no reason at all?" asked Kolodzi suspiciously.

Herbig stuck out his jaw. "Let's get one thing clear. It was his own fault. You know well enough that he never listened to anything I said. Why didn't you tell me where you were going?"

Kolodzi did not answer. His fury subsided abruptly,

like a fountain when the water is turned off. He felt he was doing Herbig an injustice. The idea that Vöhringer might still have been alive if he hadn't left him alone with Herbig, made him feel more and more remorseful every minute. The pressure of guilt was so strong in him that it stifled every other emotion. Wearily he moved away from the wall and back to the window.

"He was too trusting," he said. "Unless one actually beat him over the head, he thought everybody was a decent fellow."

"He didn't think that of me."

"You never understood him."

"He never understood me."

"You made it too damned hard for him. But the swine over there shall pay for this."

"But they're your dear fellow-countrymen."

"So dear they hanged my father."

"Your. . . ." Herbig's face turned very red. "The bastards!"

"Yes," said Kolodzi and looked again into the street at the dead civilian, or rather the heap of snow covering the body. Although this was all he could see, he felt oddly uneasy all of a sudden. "If the man was from Košice," he said to Herbig, "I may know him. Did you hear what his name was?"

"No, but you can ask the M.P.s. He had red hair, too. Perhaps they're related."

Kolodzi's face grew pale. He rushed to the M.P.s. "What was the name of the dead partisan?"

"Oh, hell, I don't know," the Fat One scratched his head and turned to the Redhead. "Wasn't it something like Krasko?"

The Redhead's voice reached Kolodzi as though through a padded wall. He returned to Herbig, who took the cigarette out of his mouth as Kolodzi came up.

"D'you know him?" asked Herbig.

Kolodzi looked through the window on the heap of snow. "He was my fiancée's father."

"This is getting too thick for me," said Herbig. "Did you know he was with the partisans?"

"I guessed."

"Then I'd have told him where he got off, if I'd been you." Kolodzi's face looked so empty and pale that Herbig felt sorry for him. "What'll you do now?" he asked.

"No idea," said Kolodzi. "My fiancée and my mother are at Košice. If the front goes back any further, I'll be leaving them stranded there."

"They can go back too, can't they?"

"My mother is very sick."

"Then they'll just have to wait till we return to Košice."

"Do you seriously think we'll get back to Košice once we've lost it?"

"Why not?"

Kolodzi looked at his indifferent face and from there toward the body of Vöhringer, whom he had stopped from deserting, and who now could not desert any longer. He thought of Vöhringer's wife, and when he tried to imagine her face, it suddenly turned into Maria's face, and it was her voice, sounding as distinctly in his ears as if she were there before him, as if he only needed to take her by the hand and go with her to Baska.

He turned to Herbig wearily. "One of us should go to Szomolnok."

"Suicide," said Herbig.

"The whole war is suicide. There's only one explanation for things over there being so quiet: the partisans are expecting more men. Once they're there it will be hopeless trying to get out even by night. Two hours to Szomolnok and two hours back—you can easily do it before dark."

203

"Here, wait a moment," Herbig swung around. "You said one of us."

"What is the difference," Kolodzi said tiredly. "Now I happened to say *you're* going. Are you afraid?"

Instead of answering, Herbig said: "I suppose you don't want anyone left who might mention that you were in Košice."

"You'll have enough chance of mentioning it in Szomolnok."

Herbig grinned. "One chance in a thousand. You always did know what you were doing." He stuck his thumbs in his belt. "I'm not going. Try it yourself."

Kolodzi raised his eyebrows. "You mean you refuse?"

"I most certainly do."

"In that case," said Kolodzi, "this is an order."

"You've no right to give that order."

"No right!" Kolodzi looked at him. "Didn't they teach you in the Hitler Youth what an order is?"

"It's nothing like this. This isn't a proper order, it's a piece of personal spite."

"Oh, yes? Schmitt ordered me to send someone with a signal as soon as we ran into partisans."

Herbig felt himself being driven into a corner. "When Schmitt gave that order," he retorted fiercely, "he naturally didn't know how things were going to look here. I mean, it all depends on the situation."

"Nothing depends on the situation," said Kolodzi. "You've been in the army long enough to know that with an order nothing depends on the situation. Did they ask what the situation was at Turka when they gave orders we should hold our positions, although we hadn't any ammunition left?"

"That was different," said Herbig lamely.

"You won't get far that way," Kolodzi grinned. "Where do you think we'd be now if anybody could refuse an unpleasant order by saying he regarded it as personal spite? Attack! What? Personal spite, I won't do it! Go on patrol? Personal spite, I object! Hold a position? Personal spite again, refused. What do you say to that?"

"You're twisting things around. The circumstances are quite different."

"Think so? You're against deserting, aren't you? Now why? Because they've given us orders to win the war? And when we don't win it, that's refusing an order, isn't it?"

"There's a limit. . . ." Herbig muttered between clenched teeth.

Kolodzi abruptly calmed down. "Ah!—that's just what I was driving at!"

"If we should lose the war," Herbig interrupted furiously. "That would be a sort of higher power. But if I desert, there's no higher power about it. It's sheer disloyalty to the others."

"If you put a bullet through your brain, and I don't, does that make me disloyal?"

"For every man who deserts, others are bound to get killed."

"Bound to? Who says they're bound to? What's to stop them from deserting as well?"

"It's pretty sad that you don't know the answer yourself."

"Their conscience, I suppose," said Kolodzi with deep scorn. "Their conscience stops them. Your conscience, my conscience. We have a conscience about not saving our skins, while the people at the top haven't the least conscience about letting whole armies be wiped out. That's just. . . ." He broke off, overwhelmed by these ideas which, without his knowing it, had been boiling up inside him for years. Seizing Herbig fiercely by the coat he dragged him over to Vöhringer's body and pulled the blanket off the dead man's face.

"Let's get this clear once and for all," cried Kolodzi.

"You may think that was my fault, but let me tell you *you've* got him on your conscience—him and all the others who are still to go. Main thing is *you're* still alive; main thing is, you can go on blubbering about loyalty and don't have to worry about their families. Why should an idiot like you bother to think what this means for somebody's wife? But I'm fed up with you now, and unless you're outside in two minutes I'll damn well shoot you myself. So beat it."

Herbig tottered back white-faced. He stopped in the middle of the room and did not move even when Kolodzi leveled the tommy-gun at him. "Are you going or not?" panted Kolodzi. Herbig saw his finger curl over the trigger. But he did not stir from the spot, and merely said: "You've lost your mind. But you'll have to shoot me before I let myself be killed by the partisans just because you don't like my face."

"Your face!" Kolodzi sneered. "Why not? How many men do you think have croaked in the army just because somebody didn't care for their face? Quite legally and quietly: a hopeless patrol, an outpost duty, a rearguard action. No one will ever know. Oh yes, you can do that in the army. Anyone who likes killing people need only become an N.C.O., and he can put away all his men one after the other, without causing the slightest stir. He needn't lift a finger himself."

"Just like you," said Herbig.

"Just like me? Nobody can ever accuse me. . . ."

"Perhaps I can," suggested a voice.

Kolodzi looked toward the door, where the red-haired M.P. was standing. He went up to him and asked: "And what's biting *you?*"

"I'll tell you that later."

"Why not now?"

The Redhead looked across at Herbig, who stood with a wooden expression on his face. "Lucky I heard all that," he said to Herbig, before answering Kolodzi. "Because later there'll be a few more listening."

"I see," said Kolodzi, and without stopping to think punched him in the face; the Redhead toppled back into the passage. Before he could get to his feet again, Kolodzi was on him, and this time caught him on the head so that he sailed several yards down the passage. Rushing after him, Kolodzi found himself impeded by the gun. He dropped it, and at that moment saw the second man, who came rushing out of the other room with Vöhringer's tommy-gun in his hand. Kolodzi chased up to him and caught hold of the gun by its barrel. But the Fat One was stronger than the Redhead and defended himself fiercely. Kolodzi got a blow on the nose which made the blood spurt. Infuriated by the pain, he let go of the gun and hammered with his fists at the face before him. Suddenly there was a crack behind him which sounded as if a piece of rotten wood had snapped. He swung around to find the Redhead lying on the ground, his pistol at his side; Kolodzi noticed the thin trickle of blood flowing slowly down from his head. A yard away Herbig stood motionless, holding his tommy-gun like a club. Their eyes met.

Kolodzi bent over the Redhead and hastily examined him. "You've smashed his skull."

"He was about to shoot you in the back," Herbig said tonelessly. He looked at the butt of his gun and wiped it on his white camouflage trousers, where it left a red streak. "I didn't mean to kill him. It all happened so fast."

"You don't have to apologize to me," said Kolodzi. The Fat One stood in the doorway, gazing at the dead man in horror. Contemplating him Kolodzi wiped the blood from his nose and said over his shoulder: "He's the only one who can tell people it was us."

207

"That's true," said Herbig. He stepped to Kolodzi's side, and they both looked at the Fat One, who stared back at them with an ashen face. His lower lip sagged, and great beads of sweat emerged on his forehead.

"If I knew we were getting out of here," observed Kolodzi, "I'd say it was better he wasn't left to tell anyone anything."

"You can't gag him."

"No, I can't. But I can't get used to the idea that a fellow like you should be hanged by the very people you've always stood up for so much."

"They won't hang me."

"Well, you may get extenuating circumstances, I suppose, but that depends on what this bastard says. And they won't worry about whether you believed in final victory or not, or what a fine soldier you were. They'll simply hang you and won't bother much about the fact that the others will have to fight just that much more hopelessly without you." He broke off to look again at the Fat One, who had been listening to the conversation with an expression of terror on his face.

"We must get rid of the man," Kolodzi said firmly. "We're both in this mess up to our eyes."

"Perhaps the fellow will hold his tongue," said Herbig.

As though the Gestapo man had been waiting for this, he now came running over to them, and in a voice shrill with fear said: "My word of honor, I give you my word of honor. . . ."

"To hell with your word of honor," answered Kolodzi.

"May I be struck dead. . . ." the Fat One began.

"I wish you were," Kolodzi interrupted. "Now I'm going to tell you something. I don't know when the partisans will come. Probably they're waiting till a few dozen more roll up. We can't deal with them on our own, but our men are at Szomolnok, and you're

going off now to fetch them. The exercise will be good
for your figure . . . shut your mouth," he said sharply,
as the Fat One was about to interrupt. "Your chances
of getting through are ten times better than ours of
surviving the night in this hole."

Kolodzi turned to Herbig. "Post yourself at the window."

"Is he leaving through the door?"

"Yes." He took the Gestapo man by the arm. "You
must go over there to the right. When you're past the
car, you've made it."

"I won't do it," said the Fat One horrified.

"You can choose between that and a bullet from
me."

"They'll shoot me into little bits. . . ."

Kolodzi ignored the man's continued whimpering
and went into the room where Herbig was. "Don't you
fire a shot."

"What d'you mean? Shouldn't I give him covering
fire?"

"The partisans will do that much more efficiently,"
Kolodzi said with a meaningful smirk and returned to
the Gestapo man. "Now jump to it."

"I can't," the man said desperately. His bruised face
with the unhealthy bloated skin was distorted. "You
swine want to kill me."

Losing patience, Kolodzi seized him by the coat.
"If we'd wanted to kill you we'd have done it long
ago. I'll break every bone in your body if you make any
more fuss."

The fat man dug his knee hard into Kolodzi's stomach and tried to get the tommy-gun up. Kolodzi swiftly
thrust him back on the wall. Grasping the barrel of the
gun, he pressed the muzzle against the Fat One's neck,
and felt for the trigger. The man screamed in terror
and began thrashing about him like a madman. His
bulky shapeless body seemed transformed into a ma-

chine gone berserk, against which Kolodzi could do nothing except try and protect his face and body from the terrific rain of blows. Even then he would have been overpowered, had Herbig not been drawn by the noise, and rushed into the fray. The two of them struck at the fat Gestapo man till they had him on the floor.

Kolodzi wiped the blood off his face, feeling a deep disgust. It had been an unfair fight. He had never met an adversary who had battled like the fat man. "Nothing to be proud of," he said to Herbig, who leaned panting against the wall.

Herbig shrugged his shoulders. "Oh, I don't know—after all, those guys are trained for it. Besides, they keep their muscles fueled. Just look at him. No one could put on that amount of fat with the muck we get."

They watched the Fat One moving his head. He groaned, and made two attempts to get to his feet, but fell back both times. Finally Herbig held out a hand and pulled him up.

"What do we do next?" asked Herbig.

"I swear to you. . . ." the Fat One groaned. There were tears in his eyes.

"My God!" said Kolodzi in disgust.

Herbig grinned lamely. "I read once that all fat people are sentimental." They looked helplessly at the weeping man.

"I can't do it," said Herbig. "I'd rather risk getting hanged." His eye fell on the Redhead, from whose battered scalp blood was still trickling. Suddenly he felt sick and went white-faced from the room.

Kolodzi took hold of the Fat One and pulled him so close that their faces nearly touched. "If you mention a word of this I'll get you. Some time or other, but I'll get you, remember that."

The Fat One started once more: "I give you my word of honor. . . ." Kolodzi made a gesture as if to hit him on the mouth. Then he released him, picked up Vöhr-

inger's gun which had fallen on the floor during the
melee and threw it over to the fat man. "Watch out at
the bedroom window, and don't dare move a foot
away."

"You can rely on me," said the fat man, wiping the
tears from his face. "You won't regret this." His battered face worked painfully.

After watching him run off into the bedroom,
Kolodzi joined Herbig. Kolodzi saw that he had pulled
the blanket off Vöhringer's face and was looking at him.
"What the devil are you doing?" he snapped. He put
the blanket back and walked over to the window. "Still
nothing," he said impatiently, after a glance at the
street.

"I think it's best after all if I went to Szomolnok,"
said Herbig suddenly.

"You do, do you? Then why did you make such a
fuss just now? What's come over you all of a sudden?"

"I'm feeling damned queer," Herbig admitted.

"Not half so queer as you'd feel with a rope around
your neck. Since when have *you* been squeamish?"

"I don't know myself. I got too much to think about.
It's all because of this blasted sitting around."

"We'll soon do something about that," said Kolodzi.
He looked out for a second, then took his tommy-gun
and fired a magazine at the right window of the house
opposite, where he thought he saw faces. "Just to wake
up those crafty bastards." With two quick steps he was
away from the window, waiting. After a minute had
passed without the fire being returned, he pushed his
cap back from his brow and said: "Well, what d'you
know?"

"I know I can't stand this much longer," said Herbig.

In the doorway the Fat One appeared, his face grey
with fear. "Was it you shooting?"

"The swine has left his window," said Herbig. He
made for the Fat One who turned in alarm and dis-

appeared again. "The swine," Herbig repeated, resuming his position at the window. "And for a swine like that you can get hanged." He stopped abruptly. By the time he had his finger properly on the trigger of his tommy-gun, Kolodzi was already shooting away at his side. They did not worry about the fact that they were standing at the window without cover. As if by a pre-arranged plan, they each fired at a different target, Kolodzi at the window and Herbig at the man who came running across the street, but now stumbled, fell on his knees and collapsed in the snow. The longish object which he had been holding in his hand exploded with a loud report. While the rear end of it hid the man's body in a fiery cloud of smoke, its cylinder-shaped point sailed high over the street, disappeared on the right of the house, and then there was a booming crash as if a bomb had hit. Herbig and Kolodzi jumped away from the window. They looked at each other. Kolodzi said: "I'd give a lot to know where those bastards got a German mortar-bomb from."

"And I'd like to know whether they've got any more. Think what would have happened if we hadn't seen the guy."

With a listless gesture Kolodzi wiped the shock off his face. "God almighty!"

After that they did not take their eyes off the street for a second, until a sub-machine gun started up behind the house. "You go to the Fat One," said Kolodzi. "I'll deal with things here on my own." He went to the other side of the window, and waited. It was beginning to get dark. If only I'd stayed with Maria, Kolodzi thought.

11

Soon after Kolmel had gone, the medical officer of a dressing station came to General Stiller, complaining that there weren't enough vehicles to take the wounded back. "There are sixty stretcher cases left in the houses," he told the general, who was busy working out plans for the counter-attack.

"Wait a moment," Stiller told him, and turned to Kreisel. "How high were your casualties?"

"About a hundred. Half of them are at Rozhanovce."

"Dead?"

"I hope so, sir."

Stiller looked at him for a moment, and then understood. "How do things look with you?" he asked Wieland.

"Appalling, sir. Not counting the battalion the division took away from me, I had three hundred men on my strength. I've got a hundred here, two hundred are missing."

"Perhaps some are stragglers."

"Possibly," said Wieland.

Stiller took out his fountain pen. "Let's see what we've got altogether." He considered the numbers given him, then said: "Right, we'll attack as soon as Herr Wieland engages with the Russians."

"Then the Russians will slash me to pieces," cried

Wieland indignantly. "With a mere hundred men I'll never get into Rozhanovce."

"You're not meant to. On the contrary, you must draw the Russians out of there. As soon as your attack bogs down, they'll make a counter-attack."

"And drive right through to Košice!"

"That won't hurt. If I can cut their lines of communication, I don't mind their going even further. The main thing is to get them out of Rozhanovce."

"And me into it, I imagine," said Kreisel.

"That's right, you and the reserve battalion. And you," he told Wieland, "will go back to the road fork. Send the reserve battalion off at once, to attack Rozhanovce from the north with the battalion Scheper has covering the flank."

"Does Herr Scheper know about it?" asked Wieland.

"He's getting a radio signal. Now for the distances and times."

When they had finished, Kreisel asked: "And what happens afterward?"

"Straight to the pass," said Stiller. "The Russians mustn't be given any time to establish themselves up there. You'll push forward with your regiment into the old positions, while Scheper and the reserve battalion stay in Rozhanovce covering the flank to the west."

"What about the pioneer battalion, sir?"

"I need that for Slancik, to establish contact with Höpper. He'll be attacking in the direction of Durkov. As soon as he connects with the pioneer battalion, he'll wheel eastward and climb to the pass with you." Stiller's eyes fell on the medical officer, who had been standing in the background all the time. "I'll send you some trucks," he said. The officer thanked him and left. Stiller turned back to Wieland. "Off you go."

"This business will cost me all my men," muttered Wieland. "Why don't you let the reserve lot do it, sir?"

"The mock attack must look genuine enough for the

Russians to believe in it, and that's a job for which I don't consider the reserve unit sufficiently reliable."

"I've lost two-thirds of my regiment."

"You should have trained your men to stay in their holes instead of running away. Have you still got officers?"

"Six," Wieland admitted reluctantly.

"Send forward all you can spare from your staff. Only you must leave your signal platoon here with me, and two or three officers also. You'll probably have to launch your attack in an hour from now." He looked at Kreisel. "Now for the artillery. What have we got here?"

Wieland regarded him angrily, and turned to leave the room. "No salute?" asked Stiller.

Wieland swung around, his face scarlet. "I didn't think you considered it important, sir."

"As a point of good manners, certainly—unless you don't think those important."

Wieland saluted and went out. When the door had closed behind him, Stiller resumed in a normal voice: "How many artillery men did you say?"

Kreisel suppressed a laugh. "Altogether, sir, or only on my own?"

"Altogether."

"I can't tell you that, sir. But we have two artillery officers here."

"Have them sent for," Stiller ordered.

They arrived just after the regimental signals office reported that Captain Hepp was on the phone. He told the general that he had three hundred and twenty men with him in the new reserve battalion.

"Wait till Colonel Wieland arrives," Stiller instructed him. "He'll give you full details. Meanwhile get your men to take up positions near the anti-tank gun. Send the empty trucks up here, they're to pick up casualties. Is there anything else?" He listened to what Hepp said, then turned to the artillery officers. "There are four trucks with ammunition for you down there."

"At last." One of the lieutenants took the receiver eagerly. While he was telephoning, Stiller told Kreisel: "You can start too now. Make sure that. . . ." He broke off. Shells were exploding quite close. Through the window he could see everyone running for the houses.

"Now it's beginning here as well," said Kreisel. "If we don't hurry, they'll smash up my men." '

"Then hurry up. You can take the assault gun with you at once. Who's the signals officer here?"

One of the officers came forward, clicking his heels. "Lieutenant Schleippen, sir."

Stiller told him: "I need continuous contact with Colonel Kreisel." He looked toward the window. Shells were again bursting on the street.

"Russian mortars," said Kreisel.

The artillery lieutenant was still on the phone. Stiller gave him an impatient glance. At last he hung up, remarking with satisfaction: "We've got enough now to make things hot for the Russians."

"Then it's time you got started," said Stiller.

After Kreisel and his officers left, the Russian fire became increasingly fierce. One of the remaining officers expressed a fear that the Russians had an observer somewhere, following movements in Durkov.

"Don't talk nonsense," said Stiller crossly. "How could an observer have got in here?"

Ten minutes later Wieland was on the phone. "I'm at the road fork," he reported. "I've just sent Captain Hepp off."

"Good. Then start your attack in a quarter of an hour. Any sign of the Russians?"

"Not their infantry. There's been some firing from their anti-tank guns."

"Send the assault guns ahead," ordered Stiller. "The

Russian tanks are bound to be west of Rozhanovce by now. Are you getting artillery fire?"

"Not here, sir. Further behind us, somewhere round the battery position."

"All right. Now listen," said Stiller, "when the Russians counter-attack, withdraw slowly back to the road fork and from there to the main Durkov road. In case I shouldn't be here any more, take up positions at the outskirts and cover westward."

"What with, sir?" Wieland asked scornfully.

For a moment Stiller was taken aback, then he said sharply: "With your staff, if that's all you have left."

He hung up, and went out into the street. The Russian mortar fire was landing all over the place. He saw the snow rising high between the trees in the direction of Rozhanovce. A Russian battery must be ranged directly on the street. Heavy fire could also be heard inside the wood, and further right came muffled explosions near the last houses on the road to Slancik. There was nobody left outside the houses. Stiller looked at his watch. When he went back into his headquarters Kreisel was on the telephone, reporting that he had reached his starting line. Stiller asked where the artillery fire was landing.

"Behind us luckily," replied Kreisel. "It's high time we got away from here."

"You must wait another half hour. Wieland is just getting ready to attack." He looked at his watch again. "It's now one-thirty. You'll attack at two. Can you see anything of the Russians?"

"Not see them, sir, but I can hear them all right. They're banging away pretty hard."

"Tanks too?"

"Not so far."

"Right, in half an hour then." Stiller replaced the receiver with a sigh of relief and dismissed the officers who had stayed in his room, including Giesinger who had kept himself silently in a corner. Then he went to the window to look out. Two women and an old man were herding some sheep across the street. The women's faces were full of fear and it occurred to Stiller that these were the first civilians he had seen in Durkov. He summoned an officer, who explained that the place had not been evacuated; the people were sitting in their cellars.

"They should have been sent away," said Stiller.

The officer closed the door behind him: a second later a heavy shell exploded in the vicinity. Stiller, who had ducked instinctively, straightened up and looked into the street again. The women and the sheep had disappeared but the man was lying in the snow, not moving. Near him was a huge crater. The snow all around was black and strewn with wooden shingles torn off the roofs by the blast. Stiller recognized the old man by the thin, patched coat; the trousers had a long tear at the side, perhaps from a shell splinter. Regarding him, Stiller registered the increasing frequency with which shells were now raining on Durkov. He glanced at the ceiling: one of them would be quite enough to blow up this wretched hovel.

He looked at his watch again, and at that moment the windows began to rattle. The batteries behind Durkov had opened fire—so things had started. Now the assault regiment must be going into attack too, and with it the reserve unit and Scheper's covering battalion. And on the other side the pioneer battalion, which was marching toward Slancik, where at the same time Colonel Höpper and his regiment were pushing north. Three-quarters of the division were now on the move.

With his eyes closed Stiller heard the other batteries opening up. Forty-eight heavy and light howitzers were firing all they had, and then there were the assault guns, heavy and light artillery guns and several dozen mortars of all calibres. The general felt he could hear them all. He stood at the window, leaning forward, abandoning himself to the oppressive feeling which always came over him when an attack was beginning. He never found the power which lay in his hands more overwhelming than in such moments. An order from him set in motion two thousand men, who at this second were climbing out of their snowdrifts and running into the fire of the Russian tank- and machine-guns.

Then he noticed the two women in the street. They stood by the body of the old man, now almost covered with snow, and screamed. He thought he heard the screams through the closed windows and in spite of the booming of the heavy howitzers on the edge of the wood. Staring at the women, he thought again of the two thousand men who were now running for their lives: two thousand men whom he'd set in motion. Outside the two women still stood and screamed.

He pressed his hands against his temples, and forced his mind away from the sight and back to all the things he had to attend to. The attack demanded precision. There were a hundred things that had to happen almost simultaneously, beginning with the reserve unit, which mustn't start marching through the valley a minute before the assault regiment reached the southern edge of Rozhanovce—because otherwise they'd be running into German artillery fire; going on to Wieland and his hundred men, who must be rolled back by the Russians so that Kreisel could get to Rozhanovce. Then there was Höpper, who must break out of Slancik, and the pioneer battalion, which had to open the way for him before the Russians noticed that there were only two companies left in Durkov. And a whole host of other decisions besides, which no one could take off his shoulders. . . .

The officers in the next room jumped from their places as Stiller flung open the door, shouting at them. In response to his command they rushed out into the street, caught hold of the dead civilian's arms and legs and flung him headlong into the nearest house, driving the women after him with curses. When they returned to Stiller, he was sitting at the table with a relaxed expression on his face, reading the first reports about the attack.

So far things were going according to plan. Kreisel had only met weak enemy forces, which had no tanks with them. The assault regiment had overrun them, and Kreisel reported a swift advance toward Rozhanovce. The reserve unit had joined Scheper's covering battalion without making contact with the enemy, and was also on the way to Rozhanovce. In fact there was news in from everyone but Wieland.

For a while Stiller stared at the reports, sunk in thought; then he reached for the phone and ordered the artillery to move its fire up to Rozhanovce. He sent a radio signal to the reserve unit, telling it to dig in with Scheper's battalion five hundred yards north of Rozhanovce and there await fresh orders. Lieutenant Schleippen brought him a report that the pioneer battalion had met strong enemy forces about a mile south of Durkov and could not go on.

"They *must* go on," said Stiller. "What about Höpper?"

"Colonel Höpper's making good progress, sir," said Schleippen cheerfully, handing him a radio signal.

Stiller gave a satisfied nod. "The pioneer battalion can dig in. If Höpper goes on at this rate, he'll be at the pass in an hour."

"There's only one thing I'm worried about, sir."

"What's that?"

"That instead of going back to the pass the Russians will break through to Durkov."

"We've always got the pioneer battalion to stop them."

"But suppose the Russians attack in great strength."

"I doubt if they will. They haven't any heavy guns on this side, so they're bound to choose the way where there's least resistance—in this case no apparent resistance at all. Only Höpper must swing east with his left wing in good time, so that they'll be driven back to the pass. Send him another signal."

Schleippen ran off. Stiller turned to the other staff officers. There were five with Giesinger, two from the assault regiment and two from Wieland's staff. Stiller sent one of them to the pioneer battalion. "I want to know the battalion's exact position. Tell the officer commanding that he mustn't give a single yard, however strongly the Russians attack." He turned to the next officer. "Go to the road fork and see what's happened to Colonel Wieland and the assault guns. He should be making direct for Durkov." He noticed Giesinger, who was standing by the window. Waving him over, he took him into the other room. "I hope you're beginning to see what you've done."

Giesinger said nothing. He had no wish to bring further humiliations on his head. Nor did the general seem to be expecting any answer, for he went on quickly: "As soon as the assault regiment is in Rozhanovce, I'm moving my headquarters there. Meanwhile you can go ahead and start looking for a suitable house. Take everything with you that isn't needed here."

"Right, sir," said Giesinger with relief: he was immensely pleased to get away from the general. But before he reached the door, the hated voice nailed him down again. "I'm still waiting for the battalion from Szomolnok."

"It should have been here long ago," said Giesinger.

"So should the reconnaissance unit. You didn't by

221

any chance send that off to Szomolnok too?" The sarcasm sent the blood to Giesinger's head. "If the battalion isn't here by this evening, you've got a long night's march ahead of you."

"You'll be doing me a favor, sir, I assure you," said Giesinger.

Stiller gave him a cold stare. "I'll cure you yet of your impertinence. You will be receiving particular attention from me."

Schleippen came in and Giesinger took this as a dismissal. "Well, what have you got for me?" Stiller asked the lieutenant.

Schleippen put a signal down on the table. "Colonel Kreisel is just outside Rozhanovce, sir. He's asking what's happened to the artillery fire."

Stiller looked up in surprise. "But I gave him eight batteries."

"They can't fire any more," said Schleippen, putting a second signal down in front of him.

The general stared at it. It was from Colonel Conrad, the artillery commander, and stated bluntly that he had ordered his batteries on both sides of the road to stop firing, so as not to attract the attention of the Russians, who were pouring down the road to the west with over a hundred tanks and almost unending infantry columns. Stiller read the signal through three times before pushing it aside with a wooden movement. "Inform Košice and corps, and report that in about ten minutes we shall be in Rozhanovce, cutting the Russians off from their only supply line. Got that?"

Schleippen scribbled the message on a piece of paper. "Right, sir."

"Then send off radio signals to Colonel Kreisel. He's to launch the attack on Rozhanovce immediately."

"Without artillery support, sir?"

"Yes. The artillery will take their guns to Rozhanovce as soon as the road is clear. Then I want a radio signal sent to Colonel Höpper, telling him to push through to Durkov."

"To Durkov," Schleippen repeated, writing it down, and left.

Stiller realized that the crucial point had been reached: if Conrad's report was right, Wieland and his hundred men must have met vastly superior forces, and the Russians might be in Košice in two hours. A hundred tanks—it was far more than he'd imagined. They seemed to set great store by the attack on Košice. If corps hadn't any more reserves, they'd not only take Košice but also get the next fifty miles thrown in for free.

Schleippen's worried face appeared at the door. "The pioneer battalion, sir."

"What about them?"

"They're coming back, sir."

Stiller had guessed as much. "Have the signals gone out?" he asked calmly.

"Yes, sir."

"Right, go and find me a tommy-gun, will you?" He got into his greatcoat, strapped the pistol on to his belt, and called the two officers from the next room, sending one to the two batteries behind Durkov and the other to fetch back the companies covering east. Then he went out into the street and waited till Schleippen returned with a tommy-gun.

A long file of men appeared behind the houses on the other side of the street. They were Kreisel's two companies which had stayed in Durkov to guard the village. Their commanders reported to Stiller, who sent them and their companies to the southern outskirts. Then he beckoned the other officers over to him, and looked impatiently across the street at the signals headquarters, where Schleippen and his platoon were just coming out. Collecting all the men standing around, the general led them off behind the two com-

panies in the direction of the firing, which was increasing in violence. The tommy-gun shots sounded as
if a hundred detonators had been thrown on to a hot-
plate simultaneously. In between came the cracking
reports of the artillery, which had now concentrated its
fire further south. The faces of the men behind Stiller
betrayed their anxiety.

The village was about six hundred yards long,
stretching along the valley in two rows of houses.
In some places the valley was so narrow that there
was only room for the road, which wound south with
many bends. On its left, where the hills rose steeply,
the wood came right up to the houses; but on the right
several clearings made the land more visible. Looking
south, Stiller could only see the last men, because
the road was curving again. The houses were further
apart now, and the ground fell away on one side to a
small stream. He noticed a horse-drawn field howitzer
rolling out into the road, and about thirty men mounting the rest of the guns on his side of the stream. He
beckoned over the company commander, a lieutenant,
and asked: "Where's your second battery?"

"At the northern end of the village, sir."

"I need it here in front," declared Stiller, pointing in
the direction of the gunfire. "Bring it up to the last
houses."

"But sir," the lieutenant protested in a shocked voice,
"if we lose the horses, I'll have to leave the guns here."

"Harness your men to it," said Stiller brusquely. "I
need the guns for direct firing."

Lieutenant Schleippen came up. "There's something
moving up there, sir."

"Where?"

"Over to the right, sir."

Stiller looked, then narrowed his eyes and raised his
binoculars: now he could see it distinctly. High above

them there was a clearing in the wood, about a hundred and fifty yards wide. Right in the middle of it a dark line went through the snow; in the distance it seemed like a moving string of beads. It came out of the wood from the left, and disappeared again on the other side beneath the trees. When he adjusted the binoculars into clearer focus, Stiller saw that they were Russians. He watched them long enough to be sure it was at least a regiment. Perhaps it had been moving through like this for an hour already. They were marching from south to north and must come out on the road to Durkov—to Durkov or to Košice.

He dropped the binoculars. Suddenly he realized something else. The Russian artillery fire was coming from due south, this was clear enough from the sound of the reports; so the batteries must be on the road somewhere between Slancik and Durkov—he was appalled. He rushed down the road, and when he got round the bend he saw the two companies. The men stood tightly pressed against the houses. He ran past them to the next corner, from where he had a good view of the landscape. It was only a few yards to the last houses, then came a long narrow gap; beyond it more wood, and the artillery fire was hitting between the wood and the end of the village. The place where the road went off into the wood seemed to have turned into an exploding powder barrel. Stiller was stunned. When he noticed the two company commanders by the last house, he asked: "What goes on here?"

"No idea, sir." The two officers had to shout to make themselves heard. One of them pointed forward. "Impossible to get through."

"Where's the pioneer battalion?"

"At the edge of the wood—they can't get back."

"But the artillery fire is coming from the south."

"The whole fireworks is coming from the south. If

225

the Russians move their fire this way, we can pack up."

"But there's one of our regiments in the south," cried Stiller.

The lieutenant shrugged his shoulders. "That's Russian artillery, sir."

"Impossible. The Russians haven't any road, except the one here. How should they get their artillery over the hills?"

"I don't know, sir, but that's Russian artillery. They dismantle their guns and drag the parts across."

Stiller thought quickly. "Bring your companies back to the crossroads and take up positions there, facing west. You can take the artillery with you, it doesn't need to come here."

The two company commanders looked at each other significantly, then they ran back to their men. Stiller beckoned Schleippen over. "I hope you've left a receiving set behind."

"Two, sir."

"Then see what's come in. I particularly want to know how things look with Höpper." He watched the artillery fire, realizing that it couldn't possibly come from Höpper, as he had half hoped: ten batteries firing at once could never have produced a barrage like this, and Höpper had only three. The bit of road between Durkov and the wood was practically plowed up, there was no more snow to be seen—the earth was black, ripped open by innumerable craters.

Stiller had seldom seen such marksmanship. The fire ranged about fifty yards from the village over the whole road along the left of the valley. At the edge of the wood it swung at a right angle straight across to the other side of the valley. Now he could watch it closely, he thought he had found its objective: to stop anyone coming in or out of the wood. It might have been meant to cut off the pioneer battalion's retreat, but seemed too great an effort for that purpose alone.

As he was pondering the point, he remembered Höpper again: perhaps the fire had something to do with his counter-attack, though he couldn't see why it should . . . Raising his binoculars, he scanned the edge of the wood, but there was nothing to be seen of the pioneer battalion; they must be still in the wood. The continuous gunfire gave an indication of the ferocity of the battle. Now and then single shots, or a whole salvo, whistled over the houses. The men behind Stiller would draw their heads in, while the officers shifted uneasily from one leg to the other.

He knew they were waiting for an order, but the decision he had to make was such a heavy one that he still hesitated. He had come up forward because he thought a battalion fleeing in disorder had to be made to stand firm. There was no longer any question of that; on the contrary, he now had to get the battalion back as quickly as possible. It it hadn't been for the artillery fire, he would have given the order for withdrawal already. He was quite aware that at least half of the pioneers would fall in the fire; but he was equally aware that unless he gave the order, none of them would get back at all. With a movement of his head he called over an officer, and ordered him to send three men into the wood. "They must keep over to the right, that's the best chance."

"They'll never make it, sir," said the officer.

Stiller looked past him. "I didn't ask for your opinion." He watched the officer detailing three men from the signal platoon. The men looked across at him furiously, and trotted along the road. "Hurry!" cried Stiller. They quickened their pace. After a bit they swerved half right off the road, running across the open space to the stream. Their pace became slower and slower, the nearer they came to the belt of fire.

Through the binoculars Stiller could see them lie down on their stomachs side by side, pressing their

227

heads into the snow. Nor did they move when he sent an officer after them, who stopped about twenty yards behind and yelled at him. Stiller took the tommy-gun off his shoulder and rushed along himself. When they saw him, they got up quickly and hurtled onward. Now they were coming into the artillery fire. A shell exploded to the right of them. Two threw themselves on the ground again, while the third shot off toward the wood with head thrust forward, vanishing soon afterwards in a cloud of black smoke. The others crept along on their stomachs and reached the place where the first had disappeared. For a while there was nothing more to be seen of them, but then they suddenly reappeared, amid spurting fountains of snow, sprinting the last few yards to the wood.

Stiller returned to the houses, and waited. After a while the first men from the pioneer battalion came running out of the wood; Stiller had to stand by and watch them being pounded down by artillery fire. More men came swarming from the wood—and suddenly there was a new noise in the air. It began with an angry hiss, which seemed to come out of the dark snowy sky, and increased to a shrill howl. The men behind Stiller ran into the houses. For a second or two he felt tempted to give in to the instinctive movement of his legs, but by then it was too late to look around for cover; the air was already full of the screaming noise of shells.

He flung himself to the ground, pressed his face into the snow and held his breath. The explosions were so violent that he felt his head was going to burst. Half numb, he looked up. The village was in flames. Among the burning houses a swarm of screaming men and women was running to and fro in confusion and fright. He saw the next shells burst right in the middle of them, then he scrambled to his feet. The whole snowy plain just outside the village was crammed full of yelling, running, leaping men, fleeing toward the houses between the bursting shells, tumbling over each other in writhing clusters and being literally torn apart.

Stiller turned and ran back. He blundered into a civilian, who was dragging a burning woman across the street; he stumbled over horrible bundles which lay in his path; he raced past houses, where appalling screams came from women and children; and when he reached his headquarters he found it blazing from top to bottom. The house with the signals office was still intact; he tore up the few steps. A door was open, he saw Lieutenant Schleippen there with a few men, packing up their radio sets and equipment. They swung round as Stiller came in, and Schleippen said quickly, "The assault regiment is in Rozhanovce."

Stiller took the signal from his hand and scanned it hastily. Then he looked up. "How about Höpper?"

"He can't go any further, sir. The Russians have penetrated into Slancik behind him. He asks if he may break through to Košice."

"Let me see."

While he was reading the signal, Schleippen said: "And here's one from corps." This came from Kolmel and ordered that the positions be held at all costs. Stiller thrust the paper carelessly into his pocket. "Signal Höpper that we are waiting for him in Rozhanovce."

"Not Durkov, sir?"

"The Russians will be waiting for him in Durkov. He must push past them on the right or the left. Report to corps that I can hold Rozhanovce till this evening at the most. And Colonel Kreisel is not to go to the pass but to wait for me in Rozhanovce. When you're through with that, come to the crossroads."

He ran outside again and stopped on the steps. The street had completely disappeared under clouds of black smoke. Another salvo of shells was just whistling over; the gun that fired them must also be somewhere in the south. There was no further doubt: the Russians had found a way over the mountains. If Durkov fell into their hands, it would be senseless to stay any longer in Rozhanovce. As the shells crashed into the village, Stiller raced back to the signals room. "Has the signal already gone off to Höpper?"

"Not yet, sir."

"Then cancel that one, and tell him he's to make for Durkov."

"Not Rozhanovce?"

"I said Durkov! The Russians must on no account get to the crossroads. Do you hear me?" Stiller shouted.

Schleippen gave him a terrified look. "Yes, sir—Durkov, sir."

"He must go on attacking until he gets to Durkov, and on no account is he to break through to the west. I forbid him to try that."

"Right, sir."

"Have you still contact with Scheper?"

"Yes, sir."

"Send him a signal too. He's to make for Rozhanovce with every man he's got, in double-quick time."

"Fill his staff, sir?"

"With every man he's got, I said. Open your ears. Scheper is to evacuate his positions and march to Rozhanovce with his whole regiment."

Paying no heed to Schleippen's bewildered face, he rushed outside again. The artillery fire was now trained on the village full force. Sweating profusely—never had he run like this before—he reached the crossroads, panting. It was another fifty yards to the wood. He looked quickly round for the companies: as ordered, they had dug in on both sides of the road to Košice. He shouted for the company commanders.

When they came, he snapped at them: "Where's the artillery?"

"Moved into the wood with their guns, sir," one of them answered.

Stiller gripped his arm. "I'm leaving you one battery. See that you get all the men still to come from the pioneer battalion here to the crossroads. The Russians must on no account take the crossroads. Understand?"

The lieutenant said nothing.

"I asked if you understood," Stiller yelled.

"Yes, sir."

"You're being reinforced. Colonel Höpper will be arriving with his regiment. Don't dare to move away from here. Anything else?"

"From which direction are the Russians actually coming, sir?" asked the lieutenant.

"How should I know? You must watch on all sides." Stiller ran across to the wood.

On the way he wondered what could still be done. Not much, he told himself; what he needed now was luck, that was all. He couldn't really count on Höpper and his regiment. With the pioneer battalion gone, the Russians had their rear free and only needed to turn their guns round. When he thought of the distance between Durkov and Slancik and remembered that they were already in Slancik, the space Höpper's regiment was confined to could be reckoned in square yards. His only chance was an attempt to break through to the west—as his signal showed he realized. But for corps' express order, he would have let him do that without hesitation but now he needed him. So long as he was sitting in the wood between Durkov and Slancik, he kept the Russians busy there. Otherwise they could simply turn back and not only overrun the two companies but also attack Rozhanovce from the south. Stiller no longer considered sending the assault regiment on to the pass. In an hour and a half at the latest, with Scheper's regiment, there would be over fifteen hundred men in Rozhanovce, so they should be able to hold it till dark—and he had no intention to stay there any longer than that, not even if corps insisted, which he doubted they would. Once the Russians were in Košice, it wasn't far to Dobšina; new orders from corps could be expected any minute . . .

He glanced ahead of him into the wood, and saw a long convoy standing on the road to Rozhanovce: trucks, ambulances and guns. He remembered that he had ordered the ammunition column to advance to Durkov. There were a few officers standing round, and on recognizing an artillery lieutenant among them, he ordered him to go into positions at the edge of the wood and support the two companies guarding the crossroads. The other battery he dispatched to Rozhanovce with the ammunition column. Then he looked over the remaining vehicles and noticed a closed command car, whose driver was sitting at the wheel. Stiller went up to him and said: "Who are you waiting for?"

"For the colonel, sir."

"Which colonel?"

"Colonel Wieland, sir."

Stiller started. During the last half hour he had not thought at all about Wieland. And why should he have? Against a hundred tanks Wieland and his men had had no sort of chance. Presumably the three assault guns could also be written off. He walked round the car once, and then said: "From now on you'll be driving me."

The man looked shocked. "But the colonel, sir. . . ."

"The colonel," Stiller interrupted, "will never have enjoyed walking so much as now, if he still can." He looked toward the houses, where Schleippen had just appeared with his signals team. Behind them, filling the whole breadth of the street, a great mass of men was pouring forward: it must be the pioneer battalion —what was left of them. Stiller waited till they came up. There was an officer with them, and when he noticed the general, he started to give a report. Stiller stopped him with an impatient gesture, "Where's your battalion commander?"

"He was killed, sir," the officer answered breathlessly.

"I see. You'll take over the battalion at once, they're to dig in here. Come with me." He showed him the place where the two companies of the assault regiment were, instructing him to establish contact with their officers. Then he called over Schleippen and his men, and climbed into the car with them. Before it could move off, another officer came rushing up. "The wounded, sir."

Stiller regarded him coldly. "What d'you expect me to do? Can't you see the ambulances?"

"There aren't enough of them, sir. Up there are wounded lying everywhere."

"The Russians are already settling in where the wounded are."

Stiller leaned out of the car and looked over at the houses, which were still being pounded by the Russian artillery. The fire had caught all the roofs, clouds of pitch-black smoke were billowing up toward the sky. Single men from the pioneer battalion still came stumbling out of the village, and he saw that most of them were wounded. Some crawled on their hands and knees, others hopped on one leg, one dragged behind him the remains of a foot which had been shot off and was hanging on by a strip of skin. The general looked away from him and returned his stare to the officer's haggard face. He asked: "Do you belong to the pioneer battalion?"

"Yes, sir."

"The battalion did not fulfill its task. If you and your men had pushed forward a mile or two further instead of retreating, you wouldn't need to be worrying about the wounded. Because an entire regiment of ours is trapped there, over seven hundred men, and I can't be sure they'll get out at all." Stiller gave his driver the order to leave.

He did not speak a word the whole way. They overtook the supply column and some howitzers. The road led straight through the wood, no gradients or bends obscuring the view. On the right the land rose steeply towards the pass, while on the left it fell away equally steeply. After less than half an hour they met a sentry from the assault regiment, who diverted them from the road to a forest track. Between the trees lay dead soldiers; Stiller saw they were mostly Russians. He glanced at them indifferently, his mind occupied with the gunfire coming from the northeast, which had begun to arouse his attention during the drive, and now became more distinct: it sounded as if the Russians were already counter-attacking. The forest track rounded a bend, and a single house appeared between the white trees; there were a lot of cars lined up by it —evidently Kreisel's headquarters. Even before Stiller could get out, the young colonel emerged from the house. "Thank God you've got here, sir," he cried.

Stiller looked at his tense face. "Where's the trouble?"

"Everywhere, sir. I can soon show you."

"Straight away." Stiller turned to Schleippen and told him to establish contact with corps and with Höpper. Then he climbed out of the car and walked along the forest track with Kreisel till they came upon a road.

"The pass road," said Kreisel. "We must be careful, it's watched."

It was on the tip of Stiller's tongue to ask from which

side, but he refrained, in case Kreisel should regard the question as a sign of fear. They passed four field howitzers, which stood on both sides of the road with their barrels directed westward.

Kreisel pointed over his shoulder with his thumb. "I've sent the reserve unit into positions further behind. It's still possible the Russians who have broken through may return when they find there's nothing coming after them."

"That's not only possible, it's very likely. Do you know by the way how many of them there were?"

"I've no idea, sir."

"You can be glad you don't. Over a hundred tanks apparently, and more infantry regiments than one can count."

Kreisel came to an abrupt halt. "A hundred tanks. But that's. . . ." He broke off, shaking his head. "And I attacked Rozhanovce with two assault guns! If the tanks had still been here. . . ."

Stiller smiled slightly. "My recipe worked. It was like a champagne bottle, where you can't say beforehand how great the pressure on the cork is. Sometimes you have to pull it out by force, while at other times it's enough if you take off the wire."

"Poor Wieland!" said Kreisel. They fell silent as they stamped through the deep snow side by side. Keeping in the wood to the right of the road, they could see nothing of the village; but the nearer they came to it, the fiercer grew the gun and mortar fire. Stiller listened intently. "Am I mistaken, or is the fire coming from the north as well?"

"You're not mistaken, sir. At first our only front was to the east, and that was all right till the Russians realized we had no contact to the left or right of us. At present my regiment is trying to dig in, but if the Russians are coming from the west as well, we'll be plumb in the middle of them."

"I've ordered Colonel Scheper here with his regiment."

Kreisel looked up. "To Rozhanovce?"

"Yes. Also, Colonel Höpper is on his way to Durkov. Only I'm afraid we shan't see him again."

"Do things look as bad as that down there?"

"Even worse."

"Then we might as well pack up at once," said Kreisel. "What does corps think?"

"That makes no difference to me. They signaled that we should hold the position in all circumstances."

"First we've got to have it again—and we can't manage that without reinforcements."

"Try and make the gentlemen at corps see that."

"But you're not going to. . . ."

"I'm not going to anything. It's enough for me that the division on our left has had an exposed flank since Scheper evacuated his positions. It's just the same in the south, the Russians can now march to Slancik quite unhindered. If he doesn't want to lose his whole corps, the commanding general is bound to order a withdrawal."

"Yes, of course, sir," said Kreisel, smiling respectfully. "The only question is—suppose the order comes too late?"

"We'll leave as soon as it's dark, probably to the north or south of Košice. With fifteen hundred desperate men, I'll break through to Dobšina if need be. Is this fellow Giesinger with you?"

"Yes, he's at my headquarters, with a face as black as thunder."

"It well may be," said Stiller.

They reached the edge of the wood, where there were about a dozen houses. Kreisel took the general past these, and then Stiller saw Rozhanovce ahead. Stiller suppressed an exclamation. The village street led to a bridge, in front of which three burned-out

T.34s were standing. Behind it, the whole street was crammed full of vehicles, horses which had dropped dead in their harness, and dead Russian soldiers piled on top of each other.

"You certainly surprised them," Stiller said in a tight voice.

Kreisel smiled, though his eyes remained serious. "If we have to pay for this, there won't be much left of us. The credit's really Wieland's of course. The Russians must have counter-attacked almost as soon as he went in. A hundred tanks!" He shook his head. "Were you expecting that, sir?"

"Not quite."

"Nor did poor Wieland, I'll bet. His handful of men must have been cut to shreds."

"Better they than the whole of your regiment. Where are your assault guns now?"

"Up in the wood. The Russians are collecting tanks on the road again. I've sent two guns off from the artillery, the others are over there." He pointed to the next house, behind which two heavy field howitzers were standing.

"And the others?"

"What others? There are only four."

"That's all you have here in the way of artillery?"

"Yes, sir."

"But that's impossible. I ordered all the batteries to come up to Rozhanovce as soon as the road was clear."

"I've not seen any of them so far. Perhaps they're still on their way."

"They should have been here long ago," said Stiller nervously.

While Kreisel was giving him a full report, the general studied the terrain. Stiller decided he did not like the look of it; indeed, the more he contemplated his surroundings the uneasier he felt. Moreover, there was the continuous din, which, flaring up here and there like a forest fire, crackled for a few seconds over the horizon before shrinking again to single gun shots. Up in the woods a Russian machine gun was rattling away steadily, and Stiller registered absentmindedly the lash of its fire, followed as if in echo by the duller impacts of the bullets. All of these noises, coming from behind the fluid curtain of the snow storm and the ghostly backdrop of the soaring mountains, sounded unspeakably menacing and oppressive.

Stiller caught himself toying with the thought of not waiting a moment longer, but evacuating Rozhanovce at once without regard for the consequences—before it was too late. He realized that with the troops and arms available even the ablest divisional commander couldn't possibly hold up the Russian attack. Perhaps a more skillfully launched counter-attack might have regained the old positions once more, but against a hundred tanks Stiller was powerless. A few dozen assault guns and a whole new infantry division would have been needed to get anywhere against the Russians' numerical superiority. From this point of view Giesinger could hardly be blamed; it was the old ten-to-one proportion, with which every individual divisional commander had to battle along as best he could, till one day he was court-martialed for incompetence or sabotage.

He turned to Kreisel: "How many Russian divisions, do you think?"

"Three or four. But there may be at least twice as many. What do you think about the artillery fire?"

"It's increased," said Stiller, watching the heavy shells exploding in the street and above at the edge of the wood.

"I didn't mean up there, sir, but further left. That must be where Scheper is."

"Indeed?" said Stiller in dismay. He could distinctly hear the fierce rumbling in the north.

238

"If it *is* in Scheper's sector," Kreisel added, "I don't think much of his chances."

"He should have been here by now," remarked Stiller with an anxious look at his watch. He listened again to the artillery fire, which was getting worse and worse; he thought he could hear fire from multi-barrelled mortars. "We must get back to your HQ," he said abruptly. "Perhaps there'll be something in from corps."

On the way to Kreisel's headquarters they almost ran into a mortar salvo. It came so silently they had no time to hurl themselves into the snow until the splinters were actually whining through the air.

"You might think they were aiming right at us," observed Stiller as he got up. He had a horrible feeling at the pit of his stomach.

Kreisel beat the snow off his camouflage coat. "Perhaps they *were*. I'd give one of the two assault guns up there to know from where we're being observed."

They raced on, and Stiller breathed a sigh of relief on reaching the headquarters. The interior of the house consisted of two rooms, the larger of which was crammed with soldiers to the last corner.

"My staff," said Kreisel, making for the other room, where there were two officers and two signal teams. They jumped up when Kreisel and the general entered. Schleippen came running over to Stiller. "We haven't got any contact, sir. Colonel Höpper's signals aren't coming through, nor is corps."

"But that's impossible," gasped Stiller. "Corps must still be in Dobšina."

"Our sets don't reach as far as Dobšina," Schleippen explained. "We were only connected with corps through division. The signals office in Košice must have left."

"I see." Stiller lowered his head. His voice sounded suddenly weary. "Probably the Russians are already there." He glanced at the officers' pale faces. Then he stared at Giesinger, whom he had discovered among them. "You've made military history. When the historians one day describe how Košice was lost, they won't forget your name." He turned to Kreisel. "Send off a few of your men to make contact with Scheper, and bring him here. We'll wait another half hour for him, and if he's not turned up by then, we'll leave at once. We must leave here before the Russians have left Durkov. Your two companies there will be thrown out of their positions at the first attack."

"Then you're no longer counting on Höpper, sir?"

"No." Stiller lit a cigarette, found he did not like its taste, and stubbed it out. "Got any food here?" he asked. "I haven't had a thing to eat since last night."

"I'll have something sent up for you, sir." Kreisel left. When he returned, he had two men with him, bringing reports from the battalions which had moved into their new positions. "We're spread all along the edge of the wood now," he told Stiller.

"To the south as well?"

Kreisel dismissed the men and answered: "Yes, to the south as well. I've kept Scheper's battalion in the village as reserve. It's up by the last houses."

"Reinforce it with Hepp's reserve. I doubt if we've anything more to fear from the west, but if things start up above, we'll need every man."

He sat down at the table, and for the next few minutes concentrated on the sandwiches which a man had brought in. The officers watched him eat. They were on edge and listened uneasily to the Russian artillery fire. Only Giesinger sat calmly in his corner on an empty ammunition chest, apparently indifferent to what was going on.

Kreisel picked up the telephone, and the report from his second battalion, which was up on the road, confirmed his worst fears. The Russians were hammering at the company positions almost continuously with mortars and artillery fire. The soil in the wood was frozen hard, so that the men could not dig in; they were suffering heavy losses.

"You must hold on for another half hour," Kreisel told him. "Can you hear the fire to the left of you?" When the captain said he could, Kreisel went on: "There should be one of our regiments coming from that direction. Tell your companies to keep their eyes open and not shoot in case they're some of our own men." He hung up, and said to Stiller: "You're right, sir. We dare not wait more than half an hour. I only hope Scheper arrives in time."

Before Stiller had time to answer, a man came rushing into the room. He looked around till he discovered the general, when he announced excitedly: "I've come from Durkov, sir. Lieutenant Stolzenthal sent me."

"Who's that?"

"The commander of one of the two companies you left in Durkov, sir," Kreisel answered for the man.

Stiller looked at the messenger. "How did you get here?"

"With an ambulance, sir. The lieutenant says he can't hold the position much longer."

"Are the Russians already attacking?"

"They certainly are, sir, from three sides. Lieutenant Stolzenthal. . . ."

"Wait outside," Stiller interrupted. Getting up, he remarked to Kreisel: "One more reason for not waiting any longer. I reckon the Russians will take at least an hour to reach Durkov from here."

"They'll get to the road fork in half an hour, though," Kreisel observed.

"I know. It's not going to be any picnic even now."

"It certainly isn't. Won't you send for the two companies, sir?"

Stiller's thoughts were already elsewhere. He an-

241

swered distractedly: "It's too late for that. You heard what the man said. If the Russians were attacking from three sides when he left Durkov, they'll be at the cross-roads now."

"Then we can write the two companies off, sir."

"I wrote them off when I told them to stay at the crossroads."

The telephone rang. Kreisel picked up the receiver. After a few words he looked at Stiller and said in an unnaturally quiet voice: "Russian tanks, sir."

"On the road?"

"On both sides of the road. The wood is thin up there, only pines. The Russians are rolling right through it."

His words caused a stir among the officers present. They watched the general, who put on his cap and looked toward the window. "Take everything here along," he ordered. When he got outside the door, he stopped for a moment and listened to the battle. The sharp claps of tank guns could be picked out distinctly from the crashing explosions of the artillery. There was a constant whining, howling and whistling in the air which mingled with the thousand-fold echo from the mountains to form a monstrous pandemonium. So far as Stiller could judge, the fire was landing on the village and further up in the wood. Only single shells were coming down near the headquarters.

Glancing across to his car, Stiller saw the driver who stood between the trees gesticulating to three other men. Stiller called him over: "Drive to the pass road, and wait for me there."

He turned to Kreisel and gave orders that all the vehicles should assemble on the road. "If there were more of them," he declared, "I'd say they should carry the whole regiment."

"There aren't even enough for a battalion," Kreisel answered. "By the time we've got the wounded on they'll be full." He passed the order to one of his officers, and then accompanied Stiller, his staff trudging behind him in a long file, to the shacks on the edge of the wood. There Kreisel distributed his men among the few houses and sent one man to the dressing station to arrange for loading the wounded on to the empty ammunition trucks.

Meanwhile Stiller had gone ahead into a house near the bridge together with the officers and signals men. Standing at the window, he scanned the street through binoculars. At present there was not much to be seen. Some houses were burning at the center of the village. The fire of the tank guns was now booming continuously, and Stiller expected the tanks to come out of the wood any minute. He looked over to the next house, where the two heavy field howitzers stood. The men were sitting on the gun carriages, staring up the street. Behind him he heard Kreisel talking to his officers. A specially loud explosion made him return his attention to the road. Right above, in the wood, a cloud of bluish-black smoke was rising almost straight towards the sky.

"Direct hit on a tank," said Kreisel.

Stiller put down his binoculars. "Or else one of your assault guns. That must be right on the road."

"Looks like it," Kreisel answered grimly. The smoke cloud up above grew thicker, spreading like a mushroom and moving slowly over the wood, where it merged into the snowy sky.

"Have we still got telephone contact?" Stiller asked.

Kreisel looked at the door. "I've had the wires laid to here. The men should come any minute."

"Send a messenger off for safety's sake. I must know. . . ." He broke off. While studying the country through his binoculars, he happened to look north, and there saw a dark mass of men pouring out of the wood on to the snowfield; the mass spread like an avalanche

until in a minute it was covering the whole expanse.
Stiller's heart almost stopped beating. He caught Kreisel by the shoulder. "What's that?"

Kreisel raised his binoculars, looked and then said:
"They're our men. Either my third battalion or. . . ."

"Or?"

"Colonel Scheper and his regiment," said Kreisel.
"We'll know in ten minutes." He turned to his officers.
"Send off runners."

"To the other battalions as well," said Stiller.
"They're to assemble in the wood behind the bridge
in fifteen minutes. Not forgetting assault guns and
artillery."

Two officers ran off. Stiller watched the movements
of the approaching mass of men. It must be Scheper, he
thought in agitation; if they were men from the assault
regiment, the Russians would be at the bridge in ten
minutes. He looked tensely through the binoculars, and
suddenly saw that the Russian artillery had shifted its
fire from the edge of the wood to the open space.
Mushrooms of smoke shot up from the hollow all the
way up to where the men were emerging from the
wood. Despite the distance he could see the running
men stop, hurl themselves to the ground, get up, run
a few yards further, and then drop again. There were
so many, and they were packed so tight that every one
of the bursting shells must tear to pieces several of
them.

Stiller took the binoculars from his eyes and glanced
at Kreisel, who stood by him mute and still, his face
deadly pale, staring straight ahead. Following his stare
with a sense of grim foreboding, Stiller saw the Russian
tanks. It took him some time to count them. Six were
on the road, approaching the first houses, now occupied by the battalion from Scheper's regiment and the
reserve unit; further to the left there were no less than

244

ten tanks rolling down the snowfield; and still more appeared above from the wood.

Stiller watched as if hypnotized. He saw the two field howitzers, whose crews had just turned their guns and were aiming them at the advancing tanks. Now they fired, first one and then the other. The shells landed in the snow ten yards in front of the first tank, which rolled on unswervingly until it suddenly vanished in a cloud of fiery smoke. The crash drowned out even the artillery fire. The men at the guns waved their arms in the air and yelled. Stiller dug his nails into the palms of his hands in a frenzy; a sort of intoxication came over him. He paid no more attention to Kreisel, he took no notice of the officers who shouted encouragements to the men at the guns or rushed senselessly to and fro; his whole attention was absorbed by the gunners, who now fired one shell after another, hitting a second and then a third tank.

The other tanks suddenly swerved north and rolled straight on towards the men who might be Scheper's regiment or part of Kreisel's. The men had meanwhile come within about two hundred yards of the village. When they saw the tanks they tried to escape into the hollow. Five or six hundred men, Stiller thought: they *must* be Scheper's regiment and he couldn't do anything to help them.

No one could help them, not even the howitzer crews, because there were now houses between them and the tanks, and because more and more tanks came rolling down the slope, and because, as if the wood had spewn them forth, there were suddenly running men everywhere. Between the tanks, in front of and behind them. Everywhere Stiller looked, men were running. The whole assault regiment fled down the hill, from all the houses, from behind every tree, running, stumbling, hurtling towards the bridge; while over to the left three tanks had edged in between Scheper's regiment and the hollow, and four others were already careening among the men, shooting and mashing down everything in their way.

The general watched his division dying. He watched their death with the impotent rage of a man who has to watch his house burning down. He saw the tanks come nearer and the Russian infantry rolling behind like an avalanche. He saw the men at the howitzers swinging their barrels to left and then to right and then left again; and then the men burst apart as if the earth had exploded beneath them, and the guns stretched their dark muzzles toward the sky and were silent.

He did not notice a hand gripping his arm. A T-34 rumbled past the dead gunners, and beside it ran Russian infantry. Russian infantry were running everywhere, as if they had dropped from the sky. The German officers, Stiller with them, rushed to the door. They ran straight into a crowd of Russians, who were just coming up the few steps and had no time to shoot because the officers fell upon them with a single cry. The officers did not even reach for their pistols, they all acted on impulse, including Stiller, who kicked a Russian in the chest so that the man fell back down the steps. He clawed his fingers into the face of the next man until he felt a glutinous substance under his nails—which revolted him so much that he lost control and yelled. He let go of the Russian's face, stumbled over the head of another, dug the heels of his boots into yielding flesh, and raced for the wood, still yelling. And while the last men of his division were being mashed to pulp by the Russian tanks and mown down by the Russian infantry, he reached his car, together with Kreisel and a few other officers. Shaken with terror and revulsion, he threw himself onto the seat and began to wipe his hands like a madman on the

246

upholstery. Not until the car was speeding along the road amid the whine of tank shells, the crashes of the explosions and the rattle of Russian machine guns did his hands come to rest.

He was sitting right behind the driver, whose bent back masked the steering wheel. An officer with blood pouring from his face was lying at the driver's side, not moving; Stiller recognized him as Lieutenant Schleippen. On the back seat, squashed so tight that Stiller was almost being squeezed out of the car, sat three other officers, of whom the middle one was Colonel Kreisel, who sat with his face buried in his hands. The two others belonged to Kreisel's staff.

Stiller looked down at his hands, with which he had squeezed the Russian's eyes out of their sockets. He rubbed the fingers together and felt how sticky they were. But he no longer felt any disgust. His whole being was pervaded with a glow of satisfaction, and the more he thought about how he had survived, the more this mood swelled into exultation. Remembering the way he had battered at the Russians with his bare fists, he was overcome by amazement and admiration. In his military career there had been many situations he could remember only with an uneasy shudder; but never before had he been involved in hand-to-hand fighting with the Russians. For a general it was a rare and, as he thought, a notable experience, which many could envy him. He suddenly noticed that the driver was reducing speed and staring hard ahead, where the burned-out remains of two assault guns emerged from the snow storm, now somewhat abated. The guns were near the road at the edge of the wood, and it looked as if they had been taken there after being knocked out. Further on there was another, and in between, almost covered by the snow, lay vast numbers of men.

He leant out of the window and looked at all that remained of Colonel Wieland's regiment. Horror seized

247

him as he remembered that he himself might meet
Russians again any minute. The kindly indifference in
which he had wrapped his exhausted body, the genial
images with which he had soothed his wounded spirit
and distracted his mind from ghastly memories, now
burst like punctured balloons, leaving him with a
dreadful sense of disillusionment and shock. But then
he was once more the general, whose sharp voice
lashed the other officers out of their lethargy and made
the driver step on the brake, so that the car began to
skid and came to a halt.

In a bound Stiller was out of the car, looking around.
They could not have covered more than a mile and a
quarter at most, and it was another two miles to the
road fork, where the assault guns had been in the
morning. Stiller supposed that the Russians had a few
men posted there or perhaps a tank. Also, they might
have marched westward from Durkov after crushing
the assault regiment's two companies, in which case
they would come out on the pass road at the fork—
unless they preferred to relieve their regiments fighting
at Rozhanovce. Furthermore the other lot of Russians
must still be somewhere around—the ones he had
watched in Durkov when they were marching north
through the wood.

All these reflections flashed through his brain, and
by the time Kreisel had got out of the car, he had
already made up his mind. His eye fell on Lieutenant
Schleippen, with whom nobody had so far bothered,
slumped on the front seat next to the driver. But Stiller
could not stop for that now. Behind them, in place of
gunfire, the noise of powerful engines could be heard.
The Russian tanks would be on them any minute, and
he turned to Kreisel with an abrupt movement. The
young regimental commander's face was grey; he was
staring past Stiller in the direction they had come from.

"We must leave the car," Stiller said. "We shan't get any further on the road."

A captain pointed to Schleippen: "What's to happen to him, sir?"

"We can't drag him with us," the general answered in an impatient voice. "Is he still alive?"

The captain turned Schleippen's head so that he could look into his face. "He's dead."

It was on the tip of Stiller's tongue to say, "Good," but he swallowed and merely remarked: "Best thing for him." He noticed Kreisel still staring back down the road, grey-faced. "What are you waiting for, eh? The Russian tanks?"

"There's a truck coming, sir," said Kreisel.

Stiller swung round. Emerging from the snow storm, the truck came careening along the road. Now it reduced speed and pulled up in front of them. It was an ambulance.

The door flew open, the driver and three other men jumped out, ran up to the general and clicked their heels. "The tanks are behind us, sir," they cried.

Stiller looked at their scared faces and at the sides of the ambulance; it was riddled with holes. "Have you casualties inside?" he asked.

The men nodded. "Crammed full of them, sir," answered one.

"Are there any more of our vehicles coming?" asked Stiller.

The men looked round doubtfully. "There were a few more behind us, sir," answered the one who had spoken before. "But I don't think they're still coming."

"Most of them left earlier, sir," the driver of Stiller's car put in. "The major took them along."

"Which major?"

"Major Giesinger, sir. Before the Russians came, he got into a command car—and the rest drove off after him."

"My car, I suppose," said Kreisel. "I noticed it wasn't there any more."

"Yes, sir, I think it was," their driver confirmed. "He wanted to take mine at first, but I told him the general was going in that."

Stiller turned to Kreisel. "When did you last see Major Giesinger?"

"When we left my headquarters, sir."

"Not since then?"

"No."

"That's what I wanted to know," said Stiller, climbing back into the car with the other officers. "Drive slowly on," he ordered.

Dead men were still lying on both sides of the road. The snow had settled over their uniforms, making it impossible to see whether they were Germans or Russians. The officers stared tensely ahead. A few minutes later they noticed a single command car standing deserted on the road.

"Stop here," Stiller told his driver. He climbed out. "Is this yours?" he asked Kreisel.

"Yes, that's mine, sir."

Their eyes followed the prints of two men's boots, which went off to the right into the trees, and disappeared into the wood. If I were in his shoes, I might have done the same, thought Stiller, and cleared his throat: "Herr Giesinger allowed the other vehicles to drive on till they ran into the Russians—probably at the fork. When he heard the fire, he left his car and escaped over there with his driver."

"He ought to hang for it," exclaimed the captain.

"He will," said Stiller, looking back along the road. Apart from the ambulance, which was now following them, there was no sign of anything. "Take the dead men's personal belongings and paybooks, we're marching off at once." He went to the edge of the wood and watched the officers pulling Lieutenant Schleippen from the car and turning out his pockets. The ambulance men opened the back door and climbed in. One of them came running up to Stiller. "There are a few still alive, sir."

"Can they walk?"

"I don't think so, sir. They're all seriously wounded."

"Then we must leave them here," said Stiller.

Kreisel, who had listened, stared at the general. "You're not serious, sir?" he gasped.

"We've no choice. There's only one thing we can do," he said, turning to one of the orderlies. "Have you a Red Cross flag with you?"

"Yes, sir."

"Good. Then take it and wait till the Russians come. As soon as the first tank appears, go toward them."

"They'll kill me," said the man in shocked tones.

"As a medical orderly they won't kill you. You've only got to hold the flag up high—it's the surest way of saving the lives of the wounded."

"I don't want to become a prisoner, sir," the man said doggedly. "I'll do anything you tell me, but. . . ."

"Quiet," roared Stiller. "As a soldier all you have to do is carry out the order given you by your general." He turned and walked off into the wood. Everyone followed him except for Kreisel, who was looking uneasily at the man who was supposed to stay behind.

The man said: "I've got an old mother, sir."

"We've all got old mothers," Kreisel answered, gazing down the road where the drone of engines grew more and more distinct.

He heard his name called. Stiller had come back to the edge of the road and was standing with his fists clenched. In a furious voice he yelled: "How much longer do we have to wait for you?"

Kreisel straightened up with a jerk and said: "I'm

waiting here, sir; there may still be some men from my regiment coming. I'm not returning to Dobšina alone."

"Don't be a damned fool," Stiller snapped. "In that case, you could have stayed in Rozhanovce in the first place."

The orderly began to whimper again. "Take me with you, sir. What can I do alone against. . . ." The rest of his sentence was drowned in a shrill howl which suddenly came roaring over their heads to be cut short in a deafening crash. A cloud of smoke rose a few yards away from them.

Stiller bounded away into the wood and the orderly shot across the road in the same direction. Kreisel alone stayed by the ambulance for a few seconds longer. Now he saw the tanks coming through the snow like shadowy monsters; they were piled high with infantrymen. He watched them without moving while his thoughts veered between the intention of staying where he was and the knowledge that it was a senseless sacrifice. When the next shell whined low over his head he made up his mind instinctively, and sprinted after the general into the wood. There was a thunderous crash behind him; a direct hit on the ambulance. Kreisel saw Stiller plunging down through the wood with the other men. They did not stop till the descent ended in a narrow ravine leading northward, where a mountain peak could be seen above the trees.

Stiller waited for Kreisel to catch up with them, then went on without saying a word. For half an hour they marched through the ravine, and with each step they took, the peak ahead soared higher into the black sky. It began to grow dark. But with the beginning of dusk, which filled the forest with its grey veils, the snow's intense gleam grew stronger; and the solemn silence over the whole mountain stirred the men's shaken hearts. They walked with hanging heads, engrossed in their troubles and painful memories, worried by the grim prospects of the coming hours; yet they were glad to have survived the terrible day. They placed their reliance entirely on the general, who marched ahead with long strides.

And their confidence was rewarded. For ten hours Stiller led them westward. They plunged into deep valleys where the forest was so thick they had to force their way through it; waded across icy mountain streams; bruised their knees and elbows on jagged rocks; by-passed hills too steep to be climbed; panted up endless new ridges; and trudged through snowdrifts several feet high.

Stiller himself felt utterly worn out. His whole body was nothing but a mass of cramp-ridden muscles, and he could scarcely stand upright. Yet the thought of the Russian tanks driving further and further west blasted his failing powers to new action, inspiring an almost superhuman energy. He maintained the same fast pace as he started with, forcing the tired men to efforts beyond anything they had ever known or thought possible. He had hoped to reach the road by midnight, but it was three o'clock before they heard the drone of a great many vehicles. After stumbling down one more steep slope, they reached the edge of the wood and saw the road ahead, with a long line of convoys driving along it in a northerly direction. Despite the darkness Stiller recognized the lances painted on their sides, and as he stood there with sagging shoulders, his face slack from strain, he realized they belonged to his division.

He was too exhausted just then to feel even relief. For ten hours he had been lashed onward by the obsessive fear that the Russians might be already on the road; now that this fear had proved groundless, it left behind only a complete lassitude. He stalked out on to the road, and took up his stand in the headlight beams of the next truck. It drew up in front of him, and he opened the door. He and Kreisel got into the cab, the others climbed into the back. "Drive on," he told the man at the wheel, who was staring in awe at this general who had so suddenly materialized.

"Where have you come from?" Stiller asked.

"Banko, sir."

"That's near Košice," said Kreisel. Stiller asked the driver a few more questions, and soon formed a fairly clear picture of the situation at Košice. After the Russians had taken the town, they had evidently been thrown out again by an armored division, and were now regrouping their forces a few miles to the east. The armored division was to move out of Košice again at eight o'clock that morning.

"I suppose," he remarked to Kreisel, "they only retook Košice to carry out corps' withdrawal operations according to plan. Interesting, isn't it, that there's a whole armored division here all of a sudden. If they'd brought it up a few hours earlier, your regiment wouldn't have been lost, nor my division."

Kreisel nodded. "Too little and too late, as usual—and then only when corps is starting to get it in the neck."

"The whole town's burning, sir," said the driver. "We could see the smoke from Banko."

"I must find a phone," said Stiller, paying no attention to this unsolicited remark. "Perhaps corps are still at Dobšina."

"We're heading for Iglo," said the driver.

Kreisel yawned. "Herr Kolmel will get a bit of a surprise."

"I doubt that. Probably they expected something like this at corps."

"Corps are going to Novy Sul, sir," said the driver.

Stiller looked at him irritably. "Who asked· you? Try keeping your eyes on the road."

"Yes, sir," the man stammered; and proceeded to concentrate on the wheel. After a few minutes, when he cautiously glanced across at the two officers, he saw that they were both asleep.

After an hour the general stirred and looked at his watch. "Keep your eyes peeled for somewhere I can phone," he said to the driver.

"There may be a place at Margitfalva," the driver replied.

"Is that far?"

"Ten minutes at most, sir," was the reply.

Shortly afterward the first houses came into view. A lot of vehicles stood in the road. It was a rather large village, and they had to drive almost to the other end of it before they discovered the small rectangular flag indicating a field telephone. Telling the driver to wait, Stiller got out and went into the house with Kreisel. Inside they stumbled over a number of feet, and several voices swore soundly in the darkness.

The telephone belonged to the supply column of an artillery regiment. When Stiller heard from the switchboard there that they could still get through to corps, his heart began to thump.

"The colonel is not here," said the man at the switchboard, when Stiller asked for Kolmel.

"Then give me the corps commander," Stiller ordered, announcing who he was. There was a moment's silence at the other end. Then the voice said hastily: "I'll put you on to Colonel Kolmel, sir."

"Why didn't you in the first place?" said Stiller. At last he heard Kolmel's incredulous voice: "Is it really you?"

"I suppose you'd already written me off?"

Kolmel did not answer at once, and Stiller heard

him talking to someone. Then he said: "To be frank, yes. Where are you now?"

"Margitfalva. My whole division has been wiped out, including the assault regiment."

"So I've heard."

"Then I don't need to tell you anything more. What's happened to my HQ at Košice?"

"Ask the Russians—they know better than I do. After all, you gave orders that no one should leave the town without your express permission."

Stiller gripped the receiver so tightly that his fingers hurt. "I lost all contact with Košice. We had to fight our way through the Russians with our bare fists."

"Really? You must have been damned lucky. And you're now in Margitfalva?"

"Yes."

"I was just going off myself," said Kolmel. "The commanding general's already gone to Spišská Nová Ves. We'll expect you there."

Stiller noticed that he wanted to end the conversation, and said: "Why didn't you send me the tank division? We'd have taken the pass back with that."

"The pass has lost its importance, we'd have evacuated it tonight anyhow."

Stiller's voice was hoarse with rage. "Then why the devil did you send that signal to me at Rozhanovce?"

"Which signal, sir?"

"The one ordering me to hold the position."

"That came from the general. Security cover for withdrawal operation. The whole army's going back—rectification of the front. That was why I had to go to Košice."

"Then the tank division's counter-attack on Košice was only launched to camouflage operations?"

"That was more than camouflage. If we hadn't held Košice, we couldn't had got corps out. I'll explain it all to you in Spišská Nová Ves. You say you fought your way out with your bare fists?"

He sounded incredulous. Stiller lost his temper again. "Colonel Kreisel, who is here with me now, can confirm the facts if you like. He hasn't a single man left from his whole regiment. Frankly, I can't get over the fact that my whole division had to be wiped out for security reasons."

"You'll get another."

"So I should hope. I trust I'm not being left high and dry. You may as well tell the commanding general that I refuse to take responsibility for the loss of Rozhanovce. Major Giesinger . . ."

"Bring him along," said Kolmel curtly. "The general knows all about it. And now, you'll really have to excuse me. If you hurry, we can have breakfast together in Spišská."

Stiller heard him hang up. For a moment he stood looking at the telephone in disgust. Then he turned to Kreisel. "We're going to Spišská Nová Ves."

"How did he take it?" asked Kreisel.

"As I expected. They mean to hold Giesinger to account."

"Thank God for Giesinger," remarked Kreisel, rising and putting on his gloves. Stiller regarded him thoughtfully. "Yes, if it hadn't been Giesinger, it might have had to be you."

He turned on his heel and went ahead through the door.

12

Early in the afternoon, Kubany and his men arrived. They were in a state of excitement. Just before they reached the house they had seen a man, apparently a German, race along the edge of the wood on the other side and disappear into the house across the street.

"That must be the third man from yesterday," said Andrej.

"And he's still alive—fumblers!" Nikolash regarded Kubany with contempt.

"How was I to know. . . ." Kubany looked from him to Andrej in bewilderment. Andrej explained about the Germans in the house across the street and Kubany whistled through his stubbly beard. He and his men could hardly be distinguished from one another. They all wore fur caps, long sheepskin coats and their bearded faces were hoary with snow that now began to melt and dribble to the floor.

Margita entered carrying a tray with glasses and a large bottle. "You must drink something to warm up," she said to the men, putting the glasses down on the table. Andrej looked at her with admiration. She always brought a friendly touch into this business so that one was reminded they were all friends and neighbors who had known each other for a long time and who were now fighting for *their* village, and their old peaceful, peasant life. At moments like that he was proud of her and thought what a good wife she would make for some better man than Nikolash. Before Nikolash came into the house she often said she would only be interested in a man if he were something like Andrej—whom she had loved with all a sister's hero-worship of an elder brother. They had quarreled badly three years ago when he had first become involved with his girl Elizabeth: she told him Elizabeth was too simple for him, that he must marry some fine lady if he was one day going to move to Prague. Remembering that Margita had suggested selling the farm after the war and starting a new life with him in Prague, Andrej looked up at her and grinned. Noticing his expression she looked puzzled and then pleased and, giving him a scuff on the head while passing, she left again.

Nikolash was explaining to the men that he had sent for Matuska's group, who should arrive within two hours. The men nodded gravely and raised their glasses with an air of relief. Matuska had a truck. He was the owner of a sawmill, and when he and his men had a partisan's job on hand, he loaded them on his truck dressed as lumberjacks and drove to the site of the operation. So far the Germans had never guessed that this sawmill, so important for their war effort, was the cover for the partisan band which for years had given them a lot of trouble. Matuska was a man of iron and just now you couldn't have wished for a better support.

Nikolash yawned and went into the next room to speak to Margita.

"Did you know that Andrej means to stay here?" he asked.

"Where—in Oviz?"

"Yes. He's not going to Dobšina."

"I never expected he would. Andrej can't think of

anyone but Elizabeth, and I don't want to spend the rest of my life under the same roof with her. Nor do I want to spend the rest of my life in Oviz."

"Of course not. A woman like you shouldn't be condemned to this one-horse village. I'll talk to Pushkin. He has connections in Prague. He knows people there with so much money they could buy up half the town."

"That's the sort of man one wants," said Margita.

So it's like that, is it, thought Nikolash. His vanity was hurt that all this time, while he had thought she was in love with him, her whole idea was to marry some rich man in Prague. "So that is what you're after," he said furiously, digging his fingers into her shoulder. "Do you really think I'll let you go so easily?"

"You're not intending to marry me, are you?" she mocked.

He started, then released her arm. "Suppose I were?"

"Oh no!" her mouth opened wide. "Nikolash thinking of marriage!"

"Why not? Aren't I good enough for you?"

"Oh, certainly. I'm just surprised, that's all. Yesterday you wouldn't hear of it. . . . You're joking."

Yes, of course I'm joking, Nikolash thought, sobering up. I'm beginning to get old, and when men get old, they should stop going with young women. . . .

Margita regarded his somber face with curiosity. "What's the matter with you all of a sudden?"

"Nothing," he answered curtly.

"You men are all the same," she said in a contemptuous voice, "when you've had enough of a woman, you don't mind how you treat her."

She left him standing and went out to the others. Looking around she asked where Andrej was. One of the men pointed up at the ceiling. "Up in the attic with Karasek, I think." Margita went to look for him and met him as he came down the stairs. "Take something up for Karasek to drink," he told her. "I've put him up in the loft to keep watch and it's very cold." She nodded and went into the kitchen while Andrej re-entered the room where the men greeted him with an air of exuberance. Kubany was grinning from ear to ear. "I forgot to mention," he said. "I've brought a present for you."

Andrej gaped at the object in his hands. "A mortar bomb," he said in amazement. "Where did you get it?"

"I've had it in my house for a few weeks now," declared Kubany. "I just remembered this morning. Kubany, I said to myself, didn't you pick up a mortar bomb at Vereshegy a few weeks ago? Haven't you got a mortar bomb somewhere right in this house?—and sure enough, it was still lying there. Here it is. Isn't it just the thing we need?"

He pressed it into Andrej's hand.

"Yes, it is, by God," said Andrej, studying it from all angles. "We can blow up the whole shop with this."

"Not my house?" cried Sztraka, who had returned a little earlier and was listening with a more and more worried face.

Andrej laid a hand on his shoulder. "You still haven't realized what this is all about. If only one of the Germans escapes, we'll all hang for it and so will you. If your furniture is more important to you than your neck, then you can get yourself hanged for all I care."

Going very pale, Sztraka sat down and looked despondently at the window. "I wish I'd known," he said.

"Well, you know now," Andrej turned to one of his men: "Look here, Hilbert. With the bomb we don't need to wait till it's dark. Two of us will keep the window under fire. When you're near enough to the house, we'll stop shooting."

"I'd rather you didn't shoot at all," said Hilbert. He

rose, and went to the window, carrying the bomb in his hand like a club. He peered across the street from the side, and said: "Just watch." He took a stride so that he was standing with his whole body in front of the window. The men crouched, staring at him in horror. He stood there for a full minute, then he turned round with a smirk. "Nothing. If they'd been sitting at the window, they wouldn't have missed the chance."

"You've got more guts than brains," muttered Andrej, still shocked.

Hilbert stuck the bomb under his arm. "I know what I'm doing. I only had to keep a good watch on the window. If I'd seen any movement, I would have jumped. Anyhow, now we know where we are. My idea is that they don't dare show their faces. They're lying low somewhere in the house, waiting for us to try and get in. After all, they can't expect us to have a mortar bomb."

"Who knows!" Andrej moved up to the window and looked across. The others came up behind him, and stared at Sztraka's house. Andrej hesitated. In an hour it would be dark, and he suddenly felt it would be better if they waited that much longer before using the bomb. Better speak to Nikolash. . . . "Watch out!" yelled Kubany.

That was the last they heard before a lash of steel swept them away from the window. Andrej toppled backward, falling heavily on Sztraka.

Next to him one of Kubany's men staggered back; his hands clutching wildly about him caught hold of a head, dug fast into its hair and pulled Kubany down with him. Hilbert, who had been standing thunderstruck looking down at the men on the floor, suddenly rushed through the door, down the hall and into the street. Immediately afterward there was a terrific explosion.

Nikolash, who had come in from the other room, rolled Andrej's body out of the way and crept to the window. He brought his head cautiously up to the shattered panes, and saw what was left of Hilbert lying in the snow like a fire-blackened log. He spat, then crawled back to Andrej, who lay on his side with closed eyes, neither moving nor making any sound. With a few practiced movements Nikolash had unbuttoned his coat and shirt, to discover two round holes where the right nipple had been, from which blood was trickling. Hastily feeling the pulse, he found that Andrej was still alive. He got up, went over to Sztraka, and gave him a kick, saying: "Get Margita."

When she came, there were again shots being fired outside. This time they sounded as if they came from the edge of the wood, where Dobrovský and his men must be. Nikolash watched as Margita ran to Andrej and stared at the holes in his chest. Her face turned dead white, but she made no sound and at once tried to lift her brother's body. She and Sztraka dragged him into her room and on to her bed.

Karasek appeared. "Where have you been?" Nikolash greeted him.

"Up in the loft. We watched from there. Hilbert got the whole volley in his stomach."

"Who's we?"

"Margita and I. What's happened to Andrej?"

Nikolash pointed with his chin to Margita's room. We're all to blame, he thought, and he couldn't help feeling a reluctant admiration for the Germans who had known exactly what they were doing and had shown such discipline and intelligence.

He went into Margita's room. One glance at the face on the bed told him that Andrej was as good as dead. The skin looked brittle, and shone like chalk above the black beard. Karasek and Sztraka stood near the bed, and Margita sat motionless on a chair, gazing into her brother's face. She did not move even when Nikolash cleared his throat, and asked the two men impatiently: "Why stand there gaping? You'd do better to go to the window and keep your eyes open there. They may try to come over when it's dark."

"Shall I go back to the loft?" asked Karasek.

"No, not you, you stay at the window with Kubany. Sztraka can go to the loft, he's useless anyway."

Nikolash turned to Margita. "Now pull yourself together. You can see there's nothing much to be done for him now." She did not answer, and he shook her by the shoulder. "Didn't you hear me?"

"Take your hands off," she said.

Her voice was so hostile that he obeyed, looking doubtfully at Andrej. "You're behaving as if he were your husband. What's happened to him has happened to millions of others before him."

"They're no concern of mine."

"All right. But you knew it might get him some time. If I were you, I'd leave the blubbing to Elizabeth."

"I'm not blubbing." She turned her face towards him. "You're glad about it, I know. Yes, I know," she repeated loudly when Nikolash made a gesture of protest. "You don't have to put on a sympathy act, I don't need that. But I can't bear the sight of you, so get out."

Nikolash looked at her in amazement, then hit her in the face so hard that she fell off the chair. "You won't treat *me* like that," he declared coldly. "You can give your shepherds the boot when you want to, but not me." He watched her scrambling to her feet in silence and looking around. "Your gun's in my room," he said.

"If only I had it here!" she answered, and kicked him in the stomach, then ran toward the door. She had her hand on the handle when he caught her. Dragging her back to the bed, he pushed her down on the pillows with one hand, gripped her legs between his own and began hitting her unmercifully with the other hand. She did not utter a sound. When he let her go, her nose and mouth were bleeding. "Come to your senses now?" he said.

Instead of answering, she bent down over Andrej, whose rattling breath suddenly stopped. Then there was a sound as if a spring had been released, and the room was silent.

Nikolash sat down at Margita's side. "Andrej's lucky in spite of everything," he remarked indifferently. "At least he could die in bed. That's a thing that doesn't often happen these days to a man of his age."

"Dying in bed isn't so easy either," said Margita, touching her face. "You bastard!"

He was surprised to see that she was crying. After all she wasn't a child any more. He caught her angrily by the arm and said: "What on earth's the matter with you? Do you expect to be pitied?"

"Let me alone." She tore herself free. "You don't understand."

He tried to look directly into her face. "Elizabeth couldn't make more of a fuss than you. Why do you have to cry about him? We've all got our own lives to lead."

"I've already said, you don't understand," she returned fiercely. "What's going to happen to the farm? Father can't manage on his own. I'll have to sell the place."

"You work things out fast," said Nikolash. "The only question is, will you find anyone to buy it?"

"I'll find someone, and once I've got money, I'll soon find a husband in Prague."

Nikolash laughed in the darkness. "You've got over this pretty quickly, didn't you?"

"We all have our own lives to lead," she quoted him.

He got up and went to the window; the snow was whirling noiselessly outside. I'll bet she carries out her plans, he thought. She was a cunning bitch, and knew just how to play her cards. For a while he had believed that it would be hard to carry on without her. Nobody would find it easy to part from a woman with whom he's slept with for two and a half years without getting tired of her. But now he knew what to think of her, he was only sorry he hadn't hurt her more just then. He had to watch out. He was not deceived by the calm way she took it—he knew her too well. She was proud and vindictive, and if he were to stay any longer, she'd certainly cut his throat one day.

He gave an impatient glance at his watch. What on earth could be keeping Matuska?

He turned to Margita, who stood near the bed, not moving. "Do you want Andrej left here?" he asked her.

"No, take him into the kitchen. I'll go and attend to my father meanwhile."

As she entered the other room, the men at the window looked toward her. "How is he?" asked Karasek.

"He's all right," she answered. "He's dead."

She went past the dismayed men into the hall and up the dark stairs. Her plans were settled in her mind. Now that Andrej was dead, it was her task to save the house. She would tell the Germans she had nothing to do with the partisans, and if she gave them the secret of where the general was hidden she could be certain they wouldn't do anything to her. But she must get rid of the men first, or else the house would be blown to pieces. For the first time, she noticed it was growing dark.

"Everything's all right," she told her father. "Stay here in this room. When the Germans come, pretend you don't know anything."

"Where's Andrej?" asked Jozef Zarnov.

Margita pressed her hands to her breast. "Downstairs. We'll come up to you later. Don't turn the light on."

Returning to the three men below, Margita first went to the table where she had left her sub-machine gun. She could feel them watching her.

Margita furtively wiped her eyes, and then picked up her gun. She looked at the men. "What are you going to do now?" her voice sounded calm.

"Nikolash thinks we should wait for Matuska," answered Karasek. "But suppose he doesn't come?"

"That's what I feel," Kubany whispered anxiously. "We don't want to leave you on your own," he said to Margita, "but anything might happen to us if we stay here, so I'm for clearing out as quickly as possible."

"They want to save their own skins," said Nikolash.

Karasek swung around angrily. He was a medium-sized man with broad shoulders and a commanding voice. "Margita knows very well that we've never yet left anyone in the lurch. If we go off we take Margita with us."

"No," objected Margita. "I'll just go over to Elizabeth's, then I'll only be a few yards away if I'm needed in the house."

"By the Germans?" Nikolash asked suspiciously.

Before she could answer, Sztraka burst into the room. "Three men," he cried.

Nikolash pounced on him. "Where?"

"Coming down the hill."

They ran into Margita's room and looked through the window. In spite of the dusk they saw the men at once, heading straight for the house. When Nikolash recognized the first man, his heart seemed to miss a beat. He leaned forward incredulously. Now he could see their faces distinctly, and there was no mistake. The one with the white winter uniform was Safarik, behind came Arbes and Novakova—the guards at the prisoner's cabin.

Nikolash stood as if turned to stone. A few seconds later the men were in the room, panting. Margita was the first to recover. She pushed through between Kubany and Sztraka, asking loudly: "What are you doing here?"

Arbes took off his cap and beat the snow off it, then put it back on his head. "We couldn't help it," he said.

"Couldn't help what?" asked Nikolash.

"The Germans came with a whole company. We resisted, Tyl was blown up by a hand grenade. . . ." Arbes was still struggling for breath.

Nikolash's voice shook as he asked: "Where are the prisoners?" When nobody answered, he caught hold of Arbes' coat and shouted: "You let them escape?"

"Keep calm," said Karasek. "They couldn't do anything against a whole company."

"We knocked off half of them," said Novakova.

Nikolash pounced on him. "Half of them?"

"Yes."

"How many?"

"I can't tell you exactly. We . . ."

"How many?" yelled Nikolash.

"At least five," stuttered Novakova.

Letting go of Arbes, Nikolash turned to Karasek, his face distorted with rage. "There's your whole company for you. I'll bet there were no more than a dozen."

"Is that right?" asked Karasek.

The three men looked at each other uncomfortably. Novakova, the oldest of them, a man strong as an ox, cleared his throat. "Even if it was only a dozen, there was nothing we could do against them. The moment they'd found the hut, we couldn't keep an eye on the prisoners any longer. In the hut it was. . . ."

"That doesn't interest us now," Karasek interrupted irritably. "You say you shot five?"

"It might have been four."

"Then there aren't more than maybe eight coming after you. How much start have you got?"

"Perhaps half an hour."

Karasek considered. "I don't think we ought to wait for them," he said to Nikolash. "They'll find the tracks even by night. What do you think?"

"We stay here," answered Nikolash savagely. He turned to Novakova. "Not enough to let the prisoners escape, is it, you have to draw the Germans down on top of us as well. Who told you to come to Oviz?"

Novakova had recovered by now. "Where else would we have gone?" he said rebelliously. "To Košice? Let the bastards come. I'll shoot them down by myself if need be. Where's Andrej?"

"Andrej's dead," answered Margita. "We haven't only the eight chasing you—there are five others in the house over there. You couldn't have acted more stupidly." She took a step toward Nikolash. "You must accept the facts. More important now than the prisoners is. . . ."

"The devil is more important," Nikolash broke in. He felt completely put out by what had happened. This time the Germans had struck back at once which meant they were well informed. He could get over the ten officers but if the general was freed as well, he could never face Pushkin again. Nikolash assumed that the Germans who had run into Novakova and his men were part of a larger unit, as were the five in Sztraka's house. They had divided their men up into small sections to go snooping over the mountains and sooner or later they would come swarming along to Oviz . . . Oviz, well, Nikolash thought, why shouldn't they? As long as they were in Oviz they couldn't cause any trouble on the Golden Table. One must throw them some bait to distract them and meanwhile he could take the general elsewhere. The only problem was, he realized, how to persuade the men to stay in the house instead of clearing out. He looked at them and thought contemptuously: that oughtn't to be too difficult!

"The thing that makes me maddest," Karasek was saying, "is the general having escaped. You should at least have taken *him* along with you."

"General?" exclaimed Novakova in surprise. "But we had no general with us up there."

"The general is safe," Nikolash interjected hastily. He turned to the men and said: "We'll stay here and wait for the other eight Germans to come. Or are you scared of them?"

Karasek shook his head. "If it were only the eight, I'd be for staying here too. But with the five in our rear it's too risky."

Nikolash drew up a chair and threw himself on to it. "Assuming we clear out of here," he said quietly, "what do you imagine will happen?"

"What *can* happen?" said Margita.

"You ask that? If you were a man, I'd knock you down for being so stupid." He turned to the others. "Imagine if the Germans found nobody they could string up. We've shot four of their people, and you know what that means. They drive together all the men, women and children from Oviz they can lay their hands on, fetch the cattle from the stables, and finally set fire to the houses. The men are shot, the women and children are taken to a camp, to be buried there a few weeks later. What do you say to that?"

The men looked at him in dismay. Sensing their uncertainty, he went on in a casual voice: "It was like that in Murán, and also in Dobra. In Dobra our people had only shot one German. The next day there wasn't a stone left standing. In Oviz we've shot four; so if we clear off, it'll be even worse. The Germans know very well that the Red Army will get to Oviz tomorrow, so

271

they don't have to consider the consequences. They'll vent their fury on everyone and everything they can find. In an hour the whole village will be in flames, as sure as my name's Nikolash." He rose slowly and concluded: "All right, it's not my village, and not my people. I don't have any relations here. As far as I'm concerned, we can clear out now. I'm going to get my things."

Without a glance at the silent men he went into the front room. In the darkness he took a large bag out of a chest and put on his best coat. When he returned the men were standing around uncertainly. Nikolash went to the window and dumped his bag outside. He slung his sub-machine gun over his shoulder in such a way that it wouldn't impede his walking. Then he looked at the men. "Well, what about it?" he asked.

Karasek cleared his throat. "Supposing we do stay here, what then?"

"But you don't want to. . . ."

"Well, Kubany and Sztraka think it's best we do stay and I understand that. They both have a house and family in Oviz, and I wouldn't like to be blamed either if anything happens to those. The only question is, are we in a position to stop it happening with the few men we've got? Do you see any chance?" He had spoken quickly and quietly. Now the men turned their eyes to the dark massive figure of Nikolash standing at the window.

He folded his arms. "I've already told you," he answered in a bored voice. "Matuska and his men should be here any minute. Then there'll be forty-three of us. That means we can hold the house for the night, and tomorrow morning our divisions will be here."

"I keep hearing: we," said Margita. "But you're going to Dobšina tonight, aren't you?"

"If you'll stay here," Nikolash declared calmly, "so will I."

His words impressed the men. Karasek breathed a sigh of relief. "That changes matters," he said. "Then we've only got to consider what will happen if first, the Germans bring reinforcements, and second, the Russian divisions don't come tomorrow."

"I can straighten you out on that. For the moment, we've only got to worry about the eight Germans. If they wanted to bring reinforcements, they couldn't turn up before morning. And as for our divisions, they are on the way to Szomolnok right now. I wouldn't risk my own neck if I didn't know it was a certainty. Of course one could. . . ." He paused and looked pensive. "I'll make you another suggestion. If I went on to the road, I could meet Matuska. In case the Germans come first, you'll hear from me how many of them there are."

"That sounds a good idea," said Karasek; "what do you think, Novakova?"

Novakova nodded agreement. "If Nikolash is on the road, the eight men can't take us by surprise." He looked at Nikolash. "It'll be best if you go up there straight away. Meanwhile we can put on a little heat for the others. Are they still over there, by the way?"

"Let's see," said Nikolash. They all went into the front room, where Nikolash approached the window from the side. He took the gun off his shoulder, pushed the barrel through the broken panes, and fired a few shots across the street.

The fire was returned at once. For a few seconds a furious rain of bullets rattled into the room, accompanied by a flare of pale lights: the Germans were using tracers. As Sztraka's house stood on lower ground, the shots entered at an angle, crashing into the back wall or through the open door into the ceiling of Margita's room.

The men pressed fearfully against the wall, waiting for the fire to stop. Nikolash slung the gun back over

273

his shoulder, remarking: "Damn. They're still over there."

"So I noticed," said Novakova thickly. "Have you got tracer ammunition too?"

"A whole chest full," said Nikolash. "In Andrej's room. Margita can show you."

He looked around for Margita. "Novakova wants tracer ammunition," he told her. "Show him the chest."

"You must watch her," Nikolash said to the others. "Since Andrej died, she's thought of nothing but her own skin."

Nobody answered.

"We can shake them up with this all right," said Novakova, re-entering the room and putting a dozen magazines down on the table. He picked up his sub-machine gun eagerly, and noticing Nikolash, asked in aggressive tones: "You're still here, are you?" Since he knew Nikolash was not staying in the house, he considered himself as the men's leader.

Karasek, who did not like to see Novakova assuming this role, said: "I'm against any superfluous firing."

"This is by no means superfluous," said Novakova loftily. "We won't have half the trouble with the boys over there if we soften them up a bit first."

"If they let you," growled Kubany.

"Oh, don't try to put him off," protested Sztraka, impressed by Novakova's self-confident bearing. He wanted to get back into his house as swiftly as possible, and Novakova seemed the right man to chase the Germans out of it. "We're having far too much talk," said Arbes. "Novakova knows the best way to deal with the Germans."

"Is that why he ran away from them?" jeered Karasek.

As they went on quarreling Nikolash quietly went into Margita's room, jumped out of the window, and picked up his bag. Then he started to climb the hill, choosing the nearest way to the wood, so that after a few yards he had already diverged from the tracks Novakova and his men had left behind. He was not worried about the Germans in Sztraka's house, it was too dark now for them to be able to see him. There wasn't a light in the whole village. The snow-covered houses hardly stood out from the white valley, and all that could be seen of the mountains on the other side were dim shapes.

He had reached the edge of the wood when he heard shots being fired in the valley. The snowfall had again abated a little. Below to the right, where the men were, he saw tracer ammunition hissing through the air in glowing arcs. The rattle of sub-machine guns came to him clear and sharp. Nikolash watched a moment and then turned and started climbing through the wood.

The sound of gunfire behind him grew gradually fainter till after half an hour he could no longer hear it. He walked on steadily until he had almost reached Svedler. There, where the road led steeply downhill, he could see lights glimmering between the trees further below.

He threw away his cigarette and went into the trees alongside the road. Now he could hear the motor of a truck. The road rose steeply here, and the truck was climbing it at a walking pace. A moment later he saw the headlight beams between the trees. Sticking out his head he peered toward the car and noticed the peculiar-shaped red bumper. Taking his bag, he came forward on to the road. Even before the truck stopped, Matuska had jumped out.

Nikolash went up to him and said: "We've been waiting for you people two hours."

"Hodscha only got to me two hours ago," answered Matuska, withdrawing his outstretched hand.

Nikolash ignored the unfriendly gesture, and looked

275

at the truck. Its canvas was being pushed aside in some places, and a few men peered out. "How many people have you got with you?" he asked.

Matuska turned his gaunt face toward the truck. "Twenty-eight. But no one wants to go to Dobšina."

"Is that so." Nikolash suppressed his anger with difficulty.

"Your own fault," retorted Matuska. He had a shrill voice, and when he spoke, his upper lip drew back, showing his white teeth. "I can't go either," he added.

"Oh, really! You were talking differently a month ago."

"Maybe. But I can't leave my work from one day to the next."

Nikolash tried to get over his disappointment. "You have to turn around," he said.

"Turn? I thought we had to go to Oviz."

"No longer necessary. We're going to Lassupatak."

Matuska walked over to the truck. "To Lassupatak," Matuska told the driver and then remarked to Nikolash: "It was damned hard getting here, the roads are full of German trucks, we were jammed all the way to Szomolnok. I talked to people from Košice. Your divisions have already been inside the town today, but the Germans sent in an armored division and took it back. I doubt if they can hold it for long, though."

"Hope not," muttered Nikolash. The news alarmed him: he hadn't known anything about an armored division. According to his reports, the Germans had little in the way of reserves: a regiment at Jaszo and two or three battalions in Košice. "Why do you think they can't hold it for long?"

"Perhaps it's more don't want to than can't," said Matuska. "You should have seen the traffic: there must have been at least two divisions on the roads. I looked at the signs on the trucks: lance and pine, mostly. And

276

loaded. If they wanted to hold the front, they wouldn't have sent all their trucks back."

"Then why would they have attacked again?"

Matuska lit a cigarette. For a few seconds Nikolash could see his emaciated face, then the match went out. "In this snow they need the roads. Without Košice they'd never get their trucks out of the mountains. And now I'd like to know what you've got on in Lassupatak."

"You have to bring a captured general from there," Nikolash answered, and gave an account of the situation, which he had rehearsed beforehand. Matuska mustn't hear how things looked in Oviz, or he would have turned on the spot and driven to that village. Nikolash told Matuska that the men had been able to take care of the Germans who had been holed up in Sztraka's house. "And do you know why we were able to take care of them?" he continued. "Because we were reinforced by Arbes and his men—they were surprised by a German patrol and let their prisoners get away! Then they came straight to Oviz. When you get to the hut where the general is, make sure you have men watching every single minute. There may be more Germans in the mountains."

"Do you think it's possible some Germans might get up there before us?" asked Matuska.

"Not if you leave for Lassupatak at once. Even so you must watch out."

"I always do."

The driver turned off the road and on to a wide track leading into the woods to the left. The snow was glittering beneath the headlights but it had stopped falling. Nikolash wound his window down, and looked up at the sky: it was full of stars. The mountain peaks gleamed a bluish white, as if they were covered by glacier ice. "You're getting a bright night for it," he remarked.

Matuska nodded absently. He seemed to be considering something, and in the end said: "You're disappointed."

"Why?"

"Because none of us is going with you."

"Do you expect me to be pleased?"

"It's your people's own fault. You couldn't have picked a more awkward time. Over Christmas men want to stay with their families."

"If that's the only reason," said Nikolash, "I really feel sorry for you. And besides, you've no family."

Matuska gave a thin-lipped smile. "No family, but a business. I have to think of the future. In another six months' time I'll have to fight for my share. There are three saw mills in Meczenef. Before the war I employed two hundred workers, today there are only sixty. I need more men again; you don't pick up skilled workers off the streets. You've no idea, man, how much work is involved in a business as big as this. . . ."

Nikolash listened with mounting irritation. They're all the same, he thought with contempt, none of them can think of anything but their future, their business, their farms, their women and their sheep. Even Matuska, who had started fighting the Germans on his own initiative, before the organization existed! Matuska, of whom Pushkin had once said that he was a cruel, cunning beast, who happened to look like a man. Yet now he seemed no longer able to think of anything but his own petty interests. . . .

The truck moved slowly to a narrow bridge and stopped. Beyond the bridge there was a steep grade. Matuska jumped out and called his men down.

"Everything is clear then, isn't it?" said Nikolash.

"Yes, I think it is." Matuska gripped the lowered window. "In case you come to these parts again sometime, you know my address."

278

Nikolash nodded. He did not say good-bye to the men.

"When the Germans are out of Prague," Matuska said chattily, "I'll go and visit it. There are a few people there who may know what happened to my brothers."

"I wouldn't be too optimistic," said Nikolash.

"I'm not." Matuska took a step back. The truck began to move off. Something inhibited Nikolash from looking out the window again.

In less than half an hour Schmitt met up with Sergeant
Roos, Corporal Baumgartner and the rest who had
followed his tracks breathlessly. Although he could
hardly keep on his feet, he turned at once and hurried
back with them toward Oviz from where he had
come. To his intense relief the gunfire was still continuing. Kolodzi and his men were still in action.

Counting himself, they were fourteen men in all;
Schmitt divided them into three teams. His own team
would go straight to the house where the Russian
sub-machine gun fire was coming from, while Baumgartner attacked the house from the east. Roos with
the third team crossed the road and managed to slip
safely into the house where Herbig and Kolodzi
greeted him enthusiastically.

Across the street many things then began to happen.
Kubany had spotted Schmitt's team approaching
the house, and warned the others. Novakova insisted
that they should ambush the Germans, and in conse-
quence the team were allowed to enter the kitchen
unmolested after breaking in the window—just as Kubany was climbing out of the window of Margita's
room to cut off their retreat.

Schmitt discovered the two bodies, made sure there

was no one else in the kitchen, then turned to the door, but could see nothing in the darkness. From somewhere there came the bark of a sub-machine gun, which stopped now and then as if recovering its breath before starting again. He stood there for a few seconds, wondering where Baumgartner was. Since the rear windows had apparently not been watched, it seemed improbable that the partisans had been looking out toward the east side—he shook his head over such negligence. There was something wrong here, and he was about to look around for his men when a tommy-gun rattled off inside the house.

After that he had no time to think: he watched one of the two doors being thrust open, and instinctively dropped on to the floor of the kitchen, feeling for the kitchen door with his foot and kicking it shut. A frightful din started behind him. A rain of sub-machine gun bullets pelted into the kitchen, a voice somewhere yelled his name, a man shrieked as if he had powdered glass in his throat, and finally there were two tremendous explosions in quick succession, which shook the whole house. The silence after that was so complete that Schmitt closed his eyes and lay there for a while in stunned immobility. Then the door opened, and he blinked into the glare of a light. Before him stood Baumgartner. "We've got them, sir."

"Got who?" asked Schmitt.

"The partisans," said Baumgartner, turning round.

Schmitt picked himself up. In the light of the torch he saw two men and a woman. On the floor lay three others, horribly mutilated. Baumgartner had climbed in with his team over the garden shed. Hearing something in the darkness, he fired his magazine empty in the direction of the noise: when he found he had shot an old man, he breathed again, and clambered over the body, coming out on to the landing just in time to save Schmitt from attack by Novakova and the others.

"We gave them the works," Baumgartner explained now, pointing up the stairs. "We were up there when they came out of the door. I threw two hand-grenades down."

"You're a genius," said Schmitt, and then something occurred to him. He ran to the kitchen window and leaned out. Apart from a few footprints and empty cartridges lying around, there was nothing to be seen: the insidious marksman had made his getaway in time. Schmitt only noticed now that the firing had cost him two of his men. They lay in the kitchen, and one was groaning. Baumgartner turned the man on his back. "You won't die," he said, going on to examine the other. "It's caught *him* all right."

Schmitt came up, "Dead?"

"Not quite, sir. He's still breathing."

Schmitt ran to the front door. When he opened it, he saw Roos and seven men coming across the street.

Schmitt saw Kolodzi standing among Roos' men. "What, you're still alive?" he said.

Kolodzi took off the binoculars and handed them to Schmitt, who received them equally without comment, and at once turned to Roos. "We must find a sledge. There are two stretcher cases in the house. They must go to the Jelnice hospital immediately."

He looked at the shot-up car in the street. "Who does that belong to?"

Kolodzi pushed the Fat One forward. "Gestapo from Dobšina, sir. *He* belongs to them too."

"Come inside all of you," Schmitt ordered. The men went back into the house, took the dead out and threw them into the snow. While Baumgartner attended to the wounded, the prisoners were brought into the room and stood against the wall. Schmitt had a blanket hung over the empty window, and lit a paraffin lamp.

As soon as he sat down Teltschik came in with a steaming mess tin, which he put down on the table. "Like some coffee, sir?"

"The things you think of, Max. Have you any more of that stuff?"

"I took along a whole bag of coffee, sir."

"Then brew up some for everybody." Schmitt turned to Kolodzi. "Do you know anything about the general?"

"We had no time to think of the general, sir."

"How did you run into the partisans?"

"Corporal Herbig can tell you that better than I can. I was away for an hour or two."

"You were away," said Schmitt absently. His eye went to the prisoners. Margita stood in the middle. She was gnawing at her lower lip and pulling nervously at her skirt. Arbes and Sztraka hung their heads in resignation. "Well, Corporal," Schmitt went on, "how did it happen?"

"Sergeant Vöhringer was really responsible, sir," said Herbig, and gave a brief account, though without mentioning Kolodzi or the red-haired M.P.

When he had finished, Schmitt looked at the fat Gestapoman. "Where did your inspector hear that there were supposed to be three deserters in Oviz?"

"From divisional headquarters, sir," answered the Fat One.

Schmitt considered, but couldn't make rhyme or reason of it, and said to Kolodzi: "Perhaps the general's in this sanatorium."

"Maybe, sir. We can ask the prisoners."

"Yes, do that." Kolodzi spoke to them. The woman looked at him and said something. "She's asking where her father is," he interpreted.

"How should I know? Where was he?"

"In his room apparently. She wants to talk to him."
284

"If she'll tell me where the general is, she can certainly talk to him and I'll let her go as soon as I have the general."

Kolodzi spoke to Margita, then told Schmitt: "She wants to talk to me outside. Also she insists on seeing her father."

"All right, you can go with her, but take another man with you." He watched Kolodzi and Herbig leading the woman out. As he was reaching for his coffee, the Fat One came forward. "I wish to make a report, sir."

Regarding his fleshy face, Schmitt suddenly had an ugly premonition and said impatiently: "Leave it till the morning."

"The thing is urgent, sir," began the Fat One, but something in Schmitt's face warned him in time. He snapped his mouth shut, and stepped to the side, where he stood glaring at Schmitt, who took no notice.

Schmitt was unutterably weary; he waited sleepily till the two men returned with Margita.

"Her father's dead, sir," said Kolodzi. "Baumgartner shot him by mistake."

Schmitt looked at Margita: her eyes were dry. For some obscure reason this relieved him. "Of course she knows nothing of the general," he said.

"She does, sir."

"What!"

"He's in a cabin on the Golden Table. Apparently there's only one man guarding him."

Schmitt looked into Kolodzi's eyes with an expressionless face. "How long does it take to get up there?" he asked after a while.

"She says four hours. She also says that the man who was shooting through the kitchen window lives in the fourteenth house on the right. His name is Kubany."

"That's the man I want," said Schmitt, getting up. He went to the door, called Baumgartner, and told him where Kubany was to be found. "Bring the fellow here, alive or dead." Then he turned back to Kolodzi. "What else does she say?"

"Nothing else of any importance. Her name's Margita Zarnov. If we let her go and don't burn the house down, she'll lead us to the general. But she begs us to shoot the two others, because otherwise they'll denounce her later for showing us the hut."

"She's no fool, is she?"

"A little too clever for my liking," said Kolodzi. "If what she says is the truth, she hasn't anything to do with the partisans. They came into her house and forced her to do what they ordered. That's how she found out where the general's been hidden."

"Too good to be true," Schmitt grunted, and began to pace up and down the room. He was wide awake all of a sudden, and would have liked to set off for the cabin right away. But his men would have dropped after the first hour, and he with them. Besides it would be inadvisable to climb the mountain till dawn; you couldn't be too sure of the woman's trustworthiness.

He remembered the wounded and went outside: they were just being loaded on to a horse-drawn sledge. As he was watching, he heard shots, and swung around toward where they had come from; then he ran down the street, with some of the men following him. He counted as he ran, and stopped at the fourteenth house, waiting for the rest to come up. "It must have been here," panted Roos.

Schmitt went inside and found Baumgartner standing with two men in a small bedroom. He had his flashlight in his hand, and a man in a blood-stained nightshirt lay on the floor with hairy legs outstretched. A woman was sitting up in bed, also in a nightshirt, her face as white as the pillows.

"Who shoots first, dies last," commented Baumgartner, kicking the lifeless body of the man on the floor who had a Russian sub-machine gun lying near him. "He had it in bed. Tried to act stupid, pretending to be asleep, although we had to break in the front door. I pulled him out of bed and he tried to shoot, but he made a mistake."

"So it seems," said Schmitt, glancing at the woman in bed. She was still young, had full lips, and her rather slanting eyes looked green in the light of the torch. Baumgartner turned abruptly and rushed out. He waited for Schmitt outside the house. "Do you feel sick?" Schmitt inquired.

"No, sir, not sick, but. . . ."

"But what?"

"I'm married myself, sir," said Baumgartner vaguely.

Walking back, Schmitt noticed the house where Kolodzi and his men had stayed, and decided to look through it. The front door was ajar, and he shone his flashlight on to the passage. On the right he noticed a man's boots, the rest of the body being covered with a white sheet. He went over and lifted the sheet off the face: it was completely unfamiliar, perhaps the man had also been a member of the Gestapo. In another room he found Vöhringer. He looked down at him for a moment, then raised his flashlight to the shattered windows. There were empty cartridge cases all over the floor. Schmitt returned to the passage, shaking his head as he passed the body of the unknown man: he could not recall Herbig mentioning anything about *him*.

Outside it had grown lighter. Schmitt looked up at the sky to realize that the clouds had broken and the stars were twinkling through. Nice weather tomorrow, he thought indifferently.

Inside the men were sitting at the table, filling their mess tin lids with coffee from a big saucepan; the prisoners were still standing against the wall. Schmitt had Teltschik bring him something to eat, and sat down with the others.

"What are you going to do with the partisans, sir?" asked Kolodzi, chewing on a piece of bread.

"We'll see about that tomorrow," Schmitt answered. He sent Herbig out to find a safe place for the prisoners, but kept the woman in the room, afraid they might intimidate her. "One thing more"—he looked at Herbig—"Sergeant Vöhringer had a stomach wound, you say?"

"Yes, sir."

"And the other man?"

Herbig flinched. "Who do you mean, sir?"

"There's another body in that house," said Schmitt, turning to the fat man. "He's one of your lot, I suppose."

"Yes, sir. They killed him."

The men froze. Schmitt looked from one to the other. "The partisans?" he asked carefully.

"Not the partisans," said the Fat One, thrusting out his chin. "This man beat him to death." He pointed to Herbig.

Schmitt sat motionless in his chair, staring at the Gestapo man. None of the others dared to move either, till Kolodzi rose solemnly to his feet. "He was going to shoot me in the back, sir."

"Why?"

"I had a row with him," Kolodzi answered, and began to explain. When Schmitt had heard everything, he sent for Roos and told him to include Kolodzi and Herbig in the guard roster for the night.

Roos glanced in astonishment at his fellow sergeant, but did not venture any comment. Instead he said: "We've got three men with bad bloodblisters on their feet, sir. I've had a look at them myself, they won't be able to do half a mile tomorrow."

"Why didn't you report that to me immediately? We could have sent them away on the sledge."

"The sledge was full, sir."

"Then they'll just have to stay here tomorrow," declared Schmitt after a moment's reflection. He turned to the Fat One again, who had taken up a position near him and was clearing his throat impatiently. "What do you want?"

"I must go to Dobšina, sir, and make a report."

"I'm the only one to decide what you must do."

"I'm responsible only to my office at Dobšina. You can't keep me here."

"I can do more than that with you if I feel like it. You're staying here. I need you tomorrow."

"The Russians will be here tomorrow."

"Who says so?"

"Ask your sergeant."

Schmitt turned to Kolodzi, and suddenly remembered Kolodzi admitting having been away for a few hours. "How do you know that?" he asked.

"I heard it on my way back," answered Kolodzi.

Schmitt regarded him in silence, then said to Roos: "I'm making you responsible for this man staying here." He pointed to the Fat One. "Take him into the kitchen to sleep, and all the others too, except for Sergeant Kolodzi."

Schmitt sat down at the table again and said crossly: "All right now, own up—where did you hear that about the Russians?"

Kolodzi, who had been waiting for the chance to talk to Schmitt on his own, launched into his story, concealing nothing.

When he had finished, Schmitt said, "Do you know what you are?"

"I'd like you to tell me."

Schmitt took a mess tin lid, and scooped himself some coffee. After drinking it, he put the receptacle down on the table and said: "The devil. What do I care?"

Kolodzi was disappointed. He began to regret having told everything. "I know the answer without your help. I'm only worried about Corporal Herbig. If you report the matter, he'll be hanged."

"His own fault," said Schmitt coldly.

"Will you report him?" asked Kolodzi.

Schmitt avoided his eyes. "We'll talk about it tomorrow."

"He didn't mean to kill the man," Kolodzi persisted.

Schmitt said nothing. Something in Kolodzi's eyes made him feel unsure of himself. The responsibility's too great, he thought: how could he tell the man what he ought to do if he hadn't the courage to see it himself? His eyes fell on Margita. She had raised her head slightly, and he contemplated her mouth, the liquid eyes, the firm skin over her cheekbones. All at once he felt the palms of his hands growing moist, and remembered that he hadn't slept with a woman for five years. A long time, he thought: a long time for a man, even when he has a hunchback—or perhaps just because of that.

Without his realizing it, his mouth twisted into a wry smile, which seemed to kindle something in the woman, so that she suddenly began smiling too. It changed her face in a surprising way, making him stare at her—till he heard someone cough. Turning his head, he saw Kolodzi still standing at the door. "Get the hell out of here," he said, unable to endure the man's expression of contempt. When Kolodzi had gone, Schmitt brought a feather bed out of the next room and put it down near the stove. After making sure all the windows were guarded, he sent Margita to the other room. "Spát—sleep!" he said curtly.

She looked at him in surprise. "Me?" she asked.

"Don't ask questions," he growled, seizing her by

the arm and pulling her toward her bed. In the darkness he could just see her smiling as she undid her skirt. It disturbed him so much that he remained standing and watching till she was left in only the shirt. Then he almost fled back into the other room, blushing scarlet as he turned the lamp down. That would be the end, he thought.

He put his tommy-gun and pistol down under the feather bed against the wall, so that he could get hold of them at once if required. He took off his jacket, pushed it under his head, and spread the camouflage coat over him. He was so tired he could hardly keep his eyes open, yet after half an hour he was still not asleep, and kept turning from one side to the other.

Everything inside him was worked up and impatient. He tried to think of the general, of the battalion, of Menges, and of all the horrible details of the past day; but it was no use, he could not get his mind off the woman. With his eyes closed he saw her face before him, her naked legs, and the pointed breasts under her shirt. The picture had stuck so fast in his brain that he could not dislodge it. It floated on the top of his consciousness like a log of wood in a whirlpool, and when he pressed his face into the pillows, he seemed to feel the salty taste of a moist skin on his tongue, the yielding pressure of a mouth, the irresistible pull of two soft arms holding him fast. . . .

He slept so soundly that Baumgartner had to pound on the door with his fists to awaken him. Schmitt staggered off the bed.

"There's a major wants to speak to you, sir," said Baumgartner but almost before he had finished, he was pushed aside and Giesinger came into the room. "You're certainly a good sleeper," he remarked, taking a chair.

Mechanically Schmitt pushed the door shut behind him and leaned against it. He was so astounded that it was some time before he could speak. "I wasn't prepared for *you* coming," he said at last.

"I didn't expect it myself," Giesinger answered. He looked years older. His face was pale, unshaven and hollow, with rings that might have been inked in under his eyes.

"How did you find me?" Schmitt asked.

"I was with Menges at Szomolnok. He didn't know where you'd got to, but suggested I try Oviz." His eyes bored into Schmitt's face. "How are things with the general?"

"All right."

Giesinger gaped. "What!"

"We know where they're holding him," said Schmitt, sitting down at the table.

Giesinger's face began to work. "Where is he?"

"In a hut on the Golden Table. We were going to start in an hour."

"We must start off at once," said Giesinger. His eyes were gleaming. "How far is it?"

"Four hours, I'm told."

"Four hours, eh? Quite a way. In case you hadn't heard yet, the front's collapsed, and the Russians will be here some time today. Wait," he said, as Schmitt was about to spring up, "that's not the whole of it. The entire division has been wiped out, I'm the only man to come through. I sent your battalion to Dobšina, the new line will be formed there. How many men have you got with you here?"

"Eleven."

"Only that! Menges said you had at least twenty."

"And three of the eleven have bad blisters on their feet," said Schmitt; "so better say eight." He had quickly recovered from his shock at Giesinger's news. If the news was accurate, it would be irresponsible to waste any more time on the general. "I don't know

292

how you think we can do it," he went on. "We need four hours to climb the mountain, and three more coming down, so it would take at least. . . ."

"I don't care," Giesinger cut in. "We must get the general, even if it means we meet the Russians on the mountain. But there's no danger of that. An armored division of ours is still in Košice. It's moving to Rožnava in the next three hours, unit by unit, and will hold the line there till tomorrow, so the Russians can't possibly be there before this evening. Anyhow you ought to be just as interested as I am in finding the general, I can tell you. Menges has nine gentlemen with him who are gunning for you hard. They should be in Dobšina soon, and the colonel is going straight to corps to fix a noose for you."

"I should have left him with the partisans!"

"You should have thought of that earlier. As I judge the case, what you've done is likely to take you in front of a firing squad. What on earth was the idea?"

"If I'd acted differently, we wouldn't know now where the general is."

"You'll have to prove that first, and you can't without the general."

Schmitt rose with a scowl. He spread out his map and bent over it. "Our men are enough," he said. "The general hasn't more than one man guarding him. In fact it will be better if we only take the smallest possible number. Excuse me a moment." He went into the kitchen, woke the men up, and took Kolodzi back with him. "Call the woman," he said. "She's to get ready for taking us to the general as quickly as possible."

"Woman?" asked Giesinger in amazement.

Schmitt told Giesinger the essentials, including the problem of the dead Gestapo man.

Giesinger took a gloomy view. "If the inspector were still alive, I could have talked to him, I knew him quite well. Perhaps the general can do something. If we don't find him, it will be just as unpleasant for this Herbig as for you and me."

"For you least of all," said Schmitt.

Giesinger snorted. "You've no idea! I'm to be held responsible for the Russians' break-through. The new general and Kolmel think it could have been avoided if you'd been there with your battalion. They didn't like my sending you off without notifying corps."

"Herr Fuchs told you they wouldn't."

"Shut up about Herr Fuchs. If we find the general, I'll certainly have something to tell him. Frankly, I'm not too pleased at having a woman along, we'll only have her collapsing on us."

"I doubt it. These women have grown up in the mountains and are tough as nails."

There was a knock on the door. Roos came in and reported that the men were ready.

Schmitt went outside, had Roos show him the men with bad feet, and told them to deliver the two prisoners to Lieutenant Menges when they reached Dobšina. "You'll have to go on foot from Szomolnok if you don't pick up another truck." He turned to the driver of the truck, who was in the back supervising the loading of the dead. "You'll wait for us in Szomolnok."

The man shrugged his shoulders. "All right, sir. I'll drive around anywhere you say. I hope I don't get into trouble afterward, though."

"You'll only get into trouble if you aren't waiting for us in Szomolnok."

Back in the house, Schmitt found Giesinger seated at the table with Margita standing in front of him. She wore a light-colored coat trimmed with fur and a kind of Balaclava tied under her chin with a red cord. Schmitt gave her a fleeting glance, and said to Giesinger: "We're ready."

"So am I." Giesinger was still staring at Margita. "How come such a good-looking bitch lives in a hole like this?"

"I wondered about that myself," Schmitt answered. When they left the house they heard angry voices coming from the truck. Schmitt stepped up in time to see Kolodzi and Herbig pull the Gestapo man out of the back. "The man got in against my express orders," Schmitt explained to Giesinger.

"There's nothing much you can do about it," said Giesinger. "The special police have their privileges. Anyhow why do you want to keep him here? He'll only hinder us."

"I have my reasons." Schmitt beckoned Kolodzi to one side. "Keep a good eye on him. I'll put the case to the general, he may know a way of solving that business."

Giesinger was looking impatiently at his watch. "We've wasted a whole hour," he said to Schmitt. "Where on earth is that woman?"

"Here she comes now," Schmitt answered. They took Margita between them and set off through the village.

After passing the last houses of the village, Margita left the road and entered the wood to head for the mountain. It was still darker here, and Schmitt glanced anxiously at the sky, observing to his relief that it had not clouded over. A few stars hung between the snow-covered tips of the pines.

Giesinger trudged alongside Schmitt, deep in thought. Although he had marched for ten hours he no longer felt tired, being wholly absorbed by the prospect of coming face to face with the general. His burning impatience mingled with a constant anxiety about what would happen if at the last moment something should prevent its coming off—it was unthinkable. If only he knew whether Stiller was alive; Stiller was the one man with any interest in having him court-martialed. And if Stiller got out of Rozhanovce alive, he must have noticed I wasn't there with the other officers. . . . In the general excitement it had been easy enough to get away from them: with a slight feeling of shame Giesinger remembered how he had sat in the lavatory for half an hour. Then hearing the yells of the approaching Russians, he had rushed headlong for the trucks, seizing the first car he found to make his getaway. Realizing the Russians might be at the road fork, he had run off into the wood with the driver, not worrying what might be happening behind him. A sudden noise sent goose flesh down his back. Now it came again: it sounded like the protracted howl of a dog. He stopped in horror. "What on earth is that?"

Schmitt peered into the wood. "A wolf I suppose. The country is full of them."

"Damned beasts," muttered Giesinger as he walked on.

"They're not so bad," said Schmitt. "At least they only attack a man when they're hungry. Nice, sensible beasts—we could learn something from *them*."

Schmitt felt utterly dispirited, and the endless hiking through deep snow seemed more of a strain than ever. To take his mind off the march, he waited until Kolodzi came up. "Is your mother still in Košice?" he asked.

"I think so," said Kolodzi curtly. He had not forgotten how Schmitt had thrown him out the evening before.

Sensing his mood, Schmitt said: "You ought to know yourself how to act now."

"I do know."

His insolent tone annoyed Schmitt. Couldn't one have a reasonable conversation with anyone? "That's good. After all, it is not I who wants to marry your fiancée."

"What has it to do with her?"

"Everything," answered Schmitt, and went ahead to Giesinger.

It had grown lighter. The wood descended into a valley opening out ahead of them. Reaching the other side, they climbed on to a narrow ridge. Then the mist began to come up. The mountains on the other side disappeared in rising clouds of mist, and the sky seemed like a white cloth suspended low over the tops of the pines.

They called Kolodzi forward to ask Margita about the route.

When he had talked to her, he told the officers: "We have to keep on the mountain from now on. She says it's part of the Golden Table. If it weren't so misty, we could see the top from here."

"That's good enough," said Giesinger, giving Margita a sign with his hand. "I shan't have any peace till we're up there. A crazy name for a mountain anyhow."

Schmitt smiled. "Since yesterday I've been marching around and around it, and I still don't know what it looks like. First it was the snow, now it's the mist. I feel there's a sort of fate about it."

"I wish that were all you had to worry over," said Giesinger. "You can have the damned mountain. I want the general, and that's all."

They marched for another two hours without stopping. The mist had become still thicker, and the further up the mountain they came, the higher the snow lay between the trees. Later on, when the wood thinned out, they saw an immense snowfield.

The men stopped, puffing and panting. Margita turned to Kolodzi and they watched her talking and pointing straight up to the snowfield, and then over to the right, where the edge of the wood was concealed by the mist.

"What does she say?" Giesinger asked.

"We have two possibilities. We can go straight across the peak, or else around the mountain. The hut is on the other side of it. The way over the peak is tougher, but an hour shorter than the other."

"Then we'll go over the peak," declared Giesinger. He turned to Margita and pointed up the mountain. "That way."

She nodded, and began climbing.

Baumgartner scowled after her. "That woman will be the death of me," he said, as he stamped off behind the others.

During the next half hour the ascent was continuous. Giesinger kept being forced to give short breaks for all the men to catch up. They did not hurry themselves unduly, and he bawled at them.

Eventually they reached a level plain, which after about three hundred yards turned into a steep descent. The mist had thickened again, clinging stickily to the men who were weaving after the officers in a long ghostly line. Giesinger was just wondering whether to allow another rest, when the grey wall of mist was torn to shreds by a harsh glare of light so fierce that for the moment he was blinded, and had to close his eyes. Involuntarily he stopped, then opened them wide in wonder.

Below him the mountain dropped about a thousand feet, to end in a gentle curve leading almost horizontally to woodland, which ran due south for another three hundred feet and then descended into a valley. Beyond that the glittering snow made such a tremendous stream of light that he again had to turn his eyes away. In the distance the mountains flattened out, and far to the south the land rose like a vast cupola, scintillating with a thousand reflections, toward the blue sky.

Margita, her face pink with the cold, pointed down

the mountain, and made some remark. The men looked
at Kolodzi, who shaded his eyes against the sun and
stared in the direction to which she was pointing.
Then he nodded. "The hut's down there."

Giesinger was with him in two strides. "Where,
man?"

"Just where I'm pointing now, perhaps ten yards
inside the wood. I can make out the roof."

"I can see it too," said Schmitt, who had his binoculars to his eyes. Giesinger grabbed them from his
hands. The hut looked so near you could almost touch
it. Its pointed roof, with a blanket of snow on top, just
stuck out above the low pines. The blood coursed
through Giesinger's veins in excitement; he saw himself already racing up to the hut, and pushing the door
in. When he lowered the binoculars, his eyes were
shining feverishly.

Schmitt told Roos to take three men and surround
the hut.

They entered the wood in a wide arc about two
hundred yards from the hut. Now the others, who had
been watching, went down the mountain too, crossed
a flat hollow, and then had wood in front of them again.
They had covered two-thirds of the distance when
shots rang out. Automatically they went on their knees
and stared at the edge of the wood, where the tops of
the pines were moving. At that moment a savage rain
of bullets pelted round their ears. They flung themselves to the ground.

They swung their guns around, pressed the trigger,
and emptied their magazines, then crawled back a few
yards, changed the magazines, and fired again. It took
them a quarter of an hour to cover the thirty yards to
the hollow, with Baumgartner, Kolodzi and Herbig
the last ones. While these three were still firing at the
wood's edge, Schmitt and the others already lay

crouched in the hollow, where Giesinger had unbut-toned his trousers and was regarding three bleeding holes in his right thigh.

Schmitt asked Teltschik for a field dressing and bandaged the major's leg. Baumgartner came crawling into the hollow. "There are at least fifty partisans," he said, as he put in a new magazine. He noticed Gie-singer, who was lying on his back, staring up wide-eyed into emptiness. "Did he get something?" asked Baumgartner.

No one answered. They were all half stunned, and avoided each other's eyes. Now Kolodzi came down, and said to Schmitt: "We must go on."

Schmitt examined the hollow. It was fifty yards long, thirty yards wide, and shaped like a tub. In the middle it was deep enough to allow a man to stand upright without being seen by the partisans, whose bullets were still whizzing over their heads. A bit further be-yond, the mountain climbed sheer toward the sky. From where he was Schmitt could only see the enor-mous expanse of its south side with the cloudless sky above.

"I'm afraid we must write off Roos and his men," said Kolodzi. "If we wait any longer, the same will happen to us."

"You surely don't imagine we can get up there by day?"

"Not all of us, but a few. Assuming the others stay and give them covering fire."

"Which others?"

Kolodzi looked at him coldly. "I leave that to you." He went over to Margita and pulled her off the ground. "You knew there was more than one man up here," he said in Czech.

"I didn't," she answered vehemently.

"Don't lie. If we die here, you'll be the first." He let

her go, and said to Schmitt: "Who are you going to send?"

"Nobody. All of us are getting out or none."

"Then let's at least send one man to Szomolnok for help."

"It's too late for that."

"Why?"

Schmitt looked up again at the mountain. The sun was now right in the south, transforming it into a coruscating glitter of crystals. "Because we have now evacuated Szomolnok," he answered. "By midday this morning the Russians will be there. The front's being withdrawn to Rožnava."

Kolodzi stood stock still. "You're telling me that now?"

"Remember who you're talking to," said Schmitt, and bent over to Giesinger. "Anything I can do for you?"

Giesinger stopped looking at the sky. "Hopeless, is it?"

"Depends if you can hold out till this evening. Do you have any pain?"

"Very little. Only when I move my leg."

"Well, that's good," said Schmitt tonelessly. He straightened up to watch Baumgartner and Herbig firing at the wood. "Stop shooting now," he told them. "It's not doing any good, and we have to save ammunition."

Herbig looked back. "How about someone else coming up here?"

"The Gestapo man will relieve you," Schmitt decided.

The firing from the wood abated, with only single shots passing over the hollow. While the Fat One took Herbig's place on guard, Herbig sat down in the snow by Kolodzi. "What exactly are we waiting for?"

"Ask the Old Man."

"Didn't he say anything?"

"No. I think he wants to wait till evening."

"The partisans want that too."

"Of course."

"And then?" asked Herbig.

Kolodzi took a puff at his cigarette. "Then the Russians will come for us."

"Russians?"

"They've broken through. The front is going back to Rožnava today."

Herbig went pale. "Who told you that?"

"Schmitt."

"Damn!" They looked across at Schmitt. "Then we're done for," Herbig said.

Kolodzi nodded.

"I'm sorry for the woman," said Herbig.

"I'm not. She must be in with the partisans."

"Not on your life. Look at her face." Margita sat with her legs out in front of her, her head drooping.

Kolodzi became doubtful. If she really has nothing to do with them, he wouldn't be in *her* shoes now. He called her over. "Sit on my groundsheet," he said, and offered her a cigarette. She accepted it, and Herbig held out a lighter, finding her rather attractive.

Kolodzi rose and crept up to Baumgartner: "How does it look?"

"They're hiding in the wood. You can see the trees wiggling. Will you take over here?"

"Yes. Go and get warm."

"Aren't you funny!" Baumgartner crawled back into the hollow, and went to Herbig. "What's that whore doing here?" he asked roughly.

"Got anything against her?"

"Do I? It was she who led us into this shit."

"*She's* in it as much as we are."

"Serves her right," sneered Baumgartner. He pinched

302

Margita's cheek. "She's got a pair of eyes like my old woman," he said, and relapsed on to the ground with a groan, his face suddenly softened.

They gazed across at the wood. Suddenly a dark object high in the air came hurtling toward them and landed in the snow about twenty yards ahead. It made a noise as if ten hand-grenades had gone off at once. They heard the sharp hiss of the big splinters, and pressed their heads on their arms.

Kolodzi crawled back a few yards, then ran past the frightened men to Schmitt, who asked: "What was that?"

"A mortar-bomb," answered Kolodzi. "They may have more of them. If we wait till it's dark, they'll get so near that the next one will drop in here."

"We just have to keep a good watch."

"Easier said than done."

"If you keep your eyes skinned, you'll see the partisans. Go back to your post. . . . Don't you hear me?" he yelled.

"You said it loud enough," said Kolodzi, and pointed to Giesinger, who was listening with his eyes closed. "Are we to carry him back?"

"Haven't you gone yet?"

"We can't carry him back," Kolodzi went on stubbornly. "It's nearly twenty miles to Rožnava as the crow flies. Besides we'll never get him out of this hole."

"Are you trying to tell me what I must do and not do?"

"You'll have to put up with that if you don't know yourself."

Schmitt looked at him speechlessly. Out of the corner of his eye he noticed Giesinger feeling for his pistol. Seizing Giesinger's arm, he said hoarsely to Kolodzi: "I'm only sorry it didn't hit *you* instead of the major. I'd like to hear the way you would have talked then."

303

"I wouldn't talk at all," Kolodzi answered. "I'd put a bullet through my brain, so that at least the others would get through."

"You'll be the last man I send off."

"I didn't say a word about myself. If you like, I'll stay here alone with the major. Only I don't see why we should all croak for his sake." He turned round, went back to the others and sat down.

"Why didn't you let me shoot the man?" groaned Giesinger.

Schmitt squatted near him. "He'd have shot you first. Besides, he's right."

"You too?"

"Not in the way you're thinking," Schmitt answered, looking at his sunken, harshly lined face. He knew as well as Kolodzi that they wouldn't get Giesinger out of the hollow. And even if they had managed it, he'd have lost his leg, like that air-force officer in Dresden, whose wife had run away screaming at the sight of her husband's ugly stump. Strange, thought Schmitt, as he looked forlornly up the mountain, which to him was still no more than an immense white expanse of harsh glare. He felt his eyes growing moist, and let his head drop, gazing apathetically between his legs. It was warm in the hollow, the sun was incredibly strong.

Schmitt squatted in the snow, and without taking in what he saw, looked at the men sitting around brooding silently. From time to time two of them got up and relieved the posts. They exchanged a few words, then the men who had been relieved sat down on their groundsheets and lit cigarettes. He saw it all through a dull glaze. He had lost all sense of time, but at one point, when he turned his head, he noticed the dark shadow of the mountain pushing over the edge of the hollow and slowly creeping toward them. He waited till the shadow reached the tip of Giesinger's boots, then stood up and called down the posts. "I need one man to stay with me," he told them all. "Who'll volunteer?"

Teltschik took a step forward. "Me, sir." His face was pale, and Schmitt looked at him a long time. Then he turned to the others. "You can try your luck now if you like. I doubt whether you'll make it, but if you want to. . . ."

"That's madness," said the Fat One, his teeth chattering. "I'm staying here."

"Anybody else?" asked Schmitt.

No one answered. Schmitt would have liked to say something more, but the tears had come to his eyes again. And because he did not want the men to see them, he turned around abruptly and crawled with Teltschik to the place where the posts had been lying.

Glancing at Margita, Kolodzi made a silent gesture toward the mountain, then looked round for Baumgartner and Herbig. "Ready?"

"What are we waiting for?" muttered Herbig between his teeth. They looked at Schmitt again. He had two tommy-guns and some magazines lying near him. Now he picked up one of the guns and started firing.

The three men started racing up the mountain side. When they emerged from the hollow, the wood behind them became alive with gunfire. Margita, who started to follow them, lost her nerve and slid back into the hollow, where she lay stiff with terror, looking up at Schmitt who was firing at the wood with each of the guns in turn, while the faithful Teltschik changed the magazines.

He did not stop till he had run out of ammunition. Far above he saw three figures zigzagging up the mountain. Margita and the Fat One were both sitting on the ground watching the three men grow smaller and smaller. Giesinger too had managed to sit up a bit. When Schmitt came over to him, he relapsed on his back with a groan. "Why did you do that?"

"So that they'll live to tell the tale." Schmitt looked at Teltschik, who was now standing in the middle of the hollow and now slowly raising his arms. The Fat One also had jumped up and was doing the same. Margita still sat on the ground, staring in the same direction as the two men, her face white.

The partisans were standing above the hollow with sub-machine guns at the ready. Almost indifferently Schmitt watched them coming down. His gun was wrenched from his hand, fists gripped his coat, and thrust him forward. Behind him Giesinger screamed, and looking around, Schmitt saw the partisans dragging him through the snow by his feet. Then Schmitt himself got a blow in the back that made him stagger out of the hollow, where Teltschik already stood.

"Why didn't you watch. . . ." Schmitt began, and then the butt of a sub-machine gun crashed over his mouth. He could feel his teeth breaking, and he dropped whimpering into the snow. The partisans pulled him to his feet again, and half stunned, he tottered into the wood ahead of them. Snow from the pines sifted onto his head and down his neck, but he was not aware of it. They reached the hut.

Matuska stood in the doorway and watched them come up. His piercing eyes ranged slowly over the prisoners; he looked on impassively as his men dragged Giesinger along and threw him into the snow like a log of wood. Two others had Margita between them. They brought her to Matuska, who looked her up and down, and finally asked: "Who are *you*?"

She stared at him. "But you know me, I'm Andrej's sister."

"Andrej's sister!" Matuska shook his head. "Andrej's sister was a patriot, not a traitor. Do you know what they do to traitors?"

"I'm not a traitor."

"You came up here for nothing anyhow," he said,

"because the general's dead. Zepac shot him when he tried to escape from the hut."

"Where's Zepac?"

"Zepac has paid for his stupidity. Do you want to see him?"

"No."

"We put him with the four Germans you sent into the wood first. We spotted you even before you went down into the hollow."

"I led the Germans so you'd be certain to see them."

"Is that so!" Matuska grinned and beckoned to his men. One of them ran into the hut and returned with a coil of wire. Matuska regarded the roof of the hut: it rested on six strong beams, which jutted out a foot and a half. "Undress," he said to Margita.

"Don't do that."

"Why not?" he asked.

"You can't do that."

"I can do anything. Undress."

"You swine," she said, and hit him in the face.

Matuska staggered back a step, a drop of blood trickling from his nose. He wiped it away with the back of his hand, and gave his men a sign. They fell on the prisoners, tore off their clothes, drove them to the hut with blows from the gun butts, and made them stand in a row. Giesinger had been left on the ground, but his clothes were cut open with a knife; his blood-saturated bandage looked like raw meat. Schmitt watched with a stony face as Matuska wound off ten equal lengths of wire. He heard the partisans jeering at his hunchback and bursting into rowdy laughter when one of the naked men hopped from one leg to the other because the cold snow was cutting into their bare feet. Schmitt himself didn't register the cold, although every muscle in his body was taut as in a cramp. The blood still ran from between his lips, freezing to his chin in a thick crust. The blow had been so hard that he felt as if his mouth had been turned to a pulp, in which the short stumps of teeth were somewhere floating; and he could not spit them out because he couldn't work his jaw.

Almost unconscious, he found his hands being tied behind his back, and saw the same happening to the others. Finally a length of wire shaped like a figure eight was put round their legs, its lower half pressing their ankles together, while its upper half stood free. When Schmitt looked up at the ends of the roof beams, he realized what was awaiting them.

Now the others had realized as well. Teltschik was sobbing. The Fat One gaped, his big, formless body shaking with cold, and Giesinger stared up at the beams with protruding eyes that looked like marbles. Margita, next to Schmitt, seemed sunk in apathy; she no longer defended herself against the attentions of her captors, who enjoyed the spectacle of her body, pawing her and making coarse jokes. Matuska did not interfere for a while, till one of the men tried to pull her into the hut; then he raised his sub-machine gun. At his order the men seized first on Giesinger, lifting him into the air feet first till the wire loop slid over one of the beams. Then they let go of him and he dangled and screamed hoarsely. His face frozen, Schmitt watched Teltschik and the Fat One being hung up in the same way. They swung heavily and screamed.

Now it was his turn. For a few seconds he could see nothing because six or eight arms were gripping him; but his nose registered the pungent body smell of the partisans' clothes. Then the earth began to move under him, and he found himself looking through the snow-covered pines into the cloudless sky, which was blazing like a blue fire over the mountain.

He saw the mountain for the first time. With its almost sheer walls, glistening snow-fields and razor-sharp contours, it resembled a beheaded pyramid, and he could not remember ever having seen a mountain to compare with it. It exceeded all his expectations.

But then he felt the glowing pain as the thin wire cut into his ankles, and he saw the partisans again—they were just seizing Margita and hanging her to the beam. He heard her shriek.

His breath rattled. He could see the blood dropping from his nose on to the ground and turning the snow red. He heard Giesinger's animal howls interspersed with horrible oaths. He heard Teltschik's pitiful whimper, the Fat One's sobs and groans—and in between the laughter of the partisans.

The victims' heads began to swell like gas-filled balloons, hanging like bloody boils from elongated necks. Now Schmitt felt the cold as well: it ate through his skin, through his flesh, and right into his bones, making him insensitive to the burning pain in his legs. He looked at his thighs, saw the blood running down them, and groaned again. His temples began to throb. He saw everything now through a red cloud, the mountain, the white wood, and the partisans—they had fallen silent. When Matuska took his gun off his shoulder and went up to Giesinger, Schmitt closed his eyes. He heard a whip-like crack, then another, and the next moment two voices began to scream so terribly that he had to open his eyes again.

A moment later Schmitt felt the hard impact against his navel; but he did not feel the bullet which tore through his entrails. Nor did he hear Margita's delirious babbling—Matuska had thought out something special for her—nor the others' screams. He did not recover consciousness till Matuska and his men were on their way to Lassupatak; and immediately the pain returned. He felt as if his body were full of liquid fire consuming him from inside. Several times he could not get his breath, the throb in his temples had increased to a continuous booming. A turn of his head showed him

Teltschik's face near him, the soft dog-like eyes now dull and glassy, while the tongue hung out of the open mouth like a blue jellyfish. Teltschik had stopped screaming, so had the others; but they rattled and groaned, and the snow beneath their heads was red with blood.

Schmitt sighed. The pain in his guts spread to his chest, and each movement he made sent a red-hot dagger into his toes. He looked past Margita to the mountain, which gleamed in the setting sun like a huge block of ice. A wolf's long-drawn-out howl rang out somewhere, and he held his breath. But he went on looking steadily at the mountain, till the glare hurt his eyes. It increased the pain a hundredfold, causing him to utter a succession of plaintive moans; he moved his head to and fro, and clenched his bound and half-frozen hands. For a while he no longer knew what he was doing; but when he could think clearly again, he moved his swollen mouth and croaked: "Let me die, oh Lord."

Near him a voice howled out, another voice stammered a name, then there was silence again, and Schmitt hung all by himself, engulfed in his pain. The fire in his stomach and chest had now reached his legs and head. It clouded his brain. Each single pain seemed far beyond what any human being could bear. He groaned like a tree that is shaken by the storm, he cursed and prayed. The next time he opened his eyes, he saw that the snow under him had turned black; the mountain too was beginning to turn black, scarcely standing out from the sky. He heard the wolf howl again. It sounded much closer now, and a second wolf answered it. Nice sensible beasts, thought Schmitt, and all at once felt his pains abating. Sensible beasts, he thought sleepily.

The three men covered the last third of the mountain without haste. Once Kolodzi looked back and saw the partisans come out of the wood. There were nearly thirty of them, running up to the hollow, where for a time they vanished from view. When they reappeared, there were four other people with them, but the distance was too great now to pick out individuals. When the figures had disappeared into the trees, Kolodzi turned around, and led the way to the top of the mountain. There they stopped.

"I shall always have a bad conscience," said Herbig, looking across at Kolodzi and noticing that his lips were bleeding, Baumgartner hung his head.

They marched across the mountain. In the waste of snow they were like three tiny insects swimming in a jug of milk. The sun was now deep in the west, hurling its red beams into their faces. They hardly noticed.

After half an hour Kolodzi stopped. Ahead of them the mountain went down steeply to the west. In the valleys it was already dark, and further on the mountains looked as if they were painted with blood.

"This blasted war," said Baumgartner.

They stood there for a time, till Kolodzi pointed toward one of the peaks. "That's the Beggar's Patch. You must pass it on the left, then you come straight up against the big one there in the background, which is called Oköchegg. Right beyond it lies the road to Dobšina."

"I thought we were heading for Rožnava," said Herbig.

"You'll have passed Rožnava by then."

"How far is it to the road?"

"Hard to say. Perhaps twenty miles as the crow flies."

"Then I've had it. I can't feel my legs any more even now. Twenty miles—my God!" Baumgartner shivered.

"Think of the sergeant," said Herbig. "He's got at least three times as far."

311

"How d'you mean?"

"He wants to get to Košice," answered Herbig, looking at Kolodzi. "Unless he's thought it over since and changed his mind."

"There's nothing to think over," said Kolodzi.

"Just as you like." Herbig regarded him coldly. "Then you branch off now?"

"Yes."

"Will you stay in Košice?"

"No."

"Here, wait a moment," said Baumgartner uncomprehendingly. "What's this about Košice?"

Herbig did not answer, he was still looking at Kolodzi. "I thought your fiancée was waiting for you in Košice."

"No, I've sent her to a friend somewhere where we can both stay a few weeks."

"And then?"

"Then we'll go on."

"To Germany?"

"Perhaps. Anyhow some place where there's no more shooting."

"Then you've a long road ahead of you."

"So have we all," said Kolodzi, holding out his hand.

Herbig ignored it. "If you do come to Germany, stay away from Cologne. That's where I live."

The scar on Kolodzi's face looked like a fresh cut. He put his hand in his pocket, turned and tramped off. Once it seemed as if he were about to stop, then he suddenly started running. Baumgartner opened his eyes wide. "Where on earth is he going?"

"You heard, didn't you?" answered Herbig. "To Košice."

"But why?"

"He's deserting."

"What!"

Before Herbig realized what the corporal was doing,

Baumgartner had pulled his gun off his shoulder, taken aim, and emptied the magazine. But Kolodzi was already far away, zigzagging and running with his body bent forward and his head down. Baumgartner started to run after him, then he stopped and yelled all of the curses and obscenities he could think of. In the silence of dusk, which was now covering the mountain, his voice sounded thin and forlorn.

Kolodzi ran on, a speck in the distance. Now he had reached the crest of the ridge, and for a moment he was silhouetted against the pink sky; then the mountain pulled him down the far side.

Baumgartner fell silent. For a while he remained staring in the direction where Kolodzi had disappeared. At last he hobbled back to Herbig on his aching legs, sobbing with frustrated rage, and wiped the saliva from his mouth with the sleeve of his coat. "The filthy swine!" he said.

Herbig made no reply.

ABOUT THE AUTHOR

WILLI HEINRICH is a German novelist whose specialty is the look, smell and sound of military defeat. He came by his competence honestly and bitterly as an infantry officer in a fearfully mauled German division that bit deep into Russia and withdrew its remnants in broken retreat. He was born in Heidelberg and received his education in German grade and trade schools. He is also the author of *The Cross of Iron*. His hobbies are chess and fast cars. He lives in Karlsruhe.